As a child **Sarah Morgan** dreamed of being a writer and, although she took a few interesting detours on the way, she is now living that dream. With her writing career she has successfully combined business with pleasure, and she firmly believes that reading romance is one of the most satisfying and fat-free escapist pleasures available. Her stories are unashamedly optimistic, and she is always pleased when she receives letters from readers saying that her books have helped them through hard times.

Sarah lives near London with her husband and two children, who innocently provide an endless supply of authentic dialogue. When she isn't writing or reading Sarah enjoys music, movies, and any activity that takes her outdoors.

Readers can find out more about Sarah and her books from her website: www.sarahmorgan.com. She can also be found on Facebook and Twitter.

Summer Kisses

Sarah Morgan

MILLS & BOON

This edition published in Great Britain 2014
by Mills & Boon, an imprint of Harlequin (UK) Limited,
Eton House, 18-24 Paradise Road, Richmond, Surrey, TW9 1SR

SUMMER KISSES © Harlequin Enterprises II B.V./S.à.r.l. 2012

Originally published as *The Rebel Doctor's Bride* © Sarah Morgan 2008
and *Dare She Date the Dreamy Doc?* © Sarah Morgan 2010

ISBN: 978 0 263 89762 3

009-0712

Printed and bound by
CPI Group (UK) Ltd, Croydon, CR0 4YY

Flora

PROLOGUE

THEY were all staring.

He could feel them staring even though he stood with his back to them, his legs braced against the slight roll of the ferry, his eyes fixed firmly on the ragged coastline of the approaching island.

The whispers and speculation had started from the moment he'd ridden his motorbike onto the ferry. *From the moment he'd removed his helmet and allowed them to see his face.*

Some of the passengers were tourists, using the ferry as a means to spend a few days or weeks on the wild Scottish island of Glenmore, but many were locals, taking advantage of their only transport link with the mainland.

And the locals knew him. Even after an absence of twelve years, they recognised him.

They remembered him for all the same reasons that he remembered them.

Their faces were filed away in his subconscious; deep scars on his soul.

He probably should have greeted them; islanders were sociable people and a smile and a 'hello' might have begun to bridge the gulf that stretched between them. But his firm mouth didn't shift and the chill in his ice blue eyes didn't thaw.

And that was the root of the problem, he brooded silently as he studied the deadly rocks that had protected this part of the coastline for centuries. He wasn't sociable. He didn't care what they thought of him. He'd never been interested in courting the good opinion of others and he'd never considered himself an islander, even though he'd been born on Glenmore and had spent the first eighteen years of his life trapped within the confines of its rocky shores.

He had no wish to exchange small talk or make friends. Neither did he intend to explain his presence. They'd find out what he was doing here soon enough. It was inevitable. But, for now, he dismissed their shocked glances as inconsequential and enjoyed his last moments of self-imposed isolation.

The first drops of rain sent the other passengers scuttling inside for protection but he didn't move. Instead he stood still, staring bleakly at the ragged shores of the island, just visible through the rain-lashed mist. The land was steeped in lore and legend, with a long, bloody history of Viking invasion.

Locals believed that the island had a soul and a personality. They believed that the unpredictable weather was Glenmore expressing her many moods.

He glanced up at the angry sky with a cynical smile. If that was the case then today she was definitely menopausal.

Or maybe, like the islanders, she'd seen his return and was crying.

The island loomed out of the mist and he stared ahead, seeing dark memories waiting on the shore. *Memories of wild teenage years; of anger and defiance.* His past was a stormy canvas of rules broken, boundaries exploded, vices explored, girls seduced—*far too many girls seduced*—and all against an atmosphere of intense disapproval from the locals who'd thought his parents should have had more control.

Remembering the vicious, violent atmosphere of his home,

he gave a humourless laugh. His father hadn't been capable of controlling himself, let alone him. After his mother had left, he'd spent as little time in the house as possible.

The rain was falling heavily as the ferry docked and he turned up the collar of his leather jacket and moved purposefully towards his motorbike.

He could have replaced his helmet and assured himself a degree of privacy from the hostile stares, but instead he paused for a moment, the wicked streak inside him making sure that they had more than enough time to take one more good look at his face. He didn't want there to be any doubt in their minds. He wanted them to know that he was back.

Let them stare and speculate. It would save him the bother of announcing his return.

With a smooth, athletic movement, he settled his powerful body onto the motorbike and caught the eye of the ferryman, acknowledging his disbelieving stare with a slight inclination of his head. He knew exactly what old Jim was thinking—*that the morning ferry had brought trouble to Glenmore*. And news of trouble spread fast on this island. As if to confirm his instincts, he caught a few words from the crush of people preparing to leave the ferry. *Arrogant, wild, unstable, volatile, handsome as the devil...*

He pushed the helmet down onto his head with his gloved hands. Luckily for him, plenty of women were attracted to arrogant, wild, unstable, volatile men, or his life would have been considerably more boring than it had been.

From behind the privacy of his helmet, he smiled, knowing exactly what would happen next. The rumours would spread like ripples in a pond. Within minutes, news of his arrival would have spread across the island. Ferryman to fisherman, fisherman to shopkeeper, shopkeeper to customer—it would take no time at all for the entire population of the island to be informed of the latest news—that Conner MacNeil had come in on the morning ferry.

The Bad Boy was back on the Island.

CHAPTER ONE

'THE waiting room is packed and you've had five requests for home visits.' Flora handed Logan a prescription to sign, thinking that he looked more tired than ever. 'Given that they were all mobile and none of their complaints sounded life-threatening, Janet's managed to persuade them all to come to the surgery because it just isn't practical for you to go dashing around the island at the moment when you're running this practice on your own. What happens if we have a genuine emergency? You can't be in five places at once. We can't carry on like this, Logan. *You* can't carry on like this. You're going to drop.'

Logan looked at the prescription. 'Gentacin ear drops?'

'Pam King has an infection. She has her ears syringed regularly, but this time the whole of the canal is looking inflamed. There didn't seem any point in adding her to your already buckling list. I've taken off half your patients and if I can sort them out, I will. Otherwise I'll push them back through to you.'

'You, Flora Harris, are a miracle.' Logan signed the prescription. 'And persuading you to come back here as my practice nurse was the best thing I ever did. When Kyla and

Ethan left, I couldn't imagine how we were going to cope. I lost nurse and doctor in one fell swoop.'

'Well, I've only solved one half of your problem. You still need to find a doctor to replace Ethan. Any progress?'

'I think so.'

'Seriously?' Flora picked the prescription up from his desk. 'You've found someone?'

'Ask me again at lunchtime. I'm expecting someone on the morning ferry.'

'Oh, that's fantastic.' Relieved, Flora relaxed slightly. 'Is he or she good? Well qualified?'

'It's a he.' Logan turned back to his computer. 'And, yes, he's extremely well qualified.'

Flora stared at him expectantly. 'And...?'

'And what?'

'Aren't you going to tell me any more?'

'No.' He tapped a few keys and frowned at the screen. 'How are you finding Glenmore, Flora? I haven't really had a chance to ask you and you've already been here for a month. Everything going all right? Have you settled into Evanna's cottage?'

'Yes, thank you.' *Hadn't they been discussing the new doctor?* Why were they suddenly on the subject of her cottage? Why was he changing the subject? 'Evanna's cottage is beautiful. I love it.' It was true. She'd never imagined she'd live anywhere so pretty. 'You can see the sea from the bed...' she blushed '...but, of course, you already know that, given that the two of you are married. I'm sure you spent plenty of time in her cottage.'

'Actually, we didn't.' Logan glanced at her, amused. 'We usually stayed at mine because there was more room. Are you finding the work very different from the practice in Edinburgh?'

'Not really, but everything takes four times as long because this is Glenmore and people like to chat.' Flora gave a helpless shrug. 'I always seem to be running late.'

'You need to cut them off when they gossip.' Logan turned his attention back to the computer screen, searching for something. 'That's what the rest of us do.'

'I haven't worked out how to do that without appearing rude. I don't want to offend them. They're all so nice and they mean well.' Flora picked up the prescription and moved towards the door. 'Anyway, I'd better let you carry on. At this rate you'll still be here at midnight. And so will I.'

As she left the room and returned to her own consulting room she suddenly remembered that Logan hadn't given her any more clues as to the identity of the new doctor. On an island where no one kept a secret, Logan appeared to have one. Why? What possible reason could he have for being so cloak and dagger about the whole thing?

Who exactly had he appointed?

Conner parked the motorbike and dragged the helmet from his head. The rain had stopped and the sun fought a battle with the clouds, as if to remind him that the weather on Glenmore Island was as unpredictable as ever.

It was July and still the wind blew.

That same wind had almost landed him in jail at the age of sixteen.

Tucking his helmet under his arm, he strolled into the surgery. *Nice job, Logan*, he thought to himself as he took in his surroundings in one casual glance. Sleek, clean lines and plenty of light. Despite the early hour, the waiting room was already crowded with patients and he saw heads turn and eyes widen as he passed.

Without adjusting his pace, he ignored the reception desk and made for the first consulting room. As he approached the door a patient walked out, clutching a prescription in her hand. She took one look at him and stopped dead, her open mouth reminding him of a baby bird waiting to be fed.

'Conner MacNeil.' Her voice trailed off in a strangled squeak and he lifted an eyebrow, a sardonic expression in his eyes as he observed her mounting discomfort.

If he'd been in any doubt as to the islanders' reaction to his return, that doubt had now gone.

'Mrs Graham.' He was cool and polite, his neutral tone a direct contrast to her shock and consternation. He moved past her, knowing that he should cut short the encounter, but he couldn't quite help himself and he turned, the devil dancing in his eyes. 'I hope your beautiful garden is thriving. If I remember correctly, it's always at its best in July.'

Her soft gasp of outrage made it obvious that her memories of their last meeting were as clear as his and a smile played around his hard mouth as he walked into the consulting room without bothering to knock.

Mrs Graham's garden.

He still remembered the girl...

He pushed the door shut with the flat of his hand and the man at the desk looked up.

'Conner.' Logan rose to his feet, welcome in his eyes as he stretched out his hand. 'It's been too long.'

'Not long enough for some,' Conner murmured, thinking of Mrs Graham who, he was sure, at that precise moment was still glaring angrily at the closed door. 'Prepare yourself for a riot. The locals will be arming themselves any minute now.' He shook the hand of the man who had been part of his boyhood.

'Kate Graham recognised you, then? I seem to recall that you were stark naked the last time she saw you.'

The devil was back in Conner's eyes. 'Mrs Graham had extremely tall delphiniums in her border,' he recalled. 'She only saw my face.'

Logan laughed out loud. 'You have no idea how pleased I am to see you. You're looking good, Conner.'

'I wish I could return the compliment.' Conner's dark brows drew together in a frown as he studied his cousin, taking in the faint shadows and the lines of strain. 'You've looked better. Island life obviously doesn't suit you. You need to leave this backwater and find yourself a proper job.' But his tone was light because he knew that the medical care that his cousin delivered on this remote Scottish island was of exceptional quality.

'There's nothing wrong with island life, just the lack of medical staff. To run this place effectively we need two doctors and two nurses.' Logan rubbed his fingers over his forehead. 'It's been tough since Kyla and Ethan left. I lost a doctor and a nurse in one blow.'

Conner thought about his cousin. 'I never thought Kyla would leave this place.'

'She married an Englishman with itchy feet.'

'There's treatment for that.'

'Yeah.' Logan grinned. 'Anyway, it's only temporary and I've replaced Kyla. Now you're here, so we're back on track.'

'If I were you, I'd postpone the celebrations until the whole island gets wind of your little plan. The jungle drums will start beating soon.'

'They're already beating.' Logan picked up his coffee-mug and then realised that it was empty and put it down again. 'My phone has been ringing and you've only been on the island for twenty minutes. You certainly know how to make a lasting impression, Conner MacNeil. What exactly did you do on that ferry?'

'Travelled on it. Apparently that was more than enough.' Conner stretched his legs out in front of him and put his helmet down on the floor. 'There's going to be a rebellion. If looks could kill, I'd be in your mortuary right now, not

your consulting room. The natives will probably return to
their roots and take up arms to defend themselves from the
unwelcome invader. They're preparing themselves for rape
and pillage.'

'Ignore them. You know what the islanders are like.' Logan
reached for a pack of papers. 'They don't like change. Can
you read this lot quickly and sign? Just a formality.'

'And you know how much I love formality,' Connor
drawled softly, but he leaned forward to take the papers,
grimacing when he saw the thickness of the documentation.
'Life's too short to wade through that much bureaucracy.
What does it say? *Conner MacNeil must not steal, destroy
property or otherwise harass the citizens of Glenmore*?'

'All that and the fact that all single women under the age
of thirty are now considered to be in danger.' Logan's eyes
gleamed as he handed his cousin a pen. 'The men of the island are locking up their wives and daughters as we speak
and Mrs Graham is probably shovelling fertiliser on her delphiniums to increase their height and preserve her modesty
and yours. Sign the back page.'

'Single women under the age of thirty? Why thirty? That
doesn't give me nearly enough scope. I've always preferred
experience to innocence.' Conner flipped straight to the back
of the sheaf of papers and signed with a casual flourish.

Logan lifted an eyebrow. 'Aren't you going to bother to
read what you just signed?'

'I'm presuming it's a load of rules and regulations.'

'And knowing that, you're prepared to sign? I thought you
hated rules and regulations.'

'I do, but I trust you and I admire what you've built here
on Glenmore.' Conner handed the papers back to Logan, a
faint smile on his mouth. 'I promise to do my best for your
patients. I'm *not* promising that I won't bend the rules a little
if it proves to be necessary.'

Logan reached for an envelope. 'I bend them all the time. It's the only way to get things done. It's good to have you here, Conner.'

'I don't think everyone is going to agree with you. Judging from the shock on the faces I've seen so far, you didn't warn them in advance.'

'Do I look stupid?' Logan slipped the papers into the envelope and dropped it into the tray on his desk. 'I was waiting until you showed up.'

'Did you think I wouldn't?'

'Reliability isn't your middle name. I wasn't sure you'd actually do this when the time came.'

Connor gave a humourless laugh. 'Then that makes two of us.'

'But you did, so now I can break the happy news to the inhabitants of Glenmore. How have you been? Tell me, honestly.' Logan hesitated. 'It must have been hard...'

'Coming back? Why would you say that?' Conner was surprised to find that his voice sounded so harsh. 'You know how much I love this place.'

Ignoring the sarcasm, Logan watched him steadily. 'Actually, I was talking about leaving the army.'

The army?

Conner realised that since he'd stepped off the ferry, he'd given no thought to the life he'd just left. All he could think about was Glenmore and how it felt to be back. The bad memories poured into him like some dark, insidious disease, gradually taking possession of his mind. 'Leaving the army isn't my problem at the moment.' he growled. 'And, anyway, I don't believe in living in the past when there's a perfectly good future to be getting on with.'

'Are you going to sell the house?'

'You get straight to the point, don't you?' Conner rose to his feet and paced across the room, keeping his back to his cousin as he rode the pain. 'Yes.' He turned, his eyes fierce. 'Why would I keep it?'

'So that you have a place on Glenmore?'

'If I'd wanted that,' Conner said softly, 'why would I be renting your barn?'

'Good point.' Logan gave him a sympathetic look. 'This must be hard for you, I know.'

'Nowhere near as hard as it's going to be for the locals.' Conner studied a picture on the wall. 'They're going to think that you've lost your mind, appointing me as the locum.'

'They'd be less shocked if you told them the truth about what you've been doing since you stormed off Glenmore all those years ago.'

'Island gossip has never interested me.'

'You sound like Flora. Her clinics are taking twice as long as they should because she doesn't like to interrupt people when they're chatting.'

'Flora?'

'My practice nurse. She replaced Kyla.'

'Flora Harris?' Conner turned, the pain inside him under control. 'Daughter of Ian Harris, our island solicitor? Niece of our esteemed headmistresses?'

Cloudy dark hair, soft brown eyes, an impossibly shy and awkward teenager, and as innocent as the dawn...

Logan's eyes narrowed. 'You didn't ever...'

'Fortunately for her, there were enough wild teenage girls on the island who were more than happy to experiment, without me having to corrupt the saintly Flora. Anyway, she didn't take her nose out of a book for long enough to discover the existence of sex.'

'She isn't saintly. Just shy.'

'Maybe. But definitely not the sort of girl who would skip classes in favour of a practical session on human reproduction.' Conner rolled his shoulders to ease the tension. 'I'm not surprised she's a nurse. It would have been that or a librarian. Does she know I'm the new doctor?'

'Not yet.'

'She won't approve.'

'Even if she doesn't, she would never say so. Flora is sweet, kind and incredibly civilised.'

'Whereas I'm sharp, unkind and incredibly uncivilised. I'm willing to bet that the first thing she does, when she finds out about me, is remind you that I blew up the science lab.'

'I'd forgotten about that.' Momentarily distracted, Logan narrowed his eyes. 'What did you use—potassium?'

'Too dangerous. They didn't keep it at school.' Restless, Conner paced across the room again and scanned the row of textbooks on the shelf. 'But they did keep sodium. That was good enough.'

'It should have been in a locked cupboard.'

'It was.'

Logan laughed. 'I'm amazed you weren't expelled.'

'Me, too. Very frustrating, given how hard I applied myself to the task.' Conner suppressed a yawn. 'So I'm going to be working with Flora. The excitement of this place increases by the minute.'

'She's a brilliant nurse. She was working in Edinburgh until last month but we persuaded her to come back. And now you've joined us. I've been thinking—we should tell the islanders what you've been doing with your life.'

'It's none of their business.'

Logan sighed. 'I don't see why you're so reluctant to let people know that you're a good guy.'

'Who says I'm a good guy? If you wanted a good guy for the job then you've appointed the wrong man.' Conner turned, a ghost of a smile on his face. 'You'll have a hard job convincing Flora, Mrs Graham and any of that lot on the ferry that there's a single decent bone in my body.'

'Give them time. How soon can you start?'

'That depends on how soon you want to clear out your surgery.' Conner unzipped his jacket. 'I can guarantee that they won't be queuing up to see me. I'm assuming that, by appointing me, you want to encourage your patients to deal with their ailments at home. We both know they won't be coming to the surgery once they know who the doctor is. Which means I get to lounge around all day with my feet up while you pay my salary.'

'That's rubbish. You know as well as I do that the women will be forming a disorderly queue all the way to the harbour.' Logan's expression was serious. 'Tell them the truth about yourself, Con. It will help them understand you.'

'I don't need them to understand me. That's always been the difference between us. You *are* a nice guy. I'm not. You care about them. I don't.'

'So why are you here?'

'Not out of love for the islanders, that's for sure. And I'm here because…' Conner shrugged '…you rang me. I came. Let's leave it at that.' He didn't want to think about the rest of it. Not yet. He frowned, his attention caught by one of the photographs on the wall. 'Isn't that little Evanna Duncan? Are you two together?'

'She's Evanna MacNeil now,' Logan's tone was a shade cooler as he corrected him. 'I married her a year ago and if you so much as glance in her direction you might just discover that I'm not such a nice guy after all.'

'Seducing married women has never been on my list of vices.' Conner turned and looked at his cousin. 'She always adored you. Children?'

'Evanna is due in five weeks.' Logan hesitated. 'And I have a daughter from a previous marriage. Kirsty. She's two.'

'So, you're a regular family man.' Conner saw the shadows in Logan's eyes but he knew better than to ask questions. He had plenty of shadows of his own, *dark corners that he kept private.*

Logan's gaze didn't waver. 'What about you? Wife? Children?'

'I'll assume that wasn't a serious question.'

'I was just hoping you had a reason not to wreak havoc across the female population of Glenmore over the summer. Just don't touch the patients, it's strictly frowned on and definitely against the rules.' Logan rose to his feet. 'Use the consulting room across the corridor. Do you want to shave or change before you start?'

'And ruin the opportunity to shock everyone? I don't think so. I'll stay as I am.'

'I've just broken the news of your arrival to Janet, our receptionist. She's already lined up some patients. Is there anything you need to know before you start?'

'Yes.' Conner paused, his hand on the door. 'If I'm not allowed to seduce the patients, how am I supposed to relieve the boredom of being trapped on Glenmore?'

'I don't suppose you'd consider a round of golf?'

'No.'

'I didn't think you would. Well, I'm confident you'll find something or someone to distract you.' Logan gave a resigned laugh. 'Just steer clear of Mrs Graham's garden, that's all I ask.'

She needed to talk to Logan quickly.

Flora nipped across the corridor and tapped lightly on the door. Without waiting for an answer, she walked into his consulting room and immediately collided with a tall, dark-haired man whose body seemed to be made of nothing but rock-hard muscle. She stumbled slightly but his hands came out and steadied her, his strong fingers digging into her arms as he held her.

'I'm *terribly* sorry,' she apologised breathlessly, catching her glasses before they could slide down her nose, 'I had no idea Logan had a patient with him.'

'Hello, Flora.' His lazy, masculine drawl was alarmingly familiar and her eyes flew wide as she tilted her head back to take a proper look at him.

'Oh!' Her heart started to beat in double time and she felt decidedly faint. Her knees weakened and from a distance she heard Logan's voice.

'Flora, you remember my cousin Conner?'

Remember? *Remember?* Well, of course she remembered! She might be short-sighted, but she was still a woman! And it didn't matter how many rules or hearts he'd broken, there wasn't a woman alive who would forget Conner MacNeil once she'd met him.

Especially not her.

And he would have known how she'd felt because arrogance and Conner had gone hand in hand. Even as a young boy he'd known exactly what effect he had on the girls and had used it to his advantage.

But it wasn't a boy who was standing in front of her now. It was a man. And his effect on the opposite sex had grown proportionately.

Determined not to boost his ego by revealing her thoughts, Flora screwed up her face and adopted what she hoped was a puzzled expression. 'Conner…Conner… The name *is* familiar—were you below me at school? Or were you above me?'

His blue eyes glinted with wicked humour. 'I don't recall ever being above or below you, Flora,' he murmured softly, 'but that may be my defective memory.'

She felt the heat flare in her cheeks and remembered, too late, that anyone trying to play word games with Conner was always going to lose. His brain and his tongue worked in perfect unison whereas hers had always been slightly disconnected. Without fail she thought of the perfect thing to say about two days after the opportunity to say it had passed.

'Well, you do look vaguely familiar,' she said quickly, stepping back and concentrating her attention on Logan to cover up how unsettled she felt. A moment ago she'd been happily existing in the present, enjoying her life. The next she'd been transported back to her childhood and it was a lonely, uncomfortable place. If this was time travel, then she wanted none of it.

She'd had such a desperate, agonising crush on Conner. *A crush that had been intensified by the fact that her father had forbidden her to mix with him.* 'Sorry to disturb your reunion, but Amy Price just rang me. Heather has chickenpox.'

'And?' Logan frowned. 'Tell her to buy some paracetamol and chlorpheniramine from the pharmacy.'

'I'm not worried about Heather. I'm worried about your wife. Evanna saw the child in clinic yesterday.'

'And the child would have been infectious.' Understanding dawned and Logan cursed softly. 'Has Evanna had chickenpox?'

'I don't think so. That's why I thought you ought to know straight away. I remember talking about it with her a few months ago. She was telling me that her mother sent her off to play with everyone who had chickenpox, but she never caught it.'

'Chickenpox is a disease that you don't want to catch in the third trimester of pregnancy.'

'That's what I thought.'

Somehow she was managing to have a normal conversation with Logan, but her head and senses were filled with Conner. In some ways he'd changed, she mused, and yet in others he hadn't. The muscular physique was the reward of manhood but other things—*the air of supreme indifference and the ice-blue eyes*—had been part of the boy.

What was he doing here, anyway? Like everyone else, she'd assumed he'd never show his face on the island again.

Logan walked to his desk. 'I'll call Evanna now.'

'I've already done it. She's about to start her clinic, but she'll come and talk to you first. I thought you might want to delay your first patient or pass him across to the new doctor when he arrives.'

'Relax. She's probably immune.' Conner leaned his broad shoulders against the doorframe, watching them both with an expression that could have been amusement or boredom. 'Do a blood test and check her antibody status.'

She was wrong, Flora realised with a flash of disquiet. *There was nothing of the boy left.* There were more changes than she'd thought, and some were so subtle that they weren't immediately obvious. Those ice-blue eyes were sharper and more cynical, and his arrogance had clearly developed along with his muscles. *What did he know about antibody status?* Or was he one of those people who watched all the medical soaps on television and then assumed they were qualified to diagnose?

To make matters worse, Logan was nodding, encouraging him. 'Yes—yes, I'll do that, but if she's not immune...'

'Then you just give her zoster immunoglobulin. What's the matter with you?' Conner's brows drew into a frown as he looked at his cousin. 'This is why I'm careful not to fall in love. It fries your brain cells and obliterates your judgement.'

'There's nothing wrong with Logan's judgement.' Fiercely loyal, Flora immediately flew to Logan's defence and then wished she hadn't because Conner switched his gaze from Logan to her and his attention was unsettling, to say the least.

Apparently unaware of the change in the atmosphere, Logan rubbed his hand over the back of his neck. 'When you love someone, Conner,' he said, 'you lose perspective.'

Conner's eyes held Flora's. 'I wouldn't know. That's one mistake I've never made.'

She swallowed, every bit as uncomfortable as he'd clearly intended her to be. Was he trying to shock her? He'd had women, she knew that. Probably many. Was she surprised that he'd never found love? *That he considered love a mistake?*

'True love is a gift, given to few,' she murmured, and Conner's mouth tilted and his blue eyes glinted with sardonic humour.

'True love is a curse, bestowed on the unlucky. Love brings weakness and vulnerability. How can that be a gift?'

Flustered, she cleared her throat and looked away. *What was he doing here?* Why had he returned to Glenmore with no warning, looking like the bad guy out of a Hollywood movie? His hair was dark and cropped short and his jaw was dark with stubble. He was *indecently* handsome and the only thing that marred the otherwise faultless symmetry of his features was the slight bump in his nose, an imperfection which she assumed to be the legacy of a fight. He looked tough and dangerous and the impression of virile manhood was further intensified by the width and power of his shoulders under the black leather jacket.

He wasn't attractive, Flora told herself desperately. How could he possibly be attractive? He looked...rough. Rough and a little menacing. She thought of the conventional, bespectacled lawyer she'd dated for a while in Edinburgh. He'd always let her through doors first and had been completely charming. His hair had always been neat and tidy and she'd never, ever seen him anything other than clean-shaven. He'd almost always worn a suit when they'd dated and his legs hadn't filled his trousers the way that Conner's did. And then there had been his smile. His cheeks had dimpled slightly and his eyes had been kind. *Nothing like Conner's eyes.* Conner's eyes were fierce and hard, as if he was just waiting for some-one to pick a fight so that he could work off some pent-up energy.

Her heart thudded hard against her chest. Conner MacNeil wasn't charming or kind. He was— He was…unsuitable. Dangerous. A woman had to be mad to look twice at a man like him.

Why, she wondered helplessly, *was the unsuitable and the dangerous always so much more appealing than the suitable?*

'We need to get on.' With a huge effort of will, she broke the connection and turned her attention back to Logan. 'We've a busy surgery this morning. What happened to the new doctor? Did he show up? You didn't tell me who he is or when he or she can start.'

'You heard the woman.' Logan turned to Conner. 'Go and do your job.'

Conner shrugged and a slight smile touched his mouth. 'Prepare for chaos.'

It took Flora a moment to understand the implications of their conversation. 'You can't— Conner?' Her voice cracked. 'But Conner isn't—' She broke off and Conner lifted an eye-brow.

'Don't stop there,' he prompted softly. 'I'm keen to hear all the things I'm not.'

Not suitable. Not safe. Not conventional. Not responsi-ble… She could have drawn up a never-ending list of things he was not. 'I— You're not a doctor. You *can't* be a doctor.'

He smiled. 'Why? Because I didn't hand in my home-work on time?'

'You didn't hand in your homework at all. You were hardly ever at school!'

'I'm flattered that you noticed.' His soft observation was a humiliating reminder that she'd always been aware of him and he'd never even noticed her.

She was probably the only girl on Glenmore who hadn't been kissed by Conner MacNeil.

She turned away, horrified that after all this time she still cared that she'd been invisible to him. 'You're forgetting that my aunt was the headmistress.'

'I've forgotten nothing.' There was something in his tone that made her glance at him and speculate. There was resentment there and—*anger*?

He'd always seemed angry, she remembered. *Angry, moody and wild.*

Was that why he was back? Was he seeking revenge on the people who had disapproved and eventually despaired of him?

'Ann runs a wonderful school.' She felt compelled to defend her family. 'The children all adore her and they get a fantastic education.'

'There's more to education than sitting in rows in a classroom with a book in front of you.' Conner leaned nonchalantly against the table, his glance speculative. 'Still the same Flora. Conventional. Playing everything by the rules. I presume that all your affairs are still with books?'

His comment stung. He made her feel so—so—*boring.* Plain, boring Flora. And that was what they'd called her at school, of course. *Boring Flora.* Hurt, she clawed back. 'Rules are there for a reason and if you're really a doctor then I hope you've read a few books yourself along the way, otherwise I pity your patients.' She stopped, shocked at herself and aware that Logan was gaping at her in amazement.

'Flora! I've never heard you speak to anyone like that before. Usually I have to drag a response from you. What is the matter with you?'

'I don't know. I— Nothing.' Flora's cheeks were scarlet and she blinked several times and adjusted her glasses. She didn't know what was the matter. She didn't know what had come over her. *She didn't know why she felt so hot and both-ered.* 'Sorry. I apologise.'

She felt miserably uncomfortable and mortified that she'd embarrassed Logan. The only person who didn't seem re-motely embarrassed was Conner himself. He simply laughed.

'Don't apologise. I much prefer to be around people who say what they think. I'm sure most of the inhabitants of Glenmore will share your sentiments and express them far more vociferously.' He turned to Logan. 'I did warn you that this wouldn't work. It isn't too late to change your mind.'

'Of course I'm not going to change my mind.' Logan sounded exasperated. 'Flora, Conner's credentials are—'

'Irrelevant,' Conner interrupted smoothly, and Flora bit her lip.

She knew she ought to say something nice and welcoming, but her brain just didn't seem to be working with its normal efficiency. Seeing Conner again without warning was shock-ing, confusing and—*thrilling*?

Horrified, she quickly dismissed that last emotion and pressed her fingers to her chest, wishing that her heart would slow down. It was not, definitely not, thrilling that he was back on the island. If she'd been asked to choose the least suitable man to be a doctor on Glenmore, it would have been Conner MacNeil.

Over the years, she'd thought of him often.

Too often.

She'd wondered where he was and what he was doing. She'd imagined him languishing in some jail, maybe in a foreign country; she'd imagined him sitting by a pool in a tax haven, having made piles of money by some unspeak-ably dubious means.

Never, in her most extravagant fantasies, had she imagined him training as a doctor and never, in those same dreams, had she imagined him returning to Glenmore.

One thing she knew for sure; the calm, tranquil routine of Glenmore Island was about to be overturned.

She didn't know what sort of doctor Conner was going to prove to be, but she knew it wasn't the sort that the islanders were used to seeing.

CHAPTER TWO

CONNER buzzed for his first patient and braced himself for the reaction.

He wasn't disappointed.

The first man who walked through his door took one look at him, gave a horrified gasp and immediately backed out, muttering that he'd 'wait for the other doctor'.

Conner watched him leave, his handsome face expressionless. Clearly people had long memories and he understood all about that. *He hadn't forgotten a single minute of his time on Glenmore.*

With a dismissive shrug, he buzzed for the next patient and the moment Susan Ellis walked through the door, he prepared himself for a repeat performance. If he had any supporters among the islanders—*and he was beginning to doubt that he had*—this lady wouldn't be among them. She ran the shop at the harbour and she had reason to know him better than most.

'Good morning, Mrs Ellis.' He kept his tone suitably neutral but her face reflected her shock at seeing him.

'Conner MacNeil! So the rumours are true, then.' She glanced behind her, obviously wondering if she'd wandered into the wrong building, and Conner lifted an eyebrow.

'Is there something I can help you with, Mrs Ellis?' *Perhaps this wasn't going to work after all.*

'I don't know. I'll have to think about it.'

It was on the tip of his tongue to tell her to think quickly because there was a queue of patients waiting but then he realised that the queue was probably dwindling by the second so a slightly longer consultation wasn't likely to matter.

'If you'd rather see Logan, go ahead. My feelings will remain intact.'

'I'm not thinking about your feelings,' she said tartly. 'I'm thinking about my health. I assume Logan knows you're here?'

'You think I broke a window and climbed in? Looking for drugs, maybe?'

She gave him a reproving look. 'Don't give me sarcasm, Conner MacNeil. I'm not afraid to admit that you wouldn't leap to mind as someone to turn to in times of trouble.'

Clearly recalling the details of their last encounter, Conner relented slightly. 'I don't blame you for that.'

She studied him from the safety of the doorway, her mouth compressed into a firm line of disapproval. 'So you've mended your ways. Are you really a doctor?'

'Apparently.'

'There's plenty on this island who will be surprised to hear that.'

'I'm sure that's true.' Conner kept his tone level. 'Are you going or staying? Because if you're staying, you may as well sit down. Or we can carry on this consultation standing, up if that's what you would prefer.'

'Not very friendly, are you?'

'I presumed you were looking for a doctor, not a date.'

Susan Ellis gave a reluctant laugh. 'You always were a sharp one, I'll give you that.' After a moment's hesitation she closed the door and sat down gingerly on the edge of the seat, as if she hadn't quite decided whether she was going to stay or not. 'I'm not sure if I can talk about this with you.'

Conner sighed. *It was going to be a long day.* 'As I said, if you'd rather see Logan, I quite understand.'

She fiddled with the strap of her handbag and then put it on the floor in a decisive movement. 'No,' she said firmly. 'I've never been one to live in the past. Times change. People change. If you're a doctor then— I don't suppose you'll be able to help me anyway.'

'Try me.'

'It's hard to put a finger on when it all started, but it's been a while.' She glanced at Conner and he sat in silence, just listening. 'Probably been almost a year. I'm tired, you see. All the time. And I know doctors hate hearing that. You're going to say it's just my age, but—'

'I haven't said anything yet, Mrs Ellis. You speak your lines and then I'll speak mine.' He could have been wrong but he thought he saw her shoulders relax slightly.

'Fair enough. Well, I feel washed out and exhausted a lot of the time. It doesn't matter how well I sleep or how much rest I take, I'm still tired.' She hesitated and then sighed. 'And a little depressed, if I'm honest. But that's probably because I just feel so...slow. If this is getting old, I want none of it.'

'Have you gained weight?'

She stiffened. 'Are you going to lecture me on my eating?'

'Are you going to answer the question?'

Susan shifted self consciously, automatically pulling in her stomach and straightening her shoulders. 'Yes, I've gained weight, but I suppose that's my age as well. You just can't eat so much when you get older and it's hard to change old habits. Aren't you going to make notes? Logan always keeps meticulous notes.'

'I prefer to listen. I'll do the writing part later.' Conner stood up and walked towards her, his eyes concentrating on her face. 'Your skin is dry. Is that usual for you?'

'Didn't used to be but it's usual now. My hair's the same.' She tilted her face so that he could take a closer look. 'Observant, aren't you?'

'Sometimes.' Having looked at her skin, Conner took her hands in his and examined them carefully. Then he looked at her eyelids. 'You have slight oedema. Can I take a look at your feet?'

'My feet?'

'That's right.' He squatted down and helped her slip her shoes off.

'I never thought I'd have Conner MacNeil at my feet.'

'Savour the moment, Mrs Ellis. Do they bother you?'

'They're aching terribly and I wouldn't be surprised if they're a bit swollen...' She wiggled her toes. 'I assumed it was the heat.'

Conner examined her feet and ankles. 'From what I've seen, Glenmore is in the middle of a typical summer. Wind and rain. I'm not expecting any cases of heatstroke today.' He was sure that her feet were swollen for a very different reason.

'We had sunshine last week. You know Glenmore—the weather is always unpredictable. A bit like you.' She looked at him, her gaze slightly puzzled. 'You're very gentle. I hadn't expected that of you.'

'I prefer not to leave marks on my victims.' A faint smile on his face, Conner rose to his feet. 'The swelling isn't caused by heat, Mrs Ellis. I can tell you that much.' He washed his hands and picked up the IV tray that Flora had left on the trolley. 'I'm going to take some blood.'

'Is that really necessary?'

'No. I just want to cause you pain.'

His patient laughed out loud. 'Revenge, Conner?'

'Maybe. You called the police that night.'

'Yes, I did.' Susan stuck out her arm. 'You were out of control. Only eight years old and helping yourself to what you wanted from my shop.'

He ran his fingers gently over her skin, searching for a vein. 'I needed some stuff and I didn't have the money to pay.'

'And how often did I hear that from the children? Plenty of them did it.' Her laughter faded and she shook her head as she watched him. 'But I remember you. You were different. So bold. A real rebel. Even when John, our island policeman, gave you a talking to, you didn't cry. It was as if you were used to being shouted at. As if you'd hardened yourself.'

Conner didn't falter. 'You have good veins. This shouldn't be hard.'

'You're not going to excuse yourself, are you?'

'Why would I do that?'

'Because we found out later that there were things happening in your house.' She spoke softly. 'Plenty to explain why you were the way you were.'

Suddenly the room felt bitterly cold. Conner slipped a tourniquet over her wrist. 'Everyone's family is complicated. Mine was no different.'

'No?' Susan looked at him for a moment and then sighed. 'I remember how you looked on that day. You just stood there, all defiant, your chin up and those blue eyes of yours flashing daggers. Oh, you were angry with me.'

'As you said, you'd called the police.'

'But it didn't have any effect. You were never afraid of anyone or anything, were you, Conner MacNeil?'

Oh, yes, he'd been afraid. *'Don't do it. Don't touch her—I'll kill you if you touch her.'*

With ruthless determination Conner pushed the memory back into the darkness where it belonged. 'On the contrary, I was afraid of my cousin Kyla.' Keeping his tone neutral, he tightened the tourniquet and studied the woman's veins.

'She had a deadly punch and a scream that would puncture your eardrums.'

'Ah, Kyla. We all miss her. It's not good when islanders leave. It's not good for Glenmore.'

Swift and sure, Conner slipped the needle into the vein. 'Depends on the islander, Mrs Ellis. There are some people that Glenmore is pleased to see the back of.' He released the tourniquet and watched as the blood flowed. 'I'm checking your thyroid function, by the way.'

'Oh. Why?'

'Because I think hypothyroidism is a possible explanation for your symptoms.' Having collected the blood he needed, he withdrew the needle and covered the area with a pad. 'Press on that for a moment, would you? If you leave here with bruises, that will be another black mark against me.'

She looked down at her arm. 'That's it? You've finished? You're good at that. I barely felt it.' The expression in her eyes cooled. 'I suppose you have a lot of experience with needles.'

Conner picked up a pen and labelled the bottles. 'I'm the first to admit that my list of vices is deplorably long, Mrs Ellis, but I've never done drugs.'

Her shoulders relaxed. 'I'm sorry,' she said softly. 'That was uncalled for. If I've offended you...'

'You haven't offended me.' He dropped the blood samples into a bag, wondering what had possessed him to take the job on Glenmore. He could have come in on the ferry, sorted out his business and left again.

'Hypothyroidism, you say?'

'There are numerous alternative explanations, of course, but this is a good place to start.'

'I don't know whether to be relieved or alarmed. I was expecting you to tell me it was nothing. Should I be worried?'

'Worrying doesn't achieve anything. If we find a problem, we'll look for a solution.' He completed the necessary form and then washed his hands again. 'I'm going to wait for those results before we look at anything else because I have a strong feeling that we've found the culprit.'

'You're confident.'

'Would you prefer me to fumble and dither?'

She laughed. 'You always were a bright boy, Conner MacNeil. Too bright, some would say. Bright and a rebel. A dangerous combination.'

Conner sat back down in his chair. 'Call the surgery in three days for the result and then make another appointment to see me. We can talk about what to do next.'

'All right, I'll do that. Thank you.' Susan picked up her bag, rose to her feet and walked to the door. Then she turned. 'I always regretted it, you know.'

Conner looked up. 'Regretted what?'

'Calling the police.' Her voice was soft. 'At the time I thought you needed a fright. I thought a bit of discipline might sort you out. But I was wrong. You were wild. Out of control. But what you needed was a bit of love. People to believe in you. I see that now. What with everything that was happening at home—your mum and dad. Of course, none of us knew the details at the time, but—'

'You did the right thing calling the police, Mrs Ellis,' Conner said in a cool tone. 'In your position I would have called them, too.'

'At the time I was angry that they didn't charge you.'

'I'm sure you were.'

It was her turn to smile. 'Now I'm pleased they didn't. Can I ask you something?'

'You can ask. I don't promise to answer.'

'There was a spate of minor shoplifting at that time but everyone else was taking sweets and crisps. You took the oddest assortment of things. What did you want it all for?'

Conner leaned back and smiled. 'I was making a bomb.'

* * *

'He blew up the science lab!' Flora stood in front of Logan, trying to make him to see reason.

'Funny.' Logan scanned the lab result in front of him. 'Conner said that you'd bring that up.'

'Of course I'm bringing it up. It says everything about the type of person he is.'

'Was.' Logan lifted his eyes to hers. 'It tells you who he was. Not who he is.'

'You really think he's changed?'

'Are you the same person you were at fifteen?'

Agonisingly shy, barely able to string a sentence together in public. Flora flushed. 'No,' she said huskily. 'Of course not.'

Logan shrugged. 'Perhaps he's changed, too.'

'And what if he hasn't? What sort of doctor is he going to make?'

'An extremely clever one. Most people wouldn't have had such a good understanding of the reactivity series to cause that explosion. Anyway, I thought you were relieved that I'd found another doctor.'

'I was, but I never thought for a moment it would be— I mean, *Conner*?' Flora's expression was troubled. 'He's right, you know. The locals won't be happy. What if they make life difficult for him?'

'They always did. He'll cope. Conner is as tough as they come.'

'I can't believe he's a doctor. How did you find out? I mean, he vanished without trace.'

'I stayed in touch with him.' Logan lifted his gaze to hers. 'He's my cousin, Flora. Family. I knew he was a doctor. When I knew I needed help, he seemed the obvious choice.'

'Are you sure? He used to be very unstable. Unreliable. Rebellious. Disruptive.' *Attractive, compelling, addictive.*

'You're describing the teenager.'

'He created havoc.' she looked at him, wondering why she had to remind him of something that he must know himself. 'He was suspended from school *three times*. If there'd been an alternative place for him to go, I'm sure he would have been expelled. Not only did he blow up the science lab, he set off a firework in the library, he burned down the MacDonalds' barn—the list of things he did is endless. He was wild, Logan. Totally out of control.' *And impossibly, hopelessly attractive.* There hadn't been a woman on Glenmore who hadn't dreamed of taming him. Herself included.

She'd wanted to help.

She'd wanted...

She pushed the thought away quickly. She'd been a dreamy teenager but she was an adult now, a grown woman and far too sensible to see Conner as anything other than a liability.

'His parents were going through a particularly acrimonious divorce at the time. There were lots of rumours about that household. My aunt—his mother—left when he was eleven. That's tough on any child.' Logan turned his attention back to the pile in his in-tray. 'Enough to shake the roots of any family. It's not surprising he was disruptive.'

'He isn't interested in authority.'

Logan threw the pen down on his desk. 'Perhaps he thinks that those in authority let him down.'

Flora bit her lip. 'Perhaps they did. But if that's the case then it makes even less sense that he's back. He couldn't wait to get away from Glenmore the first time around and he stayed away for *twelve years*.'

'Is it that long?' Logan studied her face thoughtfully. 'I haven't been counting, but obviously you have.'

'It was a wild guess,' Flora muttered quickly, 'but either way, it's been a long time. And the question is, why has he picked this particular moment to come back?'

'Why does it matter? If he turns out to be a lousy doctor,

I'm the one who will pay the price. Or is there more to this than your concern for the reputation of Glenmore Medical Centre? Is this personal, Flora?' Logan's voice was gentle. 'Is there something going on that I should know about?'

'Don't be ridiculous.' Flora rose to her feet swiftly, her heart pounding. 'And I think it's obvious to everyone that I'm not his type. I've never been attracted to unsuitable men.' A painful lump sat in the pit of her stomach. *He'd never looked at her. Not once.*

'Then you're probably the only woman on the island who wasn't,' Logan said mildly, 'if I recall correctly, Conner had quite a following, and the more reprehensible his behaviour, the bigger the following.'

'I suppose some of the girls found him attractive because he was forbidden territory.' Flora wished her heart would slow down. 'I still can't believe he's a doctor.'

'I know you can't. You didn't exactly hide your astonishment,' Logan said dryly and Flora felt a twinge of guilt.

'I didn't mean to be rude but weren't *you* surprised when you found out?'

'No.' Logan rolled his shoulders to ease the stiffness of sitting. 'Conner always was ferociously clever.'

'He hated school. He was barely ever there.'

'And he still managed straight As in every subject. As I said—we all let him down. He was too clever to be trapped behind a desk and forced to learn in a prescribed pattern. People were too conventional to notice the brain behind the behavioural problems.'

Flora gave a puzzled frown. She'd never thought of it that way before. 'Well, he obviously learned to study at some point. Where did he train, anyway?'

'In the army.'

'In the—' Stunned, Flora swallowed. 'He was in the *army*?'

'Army medic.' Logan flipped through a pile of papers on his desk and removed a file. 'Read.' He handed it to her. 'It's impressive stuff. Perhaps it will set your mind at rest about his ability and dedication.'

'But the army requires discipline. All the things Conner doesn't—'

'Read,' Logan said firmly. 'The patients might doubt him to begin with, but I don't want the practice staff making the same mistake. The man's qualifications and experience are better than mine. Read, Flora.'

Flora opened the file reluctantly. After a moment, she looked up. 'He's a surgeon?'

'Among other things. I did tell you that the man was clever.'

Her eyes flickered back to the page. 'Afghanistan? That doesn't sound very safe.'

'No.' Logan's voice was dry. 'But it sounds very Conner. I don't suppose anything safe would hold his interest for long.'

'Which brings me back to my original question.' She dropped the file back on his desk. 'What's he doing back on Glenmore? He hates Glenmore and if he still needs adrenaline and excitement in his life, he's going to last five minutes on this island.'

'I don't think it's any of my business.' Logan leaned back in his chair. 'He's back, that's all I need to know.'

'It's going to be like putting a match to a powder keg. And I'm just worried he'll let you down in the middle of the summer tourist season. You and all the islanders.'

Logan's gaze followed her. 'They let him down. This is his chance to even the score or prove himself. Either way, he's family, Flora, and I'm giving him this opportunity. It's up to him what he chooses to do with it.'

Flora bit her lip. Family. On Glenmore family and community was everything. It was what made the island what it was. But Conner had rejected everything that Glenmore stood for. He'd walked away from it.

So why was he back?

CHAPTER THREE

CONNER WATCHED as Flora entered the room. Her eyes were down and she was clutching a bunch of forms that he assumed were for him.

Probably from Logan, he thought, *finding an excuse to engineer peace.*

The fact that she seemed reluctant to look in his direction amused him. As a teenager she'd been impossibly shy. He remembered her sitting on her own in the corner of the playground, her nose stuck in a book. What he didn't remember was her ever stringing more than two words together. But today, in Logan's surgery, she'd been surprisingly articulate.

He gave a cynical smile.

It seemed his presence was enough to encourage even the mute to speak.

'The lamb enters the wolf's den unprotected,' he drawled softly, and watched as the heat built in her cheeks. 'I never saw you as a risk-taker, Flora. Aren't you afraid I might do something evil to you now we're on our own?'

'Don't be ridiculous.' She adjusted her glasses and put the forms on his desk. 'Logan wanted you to have these.'

No, Conner thought to himself. *Logan wanted us to have*

a moment together because he doesn't want his staff at odds with each other.

He heard her take a deep breath and then she looked at him.

As if she'd been plucking up courage.

'So...' She cleared her throat. 'How is it going? Any problems so far?'

'No problems at all. The locals are refusing to see me, which means I don't have to spend my time listening to the boring detail of people's minor ailments.' He studied the slight fullness of her lower lip and the smooth curve of her cheeks. *She was pretty,* he realised with a stab of shock. She was also wonderfully, deliciously serious and he couldn't resist having a little fun with her. 'And it's really interesting to make contact with all the girls I...grew up with.'

As he'd anticipated, she flushed. What he hadn't expected was the sudden flash of concern in her eyes. *The kindness.* 'The patients are refusing to see you?' She sounded affronted. 'That's awful.'

'Don't worry about it. I'm allergic to hard work and it gives me more time to spend on the internet.'

'You're just saying that, but you must feel terrible about it.'

'I don't give a damn.'

She gave a faint gasp and blinked several times. 'You don't need to pretend with me. I'm sure you're upset. How could you not be?'

'Flora,' he interrupted her, amused by her misinterpretation of the facts, 'don't endow me with qualities that I don't possess. To feel terrible I'd have to care, and I think we both know that my relationship with the islanders is hardly one of lasting affection.'

'You're very hard on them and perhaps that's justified, but you need to see it from their point of view. Everyone's a bit shocked, that's all. No one was expecting you because Logan didn't say anything to anyone.'

'Given that this is Glenmore, I expect he'll be struck off for respecting confidentiality.'

Her sudden smile caught him by surprise. 'They do gossip, don't they? Everything takes three times as long here because of the conversation. I can't get used to it.' Her smile faded. 'Logan told me about what you've done—your training. That's amazing. I had no idea.'

Conner sat in silence and she spread her hands, visibly uncomfortable with the situation.

'I'm *trying* to apologise. I didn't mean to be rude. It was just that...' She gave an awkward shrug. 'Anyway, I really am sorry.'

'Never apologise, Flora.'

'If I'm wrong, then I apologise,' she said firmly. 'Don't you?'

'I don't know.' Enjoying himself, he smiled. 'I've never been wrong.'

Derailed by the banter, she backed away slightly and then stopped. 'I'm apologising for assuming that you weren't qualified for the job. For thinking that you being here would just cause trouble.'

'It *will* cause trouble,' Conner drawled softly, 'so you weren't wrong.'

'You knew it would cause trouble?'

'Of course.'

His answer brought a puzzled frown to her face. 'If you knew that, why did you come back?'

'I thrive on trouble, Flora. Trouble is the fuel the drives my engine.'

This time, instead of backing away, she looked at him. Properly. Her eyes focused on his, as if she was searching for something. 'You're angry with us, aren't you? Is that why you're here?' She fiddled with her glasses again, as if she wasn't used to having them on her nose. 'To level a score?'

'You think I became a doctor so that I could return to my roots and exterminate the inhabitants of Glenmore, one by one?'

'Of course not. But I know you're angry. I can feel it.'

Then she was more intuitive than he'd thought. Raising his guard, Conner watched her. 'I'm not angry. If people would rather wait a week to see Logan, that's fine by me.'

'But it must hurt your feelings.'

'I don't have feelings, Flora. Providing I still get paid, I don't care whether the patients see me or not. It's Logan's problem.' He could tell she didn't like his answer because she frowned and shook her head slightly.

'I can't believe that you're not at all sensitive about the way people react to you.'

'That's because you're a woman and women think differently to men.' This time his smile was genuine. 'Do I look sensitive?' He watched as her eyes drifted to his shoulders and then lifted to his jaw line.

'No.' Her voice was hoarse. 'You don't.' And then her eyes lifted to his and the atmosphere snapped taut.

Conner felt his body stir.

Well, well, he thought. *How interesting.* Sexual chemistry with a woman who probably didn't know the meaning of the phrase. His gaze lowered to her mouth and he saw that her lips were soft and bare of make-up. He had a sudden impulse to be unforgivably shocking and kiss her.

'Well, if you're sure you're fine…' She was flustered. He could tell she was flustered.

Normally he had no qualms about making a woman flustered but somehow with Flora it seemed unsporting. She might be older but she obviously wasn't any more experienced. With an inner sigh and lingering regret, he backed off. 'I'm fine,' he said gently. 'But thank you for asking.'

He wondered idly if she'd ever had sex.

A boyfriend?

'My consulting room is next door.' Apparently unaware of what had just happened between them, she suddenly became brisk and efficient. 'Evanna is still doing a morning clinic, but if you need a nurse to do a home visit then ask me because she's too pregnant to be dashing around the island. You know your way around, so that shouldn't be a problem. If there's anything you're not sure of, ask.'

'I'll do that.'

If she had a boyfriend, it was someone tame and safe, he decided. Someone who hadn't taught her the meaning of passion.

'Well—I've held you up long enough. Morning surgery can be a long one.' Her gaze slid to his legs, encased in black leather. 'You know, people might feel more comfortable with you if you changed.'

'I am who I am, Flora.'

'I meant your clothes.' She pushed her glasses onto the bridge of her nose. 'You could change your clothes.'

'Why would I want to do that?'

'Because the patients expect a doctor to look like a doctor.'

'Flora.' He failed to keep the amusement out of his voice. 'It wouldn't matter whether I was wearing a set of theatre scrubs or a white coat, the inhabitants of Glenmore would still struggle to believe that Bad Conner is a doctor. Just as *you're* struggling.'

'I'm not. Not any more. But I don't see why you should confirm their prejudices by dressing like a biker.' She flushed. 'Do you always have to antagonise people? Break the rules?'

'Yes. I think I probably do.' Conner watched her. 'Just as you always like to please people and do everything that is expected of you. In our own ways we're the same, you and I. We're both working hard to meet society's expectations of us.'

She looked at him, her dark eyes reproachful. 'There's nothing wrong in being part of a community.'

'True. But neither is there anything wrong with *not* being part of it,' he said gently. 'Do you really think the way I'm dressed is going to compromise my ability as a doctor?'

'No. Of course not. It's just that you look—' She broke off and he knew he shouldn't follow up on that comment but he couldn't help himself.

'How do I look, Flora? Tell me. I want to know what you think of the way I look.'

She looked hot and flustered. 'I-intimidating,' she stammered, eventually. 'I wouldn't want to bump into you on a dark night.'

'Is that right?' Conner gave a slow smile and gave up trying to subdue his wicked streak. 'In that case, we'll have to make sure that we leave the lights on, angel.'

He was impossible and she was never going to be able to work with him.

Flora tried to concentrate on the dressing and not reveal how shaken she was by her encounter with Conner. He'd played with her, toyed with her carelessly, like a predator having fun with its prey before a kill. And as usual she hadn't been able to think of the right thing to say because she'd been trying to sort out surgery business and he'd been—well, he'd been Conner. Selfish, indifferent and supremely cool. Just the thought of him seeing patients—*or not seeing patients*—in the room next door unsettled her.

She shook her head and studied the skin around the leg ulcer. 'You still have a degree of varicose eczema, Mrs Parker. Are you using the cream Dr MacNeil gave you?'

'The steroid cream? No, I forget.'

Flora studied the skin, checking for infection. 'Is this tender when I press?'

'No more than usual.'

'There's no erythema and your temperature is fine.' Talking to herself, Flora made a judgement. 'We'll leave it for now but do me a favour and try the cream, would you? If it isn't looking better in a week or so, I'm going to ask one of the doctors to look at it.'

'As long as it's Logan.' Mrs Parker's mouth clamped in a thin line of disapproval. 'I'm not afraid to say that I almost fainted dead away when I saw Conner MacNeil stroll into the surgery this morning. Bold as brass. Not even trying to hide his face.'

'Why would he hide his face, Mrs Parker?' Flora swiftly finished the dressing and applied a compression bandage. 'He's a doctor and he's come to—' *create havoc?* '—help Logan.'

'Help? Help? This is the boy who was so much of a handful that his mother left home! Can you imagine how badly the boy must have behaved for his own mother to give up on him? His father stayed, of course, but he was driven to drink by Conner's antics. Died five years ago and did his son bother turning up to his funeral? No, he didn't.'

Flora flew to Conner's defence. 'He's a man now, not a boy. And no one knows what happened in his childhood, Mrs Parker.' He hadn't told anyone.

She paused for a moment, lost in thought as she remembered the love of her own family. Just what had Conner endured? She remembered the day she'd walked along the cliffs to his house.

She remembered the shouting.

'Well, I tell you this much,' Mrs Parker said firmly. 'That boy isn't capable of warmth or sensitivity and he doesn't care about anyone but himself. I still don't believe he's a doctor.

He never did a day's studying in his life and as for the way he dresses—well, I mean, Logan's always smart in trousers and a shirt, but Conner hadn't even shaved! He looked—'

Handsome, Flora thought helplessly as she fumbled with the bandage. *He'd looked impossibly, outrageously handsome.*

'Dangerous,' Mrs Parker continued with a shudder, watching as Flora finished the dressing. 'Who in their right minds would trust him with a medical problem? He causes more problems than he solves. Not too tight, dear.'

'It has to be quite tight because we need the pressure on the ankle.'

'I couldn't believe it when I heard Janet booking patients in to see him. I said to Nina Hill, "Well, that's going to be interesting to watch. Now he'll get his comeuppance because no one will see him."' Having delivered that prediction, Mrs Parker paused expectantly and Flora glanced up at her, realizing that some sort of response was required.

'They'll see him, Mrs Parker,' she said quietly. 'That was then and this is now. Conner is well qualified. And it's great news that Logan finally has help. Super.'

'Super?' Mrs Parker gaped at her. 'You think it's great news?'

Far too loyal to reveal her own reservations, Flora secured the bandage. 'Of course. Logan is barely managing on his own. We need another doctor on the island.'

'Well, don't imagine for one moment that Conner MacNeil will make a difference! Even if he *is* a doctor now, which frankly I doubt because everyone knows that these days you can fake everything for a price, there won't be a soul on this island who will trust his opinion.'

Flora took a deep breath and tried to speak. 'Mrs Parker, you really shouldn't—'

'Anyway, enough of that conversation.' Mrs Parker apparently didn't even notice the interruption. 'I refuse to waste the air in my lungs on Conner MacNeil when there are so many more important things going on around us. I meant to say to you, John Carter was seen talking at the school gate with Meg Watson. Now, *that's* an interesting match, if you ask me. She's a single mother and he's...'

Realising that a two-way conversation wasn't required, Flora stood up and washed her hands, only half listening as Mrs Parker regaled her with all the latest island gossip.

How could Conner not be hurt by the negative reaction of the islanders?

Was he really as indifferent as he seemed?

If it were her, she'd be completely mortified.

She tugged a paper towel out of the holder and dried her hands, part of her brain listening to Mrs Parker while the other half thought about Conner. He'd built a shell around himself, and who could blame him?

'So what do you think, dear?'

Realising that this time Mrs Parker was waiting for a response, Flora turned. 'I honestly don't know,' she said truthfully. 'I couldn't give an opinion.' And even if she could, she wouldn't. 'Don't forget it's important to walk when you have a venous ulcer.'

'Yes, yes, I can't possibly forget because you keep telling me.' The elderly lady put her foot on the floor and tested it gingerly. 'Oh, that's much more comfortable. You're a wonderful nurse, dear. Simply wonderful.'

But a useless gossip, Flora thought wryly. 'That's very kind of you, Mrs Parker.'

'Not kind at all. I'm only saying what everyone else is saying.' Angela Parker slipped on her shoes. 'We're all so thrilled that you've come back to the island to take over from our Kyla. Only yesterday I was saying to Meg in the café that we could have ended up with some mainlander with no idea how things work on Glenmore but, no, Dr MacNeil managed to tempt you back. When your father died I thought you might never return but then Nina reminded me that your aunt is here. Did you miss it when you were away?'

Flora felt a sudden shaft of pain as she thought of her father. *She still missed him.* 'Well, I suppose I—'

'Of course you did and now you're back, which is perfect. And Logan has been in desperate need of a practice nurse since Kyla and Dr Walker left, and what with poor Evanna being so pregnant.' Without waiting for Flora to respond, Mrs Parker forged ahead like a ship in a force-nine gale. 'Well, we all know that Dr MacNeil is worried about her, given the tragedy with his first wife. Not that Evanna should have a problem in that direction. She's a girl with good childbearing hips.'

Flora winced and hoped that no one repeated that comment to her friend and colleague. 'Logan doesn't seem worried,' she lied, 'and Evanna is a midwife, so if anyone understands her condition, she does!'

'Do you really think she should still be working, this close to having that baby?'

Aware that whatever she said would be spread around the island by nightfall, Flora once again kept her answer suitably neutral. 'She isn't on her feet that much. She's just doing the odd morning clinic.' She sat down at her desk and updated the notes on the computer. 'It's fortunate that their house is attached to the surgery. At least she doesn't have to come far to work and I do all the community calls so she doesn't have that to cope with.'

'You see? That's what I mean. It's great that you're back.' Angela Parker picked up her bag and stood up. 'Everywhere I go I hear people saying, "Have you seen our Flora? Doesn't she look well?"'

An intensely private person, Flora felt herself shrink slightly inside. 'People are talking about me?'

'Of course,' Angela said cheerfully. 'A new nurse on Glenmore is big news. People are thrilled. We're all hoping you'll meet a nice young man and then you'll be a permanent fixture on the island. Glenmore is a good place to raise a family, dear.'

A family? 'I think it's a bit soon to be thinking of that,' Flora said faintly, deciding that it was time to end the conversation before gossip about her 'wedding' reached the pub. 'Your leg is healing well, Mrs Parker. Make an appointment to see me again on your way out.'

'Yes, I'll do that. I certainly won't be seeing Conner, that's for sure.' She sniffed. 'I value my health far too much for that.'

Flora opened her mouth to reply and then realised that no reply was expected because Angela Parker was once again answering her own question.

'I think this time Logan will discover he's made a mistake.' She slid her bag over her arm. 'If he's not careful, he'll find himself handling the summer singlehanded and that won't be an easy task with a toddler and a new bairn.'

Knowing that to comment on that statement would trigger a conversation she didn't have time for, Flora stood up, worried that she'd never finish her clinic if all her patients had as much to say as Angela. 'It was nice to see you. Don't forget to put that leg up when you're sitting down.'

'I always do that.' Angela opened the door. 'Take care of yourself and give me regards to your aunt.'

'I'll do that, Mrs Parker.' Flora waited for the door to close behind her and then sank back into her chair. A quick glance at the clock on the wall confirmed that she was now running *seriously* late and she gave a despairing shake of her head. She still hadn't adjusted to how long each appointment took on Glenmore. Everyone had something to say and a consultation involved so much more than it did on the mainland.

'Problems?' Logan stood in the doorway, a question in his eyes. 'Angela Parker was with you a long time. Is her leg giving her trouble?'

'She still has some signs of eczema around the ulcer but that's because she isn't using the cream you gave her. She's not pyrexial and there's no pain or tenderness to speak of and no obvious signs of cellulitis or infection. I'll keep an eye on it. If it isn't looking any better next week, I'll give you a shout.'

Logan walked into the room and closed the door behind him. 'If there's no sign of healing in another month or so, I'll refer her for a biopsy. We need to exclude malignancy.'

'I think it is healing, it's just that she doesn't do much to help it along.'

'So why are you looking so worried? I can't believe that Mrs Parker's leg ulcer is responsible for that frown on your face.'

'I'm hopeless at this job,' Flora confessed simply. 'Absolutely hopeless.'

'That's utter nonsense.' It was Logan's turn to frown. 'You're a brilliant nurse.'

'It's not the nursing that worries me, it's the rest of it. The gossip, the chat, the rumour machine.' Flora waved a hand in a gesture of despair. 'I'm just no good at it. I've never been any good at just chatting. When I did the clinic in Edinburgh, patients just wanted me to dress their leg or take their blood. On Glenmore, I'm supposed to have an opinion on everything from the Carpenters' divorce to Janey Smith's speeding fine.' She brushed her hair out of her eyes and shot him a helpless look. 'I don't know how to handle it. I don't want to join in, I have no intention of revealing confidential information, but I don't want to look rude. How do you do it? How do you cope?'

'I say "That's interesting" a hundred times a day and if they're really rambling on I adopt my "this could be something serious" look and that soon focuses their minds back on their medical problem. The skill is to cut them off tactfully.'

'I definitely need to work on that skill,' Flora muttered. 'And I confess that I *hate* the idea that everyone is talking about me.'

'This is Glenmore,' Logan said easily. 'Of course people are talking about you. They're talking about everyone. But it's mostly friendly talk. People care and that's what makes this island so special. You've been in the city for too long. You've forgotten what island living is all about. You'll adjust.'

'But the talk isn't friendly about Conner, is it?' Troubled, Flora looked at him. 'They're being horrid to him. I mean, I know I was shocked to see him and even more shocked to discover that he's a doctor, but boycotting his surgery...'

'Some of the patients saw him and word will spread.' Logan smiled. 'Providing he isn't too outrageous. Don't worry about Conner. He can look after himself.'

'Maybe.' She suddenly noticed the dark shadows underneath his eyes. 'You look really, really tired, Logan. Is there anything I can do to help?'

'You're already doing it. Being tired is part of the job description when you work here, as you're fast discovering.' He rubbed his fingers over his forehead. 'And on top of that I was up in the night with little Helen Peters because she—'

'Had a nasty asthma attack,' Flora finished his sentence with a laugh, 'and before you ask, the reason I know is because Mrs Abbott mentioned it when she came in to have her ears syringed and *she* heard it from Sam when she was buying fish on the queue this morning and Sam knew because—'

'He lives across the road from the Peters' sister.' Logan

looked amused. 'Relax, Flora. This is how things work on
Glenmore. Don't knock it. Sam was the one who called me
because there were lights on all over the house and he went
across the road to see if he could help.'

Flora's eyes softened. 'That was kind.'

'People are kind here. Don't worry—you'll soon get back
into the swing of it. And they'll get used to Conner.'

'I hope you're right. So what happened to little Helen? Did
you change her medication?'

'No, but I talked to her mum about exercise.' He frowned.
'It was sports day yesterday. I'm confident that the physical
exertion is what triggered it. Any chance that you could you
pop in and see them today? It was pretty scary for everyone
and I think they'd appreciate an extra dose of reassurance.
You might want to have a conversation about lifestyle.'

'I'll pop in, no problem.' This was the Glenmore she knew
and loved. Where else would the medical team find time for
that sort of visit? That level of care and attention was what
made the island special. And she was doing the job she'd
been trained to do. Feeling more relaxed, Flora added Helen's
name to her list of afternoon calls.

'I'll see you later.' Logan opened the door to leave and
Conner strolled in.

Flora's world tilted and her insides knotted with an almost
unbearable tension. 'Conner.'

He stepped aside to let Logan pass. 'Isn't Angela Parker a
little old to be training for the Olympics? She took one look
at me and ran as if the hounds of hell were after her. What's
the matter with her leg?'

'Venous ulcer. She's supposed to be mobilising but she
doesn't do enough of it.'

'Then perhaps I should stand behind her more often. She
ran so fast I could have entered her in the Derby.'

He was so confident, so easy with a situation that most

people would have found agonisingly awkward. He really didn't seem to care that the locals had been distinctly unwelcoming. *But if he'd cared, he wouldn't be the man he was.*

Flora cleared her throat. 'Mrs Parker was a little surprised to discover that you're now a doctor.'

Conner smiled. 'Sweet Flora, always coating the truth with honey. Come on, angel. Tell me what she said. The truth. It will be good for you. And my shoulders are broad. I can take it.'

She knew his shoulders were broad—in fact, she was far, far too conscious of his body.

'She doesn't believe you're a doctor and she values her health too much to see you.'

'And I value my sanity far too much to see her, so both of us are happy. If her health is that good, she doesn't need a doctor anyway. So I'm spared.'

'It's not funny.' Ignoring the amusement in his eyes, Flora kept her head down and put a box of vaccine back in the fridge. 'You have no idea what things are like here! We're overwhelmed with work and every day the ferry brings more tourists. Logan needs help. He's barely had time to see his wife and daughter since Ethan left and the baby is due in a few weeks. He needs someone he can trust.'

'And you think he can't trust me?'

'I don't think that's relevant.' Desperate to make him understand, she turned to face him. 'If the patients won't see you, then it doesn't matter what Logan thinks.'

'Relax. The tourists will see me. I'll talk to Janet and make sure she allocates me a surgery full of patients who know nothing about my wicked past.'

'Conner—'

'I wasn't expecting a hero's welcome, Flora.' He gave a faint smile. 'And now you'll have to excuse me. There's a bit of a rush on. Patients are fighting to see me and I don't want to disappoint them.'

Her heart bumped against her chest and she didn't understand it. She couldn't possibly find him attractive. It was ridiculous to find him attractive. *So why were her legs shaking so much she needed to sit down?*

CHAPTER FOUR

'GLENMORE is in an uproar. Eight patients refused to see him this morning and insisted on waiting for Logan.' In the café near the harbour, Flora leaned across the table and helped herself to one of Evanna's sandwiches. 'These are delicious. Why aren't you eating them?'

'Because there's no room in my body for anything except the baby.' Evanna shifted in her seat, obviously uncomfortable. 'They refused to see him? Really? Oh, poor Conner, that's dreadful. Were his feelings hurt, do you think?'

'Does he have feelings?' Flora glanced out of the window, watching idly as groups of tourists walked from the ferry towards the beach. 'Since when did Conner MacNeil care what people think of him? He is Mr Tough Guy.'

'Deep down, I'm sure he cares.'

'If he cared he wouldn't have done his surgery wearing black leather and half an inch of stubble.' Flora winced as a toddler tripped over a fishing rod and fell hard onto the pavement. She watched the mother scoop up the child and offer comfort. 'Believe me, he has no intention of modifying his behaviour to please anyone. He was as defiant and confrontational as ever.' *And sexy. Indecently sexy.*

'If he didn't care, he'd be living in his parents' old house up on the cliffs.'

Flora was silent for a moment. She hadn't given any thought to where Conner was living. 'And he's not?'

'Logan gave him the barn.'

'I thought it was let for the summer.'

'It is. To Conner. When Logan thought he might be coming back, he kept it free for him. I suppose he knew Connor wouldn't want to stay in his parents' house.' Evanna shrugged. 'Who can blame him? I don't suppose it has any nice memories for him. By all accounts, he had a pretty miserable childhood.'

'Then why didn't he sell it after his father died?'

'He hasn't been here to sell it. Perhaps he'll deal with it this summer.'

'Break his final tie with the island? Do you think that's why he's come back? To sell the house?'

'I wouldn't think so. He could have done that with one call to the island estate agent. Perhaps he's laying old ghosts.' Evanna gave a suggestive smile. 'Or maybe he's laying old girlfriends.'

'Evanna!' Struggling between shock and laughter, Flora sent a weak, apologetic smile towards the tourists eating lunch at the next table. 'If you're going to make obscene comments, lower your voice. We still have to work here after Conner's gone.'

'And life will be considerably more boring.'

'Pregnancy has driven you mad.'

'You might be right.' Evanna shifted in her seat. 'I can't remember what it's like not to be fat and exhausted.'

'I think Conner is trying to shock them on purpose. I suspect he wants to provoke a reaction from them.' Flora looked at her and smiled. 'Do you want to know something funny?'

'Not too funny.' Evanna patted her enormous bump gently. 'I have to be economical with laughter at the moment. Go on.'

'Mrs Ellis saw him.'

'As a patient? You're joking.'

'I'm not. I expected her to walk straight back out and call the police, but she was in there for ages and she came out smiling.'

'So he even charmed her.' Evanna sighed wistfully. 'You see? It doesn't matter how badly he behaves, women just can't help themselves. It's the danger, I suppose. The fact that he's a bit volatile and unstable just adds to his appeal. If you had a date with Conner you never quite knew whether you were going to end up in bed or in a jail cell.'

Flora gasped. 'What exactly do you know about dates with Conner? There is no way your parents would have allowed you anywhere near him.'

'Didn't stop me dreaming.' Evanna sipped her tea. 'I had fantasies, just like you.'

'I did not have fantasies.'

'Now you're lying.' Evanna grinned placidly. 'Every woman dreams about the local bad boy.'

'Conner is well educated.'

'Which makes him all the more attractive,' Evanna sighed.

'My idea of a perfect date never involved a close encounter with the police,' Flora said lightly, 'and I don't believe yours did either. You were always crazy about Logan.'

'That didn't stop me looking. I suppose that's part of the reason Conner was so attractive,' Evanna said simply. 'He was forbidden. Are you seriously telling me you've never had a few fantasies about Conner?'

'Never.' Keen to end what was increasingly becoming an uncomfortable conversation, Flora finished her sandwich and glanced at her watch. 'I have to go. Little Helen Peters had an asthma attack in the night. I'm going to call on her on my way back to the surgery.'

Evanna yawned. 'Yes. Poor Logan was up and down in the night. First it was Helen, then it was our Kirsty.'

'How is she?'

'We've moved her from a cot to a bed in preparation for the arrival of her sibling.' Evanna patted her swollen abdomen gently. 'And she's just discovered that she can leap out whenever she likes and come in with us. Which is fine, except she sleeps like a starfish, arms and legs stuck out at angles designed to cause maximum discomfort to those sharing the space.'

Flora laughed. 'She's gorgeous. Who is looking after her today?'

'Meg had her this morning and I'm going home right now.' Evanna stood up and winced. 'I can't believe this is how it feels to be thirty-five weeks pregnant. Remind me to be more sympathetic next time I run the antenatal clinic. Give little Helen a kiss from me.'

'I will. Why didn't you tell me that Logan had appointed Conner as the doctor?'

'Neither of us were sure he'd turn up. It didn't seem worth mentioning until we knew for sure.'

'So you really don't know why he's back, Evanna?' Flora tried to keep her tone casual.

'No. Logan hasn't said any more to me than he has to you.'

Flora reached for her bag. 'No pillow talk?'

'Are you kidding? Our pillow talk revolves around me telling him how uncomfortable I am and him trying not to phone for an air ambulance.'

'Is he that nervous?'

'He's hiding it quite well but, yes, he's nervous. Of course. His first wife died in childbirth and none of us are likely to forget that, myself included.' Evanna breathed out heavily.

'He wants me to go and stay on the mainland, but the baby's not due for another five weeks and if it was two weeks late I could be stuck over there for seven weeks. Even if I wanted to, which I don't, it just isn't practical. There's Kirsty to think of. I don't want her unsettled.'

'No. Well...' Flora leaned forward and gave her friend a hug, carefully avoiding her bump. 'We're all keeping an eye on you and we can get you over to the mainland at the first sign of movement.'

'That's the plan.' Evanna stroked her bump. 'Just hope the baby is listening.'

Flora drove with the windows down, humming to herself and enjoying the breeze and the sunshine. She loved Glenmore at this time of year. Wild flowers clustered on the banks of grass at the side of the road and in the distance she could see the jagged silhouette of the ruined castle.

She waved at Doug MacDonald who was out on his bike and then caught sight of Sonia Davies pushing a buggy on the pavement.

'Sonia!' She slowed to a halt and called out to the young mother. 'Everything OK? How's Rachel?'

'She's beautiful.' Sonia pushed the buggy over to the car. 'I'm due in clinic later this week for another immunisation.'

Flora nodded. 'She's twelve months, isn't she? So that will be the Hib booster. *Haemophilus influenzae.*'

Sonia handed Rachel a rattle to play with. 'I hope she doesn't freak out. It's different when they're babies, isn't it? They don't know what's happening and it's over in a flash.'

'She'll be fine. Have you booked her in for Thursday afternoon?'

'Yes.' Sonia jiggled the pushchair. 'No sign of Evanna having the baby yet, then?'

'She has a few weeks to go yet.'

'I bet Dr MacNeil is nervous.' Sonia gave a little frown. 'We all know how uneasy he gets when women get near their due date. When he had to deliver me on the island last year, he was horrified. Never saw him look nervous before that night. I still think that if Evanna hadn't been there, he would have done a runner.'

'I'm sure he wouldn't, although we all know that he prefers babies to be born on the mainland. I'm sure he'll be packing Evanna off on that ferry in good time. And I'd better go. I have a visit to do before my afternoon clinic.' Flora slid back into her car. 'See you later in the week, Sonia.'

She carried on up the coast road, called in on Helen to check on her and offer reassurance to her mother. Then she drove to the medical centre, parking next to a sleek black motorbike.

She gave a faint smile. That explained the black leather. A motorbike.

She couldn't imagine Conner with anything else. He was a man who always chose to live his life on the wrong side of risk.

Janet was at the reception desk, trying to find an appointment for a patient. 'Flora has had a cancellation so she can see him straight away, Mrs Gregg,' she was saying. 'I'll put you in with her. If she thinks Harry should see a doctor urgently, she'll arrange it.'

Looking anxious, Mrs Gregg took Harry by the hand and led him to the chairs in the waiting room.

Flora walked up to the desk. 'Problems?'

'Just the one problem. People don't want to book in with Conner.' Janet sighed and rubbed her fingers over her forehead. 'I can't believe that Logan has done this to us in the middle of summer. His afternoon surgery is bursting at the seams and how many does Conner have? Two people.'

'Two? That's all?'

'No one wants to see him, Flora.' Janet looked exhausted. 'I'm sure he's a very good doctor, but all anyone round here remembers is a boy with a lot of problems. They don't trust him.'

Remembering what Logan had said to her, Flora straightened her shoulders. 'His qualifications are excellent.'

'Well, maybe he'd like to put them above my desk in neon lights.'

'It's only his first day. People will settle down,' Flora said firmly, hoping that she was right. 'I thought the women, at least, would be queuing up.'

'I'm sure they will, but not for his medical skills,' Janet said dryly. 'If Logan was looking for help, I think he was looking in the wrong place. Anyway, the Greggs are back from holiday and Harry isn't well. He has a rash and Diane is worried. Your first patient has cancelled so I've put them in with you. If you're worried, perhaps you can persuade them to see Conner, but I don't hold out much hope.'

'Leave it with me. If you see Logan can you tell him that I popped in to see Helen and she was fine?' Flora walked to the waiting area. Harry was sitting on his mother's lap and his eyes were closed.

'Hello, Nurse Harris.' Diane gave her a tired smile. 'Janet said you might fit us in.'

'Of course.' Flora touched the little boy's forehead with a gentle hand. 'He's very hot.'

'I've spent the past two nights trying to bring his temperature down.' Diane clearly hadn't slept for days and her face was pale and drawn. 'But it's the rash that's really worrying me. It's spreading.'

'I'll take a look.'

The woman gave her a grateful smile and gently eased Harry onto the floor. 'You're too big for Mummy to carry now,' she murmured, taking his hand. 'Just walk as far as the consulting room, then you can sit down again.'

Harry murmured a protest but trotted along the corridor towards Flora's consulting room.

'Tell me what happened. I'd like to know when Harry first became ill.' Flora flicked on her computer and stowed her bag under the desk. 'Presumably it started on holiday?'

'Three days ago he developed this rash. One minute he was fine and the next he had a temperature, neck stiffness, headache.' Diane swallowed. 'He's gone from well to ill really fast and that's— Well, I'm worried.'

Understanding that she didn't want to say too much in front of the child, Flora nodded. 'And you think the rash has spread?'

'Oh, yes. Definitely.'

Flora washed her hands. 'I'll take a look, if that's all right.'

'I'm just going to take your T-shirt off, Harry.' Diane reached forward and lifted his T-shirt carefully over his head. 'I want to show Nurse Harris.'

Harry gave a moan of protest. 'I'm really, really cold.'

'That's because you have a temperature,' Flora said gently, lifting his arm slightly and turning him towards the light. 'When did you first notice the rash, Mrs Gregg?'

'Well, it didn't look like this at first. It started with just one red spot under his arm and then it spread. Then his temperature shot up and he's been feeling boiling hot ever since.' Diane pushed her son's hair away from his face and touched his forehead. 'He's hot now.'

Flora examined the rash carefully. It was scarlet and circular and she'd never seen anything like it before. 'Did you see a doctor when you were away?'

'Yes, but he said it was just a virus.' Diane rolled her eyes, her worry evident. 'Perhaps it is, but I wanted a proper opinion. It isn't until you leave Glenmore that you realise how good the medical care is on this island. I was hoping to see Dr MacNeil, but Janet says his surgery is full.'

Flora checked Harry's temperature and recorded it. 'Logan isn't the only doctor working at Glenmore now,' she said carefully, and Diane pursed her lips.

'If you're talking about Conner MacNeil, I'm not interested. I remember the time he set off that firework in the school library.'

'That was a long time ago, Mrs Gregg.' Flora checked Harry's pulse and blood pressure. 'He trained in the army. His qualifications are excellent.'

'I don't care. I—'

'Didn't you ever do anything you shouldn't when you were young?'

'Well, I—I suppose…'

'I know I did.' Flora shrugged. 'And I also know I wouldn't want to be judged as an adult by how I was as a child. People change, Mrs Gregg. And everyone deserves to be given chances. Logan wouldn't have taken Conner on if he didn't trust him. I'd like him to see Harry. I don't recognise this rash and the fact that he has a temperature makes it worth exploring further.'

Mrs Gregg hesitated and then glanced at Harry, clearly torn. 'I don't suppose Conner will know any more than that doctor on the mainland.'

'Let's give it a try—see what he says? I'll see if he's free,' Flora said cheerfully, trying not to reveal that the chances of Conner having a patient with him was extremely remote.

Hoping that she wasn't making a mistake, she went across the corridor and tapped on his door. 'Conner?' She walked in and found him absorbed in a website on the internet. She peered closer. 'Wetsuits?'

'I'm planning to do some sailing. It looks as though I'm

going to have plenty of time on my hands.' He swivelled his head and looked at her. 'Are you here to relieve my boredom?'

She flushed. 'I have a patient that needs to be seen by a doctor.'

'And?'

'You're a doctor.'

'Am I?' He lounged back in his chair, his ice-blue gaze disturbingly direct. 'So why am I sitting in an empty consulting room?'

'Because this is Glenmore and it takes folks a while to get used to change. The last time they saw you, you were stirring up trouble all over the island. I don't suppose anyone imagined you'd become a doctor. So will you see Harry Gregg?'

Conner's eyes narrowed. 'Diane's son?'

'Yes. He's eight years old and a really nice little boy. Very lively usually, but not today. Diane is frightened.'

'She always did have a tendency to overreact. I remember she slapped my face once.'

'You probably deserved it.'

He smiled. 'I probably did. So what do you think, Flora? Paranoid mother?'

Flora shook her head. 'I think it's something that needs looking at. The child is poorly, there's no doubt about that. And he has a really weird rash. I've never seen anything like it before.'

Conner rose to his feet. 'Is she going to slap my face again or run away screaming in horror if I walk into the room?'

'I've no idea.' Flora gave a weary smile. 'Let's try it, shall we? Harry needs to see a doctor and I'd rather it was sooner than later.'

Diane looked up as they walked into the room. 'Dr MacNeil.'

'Diane.' Conner's greeting was cursory, his eyes focused on the boy, who was now sitting on his mother's lap, his head on her chest. 'Hey, sport.' He hunkered down so that he was on the same level. 'What's going on with you?'

Harry opened his eyes but didn't move his head. 'Feel bad.'

'His temperature is thirty-nine degrees.' Flora gently lifted Harry's arm so that Conner could see. 'He's had this rash for three days.'

'Feel horrible,' the boy muttered, and Conner nodded.

'Well, we need to see what we can do about that.' He studied the rash in silence, his blue eyes narrowed slightly. 'Circular rash.'

Diane watched his face. 'You're going to tell me that it's just a virus and that I shouldn't have bothered you.'

Conner lifted his gaze to hers. 'You were right to bring him. Harry? Do you mind undressing down to your underpants? I want to take a proper look at this rash.'

Flora helped the child undress and Conner examined his skin carefully and questioned Diane in detail.

'It started under his arm when we were on holiday,' she told him. 'Just a red spot. And then it grew bigger and it turned into that weird thing he has now.'

'Where did you go on holiday?'

Flora glanced at him in surprise. She wouldn't have expected Conner to be interested in small talk.

'Mainland.'

'Highlands?' Conner ran a finger over the rash, his expression thoughtful. 'Were you walking?'

'Yes.' Diane looked at him. 'How do you know?'

Conner straightened and reached for Harry's T-shirt. 'It fits with what I'm seeing. You can get dressed now. I've seen all I need to see.' He gently pulled the T-shirt over the boy's head. 'Were you camping?'

'Yes. We spent a few nights in a forest. It was lovely.'

'Lots of deer around?'

'Actually, yes.' Diane frowned. 'How do you know that?'

'Because Harry has Lyme disease.' Conner washed his hands. 'He was almost certainly bitten by a tick, which is why he started off with one red spot. Did you see an insect?'

'No.' Bemused, Diane shook her head. 'No, I didn't. But we've been camping every year since he was born and we've never had a problem. Lyme disease? What is that? I've never even heard of it.'

'It's not that common in this country, although the number of cases is increasing. Ticks are tiny insects and they feed by sucking blood from animals such as deer. Some ticks get infected with the bacterium that causes Lyme disease and if they bite a human then they pass the disease on.'

Diane looked at him in a mixture of horror and amazement. 'And you're sure Harry has it? How do you know?'

'Because his symptoms fit the history.'

Flora felt the tension leave her. Clearly Conner hadn't been making small talk about holidays, he'd been verifying the cause of the symptoms he was seeing. Logan was right. Conner was a good doctor. *A clever doctor.* And Diane appeared to have forgotten that she'd ever had reservations about seeing him.

'You've seen this Lyme disease before?'

'When I was stationed overseas.' Without waiting for an invitation, he sat down at Flora's computer and hit a few keys, bringing up a list of antibiotics. 'The rash that Harry has is fairly typical.' He scrolled down, searching for the one he wanted. 'It starts as a single circular red mark and it gradually spreads. It isn't always painful or itchy and some people don't even notice it, depending on where they were bitten.'

'Is there any treatment?'

'Yes.' Conner's eyes were fixed on the screen. 'I'm going to give Harry some antibiotics.'

'And will they work?'

'They should do because we've caught it early. You did the right thing, bringing him in.'

'The doctor on the mainland thought it was a virus.' Diane's mouth tightened with disapproval. 'Virus is a word doctors use when they haven't got a clue what's going on.'

'You might be right. I usually say "I don't know" but that phrase doesn't win you many friends either. In fairness to your guy on the mainland, Lyme disease is not a condition every doctor will have seen.' Conner printed off the prescription and handed it to Diane. 'Make sure Harry finishes the course.'

'I'll do that.' She slipped the prescription into her bag and hesitated. 'Thank you.' She looked Conner in the eye. 'I wasn't sure about seeing you...'

'I don't blame you for that.' As cool as ever, Conner rose to his feet. 'Make an appointment to see Logan in a few days. Harry needs to be followed up. We need to be sure that the antibiotics are working.'

Diane took Harry's hand in hers. 'Why should I see Logan? Are you going to be busy?'

Conner gave a faint smile. 'On current form? Probably not. But it's important that the patients have faith in the doctor they see.'

'I agree.' Diane walked towards the door. 'Which is why we'll be making that appointment when you're doing surgery. Thank you, Dr MacNeil. I knew I could rely on a Glenmore doctor to get the diagnosis right.' The door closed behind her and Flora smiled happily at Conner.

'I think you're a hit. That was pretty impressive. I predict that once word spreads, your surgery will be crammed with patients.'

'And I'm supposed to rejoice about that?'

'Maybe not. But Logan will. So, tell me about Lyme disease because I'm feeling horribly ignorant.'

'What else do you want to know? You get bitten by a tick that clings on once it bites. Then it sucks your blood—'

'Don't!' Flora pulled a face. 'You're telling it like a horror story. If you carry on like that I'll never set foot outside again.'

It was the wrong thing to say to Conner. He leaned against the desk and gave a wicked smile. 'As I was saying, they suck your blood and slowly become more and more engorged—'

'You do it on purpose, don't you? Try and shock people.'

'I admit it's an extremely stimulating pastime.'

'You might not find it so funny when I'm sick,' Flora said sweetly, and his smile widened.

'Nurses aren't supposed to have delicate constitutions.'

'Doctors aren't supposed to be bloodthirsty.'

'I'm just delivering the facts.'

'Well…' She was horribly aware of just how strong his shoulders were and how much he dominated her tiny room. 'Could you deliver them with slightly less gruesome relish?'

'Where was I?' He angled his head slightly. 'Oh, yes, they were engorged with blood. Anyway, the bacteria that cause Lyme disease are usually carried in the gut and only travel to their mouth once they've been feeding for about twenty-four hours. So if you remove the tick as soon as you're bitten, you're unlikely to be infected.'

Flora shuddered. 'So you're telling me that a method of prevention is to drag this greedy, engorged creature off your skin?'

'You remove it before it's engorged. And you don't drag. If you drag, you'll just leave the mouth stuck in your body.'

'Enough!'

'The best thing is to smother it with Vaseline. It suffocates and then you can remove it with a pair of tweezers. You shouldn't use your fingers—'

'I wouldn't touch it with a bargepole! And I'm never venturing outside again without full protective clothing.'

Conner's eyes flickered to the neck of her uniform. 'You don't need to overdo it. The tick that carries the bacteria likes areas where there are wild deer.'

Her heart started to beat just a little bit faster. 'And that's why you were so interested in where the Greggs went on holiday?'

'The symptoms fitted. The fact that they'd been camping in a forest in warm weather made it highly possible that he'd contracted the disease. Ticks like warm weather and people wear less then so they're more likely to be bitten.' His eyes lifted to hers and the tension between them increased.

'Why haven't I heard of it?'

'Obviously there haven't been any cases on Glenmore. It's sensible to take precautions if you're walking or camping in an area where infected ticks are known to live.' His eyes dropped to her mouth, his gaze lingering. 'Wear long sleeves and trousers, use a tick repellent spray—all the obvious things.'

They were talking about medical matters and yet there was a sudden intimacy in the atmosphere that she didn't understand. It circled her like a forcefield, drawing her in, and when the phone rang suddenly she gave a start.

He was between her and the desk and she waited for him to move to one side so that she could answer it, but he stayed where he was. Left with no choice, she was forced to brush past him as she reached for the receiver. 'Yes? I mean...' Flustered by the fact that he was standing so close to her, she stumbled over the words. 'Nurse Harris speaking— Oh, hello, Mr Murray.' Struggling to concentrate, she listened as the man on the other end spoke to her. 'Well, no, I hadn't heard of it either, but—' She broke off and listened again before finally shaking her head. 'You'd better speak to him yourself.'

She sighed and handed the receiver to Conner. 'It's Mr Murray, the pharmacist down on South Quay. He has a question about the prescription you just gave Harry.'

Relaxed and confident, Conner took the phone from her, his gaze still locked with hers. 'MacNeil.'

Flora felt as though someone had lit a fire inside her body. She should look away. She knew she should look away but she just couldn't help herself. There was something in his ice-blue eyes that insisted that she look.

'That's right, Mr Murray, the dose is large.' He listened, his eyes still fixed on hers. 'Yes, I do know that I'm not treating a horse.'

Flora frowned and mouthed, 'A horse?' But Conner merely lifted a hand and trailed a finger down her cheek with agonising slowness.

'No, believe it or not, I'm not trying to kill him, Mr Murray,' he drawled softly, his finger lingering near her mouth. 'I'm treating a case of Lyme disease. If you look it up I think you'll find that the dose I've given him is appropriate...Yes, even in a child.' He brushed her lower lip with his thumb as he continued to field a tirade from the island pharmacist. 'Yes, I do remember the incident with the firework. Yes, and the barn—No, I don't blame you for questioning me, Mr Murray.' His hand dropped to his side and she sensed a sudden change in him. 'Of course, you're just doing your job.'

Finally he replaced the receiver. 'Apparently it isn't just the patients who have a problem trusting my judgement.'

His tone was flat and Flora stood still, wanting to say something but not knowing what. 'It was an unusual prescription.'

'You don't need to make excuses for them, Flora.' Conner straightened and walked towards the door, his face expressionless. 'You'd better carry on with your surgery. You have patients lining the waiting room.'

She stared after him as he left the room, wanting to stop him. She wanted to say something that would fix things because she sensed that beneath his bored, devil-may-care attitude there was a seam of pain buried so deep that no one could touch it.

The islanders were wary of him, that was true, but what did he think of them?

Remembering Logan's words, Flora bit her lip. When had anyone given Conner MacNeil a chance? When had anyone given him the benefit of the doubt? Why should he bother with any of them when they'd never bothered with him?

It was going to take more than one or two successful consultations to fill his consulting room with patients because no one believed that Conner MacNeil could be anything but a Bad Boy.

It was going to take a miracle.

CHAPTER FIVE

THE miracle didn't happen.

A few of the locals reluctantly agreed to see Conner, but the majority refused, choosing to wait a week to see Logan rather than be forced to consult the island rebel.

'It's ridiculous,' Flora told Evanna crossly a week after Conner had arrived on Glenmore. They were sitting on a rug on the beach, watching Kirsty dig in the sand. Finally the wind had dropped and the sun shone. 'They tell Janet it's urgent, and then say they'd rather wait than see Conner. I mean, just how urgent can something be if it can wait a week? Frankly, it would serve them right if a bit of them dropped off.'

'Well, to be fair to them, Conner was a bit wild and crazy,' Evanna said mildly, picking up Kirsty's sunhat and putting it back on her head. 'We just need to give them time to realise that he's changed.'

'Time isn't on our side. Glenmore needs another doctor. A doctor the patients will see! Your baby is due in four weeks,' Flora reminded her. 'If the patients don't stop demanding to see Logan, you won't get a look-in.'

Evanna sighed. 'I know. He's shattered. He used to always get home before I put Kirsty to bed. Now I'm lucky if he's home before *I'm* in bed.' She lifted her face to the sun. 'It's hot today.'

'I gather from Logan that your blood result was all right.' Flora lifted a bottle of water out of her bag and took a sip. 'That's a relief all round.'

'Yes, I was already immune to chickenpox, so that's one less problem to contend with.'

Flora was still pondering the problem of Conner. 'It isn't as if he's a useless doctor. He's brilliant. You should have seen him with Harry Gregg.' She leaned forward and helped Kirsty ease the sand out of the bucket. 'There! A perfect castle.' She smiled as Kirsty clapped her hands with delight. 'And he's diagnosed Mrs Ellis.'

'Yes, she told me he's given her thyroxine. He certainly seems to know what he's doing.'

'So why hasn't word spread? Why won't the islanders see him?'

'Because they see the boy and not the man? I'm guessing, but I suppose they just don't trust him.' Evanna hesitated. 'Apparently Finn Sullivan refused to rent him a yacht a few evenings ago.'

Flora stared at her. 'Are you serious?'

'Yes, but it's not all black. I saw Conner kicking a football around with the kids on the beach yesterday. They think he's *so* cool. And several women have made appointments to see him, but I don't think he was too thrilled about that.'

'He certainly wasn't.' Flora brushed sand from Kirsty's face. 'He strode up to Janet and said, "I'm not a bloody gynaecologist" or something equally unsympathetic. And Janet pointed out that as we didn't have a female doctor, he was expected to see female problems.'

'And what was Conner's response to that?'

'I don't know because he lowered his voice but Janet went scarlet.'

Evanna laughed. 'I don't suppose there was much call for gynecology in the army. According to Logan, he was dealing with a lot of trauma. Anyway, it's time we helped him settle in, which is why I've invited him to join us for lunch later.'

Flora's heart bumped hard against her chest. 'He's coming to lunch? I thought it was just your family. Logan, Meg and a few others.'

'Conner is family. I thought it might be a good idea to remind people of that.'

'Oh.' Flora concentrated on Kirsty. 'Well, that's great. Really nice of you, Evanna. So we should go back to the house. Start getting ready.' She rose to her feet and picked Kirsty up. 'Come on, sweetheart. Let's get the sand off your feet and take you home. Who knows? Your daddy might even be there.'

Conner's feet echoed on the cracked wooden floorboards and he glanced around him, feeling the memories swirl. The house smelled of damp, but that wasn't surprising because it had been years since the light and air had been allowed to pour unrestricted through its doors and windows.

He'd always hated this house and nothing had changed. It was as if the walls had absorbed some of the anger and hatred that had been played out in these rooms.

He tried to feel something positive, but there was nothing that wasn't dark and murky, and he gave a soft curse and strode out of the front door and back into the sunshine, drawing the clear air deep into his lungs.

Just walking into the house had made him feel contaminated.

He shouldn't have come.

He should have just paid someone to sell the damn place.

Beneath him the sea crashed onto the rocks and he sucked in a breath, drinking in the wildness of it—the savage beauty.

Everything about this part of Glenmore was angry. The coast, the sea, the wind, the house...

Him?

Conner stood for a moment, battling with uncomfortable thoughts until some inner sense warned him that he wasn't alone.

He turned swiftly and saw her.

Flora was standing only metres away from him, the wind lifting her brown curls and blowing them around her face, her expression uncertain.

'Sorry.' Her voice faltered and it was obvious that she couldn't decide whether to stay or retreat. 'I didn't mean to disturb you.'

He wished she hadn't, because he was in no mood for company and his desperate need for isolation fuelled his temper. 'Then why did you?'

Flora flinched at his directness, but she didn't retreat. 'You were supposed to be at Logan and Evanna's for lunch. We assumed you'd forgotten.'

'I needed some space.'

'Oh.' She took a breath. 'It's just that...you didn't ring or anything.'

'No.'

'I was worried.'

'Why?' *Since when had anyone worried about him?*

'This business with the islanders,' she shrugged, embarrassed and awkward. 'It's horrible. I thought by now they would have accepted you.'

'It's not important.'

'Of course it's important! Evanna told me that Finn wouldn't rent you a boat—'

When he didn't answer, she gazed at him in exasperation. 'Don't you *care*?'

He could feel the blood throbbing in his veins. 'What are you doing here, Flora?'

'When you didn't show up, I thought I'd bring lunch to you.'

It was then that he noticed the basket by her feet. He could see a bowl of strawberries, thick whipped cream and another bowl, this one piled high with bronzed chicken legs. And white and red checked napkins.

A traditional picnic.

It was all so civilised and in such direct contrast to this place and everything he was feeling that he felt his tension levels soar.

He wasn't feeling civilised. He wasn't feeling civilised at all.

In fact, he was in an extremely dangerous mood.

'It's pretty here,' she ventured hesitantly, glancing over to the rocks and the tiny beach. 'This is the only house on the island that has its own private beach.'

'Flora, if you have any sense, you'll leave right now.'

Her eyes flew to his. Widened. 'I've made you angry.'

There was something different about her but he couldn't work out what it was. 'I was angry before you arrived. I know you mean well, but I don't wish to take a trip down memory lane and I especially don't want to do it holding anyone's hand,' he said harshly. 'How did you know where to find me?'

'I went to your barn first and you weren't there.' She captured a strand of hair as it danced in the breeze. 'And I saw Mrs North picking blackberries in the lane outside and she said she'd seen you coming in this direction.'

Conner's mood darkened still further. 'Now I know why they don't bother with CCTV on Glenmore. They have locals stationed on every street corner.'

'I shouldn't have come. I really am sorry.' Flushed and flustered, Flora lifted the basket and stepped forward. She pushed the basket into his hands, her smile brief and shy. 'Take it. Evanna is an amazing cook. Her chicken is delicious and the strawberries are freshly picked from the Roberts' farm. If you're not hungry now, you can eat it later.' Without waiting for him to reply, she turned and walked quickly away from him, her long flowery skirt swirling around her body, outlining the soft curve of her hips.

He'd offended her. *Or had he frightened her?*

Conner watched her for a moment and then looked down at the basket and swore long and fluently. The day was *not* turning out as he'd planned. He lifted his gaze from the strawberries and stared after her retreating figure with a mixture of exasperation and anger.

He didn't care that he'd offended her.

He really didn't care.

It wasn't as if he'd invited her here. He hadn't asked her to follow him.

Caught in an internal battle, he opened his mouth to speak, changed his mind and closed it again, then growled with frustration and called out to her. 'Do you like strawberries?'

She stopped and turned—slowly. 'Yes. I love them.'

But she didn't move and even from this distance Conner sensed her wariness and remembered what Logan had said about her being shy.

'Good. Because there's a large bowlful in this basket and I hate them.' He dumped the basket on the ground and looked at her expectantly, but she still didn't move.

'Just eat the chicken, then.'

Realising that she wasn't going to walk to him, he strolled towards her and suddenly saw what was different about her. 'You're not wearing your glasses.'

She lifted a hand to her cheek and shrugged self-consciously. 'Contact lenses. I don't usually wear them at work.

I'm not a morning person and I'm never awake enough to risk putting my fingers into my eyes.' She looked over his shoulder at the basket, which now lay abandoned on the soft grass. 'I can take the strawberries with me, if they offend you that much.'

'Or you can sit down and eat them here.'

Her eyes narrowed. 'I didn't think you were looking for company.'

'If the strawberries aren't eaten, I'll hurt Evanna's feelings.'

A smile touched her mouth. 'I thought you didn't care about other people's feelings, Conner MacNeil.'

'I don't, but if I upset her, Logan will give me a black eye. And then the locals will think I've seduced someone's wife or girlfriend. And I'm already in enough trouble.'

She laughed, as he'd intended. 'You told me that you thrive on trouble.'

'That's just habit. I've never known anything else.'

Her laughter faded and she stared up into his face. 'I shouldn't have come here. It's personal for you. Stressful. And you don't want to talk about it, do you?'

He gave a twisted smile. 'Let's just say that if I talk, you wouldn't like the language I'd choose to use.'

'Use whatever language you please. I'm not as shockable as you seem to think I am.'

'It would be all too easy to shock you, Flora.' He thought of what his life had been and then he looked down at her gentle eyes and her soft mouth and wondered why he'd stopped her walking away. 'I'm not the type of man who eats strawberries with girls in flowered skirts.'

'You don't like my skirt?'

'You look…' He gave a faint smile as he searched for the word that best described her. 'Wholesome. Like an advert for that whipped cream in the basket.'

'It's Evanna's whipped cream. And I don't see what my skirt has to do with anything. Do you always push people away?'

'I don't have to. They usually run all by themselves.'

'Well, I can't run in these shoes.'

'Is that right? In that case, you can sit down and help me eat this damn picnic.'

'Where?' Flora glanced towards the house and he made an impatient sound.

'No way.' *He wasn't going back in there.* Instead, he took her hand, scooped up the basket and then led her down the path to the tiny cove at the bottom. The path was steep and stony but she didn't falter, confident and sure-footed despite her comment about her shoes.

She was a local girl, he remembered. *She'd spent her childhood playing on these cliffs and exploring Glenmore's rocky shores.*

As they reached the sand, she slipped off her shoes and stooped to pick them up. 'It's pretty here. Really sheltered.'

'Haven't you been here before?'

'No.'

'Why not?'

'Honestly?' She hesitated. 'This beach is part of your property and we were too afraid of your father. Even Kyla.'

Conner gave a bitter laugh. 'Lovely man, my father.' He sat down on the sand and then glanced at her with a frown. 'Did you bring something to sit on?'

She smiled and sat down on the sand next to him. 'This is perfect.' She reached into the basket and then glanced at him, her eyes twinkling. 'Napkin?'

'Of course,' he said sarcastically. 'I'd hate to drop anything on my tuxedo.'

She laughed and passed him the bowl of chicken instead. 'Try this. I guarantee it will taste better than anything you've ever eaten before, tuxedo or no tuxedo. I bumped into Diane Gregg in the supermarket this morning. She said Harry is feeling much better.'

'Yes. I saw him in surgery yesterday. One of the advantages of being treated like a leper is that I have plenty of time for the patients that do want to see me.' He bit into the chicken and flavours exploded on his palate. 'You're right—this is good.'

'I have a boat, if you want to sail.'

Conner lifted an eyebrow. 'Are you making a pass at me?'

The colour poured into her cheeks. 'Of course not.'

'But you're offering to lend me your boat?'

'Yes.' She delved into the basket and pulled out some crusty bread. 'Or we could sail together. You can sail it singlehanded but it's more fun with two.'

'I didn't know you sailed.'

'I suspect there's quite a lot about me that you don't know,' she said calmly, and Conner gave a surprised laugh.

'And what do you think the locals will say when they see you consorting with Bad Conner?'

Flora broke the bread in two and handed him half. 'I suppose it might be sensible to avoid getting into trouble, just in case the lifeboat crew refuse to help.'

'You'd be all right. They'd pick you up and leave me in the water.'

'No problems, then. Lemonade?'

Conner winced. 'Are you serious? What is this—nursery food?'

'It's home-made. Evanna makes it.' She poured him a glass and he heard a dull clunk as ice cubes thudded into the glass. 'It's very refreshing.'

He took the glass and stared at it dubiously. 'If you say so.'

'You'd probably prefer beer.'

'I don't drink.' He felt her eyes on his face and when she spoke her voice was soft.

'Because of your father.' Her quiet statement required no response and so he didn't give one.

They ate in silence and he found himself glancing at her occasionally and noticing things about the way she looked. Like the fact that she had tiny freckles on her nose and that her eyes were incredibly pretty.

'You should ditch the glasses,' he said softly, and she blinked awkwardly.

'Oh…' She concentrated on the chicken and suddenly he was reminded of a baby kitten he'd found abandoned when he'd been a child. It had been so soft and vulnerable that he he'd been afraid to touch it in case he harmed it. So he'd placed an anonymous call to the vet's surgery and had then hidden behind a tree, watching until they'd picked it up.

Flora had that same air of vulnerability.

They finished the picnic in silence and she packed everything away tidily in the basket. 'There's a good wind. I always find there's nothing better than sailing to clear the mind and put everything into perspective.'

'Flora—'

'Don't pretend you don't want to sail, because I know you tried to hire a boat from Finn at the sailing school. I'm offering you my boat. With or without myself as crew.'

He stared out to sea. 'I was going to clear the house out this afternoon.'

'There's no worse job in the world,' she said softly. 'After Dad died, it took me six months to even go into the house. I just couldn't face all those memories. And mine were happy ones. Are you sure you don't want to talk about this?'

'I wouldn't know what to say. I've been away for twelve years. But it seems even that isn't long enough.' Conner took a mouthful of his drink and choked. 'That is truly disgusting.'

Flora laughed. 'Some people prefer it with sugar.'

'The only way I'd drink it is topped up with gin. And given that I don't touch alcohol, there's no chance of that.' Pulling a face, he emptied his glass onto the sand. 'Where's your boat moored?'

'South Quay.'

His eyes narrowed. 'In full public view.'

'Yes.' She scrambled to her feet and brushed the sand from her skirt. 'We need to go via my house so that I can change, but that will only take a minute.'

'You seriously want to sail? I thought you hated being the focus of people's attention.'

'I won't be the focus,' she muttered, carefully stacking everything back into the basket. 'You will.'

She was being kind, he realised. Trying to show solidarity in front of the locals.

He probably ought to refuse but just as he opened his mouth to do just that, the wind gusted and he glanced at the waves breaking on the beach. 'It's a perfect afternoon for a sail.'

'Then what are you waiting for?' She walked towards the path. 'Are you coming, Dr MacNeil? Or would you rather spend the afternoon being moody?'

She'd never had so much fun. The wind was gusting at five knots and Conner was a born sailor, with a natural feel for the wind and the sea and blessed with nerves of steel. And although they came close several times, he didn't land them in the water.

As the water sprayed over the bows, Flora laughed in delight. 'Who taught you to sail?'

'Taught myself. Sank two boats in the process. Probably why Finn won't rent me a boat. I always loved being on the water. The sea was the place where everything came together.' He tightened the mainsheet as he turned the boat into the wind. 'Ready about,' he called. Flora released the jib sheet and they both ducked under the boom as the boat came swiftly around. The wind caught the sails and the boat accelerated smoothly away, the sea sparkling in the summer sunshine.

It was hours before they finally turned the boat back towards the jetty and Flora felt nothing but regret. 'Do you ever feel like just sailing away and never looking back?'

'All the time.' He adjusted the sail. 'What about you?'

'Oh, yes.' She gazed dreamily up at the sky, loving the feel of the wind and the spray on her face. 'I love being on the boat. It's just so easy and comfortable. No people. No problems.'

'You are full of surprises, Flora Harris.' Conner laughed. 'I never imagined you were a sailor.'

'I bought her with the money Dad left me when he died. He was the one who taught me to sail. I was hopeless at team sports at school because I was too shy. No one ever picked me. I think Dad realised that sailing would suit me. I love the freedom of the boat. And the fact that you're away from people.' She closed her eyes and let the sun warm her skin. 'I'm always tense around people.'

'You're still incredibly shy, aren't you?'

She opened her eyes. 'Yes. But I've learned to act. That's what you do as an adult, isn't it? You act your way through situations that would have paralysed you as a child.'

'Was it that bad?'

'Yes.' Her simple, honest response touched him.

'I didn't realise. I just thought you were studious.'

Flora stared at the quay, measuring the distance. 'If I was absorbed in a book then no one bothered with me, and I preferred it that way. I liked being inconspicuous.'

'So why did you come back to Glenmore? Logan said you

were working in Edinburgh before this. I would have thought it was easier to be inconspicuous in a city.'

'It's also very lonely and I missed the scenery and the sailing. Coming back here seemed like the right thing to do.'

'And was it?'

She glanced at him. 'I don't know. Even though I know they mean well, I can't get used to the fact that everyone knows what everyone is doing.'

They approached the jetty and she released the jib sheet and the sail flapped in the wind. Conner turned the boat head to wind and brought her skilfully into the quay.

'She's pretty.' He ran a hand over the mast and Flora felt her heart kick against her chest.

She wished she were the boat.

He leapt over the foredeck onto the quay and secured the boat to the jetty while Flora de-rigged the boat, wishing they could have stayed out on the water. Now that they were on dry land she was suddenly aware that she was with Conner MacNeil and that all the locals were watching them.

As usual, Conner was totally indifferent. 'I had no idea your father encouraged you to indulge in such dangerous pastimes. My impression was that he kept you under lock and key. He was strict.'

'Not strict, exactly. Protective.' Flora stepped off the boat and onto the quay. Hot after the exertion, she removed her hat and her hair tumbled loose over her shoulders. 'My mother died when I was very young and I think he was terrified that something would happen to me, too. He never relaxed if I was out.'

'I don't remember you ever going out. All my memories of you have books in them.'

Flora laughed. 'That was partly my fault. I was painfully shy and books stopped me having to talk to people.'

'So why aren't you shy with me, Flora?'

Her eyes flew to his, startled. It was true, she realised. She'd had such fun she hadn't once felt shy with him. Not once. 'I'm never shy when I'm sailing.'

But she knew that it had nothing to do with the sailing and everything to do with the man.

She felt comfortable with Conner.

Unsettled by that thought, she looked across the quay at the throngs of tourists who were milling around on their way to and from the beach. 'Can I treat you to a hot fudge sundae? Meg's café is calorie heaven.'

'I don't think so.' He checked that the boat was securely tied. 'I just upset the balance of Glenmore. I'm like you. Better with the boat than people. I've never been any good at platitudes and all the other false things people say to each other.'

It was so close to the way she felt that for a moment she stood still. Who would have thought that she and Conner had so many similarities? 'But you came back.'

He gave a careless shrug. 'It was time.'

But it wouldn't be for long, she knew that.

Suddenly she just wanted to drag him straight back on the boat and sail back out to sea. On the water she'd had glimpses of the person behind the bad boy. He'd been relaxed. Good-humoured. Now they were back on dry land his ice-blue eyes were wary and cynical, as though he was braced for criticism.

A commotion on the far side of the quay caught her eye and she squinted across the water. 'I wonder why the ferry hasn't left yet.' Flora glanced at her watch. 'It's five past four. Jim always leaves at four o'clock sharp. He's never late.'

'Obviously he is today.'

'What are they all staring at?' An uneasy feeling washed over her. 'Something is happening on the quay. Conner, I think someone must have fallen into the water.'

A woman started screaming hysterically and Flora paled as she recognised her.

'That's Jayne Parsons, from the dental surgery. Something must have happened to Lily. It must be little Lily in the water.' She started to run, dodging groups of gaping tourists as she flew towards the other side of the quay.

And suddenly she could see why people were staring.

Blood pooled on the surface of the water and Flora felt a wave of nausea engulf her as she realised just how serious the situation was.

Her hand shaking, she delved in her pocket for her mobile phone and quickly rang the coastguard and the air ambulance. Then she caught Jayne by the shoulders before she could throw herself into the water after her child. 'No! Wait, Jayne. What happened? Is it Lily?'

'She fell. One minute she was eating her ice cream and the next...Oh, God, she fell.' Jayne's breath was coming in hysterical gasps and out of the corner of her eye Flora saw movement, heard a splash and turned to see Conner already in the water.

A local who had seen the whole incident started directing him. 'She went in about here. Between the quay and the boat. I guess the propeller...' His voice tailed off as he glanced towards Jayne and the woman's eyes widened in horror as she focused on the surface of the water and saw what Flora had already seen.

The blood.

Jayne started to scream and the sound had a thin, inhuman quality that cut through the summer air and brought horrified silence to the normally bustling quay. Then she tried to launch herself into the water again and Flora winced as Jayne's flying fist caught her on the side of her head. She was too slight to hold the woman, her head throbbed and she was just about to resign herself to the fact that Jayne was going to jump when two burly local fishermen came to her aid.

They drew a sobbing, struggling Jayne away from the edge of the quay and Flora gave them a grateful nod. Whatever happened next, Jayne being in the water would only make things worse.

Oblivious to the audience or the building tension, Conner vanished under the water. Time and time again he dived, while strangers and locals stood huddled in groups, watching the drama unfold.

Offering what comfort she could, Flora took Jayne's hand. 'Conner will find her,' she said firmly, praying desperately that she was right. 'Conner will find her.' *If she said it often enough, perhaps it would happen.*

'Conner?' Shivering violently and still restrained by the fishermen, Jayne looked at Flora blankly, as if she hadn't realised until this point who was trying to rescue her daughter. 'Conner MacNeil?'

'He's in the water now,' Flora said gently, wondering whether Jayne was going into shock. Her eyes were glazed and her face white. 'He's looking for her, Jayne.'

'Conner? When has he ever put his life on the line for anyone? He won't help her. *He won't help my baby.*' Her eyes suddenly wild with terror, Jayne developed superhuman strength, wrenched herself from the hold of the two men and hurled herself towards the edge of the quay once again.

The two men quickly grabbed her and she wriggled and pulled, struggling to free herself. 'Get the coastguard, anyone— Oh, God, no, no.' She collapsed, sobbing and Flora slid her arms round her, this time keeping her body between Jayne and the quay.

'Jayne, you're no help to Lily if you fall in, too. Leave it to Conner. You have to trust Conner.'

'Who in their right mind would trust Conner MacNeil?'

'I would,' Flora said simply, and realised that it was true. 'I'd trust him with my life.'

'Then you're obviously infatuated with him,' Jayne shrieked, 'like every other woman who comes close to him.' But she sagged against Flora, her energy depleted by the extravagant surge of emotion.

Infatuated?

Dismissing the accusation swiftly, Flora stared at the surface of the water but there was no movement and a couple of tourists standing next to her started to murmur dire predictions. She turned and glared at them just as there was a sound from the water and Conner surfaced, the limp, lifeless body of the child in his arms. He sucked in air and then hauled himself onto the concrete steps with one hand, his other arm holding the child protectively against his chest.

Lily lay still, her soaked dress darkened by blood, her hair streaked with it.

Flora felt panic, jagged and dangerous. Oh no, please no. There were no signs of life. None.

Next to her Jayne started to moan like a creature tormented and then the sound stopped as she slid to the concrete in a faint.

'Leave her,' Conner ordered, climbing the steps out of the water, the body of the child still in his arms. Lily's head hung backwards and her skin was a dull grey colour. 'Someone else can look after her and at the moment she's better off out of it. Get me a towel, Flora. With the blood and the water, I can't see what we're dealing with here.'

A towel?

Feeling sick and shaky, Flora scanned the crowd and focused on two tourists who were loaded down with beach items. 'Give me your towel.' Without waiting for their permission, she yanked the towel out of the bag, spilling buckets and spades over the quay. Then she was on her knees beside Conner.

Lily lay pale and lifeless, her tiny body still, like a puppet that had been dropped. Blood spurted like a fountain from a wound on her leg.

'It's an artery.' With a soft curse Conner pressed down hard. 'I'm guessing she gashed it on the propeller as she fell. She's lucky the engine wasn't on.' He increased the pressure in an attempt to stop the bleeding. 'She's stopped breathing.'

Flora almost stopped breathing, too. Panic pressed in on her and without Connor's abrupt commands she would have shrivelled up and sobbed, just as Jayne had. Perhaps he realised that she was on the verge of falling apart because he lifted his head and glared at her, his blue eyes fierce with determination.

'Press here! I need to start CPR. Flora, *move!*'

She stared at him for a moment, so stunned by the enormity of what was happening she couldn't respond.

'Pull yourself together!' His tone was sharp. 'If we're to stand any chance here, I need some help, and you're the only person who knows what they're doing. Everyone else is just gawping.'

Flora felt suddenly dizzy. She'd never seen so much blood in her life. She'd never worked in A and E and all the first-aid courses she'd attended had been theoretical. *She didn't know what she was doing.*

And then she realised that *he* did. Conner knew exactly what he was doing and she knelt down beside him.

'Tell me what you want me to do.'

'Press here. Like that. That's it—good.' He put her hands on the wound, showed her just how hard he wanted her to press, and then shifted slightly so that he could focus on the child's breathing. With one hand on her forehead and the other under her chin, he gently tilted Lily's head back and covered her mouth with his, creating a seal. He breathed gently, watching as the child's chest rose.

Then he lifted his mouth and watched as Lily's chest fell as the air came out. 'Flora, get a tourniquet on that leg. She's losing blood by the bucketload.'

'A tourniquet?' Flora turned to the nearest tourist. 'Get me a bandage or a tie, something—anything—I can wind around her leg.'

The man simply stared at her, but his wife moved swiftly, jerking the tie from the neck of a businessman who had been waiting to take the ferry.

Flora didn't dare release the pressure on Lily's leg. 'If I let go to tie it, she's going to bleed.' Feeling horribly ignorant, she sent Conner a helpless glance. 'I haven't done this before. Do I put it directly over the wound?'

'Above the wound. You need a stick or something to twist it tight. Tie it and leave a gap and tie it again.'

Flora swiftly did as he instructed. The towel was soaked in blood and her fingers were slippery with it and shaking.

'The bleeding's not stopping Conner,' she muttered, and he glanced across at her, his expression hard.

'You need to tighten it. More pressure. Get a stick.'

She glanced at the uneven surface of the quay. 'There's no stick!'

'Then use something else!' He glared at the group of tourists standing nearest to them. 'Find a stick of some sort! A kid's spade, a cricket stump—anything we can use.'

'The blood is everywhere.' Flora tried to twist the tie tighter but the bleeding was relentless and she felt a sob build in her throat. It just seemed hopeless. Completely hopeless. 'She's four years old, Conner.' She was ready to give up but Conner placed the heel of his hand over the child's sternum.

'She's hypovolaemic. She needs fluid and she needs it fast.' He pushed down. 'Where the *hell* is the air ambulance?'

Someone thrust a stick into Flora's hand and she looked at it with relief. Perhaps now she could stop the bleeding. 'Do I push it under the tie and twist?'

'On top.' Conner stopped chest compressions and bent to give another rescue breath. 'Between the two knots. Twist. Make a note of the time—we can't leave it on for more than ten minutes. But if we're not out of here in ten minutes, it will be too late anyway.'

He covered Lily's mouth with his again and Flora followed his instructions, placing the stick between the first and second knots and twisting until it tightened.

'The air ambulance has just landed on the beach,' Jim, the ferryman, was by her shoulder, his voice surprisingly steady. 'What can I do, Flora?'

'I don't know. Keep the crowd away, I suppose. How's Jayne?'

'Out cold. Might be the best thing. Someone's looking after her—a nurse from the mainland on a day trip.'

Conner returned to chest compressions. 'Jim—get over to the paramedics. I want oxygen and plasma expander. And get them to radio the hospital and warn them. She's going to need whole blood or packed cells when she arrives. I want her in the air in the next few minutes. We don't have time to play around here.'

'Will do.' Without argument, Jim disappeared to do as Conner had instructed and Flora lifted the edge of the towel.

'The bleeding's stopped.' She felt weak with relief and Conner nodded.

'Good. We'll release it and check it in about ten minutes. If the bleeding doesn't start again we can leave it loose, but don't take it off—we might need it again.' He bent his head to give Lily another life-saving breath and Flora saw the paramedics sprinting along the quay towards them.

'They're here, Conner.'

Conner wasn't listening. His attention was focused on the child. 'Come on, baby girl,' he murmured softly, 'breathe for me.' His eyes were on her chest and Flora watched him, wondering. Had he seen something? Had he felt a change in her condition?

'Do you think she—?'

And at that moment Lily gave a choking cough and vomited weakly.

'Oh, thank God,' Flora breathed, and Conner turned the child's head gently and cleared her airway.

'There's a good girl. You're going to be all right now, sweetheart.'

He spoke so softly that Flora doubted that anyone else had heard his words of comfort and she felt a lump block her throat as she watched him with the child.

So he was capable of kindness, then. It was there, deep inside him, just as she'd always suspected.

But then he lifted his head and his eyes were hard as ever. 'Get some blankets, dry towels, coats—something to warm her up,' he ordered, and then looked at the paramedics. 'Give her some oxygen. I want to get a line in and give her a bolus of fluid and then we're out of here.'

'How much fluid do you want?'

Conner wiped his forearm across his brow, but he kept one hand on the child's arm. *Offering reassurance.* 'What's her weight? How old is she? We can estimate—'

'I know her weight exactly,' Flora said. 'I saw her in clinic last week. She's 16 kilograms. Do you want a calculator so that you can work out the fluid?'

'Start with 160 mils of colloid and then I'll reassess. I don't want to hang around here.' Conner released Lily's hand and started looking for a vein, while one of the paramedics sorted out the fluid and the other gave Lily some oxygen.

The child was breathing steadily now, her chest rising and

falling as Conner worked. Occasionally her eyes fluttered open and then drifted closed again.

'She's got no veins,' Conner muttered, carefully examining Lily's arms. 'Get me an intraosseous needle. I'm not wasting time looking for non-existent veins. We need to get her to hospital. We've messed around here long enough.'

The paramedic dropped to his knees beside Conner, all the necessary equipment to hand. 'You want an intraosseous needle?'

'Actually, just give me a blue cannula. She might just have a vein I can use here.' Conner stroked the skin on the child's arm, focused. 'One go—if it fails, we'll get her in the air and I'll insert an intraosseous needle on the way.'

Flora leaned forward and closed her fingers around the child's arm, squeezing gently and murmuring words of re-assurance. Lily was drifting in and out of consciousness and didn't seem aware of what was going on.

There was a commotion next to them but Conner didn't seem to notice. He didn't look up or hesitate. Instead, he applied himself to the task with total concentration, slid the needle into the vein and then gave a grunt of satisfaction. 'I'm in—good. That makes things easier. Let's flush it and tape it—I don't want to lose this line.'

The paramedic leaned towards him with tape but just at that moment Jayne launched herself at Conner and tried to drag him away. *'What are you doing to my baby?'* Her face was as white as swan's feathers, her eyes glazed with despair. 'Let me get to her— I need to hold her— *Get him away from her.'*

'Jayne, not now.' Flora quickly slid an arm round her shoulders and pulled her out of the way so that the paramedic and Conner could finish what they'd started.

'But she's dead,' Jayne moaned, and Flora shook her head.

'She's not dead, Jayne,' she said firmly. 'She's breathing.'

'Not dead?' Relief diluted the pain in Jayne's eyes but then panic rose again as she saw Conner bending over her child. *'What's he doing to her? Oh, God, there's blood everywhere.'*

'Lily cut herself very badly,' Flora began, but Jayne began to scream.

'Get him away from her! *Get him away from my baby! I don't trust him!'*

'You should trust him. He's the reason the bairn's breathing now.' It was Jim who spoke, his weatherbeaten face finally showing signs of strain. Gently but firmly he drew Jayne away from Flora. 'Flora, you help Dr MacNeil. Jayne, you're staying with me. And you'd better remember that Conner MacNeil is the reason Lily is alive right now. I know you're upset, and rightly so, but you need to get a hold. The man is working miracles.'

Conner straightened, conferred with the paramedics and together he and the crew transferred Lily's tiny form onto the stretcher. Then he wiped his blood-streaked hands down his soaked shorts. His handsome face was still damp with sea water and the expression in his ice-blue eyes cold and detached as he finally looked at Jayne. 'We're taking her to hospital.'

Jayne crumpled. 'I'm sorry, I'm so sorry.' Tears poured down her cheeks as she looked from him to Lily's still form. 'Can I come with you? Please?'

Conner took a towel that a tourist tentatively offered him. 'That depends on whether you're likely to assault me during the flight.' He wiped his hands properly, watching as Jayne breathed in and out and lifted a hand to her chest.

'I—I really am sorry.'

'No, you need to understand.' Conner handed the towel back, his voice brutally harsh. 'This isn't over. If she arrests during the flight, I'll be resuscitating her. Can you cope with that? Because if you can't, you're staying on the ground.'

Jayne flinched but for some reason his lack of sympathy seemed to help her pull herself together and find some dignity. 'I understand. Of course. And that's fine. I'm just grateful that you…' She swallowed and nodded. 'Do everything,' she whispered. 'Everything. I just—I just want to be near her. And with her when we get there. I— Thank you. Thank you so much. Without you…' Her eyes met Conner's for a moment and he turned his attention back to Lily.

'We're wasting time. Let's move.'

In a matter of moments the helicopter was in the air and Flora watched as it swooped away from Glenmore towards the mainland.

Suddenly she realised how much her hands were shaking.

She stared down at herself. Her shorts were streaked with blood and Lily's blood still pooled on the grey concrete of the quay. 'Someone get a bucket and slosh some water over this,' she muttered to Jim, and he breathed a sigh and rubbed a hand over his face.

'I haven't seen anything like that in all my time on Glenmore.'

'No. I suppose it was because the quay was so crowded. She must have been knocked off the edge and into the water.'

'I didn't mean that.' Jim stared into the sky, watching as the helicopter shrank to a tiny dot in the distance. 'I meant Conner MacNeil. He was in the water like an arrow while the rest of us were still working out what had happened. And he just got on with it, didn't he?'

'Yes.' Flora cleared her throat. 'He did.'

'Logan says he was in the army.' Jim pushed his hat back from his forehead and scratched. 'I reckon if I was fighting in some godforsaken country, I'd feel better knowing he was around to pick up the pieces.'

'Yes. He was amazing.'

'He's not cuddly, of course.' Jim held up five fingers to a

tourist who tentatively asked whether or not the ferry would be running. 'Five minutes. But in a crisis which do you prefer? Cuddly or competent?'

Flora swallowed, knowing that Jim was right. Conner's ice-cold assessment of the situation had been a huge part of the reason Lily was still alive. He hadn't allowed emotion to cloud his judgement, whereas she…

Suddenly Flora felt depression wash over her. The whole situation had been awful and she was experienced enough to know that, despite Conner's heroic efforts, Lily wasn't out of danger. 'I'd better go, Jim. I need to clean up.'

'And I need to get this ferry to the mainland.' Jim gave a wry smile and glanced at his watch. 'It's the first time the Glenmore ferry has been late since the service started. Nice job, Flora. Well done.'

But Flora knew that her part in the rescue had been minimal.

It had been Conner. All of it. He'd been the one to dive into the water. He'd pulled Lily out. And when she'd been frozen with panic at the sight of Lily's lifeless form covered in all that blood, he'd worked with ruthless efficiency, showing no emotion but getting the job done. Nothing had distracted him. Not even Lily's mother. He'd had a task to do and he'd done it.

CHAPTER SIX

SHE COULDN'T relax at home so she went back to the beach with her book and when it was too dark to read she just sat, listening to the hiss of the waves as they rushed forward onto the beach and then retreated.

She wanted to know how Lily was faring, but Conner wasn't answering his mobile and she didn't want to bother the hospital staff.

Shrieks of excitement came from the far corner of the beach where a group of teenagers had lit a fire and were having a beach party. Flora watched for a moment, knowing that she was too far away for them to see her. They weren't supposed to light fires but they always did. This was Glenmore in the summer. She knew that sooner or later Nick Hillier, the policeman, would do one of his evening patrols and if they were still there, he'd move them on. Back home to their parents or the properties they rented for a few weeks every summer.

'What's a nice girl like you doing on a beach like this? It's late. You should be home.' The harsh, familiar male voice came from directly behind her and she gave a gasp of shock.

'Conner? Where did you come from? I thought you'd still be on the mainland.'

'Hitched a lift back on a boat.'

'How's Lily?'

'Asking for her dolls.'

Flora felt a rush of relief and smiled. 'That's wonderful.'

'If it's wonderful, why such a long face?' He sat down next to her and there was enough light for her to see the dark stains on his shirt and trousers. It was a vivid reminder of just what he'd achieved.

'It would have been a very different outcome for Lily if you hadn't been there.'

'Someone else would have done it.'

'No. No, they wouldn't. And I was no use to you at all. I'm sorry. I was completely out of my depth. I've never seen anything like that before.' Just the thought of Lily's body, lifeless and covered with blood, made her feel sick.

'You were fine.' He reached behind him for a pebble and threw it carelessly into the darkness. There was a faint splash as it hit the water.

'Conner, I wasn't fine.' She'd been thinking about it all evening and becoming more and more upset. 'You always imagine that you'll know what to do in an emergency, but I didn't. I didn't know! I mean, I suppose I knew the theory but nothing prepares you for seeing a little girl you know well, covered in blood and not breathing. I—I just couldn't concentrate.'

'That happens to the best of us.'

She was willing to bet it had never happened to him. 'I've never even tied a tourniquet before.'

'Join the army,' he suggested, and reached for another stone. 'You get to tie quite a few. Believe me, it's a talent I'd willingly not have to use ever again. You were fine. Stop worrying.'

'There was so much blood.'

'Yeah—it has a habit of spreading itself around when you hit an artery.'

'It didn't worry you.'

'Blood?' He shrugged. 'No, blood doesn't worry me— but emotion...' He gave a hollow laugh and threw the stone. 'Now that's a different story. When they discharge her from hospital, you're the one that's visiting.'

She curled her toes into the soft sand. 'I remember Jayne from school.'

'Me, too. I think I might have kissed her once.'

'You kissed everyone.' *Except her.* She turned to look at him. Fresh stubble darkened his jaw and in the dim light he looked more dangerous than ever.

He flung another stone and then leaned back on his elbows, watching her through narrowed eyes. 'What the hell are you doing out here at this hour, Flora Harris? You should be tucked up in bed, having exhausted yourself with a fat book.'

Flora drew a circle in the sand with her finger. 'You think I'm so boring, don't you?'

'Trust me, you don't want to know what I think.'

'I already know.' Her heart thumping, she looked at him. 'I'm probably the only girl on Glenmore that you haven't kissed, so that says quite a lot.'

'It says that I still had some decency, despite what the locals thought of me. You weren't exactly the kind of girl to indulge in adolescent groping.' Conner glanced towards the crowd on the beach, barely visible in the darkness. 'You didn't do late-night beach orgies. I suppose you were studying.'

'Yes, I probably was.' Flora thought of the life she'd led. 'Dad hated me being out too late. He always worried about me.'

'You were a good daughter. You never once slipped off the rails, not even for a moment. That's good. Be proud of it.'

'It was easy to stay on the rails because my rails were

smooth and consistent. I lost Mum but I still had Dad.' She glanced at him, hesitant about saying something that would upset him. 'It must be very stressful for you, coming back here after so long. You had such a difficult childhood and all the memories are here.'

'Actually, I think I probably had an easier childhood than you. Everyone expected you to do well, so you had to work hard and deliver or risk disappointing them. No one expected anything but trouble when I was around, so I could create havoc and meet their expectations at the same time.' He sat up and flung another stone. 'Your father expected you to be home before dark because he loved you and worried about you, so you didn't dare go out and paint the town red in case you upset him. My father didn't give a damn what I did as long as it didn't involve him.'

'You must be very upset and angry with your mother for leaving.'

'Not at all.' His tone was cool. 'He beat her every day of their marriage. She had no choice but to get out. She should have done it sooner. Probably would have done if it hadn't been for me.'

Flora was so shocked by his unexpected confession that it took her a moment to respond. 'Oh, Conner...' She'd heard rumours, of course, but no one had ever known for sure. 'But she left you there. With him.'

'She had no choice about that. If she'd taken me, he would have followed. Her only chance was to go before he killed her.'

Flora sat for a moment, trying to imagine what it must have been like, and failing. She'd only ever known love. 'Did he ever...?' Her voice trailed off and she shook her head and looked away. 'Sorry, it's none of my business and I know you hate talking about personal stuff.'

'Did he ever hit me? Is that what you were about to ask?'

He lay back on the sand and stared into the darkness. 'Just once. And I was so angry I stabbed a hole in his leg with a kitchen knife. I was six years old at the time. After that he left me alone. I think he was always a bit worried I'd empty the contents of the science lab into his tea. Did you know that science was the only subject I never skipped? I went through a phase of making bombs—blowing everything up. You probably remember that phase. Everyone on Glenmore does.'

Flora hesitated and then reached out and touched his arm, because it seemed like the right thing to do. 'I can't imagine what it must have been like for you.'

'It was amazing fun. I was causing explosions all over the place and no one could stop me.' He showed no emotion but she wasn't fooled.

'So if it's that easy and you care so little, why haven't you come home before now?'

'Good question.' He was silent for a moment and then he laughed. 'Perceptive, aren't you? Yes, I suppose I'm back here because I wanted to see how it felt to be home.'

'And?'

'It feels every bit as bad as I thought it would.' He spoke calmly and turned his head to look at her. 'So now I've spilled my guts, what happens next? I cry into your soft bosom and get in touch with my feelings?'

'In case you hadn't noticed, I'm pretty flat-chested so that won't work.' She kept her tone light because she sensed that was what he wanted. 'I suppose I just want you to know that, well, that I'm a friend—if you need one.'

'A flat-chested friend.' He gave a slow smile. 'I've never had one of those before. Do you know what I really fancy right now?'

Her heart thumped wildly. 'I hardly dare ask.'

'A cigarette.'

It wasn't what she'd wanted him to say and she let out a

breath, not knowing whether to laugh or cry. *Drop the fantasies*, Flora. 'I didn't know you smoked.'

'I don't. At least, not for years. I just need something to relieve the tension. I'll have to find another way.'

Flora stiffened. *He was talking about sex*, she knew he was. And there was no doubt in her mind that there were any number of women on Glenmore who would be only too delighted to offer him the distraction he wanted.

And he was stuck on the beach with her.

Boring Flora.

He looked at her. 'I suppose it's a waste of time asking if you have any cigarettes?'

'Complete waste of time,' she said lightly. *Boring, staid Flora.*

'Anything to drink?'

'I have a small bottle of mineral water in my bag.'

'Mineral water?' He laughed. 'You really know how to live, don't you? Nothing like a few minerals to get a person into a party mood. Tell me, Flora Harris, what do you do to release tension? Read a chapter of *War and Peace*?'

She smiled. 'If I can't sail, then I swim.'

'You swim?'

'In the sea. Every morning. I love it. It relaxes me.'

'You take your clothes off?'

'No, I swim in my uniform.' Flora glanced at him in amusement. 'Of course I take my clothes off. What did you think?'

'I've no idea. I've made a point of never picturing you without clothes on.'

'Thanks.'

His eyes narrowed. 'If you're taking that as an insult then you're even more naïve than I think you are.'

'I'm not naïve.'

'Yes, you are. The reason I don't picture you without

clothes is because then I'll start thinking about you in a way that would make Logan punch me.'

Her heart was racing. 'Logan isn't my keeper.'

'Good point.' He rose to his feet and tugged her up beside him. 'Come on, then, Flora Harris. We'll try the swim. See if it works.'

'Now?' Her voice was an astonished squeak. 'It's one in the morning.'

'Less crowded than one in the afternoon.'

She gave a strangled laugh. 'Yes, I suppose it is. I don't have a costume.'

He gave a wicked smile and slowly undid the buttons on his shirt. 'The point of skinny dipping is that you don't need clothes.' His hands dropped to the fastening at the waistband of his trousers and her cheeks warmed as she caught a glimpse of taut, muscular stomach and dark male body hair.

'For goodness' sake, Conner...'

'What? You just said "Of course I take my clothes off." So that's what I'm doing.'

'Obviously, I wear a costume.'

'Obviously.' He grinned. 'Because you wouldn't be you if you didn't. But me being me, I'm not going to bother.' Completely unselfconscious, he stepped out of his trousers and boxer shorts and Flora gave a nervous laugh, keeping her eyes firmly fixed on the horizon.

'You're going to get yourself arrested, Conner MacNeil.'

'It's dark. No one knows we're here.' His hands were on the hem of her T-shirt. 'Come on, Flora. Take a risk. Live a little. Get naked with me.'

Take a risk. Live a little.

Suddenly the world opened up in front of her and her heart thundered in her chest. 'I am *not* swimming naked with you.'

'If the water is as cold as I suspect it's going to be, you're at no risk from me, darling, but if it makes you feel better you can leave your underwear on.' He gently pulled the T-shirt over her head and slid her shorts down her legs.

As his fingers brushed her skin and she shivered.

She knew she should stop him, but she couldn't, and when he closed his hand firmly over hers and dragged her down to the water's edge, she didn't resist.

And then the water touched her feet and she stopped dead. 'Oh, my goodness, that's cold.'

'Don't be a wimp.' He jerked her forward. 'This was your idea and you're not bottling out now. Anyway, what are you complaining about?' Conner kept walking, long steady strides that took him deeper into the sea. 'It's like bathwater. I can't imagine why anyone would travel all the way to the Mediterranean when we have this on our doorstep.' He gave her no choice but to wade in with him and she picked her way gingerly through the dark, swirling water, catching her breath as the waves licked higher and higher on her legs.

'I'm not sure if I like doing this in the middle of the night.' She peered towards her feet. 'Do you think there are jelly-fish?'

'No. It's long past their bedtime. They're all curled up asleep with hot-water bottles.' The water was halfway up his thighs now and as a wave washed over him at waist level, he cursed fluently. 'I think we've just discovered a whole new non-surgical method of vasectomy. If any of my sperm survive this experience, it will be a miracle.'

Flora giggled helplessly and wondered what had come over her. *What was she doing?* She was standing in the sea at one o'clock in the morning with Conner MacNeil, the most dangerous, unsuitable man she was every likely to meet.

And she was having the time of her life.

'This is freezing. I don't think I can go in any further.'

'The only way to do this is quickly. If you do this every

morning then I have new respect for you, Flora. You're twice the woman I thought you were, flat chest or no flat chest.'

'It's bracing. It wakes me up.'

'No surprise there. If this didn't wake you up, you'd have to be dead.'

'It's colder tonight.' She clutched him tightly, afraid that the waves would knock her over, and he steadied her and then released her hand.

'All right, let's do this…' He dived forward into the waves and she had a brief glimpse of powerful male muscle and strong legs before he vanished from sight.

She rubbed her hands down her arms, knowing that the goose-bumps had nothing to do with the cold water and everything to do with the way her body had felt next to his. *How was it possible to feel hot when she was standing waist deep in freezing seawater?*

She followed him into the waves, wondering why she'd never swum in the moonlight before. In all the years she'd lived here and swum here, she'd never done this. And it was fabulous. Magical. The stars and the moon shone in the clear sky and the water glistened.

And she felt daring and more alive than she'd ever felt.

She was so enchanted by her surroundings that she gasped with shock when Conner emerged next to her.

There was just enough light for her to see the outline of his face and the faint glitter in his eyes as he reached out and pulled her against him. 'I can't believe I'm skinny dipping with Flora Harris. Looks like I've finally corrupted you.'

'I like being corrupted.' She kept her voice light, trying not to reveal how it felt to be this close to him. She could feel the hardness of his thighs against hers and, despite his complaints about the cold water, a building pressure against her abdomen. 'And I'm not naked.'

'Not yet.'

'Conner...' To keep her balance she placed her hands on his shoulders and felt the smooth swell of hard male muscle under her fingers.

His mouth was dangerously close to hers. 'I've been thinking about what you said.'

Thinking? *How could he think?* 'What did I say?'

'That you were the only female on the island that I haven't kissed.'

'I was wrong.' She was so aware of him that could barely speak, 'I'm fairly sure you haven't kissed Ann Carne, and Mrs Parker may have escaped, too.'

'Good point.' He lifted his hands and cupped her face gently. 'Nevertheless, it's only fair to warn you that I might be about to corrupt you further. You might want to run for the beach. I'll give you a two-second start.'

Her heart pounded like the hooves of a racehorse on the home stretch. 'Two seconds doesn't sound like much.'

'It's all you're getting. Take it or leave it.'

She couldn't take her eyes from his and the anticipation was agonising. 'I'll leave it. I can't run in these waves.' *He was going to kiss her.*

Finally, after what seemed like a lifetime, Conner MacNeil was going to kiss her.

'If you can't run, then you're trapped.' His head moved closer but he didn't touch her. Instead, his mouth hovered tantalisingly close to hers, the expression in his eyes knowing and wickedly sexy as he prolonged the torture for both of them. Her stomach tumbled and her senses hummed and when finally he brushed his lips over hers, she knew that this was the most perfect and exciting thing that had ever happened to her. His lips were cool and the tip of his tongue gently caressed her lower lip.

Heat exploded inside her and she made a soft sound in her throat and leaned against him, seeking more. Her eyes closed, but still she saw stars as everything inside her erupted with excitement.

His fingers closed hard around her arms and his body shifted against hers.

'Hell, Flora...' This time his mouth came down hard, his kiss sending bolts of electricity through her body, and she clutched at him for support as he drew the fire from deep inside her with the skilled, sensual stroke of his tongue. And she kissed him back, her tongue toying with his in a kiss that was both intimate and erotic. His hands dropped from her face and slid down her back, pulling her against him in a movement that was unmistakably possessive.

It was a kiss with promise and purpose but before she had the chance to discover where it was leading, there was a shout.

With a groan of frustration and anger Conner dragged his mouth from hers and Flora clutched at him for support, dizzy and disoriented from the kiss. It took her a moment to realise that the sound was coming from the beach behind them.

'Conner? Conner MacNeil, is that you? It's Jim—Jim from the ferry and a few of the lads. We wanted to buy you a drink.'

'Oh, my goodness.' Flora shrank with embarrassment. 'They can't possibly see us, can they? It's too dark.'

Conner stared down at her for a moment, his lashes lowered, his eyes as cool and defiant as ever. 'Do you care?'

Flora didn't answer because she genuinely didn't know the answer to that. This was her island. And it was her reputation on the line. She should care, she knew she should. But his kiss had changed everything. It was as if her life had reached a crossroads and she didn't know which path to take—the safe one was back on the shore and the dangerous one was here, in the sea, with Conner's hard male body pressed against hers.

'Flora?' His voice was even and she wondered how he could sound so normal after what they'd shared. She felt far from normal. She felt churned up, confused—*different.*

She breathed in and out. She knew that it was too dark for them to have recognised her, but if she walked out of the water with Conner...

She wanted to say, *Damn the lot of them,* and carry on kissing him, but something held her back. 'I—I don't know, Conner.' Her fingers tightened on his arms. 'I suppose I do care. I have to work with these people. I'll still be living on this island long after you've left.'

He released her abruptly. 'Of course you will. Stay here. I'll get them away from you and you can get home before anyone is any the wiser. I guess that's more chivalrous than escorting you home.' He spoke with a careless indifference and she felt a flash of desperation as she sensed his withdrawal and felt her new self slipping away.

Suddenly she wished desperately that she hadn't spoken. *The person who had spoken had been the girl she'd been all her life, but now she wasn't sure if she was that girl any more. She didn't know if she wanted to be that girl.*

She wanted to be daring and careless of the consequences, like him. She wanted to live in the moment and not think about what other people thought. She wanted to kiss Conner MacNeil and enjoy every second of the excitement.

Without his hands to steady her, she almost stumbled as a wave hit her from the back and the shower of cold water seemed symbolic.

It was over.

Her moment of wild living had passed and she was back to being boring Flora. Sensible Flora. A girl who would never swim half-naked in the sea with a very unsuitable man.

But did she really want to be that girl?

'Conner, wait.' She grabbed his arm. 'I don't care about them. I don't care if they see us.'

It took him a moment to reply and when he did, his voice was rough. 'Yes, you do, angel. And quite right, too. How are you going to have a proper conversation with Mrs Parker if word gets round that you've been cavorting in the waves with Bad Conner? Be grateful to the locals. You've been saved from total corruption by the brave and persistent citizens of Glenmore.'

She didn't know what to say to rescue the situation so she tried to joke about it. 'Isn't it typical? The first time I try to be wild, I have an audience.'

He laughed, then lifted a hand and drew his thumb slowly over her lower lip, the intimacy of the gesture in direct contrast to his words. 'I've had more excitement being shot at in the desert.' His tone was sarcastic but the look in his eyes made her dizzy.

'I'm sure.'

His smile faded. 'You're not made for this, Flora, and both of us know it. You need a man you're not ashamed to be seen with, so let's end this now before we both do something that will keep the locals talking for years. I'll swim to the other side of the beach and meet them there. Stay in the water until I'm out and they won't see you. Can you make your way home safely?'

'Of course. Do I look helpless?'

'No, you look sexy.' He gave a wicked smile and lowered his mouth to hers once more, his lips and tongue working a seductive magic that made the world spin. Then he lifted his head reluctantly and gave a resigned shrug. 'Sorry about that. Just couldn't help myself. Once bad, always bad, or so it would seem. You just had a lucky escape, Flora Harris. Five more minutes and we would have been in the middle of a practical scientific experiment involving frozen body parts and libido.' Without giving her time to respond, he called to the men on the shore. 'Back off, guys. I'll be with you in a minute.' And then he plunged back into the waves and swam away from her with a powerful crawl.

Nodding to the locals who were toasting his health, Conner raised his glass to his lips and tried to decide whether he should be grateful or just punch them.

Five minutes more and he would have been completing the corruption of Flora.

So he should be grateful, obviously. If he'd followed the episode to its natural conclusion, Flora would now be steeped in embarrassment and regret.

He remembered her anguished gasp when she'd realised that they'd been spotted. Even in the semi-darkness he'd been able to see the burning colour of her cheeks.

Narrow escape for her. And for him, he told himself firmly. It was hard enough being back on Glenmore, without having that on his conscience.

He drank deeply, trying to obliterate the memory of the way she'd tasted and the way her body had felt pressed against his. She'd been lithe, slender, slippery from the seawater—

'Conner MacNeil, am I drunk or are you really sitting there drinking cranberry juice?'

Conner looked at Jim. 'You are drunk. And I am sitting here drinking cranberry juice.'

Jim focused on the glass in his hand. 'It looks disgusting.'

'It is disgusting.' *But not as disgusting as Evanna's home-made lemonade*, he thought with wry humour. Something stirred inside him as he remembered Flora standing on the grass, clutching a picnic basket.

'When I offered to buy you a drink...' Jim lifted a finger and waggled it in his direction '...I meant a *proper* drink. A man's drink. What are you? Wimp or man?'

Dismissing thoughts of Flora's soft mouth, Conner gave a careless lift of his shoulder. 'Wimp, obviously.'

'Leave the man alone.' Nick Hillier, the island policeman, slapped Conner on the back. 'A hero can relax in any way he chooses. Personally, I'm just glad it's not alcohol. It will save me the bother of arresting him for drink-driving later.'

Jim hiccoughed lightly. 'Your old man knew how to drink.'

An uncomfortable silence fell on the group of men who'd had less to drink than Jim, but Conner simply nodded. 'He certainly did.'

Jim sniffed. 'Couldn't have been easy, living with that. Duncan MacNeil had one hell of a temper.'

'You want me to cry on your shoulder?'

Jim shuddered. 'You know what I want? I want to know who the girl was, Conner. That's what I want.' He winked at the others and Conner slowly lowered his glass to the table.

So they *had* seen. 'No one.'

'Bet she was pretty. You always did get the pretty ones. Hey, everyone…,' Jim raised his voice to attract maximum attention. Then he hiccoughed again and lifted his glass in salute. 'Conner was in the waves with "no one".'

'At least "no one" can't nag at you,' someone muttered, and Jim gave a snort.

'She was real enough.'

'We can torture it out of him.' Nick suggested. 'You have the right to remain silent—'

'And I intend to,' Conner drawled, his face expressionless. Inside, a slow anger burned. *Anger towards himself and what he'd so nearly done.* If they'd seen that it was Flora, what would that have done to her reputation? She was decent and sweet and, as she'd pointed out, she was going to be working on this island long after he'd turned his back on it for ever. She was also a shy and private person who would have hidden in a hole in the ground rather than have her name tossed carelessly around a group of men in a pub.

And with his selfish actions, he'd almost destroyed everything she'd worked for.

And not just by exposing her to gossip.

He lifted his glass again, remembering the shyness and the desperate excitement in her eyes in the last seconds before he'd given in to impulse and kissed her. She'd wanted him, badly. He should have been flattered but instead he felt...disgusted with himself. Disgusted with himself for not walking away. He had no idea how much sexual experience she'd had, but he was willing to bet that her lifestyle didn't encompass meaningless affairs, and that was all he could offer her.

He stared at the bunch of locals gathered around the table, laughing and joking at his expense.

He should be grateful to them.

If it weren't for them he'd now be suffering from regret instead of sexual frustration. And Flora... Flora would have assured him in that polite voice of hers that everything was fine, but deep down she'd have been horrified at herself for indulging in a moment of madness with a delinquent like him.

Or worse—she'd be looking at him with those huge, brown eyes of hers, wanting things from him that he'd never, ever be able to deliver.

Conner drained his glass, knowing that probably for the first time in his life he'd done the right thing.

With a humourless laugh he studied the empty glass in his hand, sure of one thing. If doing the right thing felt this bad, he wasn't going to make a habit of it.

CHAPTER SEVEN

'HE SAVED the child, can you believe that? Anyway, I always knew there was good in him. It's not surprising he went off the rails with everything that he had to contend with at home.' Angela Parker watched as Flora tightened the bandage. 'I mean, his mother left when he was only ten years old. And his father was a drunk. A *violent* drunk, some say. Shocking, really shocking. It's no wonder he was wild. The poor boy.'

'Yes, Mrs Parker. I mean, no.' Flora was barely listening. Her mind was on other things. Although part of her was delighted and relieved that the entire island was now treating Conner as a hero, another part of her felt as though something inside her had been ripped out.

It was just because she was tired, she told herself. But she knew that wasn't true. It had nothing to do with lack of sleep and everything to do with the kiss she'd shared with Conner.

The kiss that had been interrupted.

The kiss that she'd totally messed up.

She kept reliving that moment and wishing she'd done things differently. She wished she'd yelled out, *It's me, Flora Harris, Jim. Yes, I'm kissing Conner so could you just all go away and let us get on with it?* She wished she hadn't been embarrassed. She wished she'd held onto the moment instead of letting it slip from her fingers. She wished...

She wished Conner felt something for her.

But he didn't.

In fact, not only had he not mentioned it, he hadn't even talked to her. Several days had passed and he'd been so busy fielding patients eager to consult him about his various problems that she'd barely seen him in the distance, let alone put herself in the position where a conversation might be possible.

At first she'd managed to convince herself that he was just very busy. She'd lingered in the surgery long after the patients had left, hoping that he'd seek her out, and she'd sat in her empty cottage at night, waiting for a knock on the door or the ring of the phone.

She'd thought up a million reasons for the fact that he hadn't come near her, but in the end she'd run out of reasons. And still he hadn't disturbed her solitude.

And she couldn't blame him for that, could she? Not after she'd made it perfectly clear that she'd be embarrassed to be caught with him. It was hardly surprising that he was now avoiding her and she wished she'd done everything differently.

She had no backbone.

She was pathetic.

'Well?' Angela peered down at her. 'You've been staring at my leg for ages, dear. Is something wrong?'

'No, nothing,' Flora said quickly, and Angela nodded.

'If you're worried, perhaps I should make an appointment with Conner.'

Remembering how fast Angela had run from Conner just a couple of weeks ago, Flora gave a faint smile. That was the other reason she was finding it hard to put him out of her head. Everywhere she went, people were talking about

Conner. And he treated their attention with as much careless indifference as he'd treated their disregard.

'Your leg is looking much better, Mrs Parker. The inflammation has settled and I think it's healing now. Keep up the good work.'

And she had to pull herself together and accept the person she was. She just wasn't someone who could cavort half-naked in the moonlight with the island bad boy. She cared too much what people thought.

And that was why a relationship between her and Conner would never work.

She cared. And Conner didn't give a damn. The more he shocked people, the happier he was.

Even that night on the beach had probably just been a game to him, seeing if his seduction skills were good enough to persuade boring old Flora to kiss him.

He wasn't interested in anything more, and she couldn't blame him for that.

She was boring Flora, wasn't she? The type of girl who kept her knickers on even when she swam in the sea at night.

Not the sort of girl who would hold Conner MacNeil's attention for more than two minutes.

Trying to block out Angela's endless chatter, Flora finished the dressing, washed her hands, completed her notes and saw the woman to the door.

Then she went across and tapped on Logan's door. 'How's Evanna?'

'Still pregnant. No change. She's going to the mainland for a check at the end of the week.'

'And presumably you can go with her now, given that the entire population of Glenmore thinks that Conner walks on water.'

'I know. It's brilliant. Overnight my life has changed.' He smiled at her. 'I actually managed to have breakfast with my wife and daughter this morning. Conner should be a hero more often. I could resign and grow my own vegetables.'

'I'm so pleased it's all worked out. His surgery is so full now Janet's having to turn people away.'

'Conner's a good doctor.'

'Yes.' She thought of him with Lily. *His sure touch. His skill. His incredible focus when the entire world around him had been panicking.*

And then she thought of his kiss. Equally sure and skilled. Did he do everything well?

She gave a little shiver and Logan glanced at her.

'Are you all right? You're a bit pale.'

'I'm fine. Absolutely fine.' Just confused. *Frustrated. Out of her depth.* She'd never felt like this before and she didn't know what to do about it. Her previous relationships had been boringly uncomplicated. She'd been out with two men and neither of them had caused this degree of turbulence to her insides. 'Tell Evanna to call me if she needs anything.'

'I'll do that.' Logan studied her closely. 'Are you sure you're all right?'

'Really, I'm fine,' Flora lied. 'Just a little tired.'

'Right.' Logan watched her. 'If you're sure.'

Flora returned to her consulting room and worked her way through her patients, only half listening to the steady stream of Glenmore chatter.

She'd just seen her last patient when the door opened and Conner stood there.

Flora felt her stomach flip and looked at his face, hoping to see something that suggested he felt the same way, but there was nothing. His handsome face was expressionless, his attitude brisk and professional.

'Lily is being discharged today. You should call on her and her fussy mother—do all the touchy-feely stuff that I can't be bothered with.'

She tried not to feel hurt or disappointed. *What had she expected?* 'You could go yourself. They'd want to thank you. Jayne is so grateful, she can't stop crying.'

'All the more reason to stay away. The one body fluid I'm no good with is female tears.' He gave a faint smile. 'If Lily bleeds again, phone me. Otherwise it's just emotional support and someone else can do that bit. Someone better qualified than me.'

He wasn't comfortable with emotion.

Flora thought of the things he'd told her in the velvet darkness. She thought about the mother who had left him and the father who hadn't cared. And she suspected that he'd been exposed to more extremes of emotion in his childhood than most people experienced in a lifetime.

Was that why he backed away from it now?

Was that why he was backing away from *her*?

'I'll call on her.'

'Good.' His eyes held hers for a moment—lingered—then his mouth tightened and he turned to leave.

But there had been something in that look that made it impossible for her to let him walk away. 'Conner!' Something burst free inside her and she just couldn't help herself. 'Wait. Can we talk?'

Conner paused, his hand on the door, a man poised for flight. 'What about?' But he knew what it was going to be about and he kept his tone cool and his face expressionless because he also knew what he needed to do. *And it was going to be the hardest thing he'd ever done.*

He stood still, hoping she'd lose courage. And perhaps she almost did because she watched him closely and then gave a confused little smile that cut through him like the blade of a knife.

Don't say it, Flora. Don't say it and then I won't have to reject you.

She rubbed her hands nervously down her uniform and took a deep breath. 'All I wanted to say was that…well, you—you really don't have to avoid me.'

'Yes, I do.' He kept his answer blunt, knowing that it was the only way.

'Why? Because you kissed me?' She shrugged awkwardly. 'Do you ignore every woman you kiss?'

'No, normally I corrupt them totally before I ignore them. You escaped lightly.'

'Is that supposed to make me feel lucky?' The colour bloomed in her cheeks but she didn't back off. 'Because it doesn't.'

Her response almost weakened him and Conner reminded himself ruthlessly that this time he was doing the right thing, not the easy thing.

He watched her for a moment, his eyes fixed on her face. Then he closed the door, slowly and deliberately, giving them privacy. 'It should make you feel lucky. If they hadn't turned up I would have taken you, Flora.' His voice dangerously soft, he closed the distance between them in a single stride. *Shock tactics.* Perhaps shock tactics would work. 'You would have been mine. That's how close you came.'

She shivered with excitement. 'Yes…'

'And then I would have dumped you, because that's what I do with women. And you would have cried.'

She swallowed. 'Maybe.'

Definitely.

Unable to help himself, Conner lifted a hand to touch her but then saw the trust shining in her dark eyes and took a step backwards, letting his hand drop to his side. 'You're the sort of woman who deserves to wake up next to a good man.' His hand curled into a fist. 'That isn't me, Flora.'

'You're a good man.'

'No.'

'Why do you say that?'

'Because a good man wouldn't do what I'm about to do,' he muttered, knowing that he'd lost the fight. He reached out a hand, yanking her against him and crushing his mouth against hers.

A kaleidoscope of colours exploded in his head and any hope of pulling away vanished as she wrapped her arms around his neck and pressed closer. He kissed her roughly but she gave back willingly and her mouth was sweet and warm under his.

And since when had sweetness had any place in his life?

He released her so suddenly that she swayed dizzily. 'Conner—'

'Don't.' With a rough jerk he disengaged himself from her arms. 'Don't offer yourself to me, Flora.'

'Why not?' Clearly sensing the tension and anger boiling inside him, she lifted a hand to his cheek, pushing aside her natural shyness. 'It's what I want.'

'No, it isn't what you want.'

She stood, looking hurt and vulnerable. 'It is. I want you.'

The blood throbbing in his veins, Conner turned away from her, knowing that he couldn't say what he had to say if he was looking at her. None of the things he'd ever done in his life had ever felt as hard as this and he steeled himself to do what had to be done. 'Well, I don't want you.' His tone was rock steady. 'I'm sorry if that hurts, but it's better to be honest up front. I don't want you, Flora. There's no chemistry there at all.'

Her soft gasp was like a punch in the gut. 'Conner—'

'You kiss like a child, Flora. You don't even turn me on.' This time he altered his tone so that he sounded careless, even a little bored. Then he gave a dismissive shrug and strolled towards the door. 'I suggest you find someone of your own age to practise on.'

Then he left the room, slamming the door so hard that the entire building shook.

Only when he was safely within the privacy of his consulting room did Conner finally release the emotion he'd kept firmly locked inside. He let out a string of expletives and thumped his fist against the wall. Then he sank onto his chair and stared at the door, willing himself not to walk back through it and tell her that he hadn't meant a single word he'd just said. Because if he did that—*if he sought her out and apologised*—he wouldn't be righting a wrong, he'd be making things worse.

Yes, he'd hurt her.

He'd hurt her so badly that he felt physically sick at the thought, and he knew that her gasp of pain and the shimmer of tears in her eyes would stay with him for a long time.

But he also knew that the pain would be infinitely greater if he took their relationship any further.

His eyes slid to the doorhandle and he gritted his teeth and looked away, ruthlessly ignoring the urge to go back and comfort her. Talk to her. What was there to say? He'd already said it. And better now than later. Better a small amount of private pain than public humiliation when the entire island discovered their affair.

They'd tear her apart and he wasn't going to let that happen to her.

There was a tap on the door and he looked up with a growl of impatience, furious at having been disturbed. 'What?' He barked the word and the door opened slowly and a woman peeped nervously into the room.

'Janet said to come straight through.'

'What for?'

She blinked. 'Surgery? I have an appointment with you.'

Conner stared at her blankly and then realised that kissing Flora had actually driven everything out of his head. *Everything, including the fact that he was supposed to be seeing patients.*

'Of course. Sorry.' He managed something approximating a smile. 'Come in.' And then he recognised her. Agatha Patterson, the elderly lady who lived in the converted lifeboat cottage on the beach. 'I expect you've come to exact your revenge. I seem to remember raiding your flower-beds one night.'

'You gave them to that girl—the pretty blonde one. I still remember how pleased she was.'

Conner gave a faint smile. 'That was at least sixteen years ago so I'm guessing you're not here because you're worried about your memory. Am I supposed to apologise for helping myself to your flowers?'

'Goodness, I don't want an apology! I should be the one thanking you.' Agatha closed the door and walked stiffly into the room. 'You livened up my life. You were always down on the beach below my property. I liked watching you.'

Remembering some of the things he'd done on the beach below her house, Conner inhaled sharply. 'How much could you see?'

'Well, my eyes were better in those days, of course.' She chuckled and walked slowly towards the chair, her body bent in the shape of a question mark. She was a grey-haired lady with a jolly smile and a twinkle in her eye that hinted at a lively past. 'I was always amazed by how successful you were. Quite the lad, Conner MacNeil.'

Conner gave a reluctant laugh. 'All right, that's probably enough of that conversation. Did you want to ask me something or are you just here to threaten me with my wicked past?'

'Oh, no, nothing like that. I heard what you did for little Lily, by the way. I think you're amazing.'

'Thanks.' *So amazing that he'd left a woman crying in the room opposite.* 'What can I do for you, Mrs Patterson?'

'Well, funnily enough, it's my eyes I've come about. They're incredibly sore.'

'Too much watching people on the beach,' Conner said in a wry tone, and she gave a delighted smile.

'There's been hardly any action since you left. These days everyone is too worried about being arrested. Not that you ever worried about that sort of thing. Anyway, I wouldn't normally bother you with anything so pathetically trivial, but my eyes are so sore that the pain is reducing the time I can spend on the internet.'

Conner stared at her. 'The *internet*?'

'And if you're thinking of telling me to reduce the time I spend on the computer, you needn't waste your breath. I'm careful never to do more than eight hours a day.'

Conner glanced at his own computer screen, searching for the information he wanted. 'You're…eighty-six, Mrs Patterson. Is that right?'

'Eighty-seven next week.'

'And you're spending…' he cleared his throat, intrigued by his patient '…*how long* on the internet?'

'No more than eight hours a day.' She curled her fingers around the strap of her bag. 'Given the chance, I'd spent longer, but with my eyes the way they are…'

Conner gave a disbelieving laugh. 'I have to ask this—just what are you doing on the internet, Mrs Patterson?'

'Everything,' she said simply. 'I mean, for an old lady on her own like me, it's a doorway to a whole new exciting life. Last week I spent a morning looking around a new exhibition in a fancy gallery in London, just by clicking my mouse, then I spent an afternoon gazing at a beach in Australia—

amazing webcam, by the way, you should try it. Last month I spent an entire week in Florence—I visited somewhere new every day. But it's not just travel and art, it's food, conversation. I just *love* chat rooms.' She leaned forward and winked at him. 'I bet you didn't know there was a chat room for the over-eighties.'

Conner started to laugh. 'No, Mrs Patterson. I didn't know that. Do you party?'

'Like you wouldn't believe.' Her smile faded. 'But these eyes of mine...'

'Yes.' He shook his head and stood up. 'All right, let's take a look, although why I would want to fix your problem just so that you can spy on me, I don't know. It's probably dry-eye syndrome. You're spending too long on the computer. And that's something I've never had to say to an eighty-six-year-old before.'

'So, which young lady's heart are you breaking at the moment, you bad boy?'

Conner stilled, thinking of Flora. 'No one. I'm being boringly good.'

'You mean you don't want to tell me.' Agatha gave him a conspiratorial wink. 'That's good. When you care about a girl's reputation, it means it's serious.'

Conner stared at her. *Serious?* 'Trust me, Agatha, it isn't serious.'

'Ah—so there is someone.'

Realising that he'd just been outmanoeuvred by an eighty-six-year-old woman, Conner gave a silent laugh and examined her eyes, trying not to remember how Flora had looked when he'd said that she didn't turn him on.

Why on earth had she believed him?

Hadn't she seen that his words and his body had contradicted each other?

Apparently not, which just proved how naïve she was.

And proved that he'd been right to walk away.

He was absolutely *not* the man for her.

'Is everything all right?' Agatha looked at him anxiously. 'You seem very grim-faced.'

'I'm fine. Everything is fine.'

And it should have been.

He'd ended a completely unsuitable relationship before it had started. He should have been feeling good about himself. But he was experiencing his first ever attack of conscience.

He'd hurt women before. Plenty of them. And it had never particularly bothered him. He'd always thought it more cruel to let a woman delude herself and spend hours waiting by the phone for a call that wasn't going to come.

Fast and sharp, that's how he would have wanted it, so that's how he'd delivered it.

The difference was that he wasn't doing this for himself. He was doing it for Flora and there was a certain irony in the fact that his first truly unselfish act was causing her pain. And he was in agony.

Suddenly realising that Agatha was watching him closely, he pulled himself together. 'Do you have the central heating on at home?'

'Of course. This is Glenmore.' Her tone was dry. 'Without central heating I'd be too cold to sit at the computer.'

'Try logging on to somewhere warm,' he drawled, examining her eyes carefully. 'Mauritius is nice at this time of year. Central heating can make the irritation and redness a little worse. Tear secretion does reduce with age, Mrs Patterson.'

'So do all the other secretions, Dr MacNeil.' She gave him a saucy wink and Conner shook his head and started to laugh.

'I can't believe we're having this conversation. What were you like at twenty, Agatha?'

'I would have given you a run for your money, that's for sure.' She leaned forward, a twinkle in her eyes. 'You wouldn't have been able to walk away from that beach after a night with me.'

'I have no trouble believing you. All right, this is what we're going to do. I'm going to start by giving you artificial tears to use. It they don't make a difference, I can refer you to an ophthalmologist on the mainland for an opinion.'

'Can I contact him by email?'

Conner grinned and sat back down in his chair. 'I'm sure he'd be delighted to hear from you. Try the drops first. They might do the trick.' He studied his computer screen, clicked on the drug he wanted and printed off a prescription.

'You're a handsome one, aren't you?' Agatha gave a cheeky smile. 'If I'd seen you sixty years ago, you wouldn't have stood a chance.'

'Now, that's a pick-up line I haven't heard before.' Conner took the prescription out of the printer and stood up. 'Try these. If you have no joy, come back to me.'

'I certainly will.' She took the prescription, folded it and tucked it into her handbag. Then she stood up. 'The beach is still nice, you know. If you fancied paying a visit.'

Conner laughed. 'Get out of here, Agatha.'

'I'm going. I'm going.' And she left the room with slightly more bounce and energy than she'd shown when she'd entered it.

Flora began to wish that Glenmore was larger and busier. After her last humiliating encounter with Conner she was the one avoiding him, if such a thing was possible on an island as small as this one.

She arrived at work, hurried to her consulting room and then straight out on her calls. She didn't spend time in the staffroom and if she needed a doctor's advice on a patient, she sought out Logan.

It should have helped, but it didn't. She felt dreadful.

On the outside she looked as she always had—a little paler perhaps, but pretty much the same. But on the inside…on the inside she was ripped to shreds. She was *mortified* that she'd misinterpreted his actions and felt foolish beyond words for ever believing that a woman like her—*boring Flora*—could ever be attractive to a man like Conner.

He was a woman's dream, wasn't he?

She might be relatively inexperienced, but she wasn't blind. Women's eyes followed him wherever he went. That wicked, careless streak that defied the opinion of society was one of the very things that made him so appealing. He was his own person. As strong of mind as he was of body.

And she had to put him out of *her* mind and move on.

So she concentrated on work and succeeded in avoiding contact with him until one afternoon a thirteen-year-old boy with a cheeky smile and long, lanky limbs tapped on her door.

Recognising him immediately, Flora waved a hand towards the empty chair. 'Hi, Fraser, come on in. How are the summer holidays going?'

'Too fast.' The boy gave a shrug and stood awkwardly just inside the door.

Aisla, his mother, gave him a gentle push towards the chair. 'For goodness' sake, she isn't going to bite you!' She rolled her eyes at Flora. 'Honestly, these teenagers. They're men one minute and boys the next. He's terrified you're going to tell him to undress.'

Fraser shot his mother a horrified look, gave a grunt of embarrassment and slunk into the chair.

Flora smiled at him. 'What's the problem, Fraser?'

'It's my legs. Well, this leg mostly.' He stuck it out in front of him and frowned down at the mud and the bruises. 'I was doing football camp up at the school but I've had to stop.'

'Both the doctors are fully booked but Janet said you'd take a look and decide what we need to do,' Aisla said quickly. 'I don't know whether he needs an X-ray or what.'

'Did something happen? Did you fall?'

'I fall all the time. It's part of football.' Fraser rubbed his leg and Aisla gave a long-suffering sigh.

'I can vouch for that. You should see the colour of his clothes. I swear that all the mud of Glenmore is in my washing machine.'

Flora smiled and dropped to her knees beside Fraser. 'Let me take a look—show me exactly where it hurts. Here?'

'Ow!' Fraser winced. 'Right there. Have I broken it?'

'No, I don't think so. Nothing like that. I'm going to ask Logan to take a quick look.'

'Don't waste your time. He's just gone on a home visit,' Aisla told her wearily. 'We were in Reception when Janet took the call and he came rushing out. Some tourist with chest pain on the beach.'

'Oh.' Flora's heart rate trebled. 'Well, we could wait until he's back, I suppose. He might not be long.'

'I want to see Conner,' Fraser blurted out. 'He knows everything about football. Can we ask him to look at my leg?'

Just the sound of his name made her palms damp. 'With Logan out, he'll be very busy.'

'Is it worth just trying? Perhaps he'd see Fraser if you ask him.' Aisla's expression was worried. 'It's just that, if he thinks it should be X-rayed, I'm going to need to make some plans.'

'Of course I'll try. Wait there a moment.' Hoping she didn't look as reluctant as she felt, Flora left her room and took several deep breaths. Across the corridor a patient left Conner's room and Flora felt her knees turn to liquid.

She couldn't do it. She really couldn't face him.

She turned backwards to her room and then realised that

she couldn't do that either. How could she tell Aisla that she was too pathetic to face Conner?

Taking a deep breath, she walked briskly over to his door and rapped hard, before she could change her mind.

Keep it brief and to the point, she told herself. Professional. And don't look at him. *Whatever you do, don't look at him.*

'Yes?' The harsh bark of his voice made her jump and she wondered how any of the patients ever plucked up courage to go and see him. Closing her eyes briefly, she took a deep breath and opened the door.

'I just wanted to ask if you'd see a patient for me. Thirteen-year-old boy complaining of pain in his leg. It's tender and there's swelling over the tibial tubercle.' She adjusted her glasses, still not looking at him. 'He's been at football camp so it's possible that he's injured himself, but I'm wondering whether it could be Osgood-Schlatter disease.'

'Reading all those books has obviously paid off.'

She had the feeling that he was intentionally trying to hurt her and she didn't understand it. He wasn't unkind, she knew he wasn't. Why would he want to hurt her? 'Obviously I'm not qualified to make that diagnosis.' Suffering agonies of embarrassment, she cleared her throat. 'He's in my room now. He's suffering from an attack of hero-worship and is desperate for your opinion on his leg.'

'Ah…' He spoke softly. 'Patient pressure. And I'm willing to bet you tried Logan first.'

'Fraser is Logan's patient so he was the logical first choice.'

'And nowhere near as terrifying as facing me. How much courage did it take for you to knock on my door?'

She stiffened. 'Please, don't make fun of me, Dr MacNeil.'

'Do I look as though I'm laughing?' With a low growl of impatience, he rose to his feet. 'There are things I need to say to you, Flora.'

'You made your thoughts perfectly clear the last time we

spoke. If you could just see the patient and give me your opinion, I can take it from there.' Terrified that she was about to make a fool of herself, Flora turned and walked quickly back to her room, her heart thundering in her chest. Aware that Conner was right behind her, she concentrated on Fraser. 'Dr MacNeil will take a look at you, Fraser.'

Conner threw her a dark and dangerous look that promised trouble for the next time they were alone. 'Can you lie on the couch, Fraser? I want to examine you properly.' He waited as Fraser winced and limped to the couch and then examined the boy, his hands gentle.

'It's not my hip, it's my leg,' Fraser muttered as Conner examined his joints.

'But your hip is attached to your leg,' Conner observed in a mild tone, 'so sometimes a problem with one can cause a pain in the other. Does this hurt?'

'No.'

'This?'

'Ow! Yes, yes.' Fraser swore and his mother gasped in shock and embarrassment.

'Fraser Price, you watch your language! Where did you learn that?'

'Everyone says it,' Fraser mumbled. 'It's no big deal.'

'It's a big deal to me!'

'I bet Conner swore when he was my age.'

'He's Dr MacNeil to you,' Aisla said sharply, and Conner cleared his throat tactfully and examined the other hip.

'I can't remember that far back. Is this OK? I'm going to bend your knee now—good. Do you play a lot of sport?'

'Yes, all the time. Just like you did.' Fraser grinned. 'Football, beach volleyball, loads of different stuff.'

It wasn't just the women who adored him, Flora thought helplessly, *it was the children, too.* They thought he was *so* cool.

Aisla looked at Conner. 'Do you think we need to have it X-rayed?'

'No.' Conner straightened. 'You can sit up now, Fraser. I'm done. As Nurse Harris correctly assessed, you have something called Osgood-Schlatter disease. It's a condition that sometimes affects athletic teenagers, particularly boys. There's inflammation and swelling at the top end of the tibia—here.' He took Fraser's hand and placed it on his leg. 'Can you feel it?'

'Yes.' Fraser winced. 'So will it go away?'

'Eventually. But you're going to need to play a bit less football.'

'How much less?'

'You need to cut down on your physical activity, because that will only make things worse.'

'All of it? Everything I do?' Fraser sounded appalled and Conner put a hand on his shoulder.

'It's tough, I know. But basically you need to stop doing anything that aggravates your condition. Ideally you should avoid sport altogether until your bones have fully matured, but I appreciate that's asking a bit much. A compromise would be to stop if you feel that whatever you're doing is making it worse.' He glanced at Aisla. 'He can take anti-inflammatories for the pain. If it doesn't improve, we can immobilise it for a short time and see if that helps. Failing that, we can refer him to an orthopaedic consultant for an assessment.'

Fraser slumped. 'No football?'

'Try cutting back. That will allow the pain and swelling to resolve. Anything that makes it worse, stop doing it.'

'Will it go?'

'Once your bones have fully matured. Unfortunately, the more active you are, the worse the symptoms are likely to be.'

Fraser looked grumpy. 'I'll have to spend the summer playing on game machines.'

'I don't think so,' his mother said dryly. 'You can read a few books.'

'Books!' Fraser's face went from grumpy to mournful. 'It's my holiday! Why would I want to spend it staring at a book?'

Aisla walked towards the door. 'Thanks, Dr MacNeil. Flora. We're grateful.'

Conner waited for the door to close behind him. 'I don't know which upset him more—the prospect of cutting back on football or the thought of reading books.'

'It was a close-run thing.' Careful not to look at him, Flora changed the paper on the couch. 'Thank you for seeing him.'

'Your diagnosis was correct. Well done. That was very impressive.'

'Thank you. I'm pleased all that studying paid off.' Although she didn't look at him, she knew he was watching her. She could feel him watching her.

'Flora…' His voice was husky. 'I know you're hurt and I'm sorry.'

'I thought you never apologised.'

'Well I'm apologising now,' he said testily, and she shrugged.

'You don't have to apologise for not finding me attractive,' Flora said stiffly, and heard him inhale sharply.

'I know you won't believe me, but I was doing you a favour.'

'Really? It's doing me a favour to kiss me and then tell me I'm boring?'

'I should never have kissed you in the first place.'

'So why did you?' She breathed in and out, forcing air into her lungs. 'Not once, but twice. The kiss on the beach—all right, let's say that was an accident. But you kissed me again, didn't you? If I'm so boring, why did you do that? Were you just teasing me? Doing me a favour, giving boring old Flora a thrill? Did you just do it to hurt my feelings? It was patronizing, Conner. You made me— I was...' She couldn't even say the words. 'If you didn't want me then you should have just left me alone. Or are you so bad that you just have to cause hurt?'

'Bad? You think I'm bad?' He pressed her against the wall, his body hard against hers. 'I'll show you what bad is, Flora.' He brought his mouth down on hers with punishing force, kissing her with raw, explosive passion, the slide of his tongue explicitly sexual and unbelievably seductive.

And she melted. Her head spinning from his skilled assault on her senses, she kissed him back, feeling fire dance inside her belly. She wasn't capable of thought or speech—all she could do was respond to his demands. She did so willingly and when he finally lifted his head she stared at him, mute.

'I've been called bad by a lot of people,' he said hoarsely, his hands planted either side of her head so that she couldn't escape his gaze, 'and most of it has been justified. But I'm damned if I'm accepting that criticism when it comes to you, Flora Harris. If I was as bad as people think, we would have already had sex.'

She was dizzy with need, unable to make sense of what he was saying. 'But you don't find me attractive.'

'No?' He slid his hands over her bottom and pulled her into him so that she felt the hard ridge of his arousal pressing against her. 'What I really want to do right now is strip you naked and take you hard and fast until we're both so exhausted that neither of us can move. And then I want to do it again. And again. Do you understand me?'

She gave a little whimper of shock and his eyes darkened.

'I'm not talking about marriage, or friendship or any of those soft, woolly things. I'm talking about sex, Flora. Sex.' He released her suddenly and took a step backwards, a look of disgust on his face. 'And that isn't the sort of person you are, which is why I'm going to let you go now. I'm going to walk out of that door into my consulting room and you're not going to follow me. You are a woman who deserves a conventional relationship with a reliable guy. I'm neither of those things.'

She licked her lips, shaken by everything he'd said to her. 'I don't think you should tell me what I want.'

'You're too naïve to play this game.'

'I am not naïve. I'm not naïve, Conner.' There was tearing agony inside her. *He was going to walk away from her again.* 'Would it make a difference if I told you that I'm not a virgin? Is that what's worrying you?'

He inhaled sharply and turned away, his profile tense. 'Don't tell me that.'

'I just thought it might make a difference.'

A muscle worked in his cheek. 'It doesn't. And you might find this hard to believe, but the desire *not* to hurt you is the reason I walked away. And it's the reason I'm about to walk away again. Because there are some rules that even I won't break.' He ran a hand over his face and then strode out of the room, leaving her shaking so badly that she could hardly stand.

He wanted her?

She sank onto her chair, staring at the door. He'd pulled back out of consideration for her? He didn't find her repulsive?

She wasn't 'boring Flora'?

Her fragile, bruised confidence recovered slightly and her mind started to race.

CHAPTER EIGHT

CONNER lay sprawled on the huge sofa in the barn, mind-lessly flicking through the sports channels on the television. On the floor next to him was a bottle of whisky and a half-filled glass. He stared at it blankly and was just about to pick up the bottle and do what needed to be done when someone hammered hard on the front door.

Conner reached for the remote control and increased the volume on the television, determined to ignore whoever it was who mistakenly believed that he might be in need of company.

There was no second knock, so he picked up the whisky bottle, satisfied that his unwelcome visitor had decided to go and bother someone else.

He stared at the television screen for a moment, too emo-tionally drained to find an alternative mode of entertainment. After a few moments some deep-seated instinct warned him that he wasn't alone and he turned his head slowly.

Flora stood in the doorway.

She was wearing a coat belted at the waist and raindrops glistened like diamonds on her dark hair. 'You didn't an-swer your door.'

Whisky sloshed over his shirt and it took him a moment

to reply, the speed of his mind and his tongue dulled by the shock of seeing her there. 'I didn't feel like company.'

'Well, that's tough because there are things I need to say to you.' She stepped into the room, her eyes burning with a fire that he'd never seen before. 'That was quite a speech you made earlier, Conner MacNeil. You said a lot of things.'

What was she doing here? 'They were things that needed saying.'

'I agree. And I've been thinking about those things.' She breathed in and out, her chest rising and falling under her raincoat. 'You've made a lot of assumptions about me.' Water clung to her eyelashes and cheeks and her hair, as dark as mahogany, curled around her face. She looked pretty and wholesome and he had to force himself not to look at her soft mouth.

If he looked, he was lost.

'You shouldn't be here, Flora.'

Her eyes slid to the whisky bottle. 'Oh, Conner...' Her gentle, sympathetic tone scratched against his nerve endings.

'Go home.'

'Why? Because you're drunk?'

He licked his lips and discovered they were dry. 'I'm not drunk.'

But she didn't seem to be listening. It was as if she was in the middle of a rehearsed speech. 'You're worried in case you lose control and behave badly?' She stepped closer, the blaze in her eyes intensifying. 'What would you say if I told you that I *want* you to behave badly, Conner? In fact, I want you to be as bad as you can possibly be.'

The breath hissed through his teeth. 'For God's sake, Flora...'

'People say you're super-bright. Shockingly intelligent— brain in a different stratosphere to most people's, and all that. I'm not sure if they're right or not. What I do know is that you're certainly very slow when it comes to knowing what I want.'

His hand tightened around the glass. 'I said, *go home*!'

'Why? So that you can get slowly drunk on your own? I don't think that's the answer.'

'Well, you wouldn't, would you?' He gave a mocking smile. 'I'm willing to bet you've never been drunk in your life, Flora Harris.'

'You're right, actually. I haven't.' Her tone was calm. 'I never saw the point. There are other ways to solve a problem.'

'What makes you think I'm solving a problem?'

Her eyes flickered to the bottle. 'If you're not solving a problem, why are you drinking?'

'Actually, I'm not drinking.'

But she still wasn't listening. 'I don't know what you're searching for but you won't find it in the bottom of a whisky bottle.'

He gave a cynical smile. 'My father did.'

'You're not your father, Conner.' She spoke quietly. 'Which is why I'm standing here now.' She let the coat slip from her shoulders and underneath she was naked apart from the skimpiest, sexiest underwear he'd ever seen. 'You think I'm a good girl, Conner? You think you're not allowed to touch me?'

The glass slipped from his hand and the whisky spilled over the floor. Conner didn't notice because every neurone in his brain had fused.

Her body was all smooth lines and delicate curves, her legs impossibly long and her small breasts pressing against the filmy lace of her bra.

He stared at her in tense silence. 'I didn't think I'd drunk anything,' he muttered to himself in a hoarse voice, 'but perhaps I'm wrong about that. For a moment there I thought Flora Harris was standing in front of me in her underwear.'

She made an exasperated sound and removed the bottle from his hand. 'You've had enough.' Her subtle, floral perfume drifted towards him and he leaned his head back against the sofa with a groan.

'Believe me, I haven't had enough. I haven't even started. But if I'm still imagining Flora naked, perhaps it's time I did. I need the image to fade to black.'

'It won't fade because it's real. *I'm* real. Oh, for goodness' sake, Conner, I came here to seduce you and you're—you're...' She sighed with frustration and put the bottle on the floor, spilling some of the contents in the process. 'Why did you open a bottle of whisky?'

'Because of you.'

'Me? *I'm* the reason you're drunk?'

'I'm not drunk. But for a brief moment it seemed like a good idea. I thought it might take my mind off ravishing you,' he mumbled, and she made a sound that was somewhere between a moan and a giggle.

'Why do you need to do that? I *want* you to ravish me. I'm desperate for you to ravish me.'

He squinted up at her. 'Am I dreaming?'

'No, you're not dreaming!' She gave a sigh and shook her head. 'You're going to take a cold shower and while you're doing that I'm going to make you a jug of very strong coffee.'

Conner rubbed his eyes with the tips of his fingers and shook his head. 'You don't need to do that. And coffee stops me sleeping.'

'Good.' She sounded more exasperated than ever. 'I don't want you sleeping. I want you awake when I seduce you. I've spent most of my life listening to other women telling me what an amazing lover you are, and just when I'm about to find out what all the fuss is about, you pass out on me.'

'I'm not going to pass out.'

'Get in that shower, Conner MacNeil, or I swear I'll throw a bucket of freezing water over you right here!'

He ran a tongue over his lips. 'You look like Flora but you're not acting like Flora. Flora never swears. She's a really sweet girl.'

'Sweet? I'll show you sweet.' She grabbed his arm and yanked. 'Stand up! You're too heavy for me to pull you.'

He wondered if she'd be as confident if she knew he was as sober as she was.

Aware that his body was betraying his emotions in the most visible way possible, Conner stood up and gave a wry smile. 'I spilt half the bottle over myself when you walked through the door, so a shower might be a good idea. A freezing one, to kill my libido.'

'I don't want you to kill your libido.' Her voice was sultry and she pulled him against her and stood on tiptoe. 'Kiss me, Conner. And then go and take that shower. I want you sober enough to remember this. I don't want to wake up tomorrow and have you mouthing all sorts of excuses about being too drunk to know what you were doing.'

He knew exactly what he was doing and it felt incredible.

He groaned as he felt her silky smooth body pressing against his. He just couldn't help himself and he brought his mouth down on hers, stars exploding in his head as her tongue met his. 'You taste fantastic.'

She pulled away from him, her eyes soft and her cheeks pink. 'Where's your bathroom?'

'I don't need a cold shower.'

'Yes, you do.'

'Where is Flora? I think you've hit her on the head and stolen her identity.' He ran a hand through his hair as she tugged him towards the bathroom and hit a button on the shower. 'Flora isn't a forceful woman.'

'There's lots you don't know about Flora.'

He was starting to agree with her, especially when she reached up and yanked impatiently at his shirt, scattering buttons around the bathroom floor. Then he felt her fingers slide into the waistband of his jeans.

His hands covered hers and he gave her a sexy smile, astonished and delighted by her new-found confidence. 'Careful, angel. That's the danger zone and Flora would never wander into the danger zone.'

She gave him a gentle push and he swore fluently and then sucked in a breath as freezing water sluiced over his back. '*That* is cold.'

'Good—it's supposed to be cold. Stay in there until you can walk in a straight line unaided and tell me your name and date of birth. I'll be in the kitchen when you're ready.'

Her hand shaking, Flora rummaged through his fridge and found a packet of fresh coffee. She spooned a generous quantity into a cafetière and topped it up with hot water.

Then she sat at the table, listening to the rushing sound of the shower.

He was taking a long time.

Was it safe to have left him there? Had he drowned?

Or maybe she'd totally misread the situation and he was spending a long time in there in the hope that she'd give up and go home.

Her nerve faltered and she caught her lower lip between her teeth.

What on earth did she think she was doing?

He was absolutely right. She wasn't the sort of woman who stripped off and issued invitations to men. Neither was she the sort of woman who made coffee for a man while dressed in silk underwear.

With a whimper of panic she was just about to sprint back into the sitting room and retrieve her coat, when he walked into the kitchen. He'd knotted a towel around his waist but droplets of water still clung to the dark tangle of curls that shadowed his chest. His shoulders were broad and powerful and his arms strong and muscular. He had a body designed to make a woman think of nothing but sin, but what really caught her attention was the look in his eyes. Lazy, sexy and ready for action.

Her nerve fled completely and she decided to follow. 'Coffee on the table,' she muttered as she backed towards the door.

A hand shot out and closed around her wrist, his fingers like bands of steel as he yanked her back towards him. 'Oh, no, you don't.' His voice was cool and rock steady. 'You told me to shower. I've showered.'

'You can't possibly have sobered up that quickly.'

'I was never drunk.'

She stared at him. 'I saw the bottle.'

'I admit I considered it. That's how low I felt.' His eyes held hers for a long moment. 'But if there's one thing that being around my father taught me, it's that drink solves nothing. I was about to pour it down the sink when you walked in.'

'You smelt of alcohol.'

His smile was faintly mocking. 'When you took your coat off, I spilled most of it.'

Her heart thumped as she re-examined the facts. He hadn't been drunk. He'd been sober. She swallowed hard, all her courage leaving her. Somehow her belief that he was drunk had made him less intimidating and now, knowing that he hadn't touched a drop, she felt suddenly shaky.

'I should probably leave now. I've just remembered that I—'

'What?' His mouth was dangerously close to hers, his tone low and impossibly sexy as he curved an arm around her waist and trapped her against him. 'What have you just remembered, Flora?'

She could hardly breathe. 'Flora? Who's she? Oh, I remember—she's the woman I left her locked in her cottage when I stole her identity. I need to go and let her out.'

He gave a slow smile and his head lowered towards hers. 'Too late, sweetheart.' He paused, his mouth tantalisingly close to hers, 'You are most definitely Flora. A whole new Flora. A standing-naked-in-my-kitchen Flora.'

'In my underwear...'

His lips brushed hers, a deliberately erotic hint of things to come. He gave a low, appreciative murmur. 'You taste good. Whatever happens in the next few hours, don't dig your fingernails into my shoulders. If this is a dream, I don't want to be woken up.'

Her entire body was throbbing but still the nerves fluttered in her stomach. He was so sure and confident, whereas she... 'I made you coffee.'

'I don't want it.' His mouth slid down her neck and lingered at the base of her throat, his tongue tasting her skin. 'I want you, sweetheart.'

Her pulse was thundering and she tilted her head back with a gasp. 'Conner...'

'You came here to seduce me...' His lips moved slowly along her shoulder. 'You want to know what sort of lover I am.'

As she felt his hands slide confidently down her back, she gave a shiver. 'I thought you didn't find me attractive.'

'I always found you attractive. But you were always off limits as far as I was concerned. Despite what everyone thought of me, that was the one line I was never prepared to cross.'

'But you're crossing it now.'

'No. *You're* crossing it.' He lifted his head and looked

down at her, his ice-blue eyes compelling. 'This was your decision, Flora. You made it by coming here.'

He was giving her the chance to change her mind. But she didn't want to do that. 'Yes.'

'So...' His hand slid slowly down her back and cupped her bottom. 'You came here to seduce me.'

She couldn't breathe. 'Yes.'

He gave a slow smile. 'Carry on, angel. I'm all yours.'

Was that it? *Was that all the help he was going to give her?* For a moment her courage faltered but then she looked at his gorgeous naked body and couldn't help herself. She leaned forward and pressed her mouth to his chest, while her fingers trailed slowly across the hard muscle of his abdomen and lower still until they brushed against the top of the towel that was all that was between her and his straining manhood.

'All right, commercial break,' he said roughly, scooping her up into his arms as if she weighed nothing, 'If you carry on like that, this whole event is going to be very short-lived. You need to slow things down, angel. Make me beg.'

Beg?

She had no idea how to make a man beg. Flora clamped her mouth shut, judging it wise not to confess as much at this point. The problem with playing the seductress was that you were expected to follow through.

He carried her up a flight of stairs to the bedroom. Dusk was falling but there was enough light for her to see open fields and the jagged ruins of Glenmore Castle.

'It's a wonderful view,' she breathed, and he gave a lazy, confident smile as he deposited her in the centre of the bed.

'The only view you're going to be looking at has me in it.' He delivered a lingering kiss to her mouth and then lay down beside her and rolled onto his back, arrogantly sure of himself, his gaze direct.

And she understood. He wanted active, not passive. He

was giving her the chance to change her mind but she had no intention of doing that.

She wanted this. *She wanted him.* And this time she wasn't going to blow it. The whole of Glenmore could sing and dance outside his bedroom window and it wouldn't make any difference.

Aware that he was waiting for her to make the first move, she reached out a hand and stroked his shoulder, shivering slightly as she felt smooth skin and powerful male muscle.

He lay still, his eyelids lowered, watching and waiting, and suddenly she felt desperately nervous and impossibly excited.

'You can stop whenever you want,' he murmured, but he sounded less cool and composed than usual and the edgy quality to his voice gave her courage.

'I'm not stopping. You have an amazing body,' she said huskily, and her eyes slid shyly to his and her insides tumbled and warmed. He was so outrageously sexy that it was hard not to stare and even harder not to touch. She leaned forward and kissed his cheek, feeling the roughness of male stubble under her lips. Then she ran a finger over his nose, exploring the bump. 'How did you break it? Were you fighting?'

'Rugby.' He turned his head and kissed her fingers. 'I'm not quite the animal everyone seems to think I am.'

'Aren't you?' She trailed her finger over his mouth and then replaced it with her lips and he slid a hand behind her head and held her there while they kissed. His mouth was hot and purposeful and she felt the excitement flash through her body, turning her from willing to desperate.

Her hand slid over his shoulder, tracing flesh and hard muscle, and then lowered her head and rubbed her cheek over the roughness of his chest and breathed in his erotic scent. Her hand lingered low on his abdomen and she felt his muscles clench in an involuntary response.

She allowed her fingers to linger in that dangerous place,

teasing and promising, and then she bent her head and kissed his shoulder, using lips and tongue to discover and explore his body, gradually moving lower until her mouth rested where her hand had been. His muscles quivered under her gentle touch and she heard the sharp hiss of his breath as she teased him with her tongue. He sank his fingers into her hair and then released her instantly. She glanced up at him and saw that his eyes were closed and his jaw was clenched. Desire burned deep inside her and she bent her head again and closed her mouth over him and he made a choking sound.

'Flora...'

She lifted her head. 'Sorry—am I hurting you? Your face is sort of...twisted.'

'You're not hurting me,' he said hoarsely, 'but—'

'Good.' She lowered her head again and used her tongue and her lips until he gave a harsh groan, grabbed her and rolled her onto her back.

'You have to stop. I'm not going to last five minutes if you...' He closed his eyes and breathed deeply, tension etched in every line of his handsome face. 'Give me a minute. Just give me a minute.'

'Did I do something wrong?' She was suddenly covered with embarrassment. 'I—I haven't actually done it before...'

He shifted so that he was half on top of her, one leg pinning her to the mattress. 'You're full of surprises, do you know that? If you've never actually done it before, where did you—?' His voice cracked and he cleared his throat. 'Learn those tricks?'

'From a book.'

'A book?' He gave a shaky laugh. 'A book. Typical Flora.' He bent his head and kissed her mouth expertly and her body trembled and ached in response.

And he hadn't even touched her yet.

Desperate for him to do so, her hips moved against him

and he put a hand on her hip to steady her. Only then did she realise that at some point he'd removed her underwear. And she hadn't even noticed. She was about to ask him about it when he lowered his head and drew her nipple into his mouth.

Sensation shot through her and she tried to move against him, but he held her firmly while he lavished attention on both her breasts. The pleasure was so intense it was almost unbearable, and when he finally lifted his head, her cheeks were flushed and her limbs were trembling. For a moment he just looked at her and she thought that she was going to be the one to beg, and then she felt his hand between her thighs and the expert stroke of his fingers as they discovered the heart of her.

His touch was so intimate that for a moment she stiffened and instantly felt him pause. And the fact that he'd paused made her realise just how much care he was taking with her.

'Conner—please— I don't think I can wait.'

With a skilled, knowing fingers he found exactly the right place and caressed her gently until the excitement grew from a slow ache to a maddening turmoil of sensation. As his exploration grew bolder and more intimate, she arched and writhed, silently begging for the possession that her body craved.

'Look at me, Flora.' He shifted over her, slid a hand under her bottom and she felt the blunt tip of his erection brushing against her. For a moment she couldn't breathe, the excitement and anticipation so great that her entire body was trembling with need. And then he eased forward slowly and she gasped because it took her body a moment to accommodate him.

He paused, his breath warming her neck. 'Am I hurting you?'

'No.'

'Relax, angel.' He closed his mouth over hers, kissed her

deeply and moved forward, driving deeper inside her. 'Relax for me.'

But she didn't want to relax. She wanted— *She wanted...*

Excitement exploded inside her and she rose instinctively to meet his thrusts.

Her heart thudded wildly and she curved her hands over his bottom, urging him on. 'Conner, Conner...' She looked into his eyes and saw primitive need blazing there.

He slowed the pace, his eyes holding hers. 'Are you OK?'

'Yes...' Talking was difficult. 'It's just that you look—' She broke off and moaned as he moved again in an agonisingly slow rhythm.

'How do I look?'

'Sort of—scary.'

'I'm trying not to lose control.' He gave a wry smile. 'And it's pretty hard.'

'Then stop trying.' She breathed the words against his mouth and felt him tense. 'I'm not delicate, Conner. Make love to me the way you want to make love to me.'

His eyes darkened and his breathing quickened. 'I never want to hurt you, Flora.'

'You won't hurt me.' But the fact that he cared enough to be careful with her increased the feeling of warmth growing inside her. 'I'm OK. I've never been so OK,' she murmured, and his mouth flickered into a half-smile and he surged into her again, this time going deeper.

And she felt the change in him. He shifted his position, altered the rhythm, and her body hummed and fizzled and then tightened around his in an explosion of ecstasy so intense that it drove him to his own completion.

Flora lay in his arms, stunned and breathless. 'I—I had no idea that it would be like that.'

He turned his head, a frown on his face. 'You told me you weren't a virgin.'

'Technically I wasn't.' Her voice was soft and her eyes were misty. 'But I suppose it depends on your definition. I've never done that before. Never felt like that before.'

'I don't think I want to hear about your past lovers.' He folded her back against him in a possessive gesture and she smiled, feeling warm and protected and—just amazing.

'Lover. Just the one.'

'I definitely don't want to hear this,' Conner muttered darkly. 'Knowing you, it must have been serious.'

'I suppose it was a serious attempt to discover what all the fuss was about. He was a lawyer—very proper. Predictable. Chivalrous.'

'All the things I'm not.' Conner's arms tightened. 'He sounds like the perfect mate. You should have stuck with him.'

She lay in the semi-darkness, staring at his profile, thinking of the care he'd taken with her. 'I didn't love him.'

'Oh, please.' He made an impatient sound and she turned her head.

'It's true. I know you don't believe in love, but I do. And I didn't love him. My feelings just weren't right. There was no chemistry.' She gave a short laugh. 'That's what you said to me.'

'I was lying.' Conner bent his head and kissed her. 'And if you weren't so naïve, you would have known I was lying, because I had a massive erection as I said it.'

She gasped and then gave a strangled laugh. 'Conner MacNeil, why must you always try and shock?'

'The fact that you're shocked proves my point. You're naïve.'

'I'm *not* naïve. And it's hardly surprising that I didn't notice anything because I was so upset, I was trying not to look at you. And it wasn't hard to believe you when you said I didn't turn you on, because I know I'm not sexy.'

It was Conner's turn to laugh. 'Angel, if you were any sexier you'd have to carry a government health warning.'

She slid her arm over his stomach and rested her chin on his chest. 'Really?'

'You need to ask?' He guided her hand down his body and gave her a wicked smile. 'You currently have a hold on the evidence.'

She smiled. 'Do you know what's amazing? I don't feel at all shy with you.'

'I'd noticed. Permit me to say that your behaviour tonight would have thoroughly shocked the inhabitants of Glenmore.'

'I don't care about them,' she said honestly, and he stroked her hair away from her face, his expression serious.

'Yes, you do, and I don't blame you for that. Glenmore is your home. Talking of which...' He frowned suddenly and then released her and sprang out of bed. 'Where did you park?'

'Sorry?'

'Your car. Where did you park your car?'

She frowned. 'Outside your barn. Where else?'

'Someone could see It.' He reached down and pulled her gently to her feet. 'You have to leave, angel.'

'Now?' Bemused, she slid her arms around his neck. 'I—I assumed I'd stay the night.'

'At least eight islanders drive past my barn on the way to work in the morning. I don't want them seeing your car.' He gently unhooked her arms from his neck and retrieved her underwear from the floor. 'You need to leave, Flora.'

His words made her feel sick and her heart bumped uncomfortably. 'So—that's it?'

He slid her arms into her bra and fastened it with as much skill as he'd shown unfastening it. 'No, of course that's not it.' He lowered his head and kissed her swiftly. 'Are you busy tomorrow night?'

'No.'

He smiled and winked at her. 'Then you can cook me dinner. Meet me here at eight o'clock.' Then he frowned. 'On second thoughts, your place is probably better. Evanna's cottage is off the main road.'

She felt a rush of excitement and anticipation but tried to hide it. 'Why can't *you* cook *me* dinner?'

'Because I'm rubbish in the kitchen and I'm assuming you'd rather not be poisoned,' he drawled, sliding her silk knickers up her legs and then giving a tormented groan. 'Why am I dressing you when all I want to do is *un*dress you?'

'I don't know,' she said breathlessly. 'Why are you?'

'Because I care about you. I care about your reputation.'

She looked at him curiously. 'That doesn't exactly sound like Bad Conner.'

'You've corrupted me,' he said roughly. And then he took a deep breath, stepped back and lifted his hands. 'Get out of here. Your coat is downstairs. For goodness' sake, remember to button it or you'll give everyone a cheap thrill. Go, quickly, before I change my mind.'

CHAPTER NINE

FLORA tried, she *really* tried, to keep their relationship secret. She made a point of not gazing at him when they were in public together and she kept their interaction brief and formal. But inside she trembled with insecurity when he didn't glance at her and she knew why.

No relationship of Conner's had ever lasted. Why should theirs be any different?

But even knowing that it was probably doomed, she wouldn't have changed anything. And if she spent her days racked with doubt as to his feelings, when night came she was left in no doubt at all.

Every evening he arrived at her cottage and spent time with her until the early hours. They ate, talked and made love, but he never stayed the whole night and Flora didn't know whether she felt frustrated by that or grateful.

On the one hand she was slightly relieved not to be the subject of local gossip, but on the other hand she was greedy for time with him. She loved the fact that he talked to her and sensed that he said things to her that he'd never said to anyone else.

Occasionally the conversation turned to the topic of his father. 'It's hardly any wonder you virtually lived wild,' she murmured one night as she lay with her head on his shoulder. 'I don't suppose there was much to go home to.'

'It wasn't exactly a laugh a minute.' He stroked a hand over her hair. 'After my mother left, he was pretty much drunk from the moment he woke up in the morning to the moment he keeled over at night. I stayed out of his way. Half the time I didn't even go home. I slept on the beach or borrowed the MacDonalds' barn. That was fine until the night I lit a fire to keep warm and the wind changed.'

Flora's heart twisted. 'I guessed things were bad. I went up there once, to look for you. And he yelled at me so violently that my legs shook for days.'

His arms tightened around her. 'Why were you looking for me?'

'After your mother left, I was worried about you. And I thought I understood what you were going through. How arrogant was that?' She sighed and kissed him gently. 'I suppose because I'd lost my mother, too, I thought I might be able to help you. But of course our situations were entirely different because I still had my dad.'

'I didn't want to be helped. I just wanted to be angry.'

'I don't blame you for being angry.' She rubbed her cheek against his shoulder. 'Was it the army that stopped you being angry?'

'They taught me to channel my aggression. Running thirty miles with a pack on your back pretty much wipes it out of you.'

'So they helped you?'

'Yes, I suppose they did.' He kissed the top of her head. 'You're such a gentle person, I don't suppose you've ever been angry.'

'Of course I have. Anger is a human emotion. But I didn't have reason to be angry—not like you. I feel so bad for you. The locals should have done something.'

'What could they have done? And, anyway, I didn't exactly invite assistance.'

'You basically grew up without parents.' She raised herself on one elbow, her expression soft as she looked down at him. 'Why did you become a doctor?'

'I don't know.' His eyes closed again. 'I spent my whole life on Glenmore being angry. I suppose it was a bit of a vicious circle. They thought the worst of me so I gave them the worst. And then I left and suddenly I was with people who didn't know me. And I realised that I was tired of living my life like that. I went to an army recruitment day and it all happened from there.'

'Did you ever hear from your Dad?'

'No. And I never contacted him either.'

'But you kept in touch with Logan.'

Conner's eyes opened. 'Logan is a good man. Always was. He was the one who told me about my father's cirrhosis. He arranged for his admission to hospital on the mainland and he did all the paperwork when he died. Logan did all the things I should have done.' He hesitated. 'He was also the one who thought I should come back and tie up some loose ends. Sell the house, bury some ghosts—that sort of thing.'

'I'm glad you came back.'

He looked at her. 'I'm not good for you, Flora,' he murmured, stroking his hands over her hair and then pulling her down so that he could kiss her. 'I'm just going to hurt you.'

'I'll take that chance.'

'Relationships are destructive, terrible things.'

'I can understand why you'd think that, given everything that happened with your parents, but theirs was just one relationship, Conner. My parents' relationship was different.'

'Your mother died and your father was devastated,' he said softly. 'In its own way, that relationship was as traumatic as the one my parents had. Both ended in misery.'

'It was traumatic, that's true. But what my father and mother shared was so special that I know Dad wouldn't have changed things, even if he'd been able to foresee what was going to happen. True love is rare and special—a real gift. You don't turn that away, even if it comes with pain.'

'Love is a curse, Flora Harris, not a gift.'

'No, Conner.' She kissed him gently. 'The best thing that can happen to anyone is to be truly loved. Whatever happens in adult life, every child deserves to be loved unconditionally by their parents, and that didn't happen to you. And I'm guessing you haven't experienced it as an adult either, given the way you stomp through relationships.'

'Don't be so sure.' He lifted an eyebrow. 'Do you want to know how many women have told me that they love me?'

'Actually, I don't.' She laughed, trying to ignore the queasy feeling in her stomach that his words had induced. 'And I was talking about love, not sex.'

'All right, it's *definitely* time that you stopped talking.' He rolled her swiftly onto her back and came down on top of her, pinning her still with his weight. 'If the only thing on your mind is love, I'm going to have to do something brutal.' But his eyes were gentle and she giggled softly.

How did he feel about her?

How did she feel about him?

She really didn't know.

Their relationship was the most thrilling, exciting thing that had ever happened to her, but at the same time she knew that there couldn't be a happy ending.

But for the time being she was just going to live in the present.

And that was what she did.

But rumours were gradually spreading across Glenmore.

* * *

A few weeks into their relationship, Flora was in the pub with the rest of the medical centre staff, including an extremely pregnant Evanna.

'At the weekend I'm taking you over to the mainland.' Logan raised his glass to his wife. 'That baby is going to come any time now.'

'No hurry.' Evanna glanced at Flora. 'Are you going to manage?'

'Of course.'

'Hey, Conner.' Jim wandered over to their table and slapped Conner on the shoulders. 'How are you doing?'

Flora studied her grapefruit juice intently, careful not to look at Conner.

'I'm good, Jim.' Conner leaned back in his chair and stretched his legs out under the table. 'And you?'

'Bit tired.' Jim winked at him. 'Woken up by that bike of yours at three in the morning every night this week. Thought to myself, Young Conner's been out on the hunt.'

Flora felt her face flame, but Conner simply stifled a yawn, apparently unflustered. 'Just relieving the boredom of being stuck on Glenmore, Jim. Do you blame me?'

'No, but I envy you.' Jim gave a delighted laugh. 'Go on, lad. Tell us the name of the lucky girl. Knowing you, it's someone different from the girl you were hiding in the waves the night we saw you on the beach.'

'Of course. That was weeks ago and I'm not into long relationships.' Conner didn't falter but Flora's breathing stopped and inside she suffered an agony of embarrassment.

People were talking. Of course they were. How could she have imagined otherwise?

How long would it take for people to put two and two together?

And how would she cope with being on the receiving end of everyone's nudges and winks?

This time *she'd* be the one that everyone was talking about when they bought their apples in the greengrocer on the quay. *She'd* be the subject of speculative glances when she took her books back to the library.

Flora tightened her fingers round her glass and tried to breathe steadily and slow her heart rate, but inside she was shrinking because she knew only too well what they'd all be saying.

That Conner MacNeil had seduced her and that it wouldn't last five minutes.

She took a large slug of her drink and then realised that Conner was looking at her, his gaze curiously intent. Unable to look away, she slowly put her glass down on the table.

He gave a faint smile and something in that smile worried her. He looked...resigned? *Tired?*

She looked away quickly, telling herself that she was reading something into nothing. Of course he was tired. They were both tired. Neither of them slept much any more. Because they weren't able to conduct their relationship in daylight, they'd become nocturnal.

'I'm going to have to make a move.' Evanna rose to her feet with difficulty, a hand on her back. 'I never realised how uncomfortable these chairs are.'

Conner drained his glass. 'I don't suppose any chair is comfortable when you're carrying an elephant around in your stomach.'

Evanna laughed good-naturedly and Flora reached for her bag, grateful for the change of subject.

Jim was back with the lads, laughing about something that had happened to the lifeboat crew, and Conner was listening to Logan talking about his plans to extend the surgery.

For now, at least, it appeared that their secret was still safe. Although how long it would take for the locals to realise that she was the girl that Conner was seeing was anyone's guess.

And then what would happen?

* * *

Restless and angry with himself, Conner paced the length of his consulting room and back again.

Why had he ever let things go this far?

Buzzing for his first patient, he decided that he had to do something about the situation. Fast. Before it exploded in his face.

'Dr MacNeil?' Ann Carne stood in the doorway and Conner gave a reluctant laugh.

'If there's one thing I don't need this morning, it's an encounter with my old headmistress.' *And Flora's aunt.*

'I don't see why. Nothing I said ever worried you when you were young,' Ann said crisply, closing the door behind her and making her way to the chair. 'And I don't suppose that's changed just because you've grown up. And, anyway, it seems that no lecture is needed. You've made quite an impression since you returned to Glenmore, Conner.'

'Bad, I'm sure.'

'You know that isn't true.' She looked at him steadily. 'Evidently you're a reformed character. I've come to find out if you're as good a doctor as they say you are.'

Conner sighed. 'Is this like classroom testing?'

'You flew through every exam you ever bothered to take, Conner MacNeil. But while we're on that subject, there's something I want to say, so I may as well get it out of the way before we start.' Ann took a deep breath. 'We didn't help you enough. *I* didn't help you. That's been on my conscience for many years.'

Conner's eyes narrowed. 'I sense that this conversation is about to make both of us extremely uncomfortable so why don't we just skip straight to the part where you tell me your symptoms?'

'In a minute.' Her voice was quiet and Ann shook her head slowly, a hint of sadness in her eyes. 'You were the brightest, most able boy that ever passed through my school, Conner MacNeil.'

'And we both know I passed through it as quickly as I could,' Conner drawled lightly. 'I made a point of not resting my backside on the chair long enough to get bored.'

'You had a brilliant brain, but you were so disruptive and angry that it took me a long time to see it. Too long. By the time I realised the extent of your abilities it was too late to harness them because you were almost totally wild. You were off the rails, fighting everyone. No one could get through to you. Not the teaching staff. Not your father.' She paused and took a deep breath. 'We didn't know how bad things were for you at home. You covered it up so well. We thought your father was the one struggling with you, not the other way round.'

'I certainly didn't make his life a picnic.'

'He let you down. We all let you down.'

Conner kept his expression neutral. 'This is history and you know I hated history. Science was my subject. I never saw the point of lingering in the past.'

'There's a point when the past is affecting the future.'

'It isn't.'

'Isn't it? Are you married, Conner MacNeil? Are you living with some warm, kind, stable woman who is carrying your child?'

Conner sat for a moment, eye to eye with his old headmistress. 'My marital status has nothing to do with my father.'

'Of course it does. Are you pretending that it didn't affect you? Your wild behaviour was a reaction to everything that was happening at home, I see that now.' She shook her head again. 'I've been teaching for thirty-one years and you were the only child who passed through the doors of my school that I just couldn't cope with. The island couldn't cope with you. We all let you down and for that we owe you an apology.'

'I don't suppose the people whose property I destroyed would agree with you.

'You certainly left your mark on the place. And you're still leaving it, although this time the damage is more subtle.' Ann straightened her shoulders. 'My niece is in love with you. I suppose you know that?'

Conner swore softly and Ann's mouth tightened.

'Behave yourself! Just because you're a grown man, it doesn't mean that I'm prepared to accept that sort of language.'

'What are you going to do? Put me in detention?' Conner gave a short laugh. 'Did she tell you that?'

'No. In fact, I doubt she even knows herself. But I've heard the way she talks about you. Her eyes sparkle and every story that falls from her lips involves something you've done. Every other word she speaks is your name. So what are you going to do about it, Conner?'

Conner rubbed his fingers over his forehead. 'I expect I'll walk out and leave her crying. That's what I usually do.'

'Perhaps.' Ann's tone was calm. 'Or perhaps you'll see sense and realise that a warm, soft, kind woman like Flora is just what you need.'

'It doesn't matter what I need. I do know that whatever *she* needs, it isn't me.'

Ann smiled. 'So you've learned to think about someone other than yourself. That's good, Conner. And don't underestimate Flora. She's shy, not weak. There's more to her than meets the eye.'

Conner's hand dropped. 'So I've discovered.' He thought of Flora half-naked in the sea. Flora turning up at his barn wearing only underwear under her coat. *Flora riding him lightly, her brown curls tumbling over her shoulders.*

Ann was giving him the look she reserved for very naughty students. 'I just thought someone should tell you that you don't have to live up to your reputation. From what I've seen, Bad Conner has a good side. Why not develop it?'

Conner gave a mock shudder. 'That sounds like the lecture you gave me when you told me I should be interested in algebra.' He stirred. 'All right, enough. Is there a medical reason that you're here?'

'I have asthma. Or so they say. Started two years ago, out of nowhere. Completely ridiculous at my age, but there you are. Anyway, Logan started me off on an inhaler, and Dr Walker—he was your predecessor—gave me another one but they're not working any more.'

'And you say that because…?'

'I'm breathless all the time. Wheezing. Tight chest.' She sighed. 'I tried to walk the cliff path yesterday and had to sit down and look at the view instead. You're going to say that I shouldn't be exercising at my age—'

'Exercise is important at every age.' Conner studied his computer screen and his face broke into a slow smile. 'Well, Miss Carne, I see you were a smoker for fifteen years. I wonder how much money I could make selling that information?'

'I haven't touched one for sixteen years,' she said briskly, 'and everyone has to have a vice.'

'I couldn't agree more. I couldn't survive without my vices.' Conner stood up and took a peak-flow meter out of the drawer. 'Have you been monitoring your own peak flow?'

'Yes. Of course. I'm a teacher. I do everything by the book.' She delved into her bag and pulled out a chart. 'Here.'

He scanned it. 'This shortness of breath—is it just on exercise or when you're doing daily tasks?'

'Exercise. But I can't do as much.'

'And have you had a chest infection? Anything that might have been a trigger?'

He questioned her carefully, listened to the answers and then checked her inhaler technique. 'You should be inhaling slowly and then holding your breath for ten seconds.'

'That's what I'm doing.'

Conner questioned her further and then sat back down and looked at the computer screen. 'You're already taking salbutamol and an inhaled steroid. I'm going to add in a long-acting drug and see if that helps. If it does, you can carry on taking it. If it doesn't, we might increase the dose of your inhaled steroid.'

'I'm not wild about taking yet another drug.'

'If your symptoms stabilise, we can reassess in a few months.'

'So I should come back and see you in a few weeks?'

'Yes, or sooner if things don't settle.' He handed her the prescription and she took it with a smile of thanks.

'You've done well with your life, Conner.' She walked towards the door and paused. 'Do the right thing by my niece.'

The right thing.

Conner watched as she left the room and closed the door behind her.

What exactly was the right thing?

The rumours grew from soft whispers to blatant speculation until all the inhabitants of Glenmore had the same question on their lips.

Who was the woman that Conner MacNeil was seeing?

'She lives up your way,' Meg told Flora as she sprinkled chocolate onto a cappuccino. 'People have heard his motorbike roaring down the lanes late at night. Do you want anything to eat with this? Croissant? Chocolate muffin?'

'No, thanks.' Flora handed over the money and took the coffee, just wanting to escape before the conversation could progress any further.

'I mean, who lives near you? Who is likely to catch our Conner's eye? Tilly Andrews? No, it couldn't possibly be her.' Meg frowned as she rang up the amount on the till. 'I just can't imagine.'

'Me neither. Thanks for this, Meg.' Almost stumbling in her haste to make her exit, Flora backed towards the door while Meg pondered.

'I don't see why everyone is so interested anyway. This is Conner we're talking about. He'll have left the island or moved on to the next woman before we've identified the current one.' She wiped the side with some kitchen paper. 'You be careful out there today. There's a storm brewing. Jim reckons it's going to be a big one.'

'Is that right?' Not wanting to think about Conner leaving the island, Flora backed out of the door and took her coffee to the quay, where she sipped it slowly, watching the tourists pick their way off the ferry, most of them a pale shade of green after a rough sea crossing. Beyond them, the sea lashed angrily at the harbour walls and the sky turned ominously dark, despite the fact it was only lunchtime.

Flora sighed. Wild summer storms were a feature of Glenmore but that didn't mean that they welcomed it. If the ferry stopped running then the tourists didn't come, and if the tourists stopped then so did the money that contributed so much to the island economy. They were already in August and the summer months would soon be over.

And then Conner would be gone.

And she'd always known that, hadn't she? She'd always known that his presence on the island was only temporary.

Determined not to think about that, Flora finished her coffee and threw the empty container in the bin. She was not going to ruin the present by worrying about the future.

They still had the rest of summer together.

Climbing into her car, she drove back to the surgery, knowing that she was facing a full clinic now that Evanna had finally stopped work.

She worked through without a break and was just tidying up after her last patient when Conner walked into the room.

As usual her heart jumped and her mood lifted. Just seeing him made her want to smile. 'The weather's awful. There's a strong chance you're going to be trapped indoors tonight, Dr MacNeil.'

'Is that right?'

'Do you fancy being trapped indoors with me?'

'I might.' He pulled her against him and kissed her hungrily. 'As long as you promise to put your book away for half an hour.'

'That depends...' she curled her arms round his neck. '...on whether there is something more exciting to do than read.'

'Is that a challenge?'

'Do you need one?'

His answer was to kiss her again and she sank against him, her body erupting in a storm of excitement. They were lost in each other, absorbed, transported, and neither of them heard the click of the door behind them.

'What the—?' Logan's voice penetrated the fog of excitement that had anaesthetised her brain, and Flora opened her eyes dizzily, trying to remember where she was.

'Logan.' She said his name breathlessly and snatched her hands guiltily away from Conner's chest.

Logan gave a low growl of anger. 'Damn you, Conner, *what the hell do you think you're doing*?'

'Kissing your practice nurse.' Conner's tone was cool, almost bored. But he released his grip on her bottom and shrugged. 'Caught red-handed.' His gaze slid to Flora and he gave a faint smile. 'Or perhaps I should say red-faced.'

Flora froze as Logan turned his disbelieving gaze on her. *'Flora?'*

She stood, trapped in the headlights of his disapproval. *This was it, then*. The moment that had been inevitable.

The moment of discovery.

She waited to feel embarrassed, but nothing happened.

Tentatively, she examined the way she felt. Did she want the floor to open up and swallow her? No, she didn't. Did she wish she could turn the clock back? Absolutely not.

Flora frowned slightly, wondering why Logan's incredulous glance had so little effect on her. And then she looked at Conner—at the hard lines of his handsome face—and everything inside her disintegrated. Everything she'd thought she was, *everything she'd thought she wanted*—it all descended into rubble and she realised that the reason she wasn't embarrassed was because she didn't *care* what Logan thought. And the reason she didn't care what Logan thought was because she loved Conner.

She loved him.

Even though it was foolish and she was going to end up in tears, she was completely and utterly crazy about Conner.

She stood for a moment, shocked, exhilarated and absolutely terrified.

Then she turned to Logan, about to tell him that she didn't care what he thought, but something in his expression caught her attention. 'Logan? Is something wrong?'

Logan was glaring at Conner. 'You just can't help it, can you? You have to cause trouble. I ought to punch your lights out.'

'You're right,' Conner drawled, 'you probably should.'

'Stop it, both of you.' Flora was staring at Logan, her concern mounting as she noticed the unnatural pallor of his skin. 'Something has happened, hasn't it? Is it Kirsty? For goodness' sake, say something! You're scaring me.'

'Kirsty's fine.' Logan's voice was harsh. 'But Evanna's waters have broken.'

'Oh...' Flora immediately stepped forward and closed her fingers over his arm, her grip offering reassurance and support. 'It will be fine, Logan. Where is she?'

'In the car. I'm taking her to the ferry.' His breathing unsteady, Logan looked at Conner. 'I just came to tell you that the two of you are in charge. And then you—'

'Forget that,' Flora interrupted him. 'What's happening to Kirsty?'

'Meg is having her, but if she needs any help—'

'That's fine,' Flora said quickly. 'Of course.'

'You're taking Evanna to the ferry?' Conner frowned. 'The last thing I heard, the ferry wasn't going to run. There's a storm brewing, Logan.'

'I know there's a storm. And that's why we're getting off this island while we still can. I've already left it too late. We should have gone last weekend but Evanna is so damn stubborn.'

'But—'

'I know what I'm doing,' Logan said harshly, yanking open the door. 'Just keep an eye on the place while I'm gone.' He glared angrily at Conner. 'And try not to kiss anybody else.'

Janet appeared in the doorway, her face white. 'Logan, you have to come. Evanna says she wants to push. I've helped her out of the car and back into the house.'

'No!' Logan raked a hand through his hair, his voice sharp with panic. 'That isn't right. I don't want Evanna in the house. I want her on the ferry. And if the ferry isn't running, we'll call the air ambulance—'

Flora took control. 'If she wants to push, Conner should take a look at her.'

'I don't want him anywhere near my wife!' Logan rounded on him like a wounded animal and Conner's eyes narrowed.

'Relax. My taste has never run to heavily pregnant women.'

Flora sighed with exasperation and waved Janet away. 'Get me a delivery pack, Janet. Evanna's room. Tall cupboard on the right, top shelf. You two...' She turned to Logan and Conner, her eyes flashing with exasperation. 'Enough. All this testosterone is starting to get on my nerves and I can't concentrate. Logan, listen to me.' Stepping forward, she closed her hand over his wrist, her voice crisp. 'You are in no fit state to assess your wife's progress in labour. Conner and I will do that.' She could feel his pulse thundering under her fingers. 'We'll do that now. If Evanna is going to have this baby imminently, we need to be prepared.'

Conner looked as though he was about to speak and Flora silenced him with a glare, her instincts warning her that he was about to say something Logan didn't need to hear.

'She's not having our baby on this island.' Logan inhaled deeply and looked at her, his eyes bright with fear. *'I am not losing my wife!'*

CHAPTER TEN

'IT WOULD really help if someone could tell me what is going on here,' Conner drawled as he and Flora followed Logan through the surgery to the door that connected with their house. 'My cousin, who I always considered to be of sound mind, appears to have lost the plot. Given that he isn't usually prone to bouts of hysterics, I'm assuming there's a reason.'

Flora paused until Logan was out of earshot. 'He hasn't told you what happened to his first wife?'

'I never asked.'

Flora rolled her eyes. 'Men! OK. Well, to keep it brief, Logan was married before. His first wife died in childbirth, here on Glenmore. There was a terrible storm and he couldn't get her off the island and she...' Flora bit her lip. 'Well, she died. There isn't time to tell you more than that. There was nothing anyone could do, but don't try telling Logan that because he still blames himself.'

'Right.' Conner lifted his eyes and stared at his cousin's retreating shoulders. 'So we can expect him to be very relaxed and calm about the whole thing.'

'If he can't get Evanna off Glenmore for the delivery, he'll probably have a breakdown. We have to be very, very sensitive about this whole situation,' Flora said quietly, and Conner shot her a look, his expression faintly mocking.

'Sensitive? Perhaps I should just leave right now.'

'Don't be ridiculous. We need a plan. You can deliver the baby, I'll reassure Evanna and Logan—'

'No way.' Conner lifted his hands and stopped her in mid flow. 'I don't deliver babies. The only thing I know about babies is how *not* to produce them.'

Flora stared at him. 'Are you telling me you've never delivered a baby before? You're a doctor.'

His gaze was sardonic. 'There isn't a great deal of need for obstetrics in the army. Of course I've delivered a few babies but let's just say that my experience in that area is limited.'

'Mine, too. But we mustn't let them know that.' Flora bit her lip and thought fast. 'It doesn't matter. I can deliver the baby as long as it's straightforward. If there's a problem, you'll have to help. It will be fine. What they really need is reassurance. We just need to be confident. Really confident. Babies come by themselves...' she glanced at him doubtfully '...usually.'

'I can do confident,' Conner said, a trace of humour in his eyes, 'but I can tell you now that Logan isn't going to let me touch his wife.'

'Logan is traumatised. He'll do what we tell him.' She pushed him through the door and he lifted an eyebrow.

'I didn't know you were capable of being so dominating. Don't ever expect me to believe you're shy after this performance.'

Flora shrugged. 'You don't know me at all, do you?'

'Evidently not.'

They found Evanna in the breakfast room, a huge sunny room at the back of the house that adjoined the kitchen and looked over the garden.

'You can't possibly want to push,' Logan was saying in a hoarse voice, his arm round Evanna's shoulders. 'This is your first baby. First babies take ages. Days sometimes.'

Evanna's face was pale and streaked with sweat. 'Not all first babies take ages.' She broke off and Flora could see that she was struggling with pain.

Agitated, Logan stood up. 'I'm calling the air ambulance.'

'The wind's too strong,' Conner said in an even tone. 'They can't fly. I've already rung them.'

Evanna lifted a hand and touched Logan's face. 'You have to calm down,' she urged softly. 'You're panicking and I need you.'

'I'm not panicking,' Logan said tightly. 'I'm sorry.'

'Don't be sorry. I understand—and I love you.'

'All right—enough.' Conner pulled a face. 'You're making me feel ill. Flora, did I hear you asking Janet for a delivery pack? I presume such a thing exists on this godforsaken island?'

'We have everything,' Logan growled, his hair roughened from the number of times he'd run his fingers through it. 'I made sure. I've got the equipment to do a Caesarean section if it's necessary.'

'It's not going to be necessary,' Conner said calmly, washing his hands. 'Evanna, I'm going to take a look and see what's happening. Logan, go and check on Kirsty.'

Logan's jaw tightened. 'I'm not leaving her.'

Conner inhaled deeply and let the water stream off his hands into the sink. 'Leave the room, Logan. All this drama is giving me a headache.'

'No.'

Conner dried his hands and then pulled on the gloves Flora handed him. 'I can't concentrate with you hovering, ready to shout abuse at me.'

'What do you know about delivering babies?'

'I'm full of surprises.' Conner turned away from Logan and concentrated on Evanna, his smile gentle. 'The problem is that no one on this island trusts me.'

She gave a wan smile. 'I trust you, Conner.'

'It's all going to be fine, you know that, don't you?'

She swallowed. 'Yes…' Her voice faltered but she returned his smile. 'Of course it is. Have you—have you ever delivered a baby before?'

'Do you think I'd be here now if I hadn't? I love delivering babies,' Conner said smoothly, moving to her right side and glancing at Flora, his gaze faintly mocking. 'Delivering babies is my favourite thing.'

Evanna clutched his arm. 'You really have done it before?'

'Loads of times,' Conner said easily, and Logan snorted.

'Oh, for goodness' sake! I suppose you're going to try and convince us that the army is popping out babies all the time.'

'Of course not.' Conner's gaze didn't flicker. 'But the locals are. And they always came to us for help.'

Evanna gave a low moan and reached for Flora's hand. 'Actually, Logan, I think you should ring Meg and check on Kirsty. She was a bit off colour this morning.'

'But—'

'Logan!' Evanna's voice was surprisingly firm. 'You have to let Conner do this. We're wasting time. *I tell you this baby is coming now, whether you like it or not.*'

Flora realised that it was the first time ever she'd heard Evanna raise her voice and Logan took several deep breaths, his face a mask of indecision. 'All right—but I'll be back.' He strode away from them and Conner crouched down beside Evanna.

'Are you comfortable there?'

'I don't think I'd be comfortable anywhere,' she gasped, wincing as another contraction hit her. 'Wait a minute. I can't— Oh, Conner, I want to push—really…'

'Just hold on.' Flora dropped to her knees beside her friend. 'We're going to take a look, see if we can see the baby's head. We need to assess what's happening.'

'I can tell you what's happening,' Evanna muttered, her teeth gritted. 'I'm a midwife. This baby is coming. I think it's called precipitate labour.'

'Well, that's good news,' Conner said lightly. 'If there's one thing I can't stand, it's hanging around.'

Janet hurried into the room with the delivery pack.

'Open it,' Conner ordered brusquely. 'We're both wearing sterile gloves.'

'Open it fast,' Flora said calmly. 'I can see the head. In fact, I'd say it will crown with the next contraction.' *It was too quick*, she thought to herself. *Much too quick.* 'Don't push, Evanna. Can you take some shallow breaths? Pant? That's brilliant. Janet, put the central heating on.'

Janet stared at her. 'It's the middle of the summer.'

'It's not that warm in here and it's stormy outside. The temperature will drop and I want to heat the room a bit. And warm some towels.' *Just in case.*

Evanna groaned. 'I have to push. I can't not push. You have no idea. I've got another contraction coming— I can feel the head, Flora.'

'I know. It's brilliant,' Flora said cheerfully, ignoring Conner's ironic glance. She used her left hand to control the escape of the head and then gently allowed it to extend, remembering the deliveries she'd observed in her training. 'It's all fine, Evanna. The head is out.' *And terrifying.*

'Is he breathing? Is the cord round the neck? It's too fast. Logan was right,' Evanna gasped, tears trickling out of her eyes.

'That's nonsense, Evanna,' Flora said. She gently felt for the cord and her heart plummeted when she felt something. Struggling not to panic, she slid her fingers under it and slipped it over the baby's head. Only then did she start to breathe again. 'Everything is fine, Evanna. And there's nothing wrong with having a baby at home, you know that. You're a midwife!'

Suddenly aware that Conner was right by her side, Flora glanced at him. 'Is someone going to call Logan? He should be here for the next bit.'

'No.' Evanna grabbed his hand. 'It will be too much for him.'

But the decision was taken out of their hands because Logan appeared in the doorway, his face grey. 'Oh, God— what can I do?'

'Pour yourself a whisky and hold Evanna's hand,' Conner advised, and Flora glanced at him.

'Actually, you can draw up the Syntometrine so that Conner can give it.'

Evanna gave another gasp. 'Flora, I've got another one coming.'

'Great.' Flora smiled at her, concentrated on delivering the anterior shoulder and then the baby slithered out, red-faced and bawling. 'Little boy. Congratulations.' She lifted the wriggling bundle onto Evanna's abdomen and covered him with the warmed towels that Janet quietly handed her.

'Oh, Logan…' Tears spilled down Evanna's cheeks as she curved her arm protectively around the baby.

Logan stared down at his wife and son, his eyes bright. He didn't speak. Then he lifted a hand and pressed his fingers to his eyes, clearly struggling for control.

Conner rose to his feet. 'She's fine,' he said softly. 'They're both fine. Your family is safe. You can relax.' He hesitated for a moment and then reached out a hand and closed his fingers over his cousin's shoulder. Flora felt a lump build in her own throat as she saw the gesture of support and reassurance.

Who said Conner wasn't capable of forming relationships? *Who said that he wasn't capable of feeling?*

Knowing that her work wasn't finished, Flora turned her attention back to the delivery. She clamped the cord twice, divided it and then attached a Hollister clamp near the umbilicus. 'Two normal arteries, Evanna,' she murmured. 'Everything is looking good here.' She gently applied traction to the cord and the placenta slid out into the bowl.

'I'll check it.' Logan stepped forward to help, his face regaining some of its colour. 'I'm feeling fine now. Thank you. Both of you.'

'He's already feeding, Logan.' Evanna sounded sleepy and delighted at the same time. 'What are we going to call him?'

They murmured together and Flora's eyes misted as she watched them with their new son. Logan's hands were gentle, his face softened by love, and Evanna looked as though she'd won the lottery.

Feeling a lump in her throat, Flora glanced towards Conner. He was standing at the French windows, staring out across the garden, his shoulders tense and his features frozen.

She wondered what he was thinking.

Was he remembering his own family, and the contrast they must have made to the scene playing out in front of him?

They'd shared enough secrets in the stillness of the night for her to know that he would be less than comfortable with such undiluted domesticity.

Wanting to help, she stood up and swiftly cleared everything away. 'We're going to leave the two of you alone for a few minutes,' she said to Logan. 'We'll be next door if you need us.' She washed her hands quickly and then touched Conner's arm.

He turned, his face expressionless. 'Yes?'

'I don't think we're needed here.' She gestured with her head. 'Let's go next door.'

'Sure.' With a faint shrug he followed her through to the surgery and they walked into her room. But he didn't reach for her or make any of his usual wry, disparaging comments. Instead, he seemed distant. Remote. 'So—I didn't know you were a midwife.'

'I'm not. That's the first baby I've ever delivered.'

Conner gave a short laugh. 'You're full of surprises. I never would have known.'

'Do you want to know the truth? I was always terrified that this baby would come when Evanna was on the island and I knew Logan would panic. So I read a few books, asked Evanna a few questions…' Flora shrugged, wishing that he'd relax with her. 'I had a nasty moment when I felt the cord but it was all fine. And it helped knowing you were there.'

'I was as much use as a hog roast at a vegetarian supper,' he drawled. 'You did it all.'

'That's not true. You were strong,' she said softly. 'You gave Evanna confidence, and if something had happened to her or the baby, you would have known what to do. You're good in an emergency.'

He looked at her for a moment and then looked away. 'Well, they're both all right, and that's all that matters.' He glanced at his watch. 'I'd better get going, or Logan will be grumbling that I haven't finished my paperwork.'

Flora felt a flicker of desperation.

Something had changed between them and she didn't know what it was.

She wanted to say something about Logan and Evanna. She wanted to show him that she understood how hard it must be for him, but he was cool and remote, discouraging any sort of personal intrusion into his thoughts or feelings. And, anyway, she didn't want to have that conversation here, where they could be interrupted at any moment. 'Are you busy tonight?'

'Why do you ask?'

Her heart skipped. 'Because I thought you might fancy skinny-dipping in the sea. It's a great form of relaxation.'

He stood for a moment and then he turned. His ice-blue eyes were serious and there was no hint of a smile on his mouth. 'I don't think so.'

Her heart plummeted. 'I'll take off my bra and knickers this time, if that would swing your decision.'

'No, Flora.' His voice held none of its usual mockery. 'I don't think that's a good idea.'

'Oh. I thought you— I thought we might—' She broke off, not knowing what to say. 'Of course. Sorry. I understand.'

Had he guessed how she felt about him?

Probably. Sooner or later it happened to every woman who spent time with him, she was sure of that.

He'd guessed, and now he was running for cover. She'd always known this moment would come, but that didn't make it any easier. In fact, the pain was so overwhelming that she turned away, not wanting to embarrass herself or him by saying anything else.

'This thing between us has to end, Flora. *Do you understand?*' He closed his hands around her upper arms and spun her towards him, his eyes fierce as he stared into her face. 'Do you?'

Even though she'd sensed this moment was coming, she felt totally unprepared. 'Yes,' she croaked. 'I understand, Conner.' If he didn't want to be with her, she couldn't change that. And she didn't want to make him feel bad by showing how much she was hurting. 'We've been together for over a month.' She gave a tremulous smile. 'That's probably a record for you. Don't feel guilty. We had a great time. I had a great time.'

He gritted his teeth. 'Don't cry.'

'I'm not going to cry.' *At least, not until she was on her own.* And she wasn't going to admit that she loved him either, because that would just make the whole situation even more embarrassing for both of them.

And what was the point of it?

His fingers tightened on her arms. 'We never should have started this,' he said hoarsely. '*I* never should have started it.'

'You didn't. I did. And, Conner, you're hurting me.'

'Sorry.' He released her instantly and let out a breath. 'Sorry.'

'You don't have to look so tormented.' Though it took all her courage, she was determined to say it. 'You never promised me anything. You haven't done anything wrong. It was just a bit of fun.'

'And will it be fun when the locals work out who the woman is that I've been seeing? No, it won't.' His tone impatient and full of self-loathing, he turned away from her and strode towards the window. 'I can't believe I thought for a moment we could have a secret affair on an island like Glenmore. I'd forgotten what the place was like. You can't sneeze without someone counting the microbes.'

'I didn't think you cared what people say about you.'

'I don't. But I care about what people say about *you*. I saw your face, Flora,' he said roughly, 'when you were looking at that baby. You watched Evanna and Logan and you wanted what they have. Admit it.'

'I admit it,' she said simply. 'Who wouldn't want that, Logan? Someone to love. A family. Isn't it what everyone wants?'

His hands dropped to his sides. 'I can't do this. I'm sorry, Flora.'

'Is this because of Evanna and Logan?' Suddenly she couldn't just let him walk away. 'Talk to me, Conner. I know you're upset about what just happened and I can imagine it must be very hard seeing all that family stuff when your own family life was so desperately bad, but—'

He jerked away from her and strode towards the door. 'Enough.'

'Please, talk to me, Conner. I can see you're upset. Come over later. Even if we don't…' She stumbled over the words. 'If we're not still together, I'm still your friend. '

He paused with his hand on the door and then he turned slowly. And then he looked at her and his eyes were bleak and empty. 'People are already talking.'

'I know.'

'They're going to find out, Flora,' he said roughly. 'Nods. Winks. Whispers. Everyone wondering what a girl like you is doing with a man like me. And you'll hate it. You hate being the focus of attention. Take that first night—you were mortified when Jim and the others turned up on the beach.'

'Well of course I was.' She defended herself. 'I was in my underwear!'

'It was more than that. You didn't want people gossiping about you. And the whispers have started all over Glenmore. Do you think I haven't heard them? In the pub the other night, you almost cracked your glass because you were so terrified that Jim had discovered just who I'd been visiting in the dead of night. Knowing this place, people are grilling you every time you go to buy eggs or milk. Am I right?'

'Yes, but—'

'And you'll hate that because you're so shy. And I don't want people breathing your name and mine in the same sentence.' His knuckles whitened on the doorhandle. 'You know what people say about me. I'm bad Conner. People expect me to go the same way my father went.'

'I keep telling you that you are *not* your father.'

'No, but you deserve to be with a man you're not ashamed to be seen with.'

'I'm not ashamed of what we share, Conner.'

'Yes, you are, because you're not the sort of woman to indulge in wild affairs, especially not with men like me. When Logan walked in and caught us kissing, you jumped like a kangaroo on a hot plate and your cheeks were the colour of strawberries.'

'Well, of course! But that wasn't about you, it was about me. I'm not used to...' she shrugged self-consciously '...kissing and stuff in public.'

'And you're not going to get used to it. I have no intention of dragging your reputation down into the dirt. You have to live here after I've left.' He took her face in his hands and looked at her. 'So far the only person who knows is Logan and he won't say anything. Our secret should be safe.'

Confused, she shook her head. 'Is that why you're ending it? Because of what people might think of me?'

'Look me in the eye and tell me you haven't spent years dreaming about finding the right man, about having babies and being a family here on Glenmore.'

Incurably truthful, Flora nodded. 'I have imagined that, of course, but—'

'Of course you have. And you deserve that. You'll be a great mother.' With a faint smile he lifted her hand to his lips in an old-fashioned gesture and then cursed softly and dragged her against him. 'Sorry, but I think I'm going to be bad one more time.' He lowered his mouth to hers and kissed her slowly and thoroughly until her heart was hammering and her legs were weak. Then he lifted his head and smiled. 'Now, go away and find a man who is going to make you happy.'

Without giving her a chance to reply, he turned and left the room, leaving her staring after him with a head full of questions and a heart full of misery.

'Conner is in such a foul mood,' Evanna murmured, tucking the baby expertly onto her shoulder and rubbing his back. 'The rumour is that whoever he was seeing has dumped him.

I told Meg that's *completely* ridiculous because when in this lifetime did a woman ever dump Conner? Flora, are you listening to a word I'm saying?'

'Yes. No.' Flora lifted her fingers to her throbbing head. 'Sorry—I didn't really hear you. What did you say?'

Three days had passed since Conner had ended their relationship. Three days in which she hadn't eaten or slept. She felt as though part of her had been ripped out.

'I was just talking about Conner.' Evanna frowned. 'I can't believe a woman has dumped him because what woman in their right mind would dump him? On the other hand, I haven't seen any broken-hearted women around the place. Everyone is behaving as they usually behave. What's the matter with you? Why are you rubbing your head?'

'Bad night.' Flora curved her mouth into something that she hoped resembled a smile. 'Too much on my mind.'

She missed him so much.

She missed sleeping in his arms, she missed their long, intimate conversations in the darkness of the night, and she missed the way he made love.

He'd ended it because he thought she wanted to get married and have children. Or had he ended it because he was afraid that the ever-increasing rumours would hurt her? She wasn't sure any more. She'd replayed their last conversation in her head so many times that she felt as though her brain had turned into spaghetti.

Evanna looked guilty. 'It's our fault. Logan and I are so wrapped up in little Charlie and you and Conner are working so hard covering for the pair of us. How has he been with you? Moody?'

'I don't see that much of him. We do our own clinics.' Flora stood up quickly. 'Great to see you and Charlie looks great, too, and—'

'Flora...' Evanna peered closely at her. 'What is the matter with you? You're behaving very oddly. Is it the baby?' Her voice softened. 'Has it made you all broody? I know how much you want your own family and it *will* happen. One day you're going to meet the man of your dreams and have a family of your own.'

'Yes.' Flora felt as though her face was going to crack. 'Absolutely.' And she realised that her dream didn't seem so clear any more.

What she wanted was to be with Conner.

And if he didn't want to get married or have a family— well, she'd live with that.

But he didn't want *her*, did he?

He'd ended the relationship.

Evanna's hand stilled on the baby's back. 'I wish you'd tell me what's wrong.' She frowned. 'Flora?'

Flora looked at Evanna and Charlie. And she thought of Logan and what they shared.

And then she thought of what she'd had with Conner.

Had he at any point actually said that he didn't want her? No. Yet again she ran through the conversation in her head, trying to remember every last detail. What he'd said was that he wasn't the right man for her. That she wouldn't want to be seen with him in public.

And when he'd said that, she hadn't argued with him because, as usual, she hadn't known what to say. She'd let him walk away because she hadn't thought of the right thing to say at the right time.

But suddenly she knew exactly what she wanted to say.

Maybe he didn't want her any more, but she needed to find out. And she didn't care about pride because some things were more important than pride.

Panic fluttered inside her. 'Evanna, where is Conner, do you know?'

'He went to the Stag's Head for a drink with Logan.'

Flora glanced at the clock on the wall. Seven o'clock. The chances were that most of Glenmore would be in the Stag's Head at this hour on a Friday night. She stood up. 'I'm really sorry to abandon you, but I'm going for a drink. There's something I need to say to Conner.'

The Stag's Head was crowded with locals and heads turned as Flora opened the door and paused, her eyes scanning the room.

'Hey, Flora.' Ben smiled at her from behind the bar. 'You look like a woman in need of a drink. What can I get you?'

'In a minute, Ben, thanks.' Finally she spotted Conner and just at that moment he lifted his eyes and saw her. Ice-blue melded with brown and for a moment she just stood still, her heart pounding and her cheeks flaming red, unable to look away or move.

'Hi, Flora,' a couple of the locals called out to her, and she gave a vague smile but didn't respond.

If she didn't do this right away, she'd lose her nerve.

She let the door close behind her and wove her way through the chattering throng towards his table.

His eyes narrowed, but his gaze didn't shift from hers and from behind her came the sound of wolf whistles and good-natured laughter.

'Hey, Conner, looks like our Flora's got something to say to you.'

'Have you been a naughty boy, Con?'

The cat calls and teasing continued and Flora stopped next to him, realising with a flash of desperation that her plan was never going to work. She *did* have something to say, but the pub was so noisy that no one was ever going to hear her. *And she needed them to hear.*

'Flora?' Conner's voice was wary and for a moment she just looked at him, wondering how she was going to do this.

She opened her mouth to speak and then closed it again, thinking rapidly.

Executing a rapid change of plan, she leaned forward, took his face in her hands and kissed him. He stiffened with shock and his mouth remained immobile under hers. Then he started to pull away from her, so she slid onto his lap, straddling him, her hands clasping his head, keeping his mouth against hers.

A stunned silence had descended on the pub and although she didn't turn her head to look, Flora knew that everyone was staring at them. And that was hardly surprising because she was creating the biggest spectacle that Glenmore had seen for a long time. Which had been her intention.

Despite the tension in his body, she felt Conner's mouth move under hers and then felt the skilled stroke of his tongue. It was as if he couldn't help himself and, as always, the chemistry flashed between them. But his lapse was short-lived and this time when he pulled away he removed her hands at the same time, clasping her wrists firmly.

He stared at her, his blue eyes blazing. *'What do you think you're doing?'*

The noise around them had ceased. The low hum of chatter had died, the laughter was silenced and there was no clink of glasses.

'I'm kissing you, Conner,' Flora said clearly. 'I'm kissing you, just as I've kissed you every day for the past month. Only this time I'm doing it in public, so there's no confusion about the facts.'

His mouth tightened and he muttered something under his breath, but she covered his lips with her fingers.

'No. You had your say the other night. Now it's my turn to talk,' she said calmly, and then she slid off his lap and turned to face everyone. And for a moment her courage faltered because what seemed like a million faces were staring at her.

Her gaze slid over the crowd.

She saw Nick and, behind him, Meg. She saw Janet and Jim.

It seemed that everyone was in the Stag's Head.

'You've all been wondering who Conner has been seeing for the last month. Well, it's me,' she said simply, speaking clearly and raising her voice slightly so that everyone could hear her. 'I'm the lucky woman.'

'Flora, for crying out loud.' Conner rose to his feet, dislodging her arm from his shoulder. 'Have you been drinking?'

'No. I'm completely sober.' She smiled up at him, aware that everything she felt shone in her eyes. Then she took his hand and turned back to face the islanders—the people she spent her life with. 'I know what you're all thinking. You're thinking that Bad Conner has lived up to his name again, that obviously he seduced good, sensible Flora because she'd never do anything as reckless as have a wild, passionate affair with a man who is obviously going to walk off into the sunset, leaving her broken-hearted and very possibly pregnant.'

The locals were too shocked to respond so Flora just ploughed on.

'You're wrong. *I* seduced *him*. And I'm not embarrassed about that because I've discovered that—' She broke off as the door to the pub opened and Evanna walked in, holding the baby.

'Charlie and I suddenly had a horrible feeling that we were missing something important so I called a babysitter for Kirsty.'

As if emerging from a trance, Logan rose to his feet and walked over to his wife. He took the baby from her and tipped one of the lifeboat crew out of his chair so that she could sit down.

Flora smiled at her friend. 'Good timing. I was just about

to tell everyone that I've discovered that I don't really want what I thought I wanted. Up until a month ago I thought I wanted a man who loved me, a home, children—all the usual things. And then Conner came back.'

Conner's eyes were on hers and he shook his head. 'Stop now, before you make things worse.'

'Things can't get any worse for me, Conner.' Flora touched his cheek gently. 'I've discovered that not being with you is the worst it can get. You're all I want.' She was speaking just to him now, suddenly oblivious to her audience who stood watching, paralysed with surprise and fascination. 'You're all I want, Conner MacNeil. And I want you as you are, for as long as you want to be with me. I know you don't want babies or a family. I know you don't want anything permanent. And that's all right. If all we ever share is hot sex, that's fine.'

Someone in the crowd gulped and she wasn't sure whether the shocked sound had come from Meg or Evanna because she wasn't paying attention.

She was watching Conner.

'I love you,' she said, her eyes misting as she looked at him. 'And I know that probably scares you. I don't think anyone has ever loved you properly before and I want you to know how I feel. And I know you don't feel the same way about me and that's fine. I understand. If I'd been as badly hurt as you were as a child, I wouldn't risk my heart either. But I'm giving you mine, Conner, for as long as you want it. And I'm telling you that in public so that there's no mistake about it. I love you so much. And I'm not ashamed of that. I don't care who knows because I'm proud of what you've become and I'm proud that I'm the one you've spent time with since you've been on Glenmore. And if turns out that you've had enough of me, I'll accept it.' She shrugged. 'But I won't accept you ending our relationship because you're worried about what people might think of me. I don't care what anyone thinks. I just care about you. Us.' She stopped and Logan cleared his throat.

'That's got to be the longest speech you've ever made, Flora Harris.'

Conner stared at her, his face unusually pale. But he didn't speak.

Flora looked at him expectantly. 'Aren't you going to say something? You're the one who's slick with words, Conner MacNeil, not me. You always know what to say.'

Still he didn't answer her. It was as if he'd been turned to stone and she gave a sigh of frustration.

'Did you hear what I said? I'm in love with you.' On impulse, she pulled out a chair, stood on it and turned to face the crowd. 'Flora Harris loves Conner MacNeil!'

Ben cleared his throat and scratched his head. 'We heard you the first time, Flora. We're waiting to hear what Conner has to say. But apparently he's been struck dumb.'

Finally Conner moved. He rose slowly to his feet, gently lifted Flora off the chair and lowered her to the floor as if she were made of porcelain. 'I thought you were shy.'

'I am shy.'

He stroked a strand of hair away from her eyes with a gentle hand. 'I've got news for you, angel. Shy girls don't stand on chairs in pubs and declare undying love.'

'They do if they mean it,' she said softly, and his hand dropped to his side.

'There are things I need to say to you.'

Her heart fluttered. Rejection? Or a stay of execution? 'Then say them.'

'Not here.' He glanced at their audience. 'I think you've had enough of a show for one night.' And then he closed his hand over hers and led her from the pub and out into the darkness.

'Where are we going?' Flora hurried to keep up with him but he didn't answer and eventually they reached the quay where her boat was moored. 'You want to go sailing in the dark?'

'No, but I want to sit and look at her for a minute. Boats always calm me.' He sat down on the edge of the quay and tugged at her hand. 'Sit down.'

She sat, her heart pumping, the surface of the quay rough beneath her legs. 'Are you angry?'

'How could I possibly be angry?' He gave a short laugh, his eyes on the boats. 'I'm not angry. But I can't accept what you're offering, Flora.'

'I love you, Conner. Nothing you do or say is going to change that fact.'

'You don't really want an affair. It isn't who you are.'

'I want *you*. And if an affair is what's on offer then that's what I'll take.' She hesitated and then put her hand on his thigh and left it there. 'There's no pressure on you, Conner. I know you were more than a little spooked by seeing Logan and Evanna. I know that family life isn't what you want—'

'You're wrong.' His voice was hoarse and he covered her hand with his and then gripped it tightly. 'I was spooked, that's true, but I was spooked because in my mind I kept seeing *you* sitting there, holding a baby. And I wanted that baby to be mine.'

His words were so unexpected that for a moment she assumed she must have imagined them. She stared blankly at the boat, afraid to breathe, move or do anything that might disturb the atmosphere. *Afraid to look at him*.

Then, finally, she dared to turn her head. 'What did you say?'

'You heard me.'

Stunned, Flora could do nothing but stare. 'I don't understand.'

'Neither do I. I've spent my entire life running from relationships. I've never given anyone the opportunity to hurt me. But you crept up on me, Flora Harris.' He gave a lopsided smile. 'Somehow you sneaked in under my radar. With you, I didn't feel angry any more. You're the only person I've ever met whose company I prefer to my own.'

She could hardly breathe. 'But if you felt like that, why didn't you tell me? Why did you end our relationship? *Why did you walk away?*'

'Because I'm not a good catch.' He lifted her hand to his lips and kissed it. 'As far as commitment goes, my track record is appallingly bad. What woman in her right mind would take a chance on me?'

'I would,' Flora said softly. 'I would, if you asked me to.'

He was silent for a moment and when he spoke his voice was husky. 'You would? You're not worried about my past?'

'I'm more worried about my future. I can't imagine what it will be like if you're not part of it.'

'Knowing who I am doesn't make a difference?'

'I love who you are,' she said simply. 'You're a man who has done tremendous things with his life, despite the most appalling start. Most people would have crumpled. Most people would have repeated the pattern they'd seen at home or allowed the past to dictate their present. You did neither of those things. You trained as a doctor. You give to others, even though you were given so little yourself.'

He was silent for a moment and then he cleared his throat and gave her a wry smile. 'Now, this is the sort of hero-worship I think I could live with,' he drawled softly, standing up and pulling her up after him. 'I'm still afraid you're going to lose your nerve any minute and change your mind.'

'I won't do that. I love you, Conner. What I feel for you isn't something I can turn on and off.'

'I make women miserable, Flora.'

'You don't make *me* miserable. These last weeks has been the happiest of my life.'

He hesitated. 'What would you say if I told you that I don't want to stay on Glenmore?'

She lifted a hand to his face, gently exploring the roughness of his jaw with her finger. 'I'd say that's fine. And I'd ask you where you want to go.'

His gaze flickered from her face to the boat. 'I want to sail. Just the two of us. And when you're too pregnant to move around the boat, we'll find some dry land and make a home.'

She felt the lump building in her throat. 'That sounds good to me.'

'You don't mind leaving Glenmore?'

'I want to be wherever you are.'

He closed his eyes for a moment and then lowered his head so that his forehead brushed hers. 'If you'll do this, *if you'll trust me with your heart,* I swear I won't let you down, angel.'

'I know you won't let me down.'

His breath warmed her mouth. 'I don't deserve you. You're such a good person.'

'Actually, you're wrong about that. I have an *extremely* bad side,' she murmured, giving a soft gasp as his lips brushed the corner of her mouth. 'Several less-than-desirable qualities, in fact.'

'Name a few.' His body was pressed against hers and it was becoming harder and harder to concentrate.

'I'm useless at gossip.'

'That's a quality.'

'I'm insatiable in the bedroom.' She tilted her head back and gave him a wicked smile. 'The problem with good girls,

Conner MacNeil, is that when they discover what fun being bad can be, they never want to stop.'

'Is that right?' He curved his hands over her bottom and brought his mouth down on hers. And then he suddenly lifted his head and cursed softly.

'What's the matter?'

'What does a person have to do to get privacy on this island?' He stared over her shoulder and Flora turned to find what appeared to be the entire population of Glenmore gathered on the quay, watching.

Several of them held torches and Flora blinked as the beam from one almost blinded her.

'Well?' It was Jim who spoke and his voice carried the short distance across the quay. 'You can't expect to make a declaration like that in the Stag's Head and not tell us the ending. What's the ending? Has she said yes?'

Conner shook his head in disbelief. 'I can't believe this,' he muttered. 'The first and only time I propose to a woman and I have to do it with an audience.'

'You should be down on one knee, Conner MacNeil,' Ann Carne said primly, appearing at the front of the crowd, and Flora's heart stumbled in her chest.

'You don't have to propose—I don't want you to feel smothered by all this. We can just live together and—'

He put a finger over her lips, his eyes gentle. 'That isn't what I want. I want to make sure you're chained to me so that you can't run off easily when you realise what you've married.' He dropped to one knee and she gave an appalled gasp.

'Conner! You don't have to go that far! The seagulls are usually pretty busy above here. Kneeling could be a messy experience.'

'If I don't kneel, I'll never hear the last of it from the locals.' With an exaggerated gesture Conner took her hand in his. His eyes gleamed wickedly and he lifted an eyebrow in question. 'Well? How daring are you feeling? Can you bring yourself to marry a reprobate like me?'

'Conner!' There was a disgusted snort from Evanna. 'You're *supposed* to make it romantic. At the very least you're supposed to tell her that you love her.'

'I'm on my knees in seagull droppings,' Conner growled. 'I think that tells her quite a lot about my feelings.'

Half laughing, half crying, Flora looked down at him. 'You haven't said that you love me. I want to hear you say it. That's the really important bit.'

'I love you.' This time his voice was serious. 'I love you, Flora Mary Harris. Will you marry me?'

'Yes. Oh, yes. *Yes!*' She choked on the word and tears spilled down her cheeks.

Instantly Conner was on his feet, his expression horrified as he scooped her face into his hands. 'What's wrong?' He brushed the tears away with his thumbs. 'All my life I've been making women cry because I wouldn't say those words. Now, suddenly, I've said them and you're crying!'

'I'm crying because I'm happy.' She pressed her mouth to his. 'I'm happy and I love you. And, just for the record, my answer is yes.'

Torchlight wavered on her face. 'Speak up, Flora! We can't hear you at the back!'

Flora started to laugh. 'Yes,' she yelled in a voice so loud that Conner flinched. *'Yes, I will marry you.'*

There was a cheer from the crowd on the quay and Conner folded her into his arms. 'I hope you know what you're saying yes to, because you can't back out now.'

'I'm saying yes to everything,' Flora said softly, and this time her words were for him alone. 'Everything, Conner.'

'Everything?' His eyes held a wicked gleam. 'In that case,

I don't know about you,' he murmured against her mouth, 'but I think I could do with a bit more privacy for the rest of this conversation. Your place or mine?'

* * * * *

Jenna

CHAPTER ONE

'I CAN'T believe you've dragged me to the middle of nowhere. You must really hate me.' The girl slumped against the rail of the ferry, sullen and defiant, every muscle in her slender teenage frame straining with injured martyrdom and simmering rebellion.

Jenna dragged her gaze from the misty beauty of the approaching island and focused on her daughter. 'I don't hate you, Lexi,' she said quietly. 'I love you. Very much.'

'If you loved me, we'd still be in London.'

Guilt mingled with stress and tension until the whole indigestible mix sat like a hard ball behind her ribs. 'I thought this was the best thing.'

'Best for you, maybe. Not me.'

'It's a fresh start. A new life.' As far away from her old life as possible. Far away from everything that reminded her of her marriage. Far away from the pitying glances of people she'd used to think were her friends.

'I liked my old life!'

So had she. Until she'd discovered that her life had been a lie. They always said you didn't know what was going on in someone else's marriage—she hadn't known what was going on in her own.

Jenna blinked rapidly, holding herself together through will-power alone, frightened by how bad she felt. Not for the first time, she wondered whether eventually she was going to crack. People said that time healed, but how much time? Five years? Ten years? Certainly not a year. She didn't feel any better now than she had when it had first happened. She was starting to wonder whether some things just didn't heal—whether she'd have to put on the 'everything is OK' act for the rest of her life.

She must have been doing a reasonably good job of convincing everyone she was all right because Lexi was glaring at her, apparently oblivious to her mother's own personal struggle. 'You had a perfectly good job in London. We could have stayed there.'

'London is expensive.'

'So? Make Dad pay maintenance or something. He's the one who walked out.'

The comment was like a slap in the face. 'I don't want to live off your father. I'd rather be independent.' Which was just as well, Jenna thought bleakly, given Clive's reluctance to part with any money for his daughter. 'Up here there are no travel costs, you can go to the local school, and they give me a cottage with the job.'

That was the best part. A cottage. Somewhere that was their own. She wasn't going to wake up one morning and find it had been taken away from them.

'How can you be so calm and civilised about all this?' Lexi looked at her in exasperation. 'You should be angry. I tell you now, if a man ever treats me the way Dad treated you I'll punch his teeth down his throat and then I'll take a knife to his—'

'Lexi!'

'Well, I would!'

Jenna took a slow deep breath. 'Of course I've felt angry.

And upset. But what's happened has happened, and we have to get on with it.' Step by step. Day by day.

'So Dad's left living in luxury with his new woman and we're exiled to a remote island that doesn't even have electricity? Great.'

'Glenmore is a wonderful place. Keep an open mind. I loved it when I was your age and I came with my grandparents.'

'People *choose* to come here?' Lexi glared at the rocky shore, as if hoping to scare the island into vanishing. 'Is this seriously where you came on holiday? That's totally tragic. You should have sued them for cruelty.'

'I loved it. It was a proper holiday. The sort where we spent time together—' Memories swamped her and suddenly Jenna was a child again, excited at the prospect of a holiday with her grandparents. Here—and perhaps only here—she'd felt loved and accepted for who she was. 'We used to make sandcastles and hunt for shells on the beach—'

'Wow. I'm surprised you didn't die of excitement.'

Faced with the sting of teenage sarcasm, Jenna blinked. Suddenly she wished she were a child again, with no worries. No one depending on her. Oh, for crying out loud—she pushed her hair away from her eyes and reminded herself that she was thirty-three, not twelve. 'It *is* exciting here. Lexi, this island was occupied by Celts and Vikings—it's full of history. There's an archaeological dig going on this summer and they had a small number of places for interested teenagers. I've booked you on it.'

'You *what*?' Appalled, Lexi lost her look of martyred boredom and shot upright in full defensive mode. 'I am not an interested teenager so you can count me out!'

'Try it, Lexi,' Jenna urged, wondering with a lurch of horror what she was going to do if Lexi refused to co-operate. 'You used to love history when you were younger, and—'

'I'm not a kid any more, Mum! This is my summer holiday. I'm supposed to have a rest from school. I don't want to be taught history!'

Forcing herself to stay calm, Jenna took a slow, deep breath; one of the many she'd taken since her daughter had morphed from sweet child to scary teen. When you read the pregnancy books, why didn't it warn you that the pain of being a mother didn't end with labour?

Across the ferry she caught sight of a family, gathered together by the rail. Mother, father, two children—they were laughing and talking, and Jenna looked away quickly because she'd discovered that nothing was more painful than being around happy families when your own was in trouble.

Swallowing hard, she reminded herself that not every modern family had perfect symmetry. Single-parent families, stepfamilies—they came in different shapes. Yes, her family had been broken, but breakages could be mended. They might heal in a different shape, but they could still be sturdy.

'I thought maybe we could go fishing.' It was up to her to be the glue. It was up to her to knit her family together again in a new shape. 'There's nothing quite like eating a fish you've caught yourself.'

Lexi rolled her eyes and exhaled dramatically. 'Call me boring, but gutting a fish with my mother is *so* not my idea of fun. Stop trying so hard, Mum. Just admit that the situation is crap.'

'Don't swear, Alexandra.'

'Why not? Grandma isn't around to hear and it *is* crap. If you want my honest opinion, I hope Dad and his shiny new girlfriend drown in their stupid hot tub.'

Relieved that no one was standing near them, Jenna rubbed her fingers over her forehead, reminding herself that this was not the time to get into an argument. 'Let's talk about us for a moment, not Dad. There are six weeks of summer holiday left before term starts. I'm going to be working, and I'm not leaving you on your own all day. That's why I thought archaeology camp would be fun.'

'About as much fun as pulling my toenails out one by one. I don't need a babysitter. I'm fifteen.'

And you're still a child, Jenna thought wistfully. Underneath that moody, sullen exterior lurked a terrified girl. And she knew all about being terrified, because she was too. She felt like a plant that had been growing happily in one spot for years, only to be dug up and tossed on the compost heap. The only difference between her and Lexi was that she had to hide it. She was the grown-up. She had to look confident and in control.

Not terrified, insecure and needy.

Now that it was just the two of them, Lexi needed her to be strong. But the truth was she didn't feel strong. When she was lying in bed staring into the darkness she had moments of utter panic, wondering whether she could actually do this on her own. Had she been crazy to move so far away? Should she have gone and stayed with her parents? At least that would have eased the financial pressure, and her mother would have been able to watch out for Lexi while she worked. Imagining her mother's tight-lipped disapproval, Jenna shuddered. There were two sins her mother couldn't forgive and she'd committed both of them. No, they were better on their own.

Anger? Oh, yes, she felt anger. Not just for herself, but for Lexi. What had happened to the man who had cradled his daughter when she'd cried and spent weeks choosing exactly the right dolls' house? Jenna grabbed hold of the anger and held it tightly, knowing that it was much easier to live with than misery. Anger drove her forward. Misery left her inert.

She needed anger if she was going to make this work. And she *was* going to make it work.

She had to.

'We're going to be OK. I promise, Lexi.' Jenna stroked a hand over the teenager's rigid shoulder, relieved when her touch wasn't instantly rejected. 'We'll have some fun.'

'Fun is seeing my friends. Fun is my bedroom at home and my computer—'

Jenna didn't point out that they didn't have a home any more. Clive had sold it—the beautiful old Victorian house that she'd tended so lovingly for the past thirteen years. When they'd first married money had been tight, so she'd decorated every room herself...

The enormity of what she'd lost engulfed her again and Jenna drew in a jerky breath, utterly daunted at the prospect of creating a new life from scratch. By herself.

Lexi dug her hand in her pocket and pulled out her mobile phone. 'No signal. Mum, there's no signal!' Panic mingled with disgust as she waved her phone in different directions, trying to make it work. 'I swear, if there's no signal in this place I'm swimming home. It's bad enough not seeing my friends, but not talking to them either is going to be the end.'

Not by herself, Jenna thought. With her daughter. Somehow they needed to rediscover the bond they'd shared before the stability of their family had been blown apart.

'This is a great opportunity to try a few different things. Develop some new interests.'

Lexi gave her a pitying look. 'I already have interests, Mum. Boys, my friends, hanging out, and did I say boys? Chatting on my phone—boys. Normal stuff, you know? No, I'm sure you don't know—you're too old.' She huffed moodily. 'You met Dad when you were sixteen, don't forget.'

Jenna flinched. She had just managed to put Clive out of her mind and Lexi had stuffed him back in her face. And she wasn't allowed to say that she'd had no judgement at sixteen. She couldn't say that the whole thing had been a mistake, because then Lexi would think she was a mistake and that wasn't true.

'All I'm asking is that you keep an open mind while you're here, Lexi. You'll make new friends.'

'Anyone who chooses to spend their life in a place like this is seriously tragic and no friend of mine. Face it, Mum, basically I'm going to have a miserable, lonely summer and it's all your fault.' Lexi scowled furiously at the phone. 'There's still no signal. I hate this place.'

'It's probably something to do with the rocky coastline. It will be fine once we land on the island.'

'It is not going to be fine! Nothing about this place is fine.' Lexi stuffed the phone moodily back in her pocket. 'Why didn't you let me spend the summer with Dad? At least I could have seen my friends.'

Banking down the hurt, Jenna fished for a tactful answer. 'Dad is working,' she said, hoping her voice didn't sound too robotic. 'He was worried you'd be on your own too much.' Well, what was she supposed to say? Sorry, Lexi, your dad is selfish and wants to forget he has responsibilities so he can spend his summer having sex with his new girlfriend.

'I wouldn't have cared if Dad was working. I could have hung around the house. I get on all right with Suzie. As long as I block out the fact that my Dad is hooked up with someone barely older than me.'

Jenna kept her expression neutral. 'People have relationships, Lexi. It's part of life.' Not part of *her* life, but she wasn't going to think about that now. For now her priorities were remembering to breathe in and out, get up in the morning, go to work, earn a living. Settling into her job, giving her daughter roots and security—that was what mattered.

'When you're young, yes. But he's old enough to know better. They should be banned for everyone over twenty-one.'

SARAH MORGAN

Lexi shuddered. 'Thank goodness you have more sense. It's a relief you're past all that.'

Jenna blinked. She was thirty-three. Was thirty-three really past it? Perhaps it was. By thirty-three you'd discovered that fairy tales were for children, that men didn't ride up with swords to rescue you; they were more likely to run you down while looking at the pretty girl standing behind you.

Resolutely she blocked that train of thought. She'd promised herself that she wasn't going to do that. She wasn't going to generalise and blame the entire male race for Clive's shortcomings. She wasn't going to grow old bitter and twisted, giving Lexi the impression that all men were selfish losers. It wasn't men who had hurt her; it was Clive. One man—not all men.

It was Clive who had chosen to have a rampant affair with a trainee lawyer barely out of college. It was Clive who had chosen to have sex on his desk without bothering to lock the door. There were moments when Jenna wondered if he'd done it on purpose, in the hope of being caught so he could prove how virile he was.

She frowned. Virile? If she'd been asked for a word to describe Clive, it certainly wouldn't have been virile. That would have been like describing herself as sexy, and she would never in a million years describe herself as sexy.

When had she ever had wild sex with a man while still wearing all her clothes? No one had ever been that desperate for her, had they? Not even Clive. Certainly not Clive.

When Clive had come home from the office they'd talked about household accounts, mending the leaking tap, whether or not they should have his mother for the weekend. Never had he walked through the door and grabbed her, overwhelmed by lust. And she wouldn't have wanted him to, Jenna admitted to herself. If he had grabbed her she would have been thinking about all the jobs she still had to do before she could go to bed.

Blissfully unaware that her mother was thinking about sex, Lexi scuffed her trainer on the ground. 'There would have been loads for me to do in London. Cool stuff, not digging up bits of pot from muddy ground. I could have done my own thing.'

'There will be lots of things to do here.'

'On my own. Great.'

'You'll make friends, Lex.'

'What if I don't? What if everyone hates me?'

Seeing the insecurity in her daughter's eyes, Jenna hugged her, not confessing that she felt exactly the same way. Still, at least the people here wouldn't be gossiping about her disastrous marriage. 'They won't hate you. You make friends easily, and everyone on this island is friendly.' Please let them be friendly. 'That's why we're here.'

Lexi leaned on the rail and stared at the island mournfully. 'Change is the pits.'

'Change often feels difficult, but it can turn out to be exciting.' Jenna parroted the words, hoping she sounded more convincing than she felt. 'Life is full of possibilities.'

'Not stuck here, it isn't. Face it, Mum. It's crap.'

Ryan McKinley stood with his legs braced and his arms folded. His eyes stung from lack of sleep, he'd had no time to shave, and his mind was preoccupied by thoughts of the little girl with asthma he'd seen during the night. He dug his mobile out of his pocket and checked for missed calls and messages but for once there were none—which meant that the child was probably still sleeping peacefully. Which was what he would have been doing, given the choice.

As the ferry approached the quay, he slipped the phone

back into his pocket, trying not to think of the extra hour he could have spent in bed.

Why had Evanna insisted that *he* be the one to meet the new practice nurse? If he hadn't known that the woman had a teenage daughter, he would have suspected Evanna of match-making. He'd even thought of mentioning his suspicions to Logan McNeil, his colleague and the senior partner in the Glenmore Medical Centre. If she was planning something, Logan would probably know, given that Evanna was his wife. Wife, mother, midwife and—Ryan sighed—friend. She was a loyal, caring friend.

In the two years he'd been living on the island she'd done everything she could to end his hermit-like existence. It had been Evanna who had dragged him into island life, and Evanna who had insisted that he help out when the second island doctor had left a year earlier.

He hadn't been planning to work, but the work had proved a distraction from his thoughts, as she'd guessed it would. And it was different enough from his old job to ensure that there were no difficult memories. Different had proved to be good. The shift in pace and pressure just what he'd needed. But, as grateful as he was to his colleague's wife for forcing him out of his life of self-imposed isolation, he refused to go along with her need to see him in a relationship.

There were some things that wouldn't change.

'Hi, Dr McKinley. You're up early—' A pretty girl strolled over to him, her hair swinging over her shoulders, her ador-ing gaze hopeful. 'Last night was fun, wasn't it?'

'It was a good night, Zoe.' Confronted with the realities of living as part of a small island community, Ryan chose his words carefully. This was the drawback of living and work-ing in the same place, he mused. He was her doctor. He knew about her depression and the battle she'd had to get herself to this point. 'You looked as though you were enjoying yourself. It was good to see you out. I'm glad you're feeling better.'

He'd spent the evening trying to keep the girl at a safe distance without hurting her feelings in front of her friends. Aware that her emotions were fragile, he hadn't wanted to be the cause of any more damage—but he knew only too well how important it was to keep that distance.

'I wasn't drinking alcohol. You told me not to with those tablets.'

'Probably wise.'

'I—' She pushed her thumbs into the pockets of her jeans, slightly awkward. 'You know—if you ever wanted to go out some time—' She broke off and her face turned scarlet. 'I shouldn't have said that. Millions of girls want to go out with you, I know. Sorry. Why would someone like you pick a screwball like me?'

'You're not a screwball.' Ryan wondered why the most difficult conversations always happened at the most awkward times. The ferry was docking and he was doing a consultation on the quay, within earshot of a hundred disembarking passengers. And, as if that wasn't enough, she was trying to step over a line he never allowed a patient to cross. 'You're suffering from depression, Zoe, and that's an illness like any other.'

'Yes, I know. You made me see that.' Painfully awkward, she rubbed her toe on the hard concrete of the quay. 'You've been great, Dr McKinley. Really great. I feel better about everything, now. More able to cope, you know? And I just wondered if—'

Ryan cut her off before she went too far and said something that couldn't be unsaid. 'Apart from the fact I'm your doctor, and I'd be struck off if I said yes, I'm way too old for you.' Too old. Too cynical. 'But I'm pleased you feel like dating. That's good, Zoe. And, judging from the way the men of Glenmore were flocking around you last night, you're not short of admirers, so I think you should go for it. Pick someone you like and get yourself out there.'

Her wistful glance told him exactly who was top of her list, and she gazed at him for a moment before giving a short laugh. 'You're refusing me.'

'Yes.' Ryan spoke firmly, not wanting there to be any mistake. 'I am. But in the nicest possible way.'

Zoe was looking at him anxiously. 'I've embarrassed you—'

'I'm not embarrassed.' Ryan searched for the right thing to say, knowing that the correct response was crucial both for her self-esteem and their future relationship. 'We've talked a lot over the past two months, Zoe. You've trusted me with things you probably haven't told other people. It's not unusual for that type of confidence to make you feel a bit confused about your own feelings. If it would help, you can change doctors.'

'I'm not confused, Dr McKinley. And I don't want to change doctors. You've got such a way with words, and I've never known a man listen like you—I suppose that's why I—' She shrugged. 'Maybe I will date one of those guys.' She smiled up at him. 'That archaeologist who's hanging around this summer is pretty cool.'

'Interesting guy,' Ryan agreed, relieved that she didn't appear to be too heartbroken by his rejection.

'What about you, Dr McKinley? Why are you waiting for the ferry? Are you meeting a woman?'

'In a manner of speaking. Our new practice nurse is arriving today. Reinforcements.' And he had a favour to ask her. He just hoped that Jennifer Richards was a big-hearted woman.

'A new nurse?' There was a wistful note to Zoe's voice.

'Well, I know Nurse Evanna needs the help. So what's this new nurse like? Is she young?'

'She's coming with her teenage daughter.' Why had Evanna wanted him to meet her? That question played on his mind as he watched the ferry dock. It could have been an innocent request, but he also knew that his colleague was obsessed with matching people up. She wanted a happy ending.

Ryan felt the tension spread across his shoulders. He knew life didn't often offer up happy endings.

Zoe's face brightened. 'If she has a teenage daughter, she must be forty at least. Maybe even older.' She dismissed the competition. 'Well, the ferry is on time, so you're about to meet your nurse.'

Shaking the sleep out of his brain, Ryan watched as a patchwork of people flowed off the ferry. Businessmen in suits, families clutching bulging beach bags, toddlers in pushchairs. A slightly overweight, middle-aged woman puffed her way towards him carrying a suitcase.

He didn't know whether to be relieved that Evanna clearly hadn't been matchmaking or disappointed that their new practice nurse didn't look fit enough to work a hard day at the surgery. 'Jennifer?' He extended a hand. 'I'm Dr McKinley. Ryan McKinley. Welcome to Glenmore Island.'

The woman looked startled. 'Thank you, but I'm Caroline, not Jennifer. I'm just here for a week with my husband.' She glanced over her shoulder towards a sweating, balding man, who was struggling with a beach umbrella and an assortment of bags, one of which popped open, spilling the contents onto the quay.

'Oops. Let me help you—' A slim girl put down her own suitcase, stepped forward and deftly rescued the contents of the bag, her pink mouth curving into a friendly smile as she stuffed everything back inside and snapped the bag firmly shut.

Ryan's gaze lingered on that mouth for a full five seconds before shifting to her snaky dark curls. The clip at the back of her head suggested that at one time her hair had been fastened, but it had obviously made an escape bid during the ferry journey and was now tumbling unrestrained around her narrow shoulders. She was pale, and there were dark rings under her eyes—as if she hadn't had a decent sleep in months. As if life had closed its jaws and taken a bite out of her.

He recognised the look because for months he'd seen it in his own reflection when he'd looked in the mirror.

Or maybe he was imagining things. Plenty of people looked tired when they first arrived on the island. It took time to relax and unwind, but by the time they caught the ferry back to the mainland they had colour in their cheeks and the dark circles had gone.

Doubtless this girl had worked all winter in some grey, smog-filled city, saving up her holiday for a couple of bracing weeks on a remote Scottish island.

Eyeing the jumper looped around her shoulders, Ryan realised that she obviously knew that summer weather on Glenmore could be unpredictable.

He watched her for a full minute, surprised by the kindness she showed to a stranger. With no fuss, she helped rearrange his possessions into a manageable load, making small talk about the problems of packing for a holiday in a destination where the weather was unpredictable.

Having helped the couple, the girl stood for a moment, just breathing in the sea air, as if she hadn't stood still for ages while the man and his wife carted themselves and their luggage towards the two island taxis.

'The brochures promise you a welcome,' the woman panted, her voice carrying across the quay, 'but I didn't imagine that the island doctor would meet everyone personally. He even shook my hand! That *is* good service.'

A faint smile on his lips, Ryan watched them pile into a taxi. Then he stared at the ferry, resisting the temptation to take another look at the girl. He hoped the nurse and her daughter hadn't missed the boat.

A hand touched his arm. 'Did I hear you say that you're Dr McKinley?' The girl with the tumbling black hair was beside him, cases by her feet, her voice smoky soft and her eyes sharp and intelligent. 'I'm Jenna.'

Ryan looked into her eyes and thought of the sea. Shades of aquamarine, green and blue blended into a shade that was uniquely hers. He opened his mouth and closed it again—tried to look away and found that he couldn't. So he just carried on staring, and he saw something blossom in the depths of those eyes. Awareness. A connection. As if each recognised something in the other.

Something gripped him hard—something he hadn't felt in a long time.

Shocked by the chemistry, Ryan inhaled sharply and prepared himself to put up barriers, but she got there first.

Panic flickered across her face and she took a step backwards, clearly rejecting what had happened between them.

And that was fine with him, because he was rejecting it too.

He didn't even know why she'd introduced herself. Was every passenger going to shake his hand this morning?

Ryan knew he needed to say something casual and dismissive, but his eyes were fixed on the sweet lines of her profile and his tongue seemed to be stuck to the roof of his mouth.

She wasn't a girl, he realised. She was a woman. A young woman.

Mid-twenties?

And she looked bone tired—as if she was ready to collapse into a big comfortable bed and sleep for a month.

'Sorry. I must have misheard—' Flustered, she adjusted

the bag that hung from her shoulder. 'I thought I heard you say that you're Dr McKinley.'

'I did.'

'Oh.' Her tone suggested that news was unwelcome. Then she stuck out her hand. 'Right, well, I'm Jennifer Richards. Jenna.' She left her hand hovering in the space between them for a moment, and then slowly withdrew it as he simply stared at her. 'What's wrong? Have I arrived on the wrong day? You look a bit...stunned to see me.'

Jennifer Richards? Stunned didn't begin to describe his reaction. Ryan cleared his throat and shook her hand, noticing that her fingers were slim and cool. 'Right day.' Wrong description. 'It's just that—my partner fed me false information. I was expecting a woman and her teenage daughter.' Someone about twenty years older. Someone who wasn't going to make his hormones surge.

'Ah—' She glanced towards the ferry, her smile tired. 'Well, I'm the woman, but the teenage daughter is still on the boat, I'm afraid. That's her, hanging over the side glaring at me. She's refusing to get off, and I'm still trying to decide how best to handle this particular situation without ruining my reputation before I even take my first clinic. I don't suppose you have any experience in handling moody teenagers, Dr McKinley?'

He cleared his throat. 'None.'

'Shame.' Her tone was a mixture of humour and weary acceptance. 'This is one of those occasions when I need to refer to my handbook on teenagers. Stupidly, I packed it at the bottom of the suitcase. Next time it's going in my handbag and if necessary I'll ditch my purse. I apologise for her lack of manners.' She flushed self-consciously and looked away. 'You're staring at me, Dr McKinley. You're thinking I should have better control over my child.'

Yes, he was staring. Of course he was staring.

All the men on Glenmore were going to be staring.

Ryan realised that she was waiting for him to say something. 'I'm thinking you can't possibly be old enough to be that girl's mother. Is she adopted?' Damn. That wasn't what he'd meant to say.

'No, she's all mine. I have sole responsibility for the behavioural problems. But it's refreshing to hear I don't look old enough. According to Lexi, I'm a dinosaur. And she's probably right. I certainly feel past it—particularly right now, when I'm going to have to get firm with her in public. Oh, joy.' The wind flipped a strand of hair across her face and she anchored it with her fingers. 'You're still staring, Dr McKinley. I'm sorry I'm not what you were expecting.'

So was he.

He wasn't ready to feel this. Wasn't sure he wanted to feel this.

Mistrusting his emotions, Ryan ran a hand over his neck, wondering what had happened to his powers of speech. 'You must have been a child bride. Either that or you have shares in Botox.'

'Child bride.' There was a wistful note to her voice, and something else that he couldn't decipher. And then she lifted her eyebrows as the girl flounced off the ferry. 'Well, that's a first. She's doing something I want her to do without a row. I wonder what made her co-operate. Lexi—' she lifted her voice slightly '—come and meet Dr McKinley.'

A slender, moody teenager stomped towards them.

Ryan, who had never had any trouble with numbers, couldn't work out how the girl in front of him could be this woman's daughter. 'Hi, there. Nice to meet you.'

Eyes exactly like her mother's stared back at him. 'Are you the one who gave my mum this job? You don't look like anything like a doctor.'

Ryan wanted to say that Jenna didn't look like the mother

of a teenager, but he didn't. 'That's because I didn't have time to shave before I met the ferry.' He rubbed his fingers over his roughened jaw. 'I am a doctor. But I didn't give your mother the job—that was my colleague, Dr McNeil.'

'Well, whatever you do, don't put her in charge of family planning. As you can probably tell from looking at me, contraception is *so* not her specialist subject.'

'Lexi!' Jenna sounded mortified and the girl flushed.

'Sorry. It's just—oh, never mind. Being in this place is really doing my head in.' Close to tears, the teenager flipped her hair away from her face and stared across the quay. 'Is there an internet café or something? Any way of contacting the outside world? Or are we using Morse code and smoke signals? Or, better still, can we just go home, Mum?'

Ryan was still watching Jenna. He saw the pain in her eyes, the exasperation and the sheer grit and determination. She looked like someone who was fighting her way through a storm, knowing that there was no shelter.

Interesting, he mused, that Glenmore so often provided a bolthole for the wounded.

He wondered what these two were escaping.

Sensing that Jenna was hideously embarrassed, he knew he ought to say something—but what did he know about handling teenagers? Nothing. And he knew even less about what to say to soften the blow of teenage rudeness. Assuming that something along the lines of *she'll be leaving home in another four years* wouldn't go down well, Ryan opted to keep his mouth shut.

He'd never raised a child, had he?

Never been given that option. Anger thudded through him and he stilled, acknowledging that the feelings hadn't gone away. He'd buried them, but they were still there.

Taking an audible breath, Jenna picked up their bags.

'We're renting a cottage at West Beach. Is there a bus that goes that way?'

'No bus. There are taxis, but before you think about that I have a favour to ask.'

'What favour can I possibly do you already?'

Ryan gently prised the suitcases from her cold fingers, sensing the vulnerability hidden beneath layers of poise and dignity. 'I know you're not supposed to officially start until tomorrow, but we're snowed under at the surgery. I'm supposed to exert my charm to persuade you to start early, only I was up three times in the night so I'm not feeling that charming. I'd appreciate it if you'd cut me some slack and say yes.'

'You do house-calls?'

'Is that surprising?'

'The doctors I worked with rarely did their own house-calls. It was the one thing—' She broke off and smiled at him, obviously deciding that she'd said too much.

'On Glenmore we can't delegate. We don't have an out-of-hours service or a local hospital—it's just the three of us.' He looked at her pointedly. 'Four now. You're one of the team.' And he still wasn't sure what he thought about that.

'Are you sure you still want me? You're sure you don't want to rethink my appointment after what Lexi just said?' Her tone was light, but there was vulnerability in her eyes that told him she was worrying about her daughter's comments.

Ryan was surprised that she was so sensitive to what others might be thinking. Out of the blue, his mind drifted to Connie. Connie hadn't given a damn what other people thought. She'd been so monumentally selfish and self-absorbed that it had driven him mad.

'Your qualifications are really impressive. We're delighted to have you here. And the sooner you can start the better.'

'I spoke to Evanna McNeil on the phone.' She turned her head and checked on her daughter. 'She's arranged for us to pick up the keys to the cottage this morning. I was going to spend the day settling in and start work tomorrow.'

'The cottage isn't far from here. And I know you were supposed to have today to settle in, but if there is any way I can persuade you to start work this morning that would be fantastic. There's a clinic starting at eight-thirty, and the girl who helps Evanna with the kids is off sick so she has to look after the children. I'd cancel it, but we're already overrun because we've been down a nurse for a few months.'

'But if the clinic starts at eight-thirty that's just half an hour from now.' Jenna glanced at her watch, flustered by his request, working out the implications. 'I want to help, of course. Normally I'd say yes instantly, but—well, I haven't made any arrangements for Lexi.'

'I'm not six, Mum. I'll stay on my own.' The girl looked round with a despairing look on her face. 'I'm hardly likely to get into danger here.'

Ryan had a feeling that the child would be capable of getting into trouble in an empty room, and Jenna was clearly of the same opinion because she looked doubtful.

'I'm not leaving you on your own until we've both settled in and found our feet. It's going to be OK, Lex.' Her gaze was fixed on her daughter's face and Ryan wanted to ask *what* was going to be OK. What had given her dark rings around her eyes? What was keeping her awake at night?

Why had she taken a job on a remote Scottish Island?

It didn't take a genius to sense that there was a great deal more going on than was revealed by their spoken communication. And he couldn't help noticing that no man had followed her off the ferry. If there was a Mr Richards, then he was keeping his distance.

With customary practicality, Ryan searched for a solution. 'Lexi can come too. The surgery is attached to the house. She can hang out with Evanna and the children. Evanna would be glad of the help, and it will give Lexi a chance to find out something about the island. And I can drive you over to the cottage at lunchtime. I'll even help you unpack to speed things up.'

'Mum!' Lexi spoke through gritted teeth. 'I'm not spending the morning looking after a couple of babies! I'd rather go to broken pottery camp, or whatever it's called!'

Ryan struggled to think like a teenager. 'Evanna has internet access, and the mobile signal is great from her house.'

Lexi gave a wide smile that transformed her face from sullen to stunning. 'Then what are we waiting for? Lead me to civilisation. Otherwise known as wireless broadband.'

CHAPTER TWO

'I NORMALLY see Nurse Evanna,' the old lady said, settling herself into the chair. 'She knows exactly what to do with my leg.'

Could today get any worse? Feeling mentally exhausted, Jenna scanned the notes on the screen.

Not only did her daughter not want her to be here, the patients didn't appear to want her either. And doubtless Dr McKinley was also regretting her appointment after that embarrassing scenario on the quay.

And to top it all, having not thought about sex for what seemed like the whole of her twenties, she'd looked into Ryan McKinley's cool blue eyes and suddenly started thinking about nothing but sex. She'd been so mesmerised by an alien flash of chemistry that she'd almost embarrassed herself.

Jenna cringed at the memory of just how long she'd stared at him. Who was she kidding? She *had* embarrassed herself. There was no almost about it.

And she'd embarrassed him.

Why else would he have been staring at her?

What must he have thought?

That she was a sad, desperate single mother who hadn't had sex for a lifetime.

He'd made all those polite noises about her looking too young to have a teenage daughter, but Jenna knew it was nonsense. People said that, didn't they? People said *You don't look thirty*, while secretly thinking you looked closer to forty. She shuddered, appalled at the thought that he might be sitting in his consulting room right now, formulating a strategy for keeping her at a distance. She needed to make sure he knew she didn't have designs on him—that a relationship with a man was right at the bottom of her wish list.

She was just trying to survive. Rebuild her life.

Knowing she couldn't afford to think about that now, Jenna concentrated on her patient. 'I understand that it's unsettling to have someone new, Mrs Parker, but Evanna has left detailed notes. If you see me doing anything differently, or anything that makes you feel worried, you can tell me.'

'You've a teenage daughter, I hear?' Mrs Parker dropped her bag onto the floor and slipped off her shoe. Her tights were the colour of stewed tea and twisted slightly around her ankles.

Jenna searched through the choice of dressings available to her, unsure what the surgery stocked. 'I only stepped off the ferry half an hour ago. Word travels fast.'

'Hard to have secrets on Glenmore. We're a close community.'

'That's why I chose to come here, Mrs Parker.' That and the fact she hadn't had much choice. She helped the woman onto the trolley. 'And I don't have any secrets.'

'Will your husband be joining you later?'

'I'm no longer married, Mrs Parker.' Jenna swiftly removed the old dressing, wondering why saying those words made her feel such a failure.

As if to reinforce those feelings, Mrs Parker pressed her lips together in disapproval. 'I was married for fifty-two years. In those days we sorted out our differences. We didn't give up.'

Great. Just what she needed. A lecture. Still, she was used to those from her mother. She'd grown up seeing her failings highlighted in neon lights.

'I admire you, Mrs Parker. I'm just going to check your blood pressure.'

Mrs Parker sniffed her disapproval. 'I'm here to have the dressing changed.'

'I know that. And I've already picked out what I'm going to use.' Reminding herself that building relationships was essential to the smooth running of the practice, Jenna was patient. 'But it's important to check your blood pressure every six months or so, and I can see from your notes that it hasn't been done for a while.'

'I don't see what my blood pressure has to do with the ulcer on my leg.'

'Sometimes ulcers can be caused by bad circulation rather than venous problems. I want to do an ankle blood pressure as well as taking it on your arm.'

Mrs Parker relaxed slightly. 'You obviously know what you're doing. All right. But I haven't got all day.'

Jenna checked her blood pressure, reminding herself that she'd always known this move wouldn't be easy. Not for her, nor Lexi.

'So you fell pregnant when you were still in school, by the looks of you.' Mrs Parker's lips pursed. 'Still, everyone makes mistakes.'

Jenna carefully recorded the blood pressure readings before she replied. 'I don't consider my daughter to be a mistake, Mrs Parker.'

There was a moment of silence and then the old lady gave a chuckle. 'Capable of standing up for yourself, are you? I like that. You're obviously a bright girl. Why have you moved all the way up here? You could be in some leading city practice. Or are you running away?'

Jenna sensed that whatever she told this woman would be all over the island by lunchtime, so she delivered an edited version of the truth. 'My marriage ended. I needed a change. And this place has a good reputation. Logan McNeil has built a good practice.' She didn't add that she would have taken the job regardless, because it was as far from Clive and her parents as it was possible to get without leaving the country.

'Logan is a good doctor. So's Ryan McKinley, of course. But we all know he won't be around for long. He's a real high-flier. Used to work as one of those emergency doctors.'

Emergency doctor?

Confused, Jenna paused. 'How long has he lived here?'

'Came here two years ago and bought the old abandoned lighthouse that Ewan Kinaird had given up hope of selling. Too isolated for everyone. But not for Dr McKinley. Apparently isolation was what he wanted, and he paid a fair price for it. Didn't see him for most of that first year. Turned up occasionally in the village to buy supplies. Kept himself to himself. Never smiled. Some thought he was antisocial. Others thought he was recovering from some trauma or other. Certainly looked grim-faced whenever I glimpsed him.'

Jenna felt guilty for listening. Part of her wanted to cover her ears but she didn't want to be rude. And she was intrigued by Ryan McKinley. When she'd met him he hadn't seemed antisocial. Nor had he shown signs of trauma. He'd talked. Smiled. But she knew a smile often hid a secret. 'So how does he come to be working as a GP?'

'That was Evanna's doing. Won't let anyone be, that girl— especially not if they're in trouble. She coaxed him into helping out after the last locum left them in the lurch. She had baby Charlie, and Logan was managing the practice on his own. When he was needed, Ryan stepped up. But we all know he won't stick. He'll be off to some high-flying job before the tide has turned.' Mrs Parker took a closer look at her leg. 'What's your professional opinion of this, then?'

'I'm just taking a look now.' Jenna wondered what trauma had made a doctor qualified in emergency medicine buy a secluded lighthouse on an isolated island. 'How did you find out he was a doctor?'

'Oh, he kept it quiet.' Mrs Parker peered at her leg. 'But Fiona Grange crashed her car into a ditch in the middle of a storm and he happened to be passing when it happened. Some say he's the reason she's alive. Bones smashed, she was unconscious, and the air ambulance couldn't take off. And there was Dr McKinley, cool as a Glenmore winter, stopping the bleeding, extracting her from the car—shocked everyone, he did. Went from hermit to hero in the blink of an eye. But there was no hiding his profession after that. And he's been a good doctor, although he's private. Keeps himself to himself. Some think he's unfriendly. A bit cold.'

Unfriendly? Jenna thought about the man who had met her at the quay. He hadn't been unfriendly. Tired, definitely. Guarded, maybe. She would have described him as cool, but not cold.

'I'm going to take a proper look at your leg now.' Trying not to think about Ryan McKinley, Jenna washed her hands and opened the dressing pack. 'Your blood pressure is fine. How long have you had this problem, Mrs Parker?'

'I had it last summer and it went away. But then it came back.'

'Did you wear your compression stockings?' She glanced down at the tan stockings that had been placed neatly on the chair.

'Not as much as I'm supposed to.'

'They're not that comfortable, I know.' Jenna cleaned the

wound and dressed it. 'That does look sore, you poor thing. Are you in a lot of pain?'

Mrs Parker relaxed slightly. 'I'm old. I'm always in pain. My bones ache every morning. The Glenmore winter is bitter. Like having your leg in the jaws of a shark.'

'I've only ever been here in the summer. My grandparents used to bring me. Tell me if this feels too tight.' Jenna bandaged the leg, applying most pressure to the ankle and gradually less towards the knee and thigh. 'Try and keep your leg up before you come and have that dressing changed next week. Have you tried putting a couple of pillows under your mattress? The aim is to let gravity pull the fluid and blood towards the heart. It will reduce the swelling. Can you move your ankle?'

'Yes. You've done a good job,' Mrs Parker said grudgingly. She stood up and put her stockings back on with Jenna's help. Then she reached for her bag. 'That dressing feels very comfortable, actually. But tell Evanna I'm sorry to have missed her.'

'I'll do that.'

Jenna watched as Mrs Parker walked slowly down the corridor, and then returned to the computer to type up the notes, sinking into the chair, exhausted. This was a huge mistake. She should have just bought a new flat in London, then she could have stayed in her job and Lexi could have stayed in her school.

Instead she'd chosen a small island where strangers were viewed with suspicion and where her life was going to be lived under a microscope.

She was an idiot.

Forcing herself to take several deep breaths, Jenna reminded herself that it was natural for the islanders to be wary of a new nurse. She just had to earn their trust.

Or maybe she should just buy another ferry ticket and get

off this island as fast as possible. She sank her head into her hands, and then sat up quickly as she heard a rap on the door.

Ryan walked in. 'I owe you an apology. I had no idea Mrs Parker was your first patient. Talk about baptism of fire.'

Somewhere between meeting her on the quay and starting his surgery he'd shaved and changed. The faded jeans had been replaced by smart trousers and the comfortable tee shirt by a tailored shirt. In the confines of her consulting room he seemed taller. And broader. Suddenly she had no trouble imagining him as a high-powered consultant in a busy emergency department.

Her throat suddenly felt dry. 'Yes, she was my first patient.'

'You're still alive?'

Oh, yes. She knew she was alive because she could feel her heart banging hard against her chest. 'We did OK.'

'But now you want to resign?' His voice was dry. 'You're about to buy a return ferry ticket and run back to London?'

Jenna sat rigid, terrified that he'd guessed how bad she felt. 'No.' Her voice was bright. 'I'm not even remotely tempted to run away.'

His smile faded and his gaze sharpened. 'I was joking.'

'Oh.' She turned scarlet. 'Of course you were joking. Sorry. I'm a bit tired after the journey.'

'The last nurse we appointed lasted three days. Didn't Evanna tell you?'

'She did mention something. Don't worry, Dr McKinley. I'm not a quitter.' Jenna said it firmly, reminding herself of that fact. 'And Mrs Parker was fine.'

'I know Mrs Parker, so you must be lying.'

Yes, she was and it seemed that these days she spent her life lying. Even her smile was a lie. 'Mrs Parker was wary at seeing someone new, and that's normal—especially at her age. She doesn't like change. I understand that.' Jenna concentrated on the computer, thinking that she was finding change terrifying and she was several decades younger than Mrs Parker.

'That leg of hers is slow to heal.'

Jenna thought about the old lady—remembered how much had been said in a short time. 'I don't know her, but at a guess I'd say she doesn't really want it to heal. She's lonely. Her leg gives her a reason to come up here and interact with people.'

'That's possible.' His eyes narrowed thoughtfully. 'Despite your college-girl looks, you're obviously very sharp.'

Accustomed to thinking of herself as 'past it', his compliment made her feel strange. Or maybe it hadn't been a compliment. 'I'm interested in people. I like looking for the reasons they do things. It's why I do the job.' Even as she said the words she realised the flaw in that theory. If she was so interested in why people did what they did, why hadn't she spotted the signs that her husband was cheating on her? Maybe she wasn't so observant after all. Or maybe she hadn't wanted to see what was under her nose.

Feeling the tension erupt inside her, Jenna hit a button on the computer and exited Mrs Parker's file, wishing she could control her thinking. She had to stop asking 'what if?' She had to move on. That was what she was doing here, wasn't it? She was wiping out the past. 'Why do *you* do the job, Dr McKinley?' Would he tell her that he was an emergency specialist in hiding?

He was leaning against the wall, his broad shoulders threatening the safety of the asthma poster stuck to the wall. 'At the moment I can't remember. You'd better ask me that question again when I haven't been up for half the night doing calls. I'm always in a snarly mood when I get less than three hours' sleep.'

'That's understandable. Could you sneak off and sleep at some point today?'

'Unfortunately, no. Like I said to you on the quay—it's

just the four of us. When we're busy, we're busy. We can't hand it over.'

'Who called you out last night? Locals or tourists?'

'One tourist with chest pains, a toddler with a febrile convulsion, and one of our own with a very nasty asthma attack.' He frowned. 'I called the mother a few moments ago to check on her and she told me the child is still asleep, but I'm going to call in later. I didn't like the look of her in the night. I gather you have an interest in asthma?'

'Yes. I ran a clinic in London.' Jenna was interested. 'Was there an obvious trigger? Did she have an infection or something?'

'They'd got themselves a dog from the rescue centre. I'm assuming it was that.'

'They didn't know that animal fur was a trigger?' Jenna pulled a face, understanding the ramifications of that statement. 'So is the dog being returned?'

'It's a strong possibility. They're thinking about it, but obviously the child will be upset.'

'It would be wonderful to have a dog,' Jenna said wistfully, and then sat up straight, slightly shocked by herself. A dog? Where had that thought come from? Why on earth would she want a dog?

'Maybe you could give this one a home?'

Jenna automatically shook her head. 'We can't have a dog. Cl—' She was about to say that Clive hated animals, but then she remembered that she wasn't married to Clive any more. His opinion didn't matter.

Glancing down at her left hand, she stared at the pale line on her finger that was the only remaining evidence that she'd once worn a ring. It still felt strange, seeing the finger bare. And it still brought a sting to the back of her throat.

'Something wrong?' His question made her jump.

'No. I was just thinking about your little asthma patient and the dog.'

'Right.' His gaze locked onto hers and she looked away quickly, thinking that Ryan McKinley was nothing like the men she usually met during her working day. For a start he was about two decades younger than the GPs she'd worked with in her last practice. She tried to imagine any of *them* extracting a seriously injured girl from the wreck of a car during a storm without the help of paramedics—and failed. Ryan McKinley was a different breed of doctor. And then there was the fact that he was indecently good-looking. Sexy.

A different breed of man.

'You look really stressed out.' Ryan spoke quietly. 'Is that Mrs Parker's doing? Or is it being thrown in at the deep end?'

'No! Not at all.' Oh, God, he'd noticed that she was stressed. And the one thing she absolutely couldn't afford to do was put a foot wrong in this job. 'I love being thrown in at the deep end. Anyway, I didn't ask why you were here. Did you want to talk to me? Is there something I can help you with, Dr McKinley?' Please don't let him say he'd changed his mind about hiring her.

'I wondered if you could take some bloods for me.' Ryan handed her a form, his eyes still on her face. 'Callum is fifteen and he's showing all the signs of glandular fever. I know you already have a full clinic, but I really need these results as soon as possible.'

'Of course you do.' As she took the form from him, Jenna's fingers brushed against his. She immediately snatched her hand away, feeling as though she'd touched a live wire. 'I'll do them straight away.' Without thinking, she rubbed her fingers, wondering whether she was doomed to overreact around this man.

'He's in the waiting room with his mum.' Ryan was looking at her fingers, and Jenna swallowed and dropped her hands into her lap.

'Fine. Great. I'll call him.'

'I appreciate it.' There was a tension about him that hadn't been there before. 'Your bikes have been delivered, by the way. I had them taken straight to the cottage. They'll be safe enough outside your front door.'

'Bikes?' Jenna had to force herself to concentrate. 'Bikes. Yes, of course. Evanna told me about this place that hires them for the summer, so I rang them. I thought it would be good for both of us to cycle.'

'I'm impressed. It's a good example to set to the patients.'

'So you'll try not to knock me off my bike when you're accelerating past in your Porsche?'

He gave a faint smile as he strolled towards the door. 'Are you accusing me of speeding or being a couch potato?'

'Neither. I'm sure you're very fit.' Her eyes slid to the hard muscle of his shoulders, clearly outlined by the smooth fabric of his casual shirt. Damn, she shouldn't have used the word *fit*. Wasn't that the word Lexi used when she found a boy attractive? 'I mean, you're obviously athletic—I mean, health-conscious—sorry, just ignore me…' Jenna had the distinct impression that he was laughing at her, but when she looked at him his expression was unreadable.

'Why would I want to ignore you?'

'Because I'm talking nonsense—' And he was super-cool, hyper-intelligent and nothing like the men she usually dealt with. She had no trouble believing Mrs Parker's assertion that he was a top doctor. He had an air of authority and command that she found mildly intimidating. 'The bikes will be great.'

'Does Lexi know you've ordered bikes?'

'Not yet.' She didn't know which impressed her more, the fact that he'd remembered her daughter's name or his uncannily accurate assessment of her character. 'Light the touch paper and stand well back. Which reminds me; I owe you an apology for her behaviour earlier.'

'What do you have to apologise for?'

'Lexi. She——' Jenna didn't want to reveal personal details, but she was unable to bear the thought he might think badly of her daughter. 'She's very mixed up at the moment. She didn't want to move from our home in London. It's been hard on her.'

He was silent for a moment, considering her words. She had a nasty feeling that he knew just how close to the edge she was. 'Glenmore has a very calming effect on people. It's a good place to escape.'

'Lexi didn't want to leave London.'

'Perhaps your needs are greater than hers at the moment,' he said gently. 'Does Lexi know you're living in a cottage on the beach?'

'No. There's only so much bad news that she can take at one time. She's going to hate me for not renting a house in the village.'

'That's not exactly a hub for entertainment, either.' He opened the door. 'When you've finished your clinic, knock on my door. I'll take you and your luggage over there.'

'I don't expect you to do that. If you have any spare time, you need to sleep.'

'I'll give you a lift.' He hesitated, his hand on the door. 'Give it a few weeks before you buy that ferry ticket. I predict that in no time this place will feel like home.'

He knew.

He knew how bad she felt. She'd done a lousy job at hiding her feelings. He knew she was panicking and having second thoughts.

Horrified that he was clearly aware of how close she was

to breaking, Jenna just sat there, not trusting herself to speak. Their eyes held, and then he gave a brief nod.

'Welcome to Glenmore, Jenna. We're very pleased to have you here.'

Ryan stood in front of his colleague, legs spread, hands dug in his back pockets. 'Tell me about Jenna.'

'Jenna?' Logan McNeil signed a prescription and glanced up, his expression interested. 'Why? Was it love at first sight? Your eyes met across a crowded ferry ramp?'

Remembering the flash of chemistry, Ryan rolled his shoulders to ease the tension. 'Just give me the facts, Logan.'

Logan put his pen down. 'She's been working as a practice nurse in England for the past six years, but I'm not holding that against her. Why are you asking? Has she killed a patient or something?'

'I'm worried about her.'

'Isn't that a little premature? She's been here for five minutes.'

And he'd been worried about her within thirty seconds of meeting her. She'd looked fragile and battered, as though she'd emerged from a terrible storm. 'Evanna asked me to meet her, remember? She looks as though she's holding it together by a thread.'

Suddenly Logan wasn't smiling. 'You're worried about her ability to do the job?'

'No. She handled Mrs Parker, which proves she's more than capable of doing the job. I'm worried about *her*!' Ryan shot him an impatient look. 'What do you know about her personal circumstances?'

With a sigh, Logan opened his drawer and pulled out a file. Scanning the papers, he paused. 'Divorced with a teenage daughter. That's all it says.'

Divorced.

Ryan prowled to the window of Logan's consulting room and stared across the fields. Remembering the white circle on her ring finger, he was willing to bet the divorce was recent. Was that why she was so pale and drawn? Divorce did that to people, didn't it? Was that why she jumped when a man touched her? 'Was her ex-husband abusive?'

'I have absolutely no idea. This is her CV, not a police statement. Are you sure you're not going a little over the top here? You seem very concerned about someone you only met a few hours ago.'

Ryan turned. 'She's a colleague,' he said evenly. 'It's in our interest to make sure she's happy here.'

'And that's all that's going on here?' Logan closed the file. 'You seem very interested in her.'

'I didn't say I was interested. I said it was in our interest to make sure she's happy.'

'Good. Then I'll leave it to you to make sure she is.' Logan pushed the file back in the drawer. 'Plenty of people get divorced, Ryan. It's a fact of life in our society. It doesn't mean she has problems. You could be barking up the wrong tree. Has she seen the cottage yet?'

'I'm taking her at the end of morning surgery.'

'Let's just hope she likes isolation, otherwise we'll be looking for a new practice nurse. Ted Walker has a flat vacant in the village if you think that would be better.'

'I know she's going to like the cottage.' He didn't know how he knew, but he did.

She was running—wounded—looking for a place to hide and recover.

And the cottage was the perfect place for her. Whether her teenager daughter would survive the isolation was another matter.

CHAPTER THREE

IT WAS the prettiest house she'd ever seen—one of four fishermen's cottages facing the sea, their front gardens leading straight down to a sandy beach.

The iron gate was rusty and creaked as she pushed it open, but Jenna felt a sudden feeling of calm and contentment. No more endless traffic jams and road rage. No more rush hour. No more litter on the streets and graffiti on the walls.

Just open space, fresh air, and the sound of the sea.

It was perfect.

Lexi gave a whimper of horror. 'This is it? It's the smallest house I've ever seen.'

Jenna felt the tension return to her stomach. 'Small, yes, but it's ours.' As long as she kept the job. The house came with the job. They had a home again. And it would be cheap to run.

Lexi was gaping at the tiny cottage. 'A whole summer here?'

'Yes.'

'You can't swing a cat.'

'We don't have a cat.' But they might have a dog. She'd been thinking about it ever since Ryan McKinley had mentioned the idea.

Lexi closed her eyes. 'Just kill me now,' she muttered, and Jenna searched for something to say that would cheer her up.

'Don't you think this is better than London?'

'Tell me that isn't a serious question—'

Jenna sighed. They'd come this far. They had to keep moving forward.

She walked up the path to the front door, her eyes scanning the pretty garden. She noticed a few weeds and her hands itched. It would be fun, she mused, to have a proper garden.

Lexi stared desperately at the house and then at the beach. 'Where's the nearest shop?'

'Walk straight down the road and you reach the harbour. If it's low tide you can walk along the beach.' Ryan strode up the path behind them, carrying both suitcases. He deposited them on the ground, gently removed the key from Jenna's hand and opened the door of the cottage.

'Sorry—I was miles away.' Jenna gave a smile of apology. 'It's so long since I had a garden. Our house in London just had a courtyard. I'm not used to so much outdoor space.' Enchanted, she stooped and touched some of the pretty pink flowers that clustered by the door. *'Armeria maritima.'*

Ryan raised his eyebrows, apparently amused. 'You're quoting the Latin names of plants at me?'

'My mother was a botanist. I grew up hearing Latin names. Some of them stuck.' She touched the flower with the tip of her finger. 'Sea pinks. They grow well in this climate, by the coast.'

Lexi rolled her eyes. 'Gosh, Mum, gripping stuff.'

Jenna flushed and stood up. 'Sorry. It's just so wonderful to have a garden.' Despite the knot in her stomach she felt better, and she was in no hurry to go indoors. Instead she breathed in the sea air and watched the plants waving in the breeze. The grass needed cutting, and there were weeds in the borders, but somehow that just added to the charm. She imagined herself lying on a rug on a warm Sunday morning, listening to the gulls and reading the paper.

When had she ever done that? Sundays were normally so busy, what with making a traditional Sunday roast for Clive and his mother, and then being expected to produce tea for the cricket club...

Aware that Ryan was watching her, Jenna flushed. She felt as though he could read her every thought, and that was disturbing because some of the thoughts she'd been having about him were definitely best kept private. 'When Evanna told me that the job came with a house, I never imagined it would be anywhere as perfect as this. I can't imagine why anyone would want to leave here. Who owns it?'

'Kyla—Logan's sister. Her husband, Ethan, was offered a job in the States. They'll be back at some point.'

But not soon. Please don't let it be soon.

A warm feeling spread through her, and for the first time since she'd left London Jenna felt a flicker of hope. Excitement. As if this might be the right decision after all.

She felt as if she belonged. She felt at home.

It's—so peaceful.' A gull shrieked above her and she laughed as she caught Ryan's eye. 'Well, not peaceful, perhaps, but the noises are different. Good noises. No car horns and revving engines. And everything is slow. I'm looking forward to just being still.' Realising that she probably sounded ridiculous, Jenna shrugged awkwardly. 'In London everything moves so fast. You get swept along with it so that sometimes you can't even take a breath—I hate the pace of it.'

'That's because you're so old, Mum.' Lexi fiddled with her phone. 'London was exciting. And our house was lovely.'

'London was noisy and smelly and our house was far too big for the two of us.' It was what she'd told herself when she'd realised that their house had been sold and she and Lexi no longer had a home. It was the only way she had coped.

Pushing away that thought, Jenna stepped into the hallway of the cottage. They had a home now, and she loved it. Light reflected off the polished wooden floor, and through an open door she could see a bright, cheerful kitchen. 'We lived right next to an underground station and every three minutes the house shook.'

'Yeah, it was so cool.' Lexi tossed her hair away from her face, her eyes still on her mobile phone. 'I was never more than ten minutes from the shops.'

But Jenna wasn't thinking about shopping. It seemed far away. And so did Clive and the whole sordid mess she'd left behind. 'This place is wonderful. We can have our breakfast outside on that little table.' She turned to look at the pretty garden, eyes slightly misty, imagination running free. 'Lexi, you can go for a swim, or a run on the beach.'

How could this be a mistake?

Maybe she hadn't done the wrong thing. They could be happy here—she felt it.

Lexi shot her a look of incredulous disbelief and checked her mobile phone. 'No signal again. How do people function around here?'

'You can usually get a signal if you walk up the hill towards the castle.' Ryan lifted their suitcases into the hallway and Lexi gave an exaggerated sigh.

'Fine. If the only place I can use my phone is at the top of a hill then I'm going to have to walk up it!' Making a frustrated sound in her throat, she stalked away.

Jenna opened her mouth to say *be careful* and then closed it again, leaving the words unspoken. She knew from experience that too much maternal anxiety was counterproductive.

But the guilt was back, eating away at her like acid, corroding her insides. She might have fallen in love with the cottage, but she knew this wasn't what Lexi wanted.

'It must be hard, letting them grow up.' Ryan was standing in the doorway, his thumbs hooked into the pockets of his trousers, a speculative look in his blue eyes as he watched her.

'You have no idea.' Keeping her tone light, Jenna walked past him into the garden, her gaze on Lexi as her daughter sauntered across the road and started up the hill. A dozen nightmare scenarios sped through her overactive maternal brain. To control them, she used black humour. *Say it aloud and it might not happen.* 'Are there any scary, dangerous individuals at large on Glenmore at the moment?'

'Well, you've already met Mrs Parker—they don't come much scarier or more dangerous than her. She's wanted in five counties.' His arm brushed against hers and Jenna felt her whole body tingle.

She stepped away from him, keeping her distance as she would from an electric fence. 'I was thinking more of axe-wielding murderers and rapists.'

'We had dozens of those last summer, but Mrs Parker saw them off. It's hard to commit a crime in a community that knows what you're planning to eat for supper.'

As Lexi's figure grew smaller, and then vanished from sight, Jenna felt a moment of panic. Catching his eye, she gave an embarrassed laugh. 'Yes, I know—I'm overreacting. It's hard to forget this isn't London. You must think I'm crazy. *I* think I'm crazy!'

'That isn't what I'm thinking.'

'It would be if you knew what was going through my mind. It's taking all my will-power not to charge after her and follow her up that hill.'

His gaze shifted from her face to where Lexi had disappeared. 'I don't know much about teenagers, but at a guess I'd say that probably isn't the best idea.'

'Well, I'd have to be discreet, of course.' She made a joke of it. 'I'd probably start by sprinting up the hill and then drop to my stomach and crawl so that she couldn't see me.'

'You're going to have a hell of a job beating off an axe-wielding murderer if you're crawling on your stomach.'

'Never underestimate a mother protecting her young.'

'I'll remember that.' He had a deep voice. Deep and male, with a slightly husky timbre that made her think things she hadn't thought for a long time.

Jenna breathed in slowly and stared at the ridge, trying not to think about his voice. 'I can't believe she made it up there so quickly. Lexi isn't really into exercise. It's amazing what the lure of a mobile phone signal can do to cure teenage lethargy. I hope she'll be OK.'

Ryan turned to her, and she noticed that the passing hours had darkened his jaw again. 'She's crossed the only road and she's still alive. She'll be fine. I'm not so sure about you.'

Her gaze met his and their eyes held.

The rhythm of her heart altered and the oxygen was sucked from the air. The world shrank to this one place—this one man.

Everything else was forgotten.

Mesmerised by those blue eyes, Jenna felt her body come to life, like the slow, sensual unfolding of a bud under the heat of the sun. Not the sultry, languid heat of summer sunshine but the fierce, rapacious scorch of sexual awareness. Like a volcano too long dormant after centuries of sleep, it exploded violently—blowing the lid on everything she believed herself to be. Excitement ripped through her like a consuming, ravenous fire, and in her newly sensitised state she found staring longingly at the firm lines of his mouth.

If she wanted to kiss him, she could...

She was a free woman now.

The shriek of a seagull brought her to her senses and Jenna took a step backwards.

What on earth was she thinking? If she did something crazy, like kissing him, he'd fire her from her job, Lexi would have a nervous breakdown, and she'd be more of an emotional wreck than she was already. And anyway, if she hadn't been able to trust someone she'd known for fifteen years, what chance was there with someone she'd known for fifteen minutes?

Jenna straightened her shoulders. 'You're right. I worry far too much about her. I intend to work on that this summer. I'm hoping it will be easier here.' Unfortunately her bright, businesslike tone did nothing to dissipate the strange turbulence inside her. She needed to be on her own, so that she could undo whatever she'd just done to herself by looking at him. And she was sure he was desperate to escape from her, albeit for different reasons.

'Thanks so much for the lift, Dr McKinley. I'm sorry to hold you up.'

'You're not holding me up.' Instead of leaving, as she'd expected, he walked back towards the house. 'Do you have any caffeine?'

Pulling herself together, Jenna followed him. 'Pardon?'

'Caffeine. I'm feeling tired, and there's still most of the day to get through.' Suppressing a yawn, he walked through to the kitchen without asking for directions or permission. 'I need coffee. Strong coffee.'

'I thought you'd need to dash off somewhere—lunch, house-calls...' She had thought he'd be anxious to escape from her—the desperate divorcee...

'We try not to do too much dashing on Glenmore.' Concentration on his face, he pulled open a cupboard and rummaged through the contents. 'It's bad for the heart. Which do you prefer? Tea or coffee?'

'Either. I mean—I haven't had time to shop.'

'The kitchen should be stocked.'

'Oh.' Jenna was about to ask who could possibly have

stocked the kitchen when the phone rang. She jumped. 'Who on earth can that be?'

'Why don't you answer it and see? Phone's in the hall.'

Jenna found the phone, answered it, and immediately wished she hadn't because it was her mother. 'Hi, Mum.' Oh, no, she absolutely didn't want to have this conversation with Ryan McKinley listening. Why, oh, why had she given her this number? 'No, everything is fine—' All her newfound tranquillity faded as her mother's cold disapproval trickled down the line like liquid nitrogen, freezing everything in its path. 'No, the doctors here don't care that I'm divorced.' She lowered her voice and turned away from the kitchen, hoping Ryan couldn't hear her above the hum of the kettle. 'No, the patients don't care, either—' She squeezed her eyes shut and tried not to think of Mrs Parker. 'And I'm not trying to ruin Lexi's life—it's kind of you to offer, but I don't think living with you would have been the best thing, Mum. I need to do this on my own—no, I'm not being stubborn—'

The conversation went the way it always went, with her mother stirring up every unpleasant emotion she could. Reminding herself to get caller ID, so that she could speak to her mother only when she was feeling really strong, Jenna gripped the phone. 'Yes, I know you're very disappointed with the way things have turned out—I'm not whispering—'

By the time the conversation ended her throat was clogged and her eyes stung. Whatever magic the cottage had created had been undone. The knot was back in her stomach.

All she wanted was moral support. Was that really too much to ask from a mother?

Knowing that she wasn't capable of going back into the kitchen without making a fool of herself, Jenna stood for a moment in the hallway, still holding the phone to her ear. It was only when it was gently removed from her hand that she realised Ryan was standing next to her.

He replaced the receiver in the cradle and curved his hand over her shoulder, his touch firm. 'Are you all right?'

Jenna nodded vigorously, not trusting herself to speak. But the feel of his hand sent a warm glow through her body. It had been so long since anyone had touched her. She'd been divorced for months, and even during her marriage there hadn't been that much touching. Clive had never been tactile. More often than not he'd had dinner with clients or colleagues, which had meant she was in bed and asleep long before him. Even when they had made it to bed at the same time he'd been perfunctory, fumbling, as if making love to her had been another task on his 'to do' list and not something to be prolonged.

She was willing to bet that Ryan McKinley had never fumbled in his life.

His broad shoulders were there, right next to her, and Jenna had a powerful urge to just lean against him for a moment and see if some of his strength could be transferred to her by touch alone.

They stepped back from each other at exactly the same time, as if each had come to the same conclusion.

Not this. Not now.

'I found the coffee.' His voice was rough. 'We need scissors or a knife to open this.'

Blinking rapidly to clear the tears misting her eyes, Jenna saw that he was holding a packet of fresh coffee in his free hand. 'Great.' Appalled to realise how close she'd come to making a fool of herself, she took the coffee from his hand and walked back into the kitchen. Keeping her back to him, she opened the drawers one by one until she found a knife.

He followed her. 'Does a conversation with your mother always upset you like this?'

'How do you know it was my mother?'

'I heard you say, "Hi, Mum".'

'Oh.' If he'd heard that, then he'd heard everything—which meant that there was no point in trying to keep the messy details of her life a secret. Jenna stared down at the knives in the drawer. 'Stupid, isn't it? I'm thirty-three. She shouldn't have an effect on me, but she does. She has a talent for tapping into my deep-seated fears—exposing thoughts I'm having but would never admit even to myself.' She closed her fingers around the handle of a knife. 'She thinks I've made the wrong decision, coming here.'

'And what do you think?'

'I don't know any more.' The tears were back in her eyes, blurring her vision. 'I thought I was doing the right thing. But now I'm worrying that what's right for me might be wrong for Lexi. I've uprooted her. I've dragged her away from everything familiar. We had to leave our home, but I didn't have to come this far away—' Taking the knife from the drawer, Jenna turned, wishing she hadn't said so much. 'Sorry. You wanted a cup of coffee, not a confessional. My call has held you up. If you want to change your mind and get on with your day, I quite understand.'

It was mortifying, having your life exposed in front of a stranger.

'I'm not leaving until I've had my coffee. I'm not safe to drive.' He leaned against the granite work surface, thumbs hooked in his pockets. 'Why did you have to move?'

'I'm divorced.' There seemed no point in not being honest. Why keep it a secret?

It had happened. There was no going back. She had to get used to it.

The problem was that once people knew you were divorced, they inevitably wanted to know why.

Jenna stared at the coffee in her hand, trying not to think about the girl with the long legs and the blond hair who had been lying on her husband's desk having crazy, abandoned

242 SARAH MORGAN

sex. When had *she* ever had crazy, abandoned sex? When had *she* ever lost control? Been overwhelmed—?

'Careful! You're going to cut yourself—' A frown on his face, Ryan removed the knife from her hand. 'In fact you have cut yourself. Obviously this isn't a conversation to have while you're holding a sharp object. Let me look at that for you.'

Jenna watched as blood poured down her finger. 'Oh!'

Ryan took her hand and held it under the tap, cleaned it and then examined the cut. 'We need to find a plaster. Call me traditional, but I prefer milk in my coffee.' He was cool and calm, but Jenna was thoroughly embarrassed, and she tugged her hand away from his, dried it in a towel and applied pressure.

'Stupid of me. I don't know what I was thinking.'

'You were thinking of your ex-husband. Perhaps I should clear the knives out of the cutlery drawer.'

'You don't need to worry about me. I'm fine.'

'Obviously not, or your hand wouldn't be bleeding now. And no one emerges from divorce completely unscathed.'

'I didn't say I was unscathed, Dr McKinley. I said I was fine.'

'Ryan—' He handed her another piece of kitchen roll for her finger. 'Call me Ryan. Round here we tend to be pretty informal. Do you always pretend everything is OK when it isn't?'

'I'm just starting a new job. I don't want everyone knowing I have baggage.' She pressed her finger hard, trying to stop the bleeding, exasperated with herself. 'It won't affect my work.'

'No one is suggesting that it would. Everyone has baggage, Jenna. You don't have to wrap it up and hide it.'

'Yes, I do. For Lexi's sake. I've seen couples let rip at each other through their kids and there is no way I'm going to let that happen. I refused to let it be acrimonious. I refuse to be a bitter ex-wife.'

'So you grit your teeth and shed your tears in private?' Ryan took her hand and strapped a plaster to her finger.

'Something like that.' She'd bottled up the humiliation, the devastation, the sense of betrayal—the sense of failure. All those years people had been waiting for her to fail. And she'd failed in spectacular style.

Feeling the familiar sickness inside her, Jenna snatched her hand away from his. 'Sorry. I'm talking too much. If you're sure you still want it, I'll make you that coffee.'

'I'll make it. You press on that finger.'

Watching him perform that simple task with swift efficiency, Jenna couldn't help comparing him with Clive, who had never made her a cup of coffee in all the years they'd been together. 'Do you live far from the practice, Dr Mc— Ryan?'

'In the old lighthouse, three bays round from this one. You can walk there in twenty minutes along the coast path.'

Jenna remembered what Mrs Parker had said about him living like a hermit. 'The views must be fantastic. If I had a lighthouse, I'd have my bedroom right in the top so that I could look at the view.'

'Then we think alike.' He poured fresh coffee into two mugs. 'Because I have a three-hundred–and-sixty-degree view from my bedroom.'

For some reason Jenna had a vision of Ryan sprawled in bed, and she felt a strange flutter behind her ribs, like butterflies trying to escape from a net.

'Lucky you.' Her image of leaning against his shoulder for comfort morphed into something entirely different. Different and dangerous.

She stood up quickly. 'Why don't we drink this in the garden?' The fresh air would do her good, and the kitchen sud-

denly seemed far too small. Or maybe he seemed too big.
Something was definitely out of proportion.

'Why did you have to leave your home?' He followed
her outside and put the coffee down on the wooden table.
'Couldn't you have bought him out?'

'He sold the house.' She felt her hair lift in the breeze and
breathed in deeply, smelling the sea. 'He put it on the mar-
ket without even telling me. I was living there with Lexi,
and then one morning I woke up to find three estate agents
on my doorstep.'

'Did you get yourself a good lawyer?'

'Clive *is* a lawyer,' Jenna said wearily. 'And I didn't want
Lexi seeing her parents fighting. I wanted it to be as civilised
as possible.'

'Civilised isn't sending round estate agents with no warning.'

'I know. But if I'd created a scene it would have been worse
for Lexi. Apparently what he did was legal. I was only eighteen when we married—I didn't check whose name the house
was in. I didn't check a lot of things.'

'Legal, maybe—decent, definitely not.' His tone was hard
and there was a dangerous glint in his eyes. 'Does Lexi know
he made you sell?'

'Yes. I told her the truth about that. I'm not sure if that
was the right thing to do or not. She was already very angry
with Clive for going off with another woman. And furious
with me for choosing to relocate to Scotland.'

'Why *did* you choose Scotland?'

'Because it's a long way from London…' Jenna hesitated.
'Clive doesn't want Lexi around at the moment. He's living
the single life and he sees her as a hindrance. I thought it
would damage their relationship for ever if she found out he
doesn't want her there, so I picked somewhere so far away

it would be a logistical nightmare for her to spend time with him. I didn't want her having another reason to hate him.'

Ryan watched her for a long moment. 'No wonder you're exhausted. Lexi's a lucky girl, having a mother who cares as much as you do.'

'I don't know. Maybe I care too much. Maybe I'm protecting her too much. Or maybe I'm protecting myself. I don't want to admit that the man I was married to for fifteen years can behave like that. Anyway, this is a very boring for you.' Tormented by guilt, and depressed after the conversation with her mother, Jenna took a deep breath. 'Sorry. I'm lousy company, I know. Take no notice. I'm just tired after the journey. I'm sure you're really busy.'

'Why didn't your mother want you to come here?'

Jenna watched the sunlight spread across the pretty garden. 'She wanted us to move in with her. She said it would save money.'

'Save money, but not your sanity. I gather you resisted?'

'Yes. I thought we'd be better off having a fresh start, away from everyone. Clive has another woman. Actually, it turned out he had several women throughout our marriage…' Her face was scarlet. 'I was the last person to know. That's another reason I wanted to get away. That and the fact that the girl he's started seeing is twenty-two. It was really difficult for Lexi.'

'And you, I should imagine.'

She didn't even want to think about how she'd felt. 'The hardest thing was seeing Lexi so hurt. I thought if we moved here we'd be right away from it. I thought it would be good—but at the moment she just hates me for dragging her away from her friends. She's worried no one here will speak to her. And I have no idea why I'm telling you all this.'

'Because I asked. And don't worry about no one speaking to her. This is Glenmore,' Ryan said dryly. 'There aren't enough people here for anyone to be ignored. It's a small community.'

'I hope she doesn't get into any trouble.' Jenna stared over her shoulder towards the grassy hill where Lexi had disappeared. 'I think she's very vulnerable at the moment.'

'If it's any consolation, there are not a lot of places to find trouble here. Mrs Parker aside, the crime rate on Glenmore is very low. When we do have trouble it's almost always tourists and nothing serious. Nick Hillier, the island policeman, has a pretty boring job. If there's a group of tourists drunk on the beach then it's an exciting day for him. You have nothing to worry about.'

'I'm a mother. Worrying yourself to death is part of the package. It never changes. From the moment they're born, you're worrying. When they sleep you check them every five minutes to see if they're breathing. Once I even woke Lexi up in the night just to check she was alive. Can you believe that?'

His eyes amused, Ryan reached for his coffee. 'Our new mothers' group will love you. They talk about that sort of stuff all the time and I just nod sagely and say it's all normal.'

'But you're secretly thinking they're a bit odd?'

'Waking a sleeping baby? I have mothers tearing their hair out because the baby doesn't sleep, so, yes, it seems a bit odd to hear mothers worrying when the baby does sleep.'

'Once you have children you worry about everything, from sharp knives to global warming. And it doesn't stop.' Jenna shook her head, finding it a relief to talk to someone. He was a good listener. 'Will they fall off that bike they're riding? Will they remember to look both ways when they cross the road? You want them to be polite to people, and then you're worried they'll be too polite and might go off with some stranger because they don't want to give offence–'

'Jenna, relax! You're going to give yourself a nervous

breakdown and you haven't even unpacked yet. You need to learn to chill.'

'Chill? What's that?' Jenna rolled her eyes in self-mockery. 'I don't know how to chill. But at work I'm sane, I promise. You must be wondering why on earth you gave me a lift. And a job.'

'Your job is safe. I can promise you that.'

'There's no such thing as safe.' She rubbed her finger over the table, following the grain of the wood. 'A year ago I had a husband, a home and a job. I lost all three.'

He was silent for a long moment. 'And now you have a home and a job again.'

There was something in his voice that made her look at him—made her wonder what personal trauma had driven him to this island.

'What I want is for Lexi to be happy.' Feeling calmer than she'd felt for ages, Jenna slipped off her shoes and curled her toes into the grass. 'I'm hoping that this will be a fresh start. I want it to feel like home.'

'If you need any help turning it into a home, give me a shout.' Ryan checked his watch and rose to his feet. 'I'm pretty good with a toolbox. Do you want any help unpacking? Is any of your furniture coming over?'

'No. No furniture.' Clive had claimed the furniture and all the belongings they'd collected over fifteen years of marriage. She hadn't had the strength to argue. She'd packed her clothes, a few books and not much else. 'I need to go shopping—oh, you said someone had stocked the place already?'

'When Evanna told the town meeting that you were coming, everyone from the village contributed.'

Jenna blinked. 'A group of people sat down and discussed my shopping list?'

'There's not a lot going on around here when the nightclubs are closed.'

'That's really kind.' Touched, Jenna made a mental note to thank everyone. 'Perhaps you could tell me the names. Then I can work out how much I owe everyone and pay them back.'

Ryan gave a faint smile, rolling up his shirtsleeves, revealing arms as strong as his shoulders. 'Oh, you'll pay. Don't worry about it. Everyone will claim a favour from you at some point. Usually at the most awkward, embarrassing moment, because that's how it works around here. One minute you're buying yourself a loaf of bread and the next you're giving an opinion on someone's rash.' He stood up. 'If we can do anything to help you settle in faster, let us know. The key to the back door is in the top drawer in the kitchen. It can be temperamental. If it jams, jiggle it slightly in the lock. And the shower turns cold if someone turns on a tap in the kitchen.'

'You know this house?'

'I stayed here for a few nights before I completed the sale on the lighthouse.'

'Oh.' Jenna had a disturbing image of him walking around the kitchen—showering in the bathroom. Naked.

Oh, God, she was losing it.

He raised an eyebrow. 'Are you all right?'

'Absolutely. How long should it take Lexi to get to the top and back? When do I start worrying?'

'You don't.' Ryan looked at the grassy ridge. 'She's on her way down now. I'll leave you to it. Surgery isn't until four. You can have a few hours to settle in. Spend some time together.'

'Yes.' Conscious that Lexi was approaching, Jenna lost her sense of calm. 'Thanks for the lift. And thanks for listening.'

He gave a brief nod and strolled out of her gate towards the sleek sports car that had transported her and her luggage from the surgery to the cottage. Without pausing in his stride, he exchanged a few words with Lexi as she sauntered past.

Watching anxiously from the garden, Jenna couldn't hear what he said, but whatever it was had Lexi smiling and that was an achievement in itself. Bracing herself for more complaints about her new home, she smiled at her daughter. 'Did you get a signal?'

'Yes, but everyone was out. Or maybe they're all still asleep after a night clubbing. Lucky them.' Lexi glanced over her shoulder as the sports car growled its way up the road away from them. 'What was he doing here, Mum?'

'He gave us a lift, remember?'

'An hour and a half ago.'

An hour and a half? Was that how much time had passed? Startled, Jenna glanced at her watch. 'Well—we were talking.'

'About what?' Lexi stared at her suspiciously and Jenna felt herself blush.

'About work,' she said firmly. 'I'm new to this practice, remember?'

'Oh. Right. I thought for one awful minute you—' She broke off and Jenna stared at her, heart thumping.

'What?'

'Nothing.' The girl gave a careless shrug, but Jenna knew exactly what she'd been thinking— *That her mother had been showing interest in a man.*

Jenna walked back into the cottage, feeling the burden of responsibility settle on her like a heavy weight. Whatever happened, she mustn't do anything to make her daughter feel more insecure than she already did.

'Dr McKinley was telling me that he lives in a lighthouse.'

'Dr McKinley is really hot.'

'Lexi! You're fifteen years old.' Appalled, Jenna cast a look at her daughter, but Lexi had her head in the fridge.

'Nearly sixteen. Old enough to know when a man is hot. Don't worry—I don't expect you to understand. You wouldn't know a good-looking man if you fell over him.' She pulled some cheese out of the fridge and then noticed the empty mugs on the kitchen table. Suddenly the tension was back. 'You invited him in for coffee?'

No, he'd invited himself in for coffee. 'He was up all night with patients.' Jenna adopted a casual tone. 'He was tired. It was the least I could do after he'd helped us.'

'Oh, Mum—' Lexi rolled her eyes, visibly cringing. 'Poor guy, being trapped by someone desperate divorcee. I suppose he was too polite to refuse.'

Wondering if Ryan saw her as old and desperate, Jenna picked up the empty mugs and washed them by hand. 'Of course he was being polite.' She didn't need her daughter to tell her that. 'I'm going to spend a few hours unpacking before I do the clinic this afternoon. Come and see your bedroom.'

They wandered upstairs and Lexi stared into the pretty bedroom. It had been decorated in keeping with the beach setting, with white New England furniture. A rug with bold blue and white stripes sat in the centre of the white floorboards. 'This is mine?'

'Yes. We can put your duvet cover on the bed and—'

'Sorting out the bed isn't going to make this my home.'

'Home is where family is,' Jenna said softly, 'and I'm here with you.' She felt a pang as she saw the vulnerability in Lexi's eyes.

'Well, that doesn't mean anything does it?' Her tone was flippant. 'I mean—Dad just walked out. What's stopping you doing the same?'

'I'm not going to walk out, Lexi. Not ever.' Jenna sank onto the edge of the bed, wanting to reassure her daughter. 'I know how difficult this has been for you—'

'No, you don't! You haven't got a clue—you have no idea how embarrassing it is that my Dad is having sex with a girl not much older than me!' Her voice rose. 'It's gross!'

Jenna resisted the temptation to agree. 'I told you—adults have relationships, Lexi.'

'*You* were in a relationship,' Lexi hissed. 'With each other. Marriage is supposed to be for ever—isn't that what you taught me?'

Jenna bit her lip. 'Ideally, yes.'

'So why didn't you try and fix it with Dad?'

'He didn't want to fix it. And—' Jenna thought about everything that had happened. *The way he'd treated her.* 'Not everything can be fixed.'

'Well, don't tell me you know how I feel, because you have no idea.' Lexi flounced out of the room and locked herself in the bathroom.

Jenna flopped onto the bed, feeling wrung-out and exhausted.

It was will-power that drove her downstairs to fetch the suitcases. Will-power that made her unpack methodically, finding homes for her pathetically small number of belongings. Unfortunately her will-power wasn't strong enough to stop her from thinking about Ryan McKinley.

It was only when she was hanging her clothes in her wardrobe that she realised that they'd spent an hour and a half together and he'd told her nothing about himself.

Nothing at all.

CHAPTER FOUR

JENNA leant her bike against the wall near the quay, waving to Jim the ferryman.

'Morning, Nurse Jenna. Finished your morning clinic?' A grey haired lady with a stick ambled past her on the pavement and Jenna smiled.

'Yes, all done, Mrs Hampton. How's the hip?'

'It's a miracle. I've had my first good night's sleep for four years. I was dreading the operation, if I'm honest—probably wouldn't have gone ahead with it if Dr McKinley hadn't encouraged me.'

'Nurse Jenna?' Someone touched her arm. 'Sorry to bother you—'

The impromptu conversations continued, so that by the time she'd walked along South Quay and up to the row of terraced houses that overlooked the water she was ten minutes late.

Ryan was already there and glancing at his watch, a brooding frown on his handsome face.

Jenna quickened her pace and arrived breathless, although whether that was from rushing the last few metres or from the sight of him, she wasn't sure. After two weeks working alongside him she knew that her body did strange things when Ryan was near. It didn't matter that they kept every exchange strictly professional. That didn't alter the chemistry. She hadn't said anything, and neither had he, but they both knew it was there.

Funny, Jenna mused, that she could even recognise chemistry when she'd been with one man all her life. 'I'm so sorry I'm late—I was waylaid.'

'You did a clinic on the quay?'

'How did you guess?' Laughing, Jenna removed the clip from her hair. Smoothing her hands over her curls, she twisted it into a thick rope and secured it firmly. 'There was a strong wind on the coast road. I must look as though I've been dragged through a hedge backwards.'

His eyes moved from her face to her hair. 'That isn't how you look.'

Colour stung her cheeks and she felt a shaft of awareness pierce low in her pelvis. 'Did you know Abby Brown is pregnant? I saw her eating a double chocolate fudge sundae in Meg's Café to celebrate.'

Ryan gave a wry smile. 'Let's hope she doesn't keep that up throughout the pregnancy. Are you ready?' But before he could press the doorbell the door opened and a woman stood there, a baby in her arms and a harassed look on her face. 'Hello, Elaine.'

'Oh, Dr McKinley—come on in.' The woman stood to one side and almost tripped over the dog which was bouncing in the hallway. As his tail hit the umbrella stand flying, the woman winced. 'Whatever possessed me to say yes to a dog? Not only does he make Hope's asthma worse, he knocks everything over.'

'He's beautiful.' Jenna bent down and made a fuss of the dog, and the animal leaped up and tried to lick her face, sensing an ally.

'Sorry—we've failed to teach him any manners.'

'I don't mind.' Giggling, Jenna pushed the dog down.
'What's his name?'

'We haven't decided—at the moment he's just called
Black.'

Jenna tried to look stern. 'Sit!'

Black sat, and Ryan lifted an eyebrow. 'That's the first
time I've seen that animal do as it's told.'

Elaine was astonished. 'You're so good with dogs! Do you
have your own?'

'No.' Jenna stared at the black Labrador, who stared back,
tongue lolling, tail wagging over the floor. It was a long time
since anyone had looked at her with such adoration and un-
questioning trust. 'I don't have a dog of my own.'

A family, she thought, didn't have to be a mother, a father
and two children.

'You should think about getting one—you're obviously
good with animals.' Elaine ushered them into the living room.
'Hope's on the sofa. She's had a much better night. We kept
Black locked in the garden shed, and I vacuumed all the dog
hairs this morning, but I haven't quite got my head round taking him back to the home.'

Jenna followed Ryan into the sitting room and noticed that
the little girl's face brightened when she saw him.

'Dr Mac—I've been eating ice cream and jelly.'

'For breakfast?' Ryan pulled a face and sat down next to
the child. He admired her doll, had a solemn conversation
about which outfit she ought to wear for the day, and then
pulled out his stethoscope. 'Can I listen to your chest?'

'It's all better.'

'So I hear. That's good. Can I listen?'

'OK.' With a wide smile, the little girl lay back on the
sofa and waited.

His hands infinitely gentle, Ryan listened to her breathing, and watching him with the child made Jenna's breath

catch. He focused entirely on the little girl, listening to every word she said as if she were the most important person in the room. 'I've been thinking about the attack she had, Elaine.' He folded the stethoscope and slid it back into his bag. 'You say she's using a normal inhaler, is that right?'

'Yes.'

'I think that might be the problem. I want to try her with a spacer—it's a device that relies less on technique, which is very useful for younger children. It makes sure they inhale the complete dose. To see you're taught to use it properly I've brought Nurse Jenna along with me.' Ryan gave a self-deprecating smile. 'I'm the first to admit that training children in inhaler technique probably isn't my forte, so I've called in the experts. Jenna used to do it all the time in her last job.'

Jenna removed the spacer from her bag and showed Hope's mother how it worked, explaining exactly what she had to do. 'It's really that simple.'

'She's due a dose now,' Elaine said. 'Could you check we do it right?'

Jenna watched, made a few suggestions, and explained to Hope exactly why it was important for her to take the drug.

'I breathe in that space thing every time?'

'Every time.'

'If I do that can I keep Black?'

Elaine sighed. 'No, sweetie. Black has to go.'

Hope's eyes filled with tears. 'But I love him. I can't send him back to that horrid place. I made him a promise. I promised him he had a home now.'

Feeling tears in her own eyes, Jenna blinked rapidly, feeling every bit of Elaine's anguish as a mother.

Elaine sank onto the sofa and shook her head. 'I have to take him back, Hope.' Her voice cracked. 'We can't keep him here. I can't risk going through what I went through the other night with you. I know it's hard, but we have no choice.'

'But I promised him he'd have a home and be loved.' Hope was sobbing now, great tearing sobs that shook her tiny body. 'I promised him, Mummy, and I can't break a promise. He'll be all on his own again. He'll think no one loves him.'

'I'll have him.' Jenna blurted the words past the lump in her throat and then stood in stunned silence, absorbing two things. Firstly, that she'd just got herself a dog, and secondly that making that decision had felt incredibly liberating.

For once she'd thought about herself. Not Clive. Not her mother. Herself.

Realising that everyone was looking at her, she shrugged. 'I'd like to have him. Really.' She looked at Hope. 'And I'll love him and give him a good home. So you won't have broken your promise...'

A tearful Elaine exchanged glances with Ryan. 'You want to take the dog?'

'I do.' Jenna spoke the words firmly, almost defiantly. Like a wedding ceremony, she thought with wry humour. *Do you take this dog...?* Only she knew without a flicker of doubt that the dog would never disappoint her. 'I really do. My daughter will be thrilled. And any time you want to come and see him, or meet up on the beach to throw a stick or two, you just bang on my front door...'

Ryan took a deep breath. 'Jenna, perhaps you should think about this—'

'I've thought about it for about thirty years. I've wanted a dog since I was a child.'

But her mother had said no. Then Clive had said no.

The advantage of being her own woman, in charge of her own life, was that there was no one to say no. And even if someone did say no, she wasn't sure she'd listen any more. She'd been weak, she realised. She'd allowed her own needs to come second. Her life had been about what Clive wanted. What Clive needed. And she'd been so busy keeping him

happy, determined to keep her marriage alive and prove her
mother wrong, that she'd stopped asking herself what she
wanted.

Jenna straightened her shoulders and stood a little taller.
'If you wouldn't mind holding on to Black for one more day. I
need to buy a book, check on the internet—make sure I know
what I'm doing. A patient I saw last week breeds Labradors—
I'd like to give her a ring and chat to her before I take Black.'
Suddenly she felt strong, and the feeling was good—almost
as if happiness was pouring through her veins.

Elaine gave a delighted laugh, relief lighting her face. 'If
you're sure?'

'I'm completely sure.' And she had no need to ask Lexi
what she thought. Lexi had wanted a dog all her life. 'I can
take him with me on my visits—tie him to my bicycle while
I go indoors. When I'm in clinic he can either play with
Evanna's dog, or just stay in our garden. I'll find someone
to build a fence.'

Elaine looked worried. 'Black rarely does what people
want him to do.'

'That's fine by me.' Jenna stroked her hand over the
dog's head, thinking of how often she'd disappointed her
own mother. 'Maybe he and I have something in common.
Welcome to rebellion.'

'That would be a good name,' Elaine laughed. 'Rebel. You
should call him Rebel.'

'Just hope he doesn't live up to his name,' Ryan said
dryly, closing his bag. 'There's a dog-training session every
Thursday night in the church hall. You might want to book
him in.'

'He ate your favourite shoes?' Laughing, Evanna leaned
across the table and helped herself to more lasagne. 'You
must have been mad.'

'With myself, for leaving them out.' Jenna was smiling too, and Ryan found it impossible not to watch her because the smile lit her face. He loved the dimple that appeared at the corner of her mouth, and the way her eyes shone when she was amused.

She was smiling regularly now, and the black circles had gone from under her eyes.

Extraordinary, he thought, how Glenmore could change people. 'What does Lexi think of him?'

'She adores him. She's the only teenager on Glenmore up at dawn during the summer holidays, and that's because she can't wait to walk him.'

Evanna cleared her plate and looked longingly at the food. 'Why am I so hungry? Do you think I could be pregnant again, Logan?'

It was only because he was looking at Jenna that Ryan saw her smile dim for a fraction of a second. Then she pulled herself together and joined in the conversation, her expression warm and excited.

'Do you think you could be? Charlie is two, isn't he? What a lovely age gap.'

Evanna agreed. 'I always wanted at least four kids.'

Ryan wondered if he was the only one who had noticed that Jenna had put her fork down quietly and was no longer eating.

Perhaps it was just that she found the whole happy family scene playing out in front of her emotionally painful. Or perhaps it was something else.

She'd been happy enough until Evanna had mentioned having more children.

Evanna lost the battle with her will-power and helped herself to more food. 'Weren't you tempted to have more children, Jenna?'

Sensing Jenna's tension, Ryan shifted the focus of the conversation away from her. 'If you're planning more children, you're going to have to build an extension on this house, Logan.'

'They can share a room,' Evanna said. 'If it's a girl, she can share with my Kirsty. If it's a boy, with Charlie.'

She and Logan spun plans while Jenna relocated her food from one side of her plate to the other.

It was the question about children that had chased away her appetite, Ryan thought grimly, reaching for his wine. And now he found himself wondering the same as Evanna. Why hadn't she had more children? She clearly loved being a mother.

Evanna heaped seconds onto everyone's plate except Jenna's. 'Aren't you enjoying it, Jenna?'

Jenna looked up and met Ryan's gaze.

They stared at each other for a moment, and then she gave a faltering smile and picked up her fork. 'It's delicious.' With a determined effort she ate, but Ryan knew she was doing it not because she was hungry, but because she didn't want to hurt Evanna's feelings. She was that sort of person, wasn't she? She thought about other people. Usually to the exclusion of her own needs.

He'd never actually met anyone as unselfish as her.

He felt something punch deep in his gut.

'Ryan—you have to fill those legs and wide shoulders with something.' Evanna pushed the dish towards Ryan but he held up a hand.

'Preferably not adipose tissue. I couldn't eat another thing, but it was delicious, thanks. I ought to be on my way.' Sitting here watching Jenna was doing nothing for his equilibrium.

Why had he accepted Evanna's invitation to dinner?

Over the past weeks he'd made sure he'd avoided being in a social situation with Jenna, and he had a feeling she'd been doing the same. And yet both of them had said yes to Evanna's impromptu invitation to join them for a casual supper.

'You can't go yet.' Evanna's eyes flickered to Jenna. 'Finish telling us about dog-training.'

It occurred to Ryan that the supper invitation probably hadn't been impromptu. Watching Evanna draw the two of them together, he had a sense that she'd planned the evening very carefully.

'The dog-training is a failure.' Jenna finished her wine. 'I really ought to go. Lexi was invited out to a friend's house, and she's taken Rebel, but she'll be back soon. I want to be there when they drop her home. I don't like her coming back to an empty house.'

Ryan poured himself a glass of water. 'I saw her eating fish and chips on the quay with the Harrington twins last week. She's obviously made friends.'

'Yes.' This time Jenna's smile wasn't forced. 'People have been very welcoming. There's hardly an evening when she's in.'

Which must mean that Jenna was often alone.

Ryan frowned, wondering how she spent her evenings.

Was she lonely?

He realised suddenly just how hard this move must have been for Jenna. Her relationship with her mother was clearly strained and her husband had left her. She'd moved to an area of the country where she knew no one, taken a new job and started a new life. And her only support was a teenager who seemed to blame her for everything that had gone wrong. And yet she carried on with quiet dignity and determination.

Unsettled by just how much he admired her, he stood up. 'I need to get back. I have things to do.'

Like reminding himself that the worst thing you could do after a relationship went wrong was dive into another relationship. That was the last thing Jenna needed right now. As for him—he had no idea what he needed.

'You can't possibly leave now! I made dessert—' Evanna glanced between him and Jenna and then cast a frantic look at Logan, who appeared oblivious to his wife's efforts to keep the two of them at her table.

'If Ryan has things to do, he has things to do.'

'Well, obviously, but—I was hoping he'd give Jenna a lift.'

'I'll give Jenna a lift if she wants one,' Logan said, and Evanna glared at her husband.

'No! You can't do it, you have that—thing—you know...' she waved a hand vaguely '...to fix for me. It needs doing—urgently.'

'Thing?' Logan looked confused, and Ryan gave a half-smile and strolled to the door, scooping up his jacket on the way. If Evanna had hoped for help in her matchmaking attempts then she was going to be disappointed.

'I don't need a lift,' Jenna said quickly. 'I brought my bike. I'll cycle.'

She was keeping her distance, just as he was. Which suited him.

Unfortunately it didn't suit Evanna.

'You can't cycle! It's late. You could be mugged, or you might fall into a ditch.'

'It isn't that late, and if I don't cycle I won't be able to get to work tomorrow. My bike won't fit into Ryan's car.' Ever practical, Jenna stood up. 'I hadn't realised how late it was. Supper was delicious, Evanna. Are you sure I can't wash up?'

'No—the dishwasher does that bit...' Evanna looked crestfallen, but Jenna appeared not to notice as she dropped to her knees to hand a toy to Charlie, the couple's two-year-old son.

Catching the wistful look on her face, Ryan felt something tug inside him. He found her kindness as appealing as the length of her legs and the curve of her lips.

As she walked past him to the door he caught her eye and she blushed slightly, said another thank-you to Evanna and Logan and walked out of the house, leaving the scent of her hair trailing over his senses.

By the time Ryan had said his farewells and followed her out of the house Jenna was fiddling with her bike, head down. Something about the conversation had upset her, he knew that. He also knew that if he delved into the reason he'd probably upset her more. He strolled across to her, his feet crunching on the gravel. 'Are you sure you don't want a lift home?'

'Positive. I'll be fine, but thanks.' She hooked her bag over the handlebars and Ryan noticed that her movements were always graceful, fluid. Like a dancer.

'Mrs Parker was singing your praises this week.'

'That's good to hear.' Smiling, she pushed a cycle helmet onto her head and settled onto the bike. 'Under that fierce exterior she's a sweet lady. Interesting past. Did you know she drove an ambulance during the war?'

'No. Did she tell you that during one of your afternoon tea sessions?'

'She told you about that?' Jenna fastened the chin strap. 'I call in sometimes, on my way home. I pass her front door.'

And he had a feeling she would have called in even if it hadn't been on her way home. The fact that she had time for everyone hadn't gone unnoticed among the islanders. 'Her leg is looking better than it has for ages. I suspect it's because you're nagging her to wear her stockings.'

'It isn't easy when the weather is warm. She needs a little encouragement.'

'So you've been stopping by several times a week, encouraging her?'

'I like her.'

They were making conversation, but he knew she was as aware of him as he was of her.

Looking at her rose-pink mouth, he wondered if she'd had a relationship since her husband.

'Evanna upset you this evening.'

Her gaze flew to his. Guarded. 'Not at all. I was a little tired, that's all. Rebel sometimes wakes me up at night, walking round the kitchen. I'm a light sleeper.'

Ryan didn't push it. 'I walk on the beach most mornings. If you want help with the dog-training, you could join me.'

'I'll remember that. Thanks.' She dipped her head so that her face was in shadow, her expression unreadable. 'I'll see you tomorrow, Ryan.'

He was a breath away from stopping her. A heartbeat away from doing something about the chemistry they were both so carefully ignoring.

What would she do if he knocked her off her bike and tumbled her into the heather that bordered Evanna's garden?

'Goodnight.' He spoke the word firmly and then watched as she cycled away, the bike wobbling slightly as she found her balance.

He was still watching as she vanished over the brow of the hill into the dusk.

CHAPTER FIVE

'Two salmon fillets, please.' Jenna stood in the fishmonger's, trying to remember a time when she'd bought food that wasn't shrink-wrapped and stamped with a date. And she'd never bought fish. Clive had hated fish.

Was that why she now ate fish three times a week?

Was she being contrary?

Eyeing the alternatives spread out in front of her, she gave a faint shrug. So what if she was? The advantage of being single was that you could live life the way you wanted to live it.

She had a dog and a garden, and now she was eating fish.

'Just you and the bairn eating tonight, then?' Hamish selected two plump fillets, wrapped the fish and dropped it into a bag.

'That's right.' How did anyone have a secret life on Glenmore? After only a month on the island, everyone knew who she was. And what she ate. And who she ate it with. Strangely enough, she didn't mind.

'How was your dinner with Dr McKinley?'

All right, maybe she minded.

Wondering if the entire island was involved in the matchmaking attempt, Jenna struggled for an answer. 'Dinner was casual. With Evanna and Logan. Just supper—nothing per-

sonal.' She cringed, knowing she sounded as though she had
something to hide. 'How's Alice doing?' Changing the subject quickly, she tried to look relaxed.

'Still rushing around. I say to her, "Rest, for goodness'
sake." But does she listen?' Hamish added a bunch of fresh
parsley to the bag. 'No, she doesn't. That's women for you.
Stubborn. Alice would die if it meant proving a point.'

'Well, I saw her in clinic yesterday and the wound was
healing nicely, so I'm sure she isn't going to die any time
soon.' Jenna dug her purse out of her bag. 'How much do I
owe you?'

'Nothing.' His weathered brow crinkled into a frown as
he handed over the bag. 'As if I'd take money after what
you did for my Alice. I said to her, "It's a good job you fell
outside Nurse Jenna's house, otherwise it would have been
a different story." You sorted her out, fed her, had a lovely
chat.' He glanced up as the door opened behind her and a
bell rang. 'Morning, Dr McKinley. Surf's up for you today.
They had the lifeboat out this morning—two kids in trouble
on the rocks round at the Devil's Jaws. Place is roped off,
but they climbed over.'

Jenna froze. He was behind her? She'd thought about him
all night—thought about the way he'd watched her across the
table. He'd made her so nervous she hadn't been able to eat.
And he'd noticed that she wasn't eating.

Adopting her most casual expression, she turned and
looked.

He was standing in the doorway, a sleek black wetsuit
moulding itself to every muscular dip and curve of his powerful shoulders.

The bag of salmon slipped from her fingers and landed
with a plop on the tiled floor.

Hamish cleared his throat pointedly and Jenna stooped to
retrieve her bag, her face as red as a bonfire. 'Good morn-

ing, Dr McKinley.' She turned back to the fish counter and developed a sudden interest in the dressed crab that Hamish had on display as she tried to compose herself. Over the past few weeks she'd had plenty of practice. In fact she was proud of how controlled she was around him.

They worked together every day, but so far she'd managed not to repeat any of the embarrassing sins she'd committed on her first day, like staring at his mouth. Even during dinner last night she'd managed to barely look at him.

And if she occasionally thought about how his hands had felt on her shoulders that day in her kitchen—well, that was her secret. A girl could dream, and she knew better than anyone that there was a world of difference between dreams and reality.

Jenna continued to stare at the crab. It was a shock to discover that, having thought she'd never trust a man again, she could actually find one attractive. But even if she could trust a man, the one thing she couldn't trust was her feelings. She knew she was hurt. She knew she was angry. And she knew that she was lonely for adult company.

This would be a bad, bad time to have a relationship even if one was on offer. Which it clearly wasn't—because, as Lexi was always telling her, she was past it. Why would Ryan want a relationship with someone like her?

'Thought I'd save you a journey and drop off that prescription.' Ryan handed it to Hamish. 'Did you know that crab personally, Jenna? You've been staring at him for the past five minutes.'

Jenna looked up, her inappropriate thoughts bringing the colour rushing to her cheeks. 'He has the same complexion as my first cousin.'

The corners of his mouth flickered. 'Yes? I can recommend a cream for that condition.'

She felt the breath catch in her throat because his smile was so sexy, and there was that unmistakable flash of chemistry that always occurred when they were together.

Imagining what it would be like to kiss a man like him, Jenna stared at him for a moment and then turned back to the crab, telling herself that even if things had been different she'd never have been sophisticated enough to hold a man like him. Ryan McKinley might be working on Glenmore, but she recognised a high-flier when she saw one. He was like one of those remote, intimidating consultants who strode the corridors of the hospital where she'd trained. Out of her league.

Hamish exchanged a look with Ryan and raised his eyebrows. 'You want to take a closer look at that crab?'

'No.' Flustered, Jenna pushed her hair out of her eyes. 'No, thanks— I— But it does look delicious.' Oh, for goodness' sake. What was the matter with her? Lexi was right— she was desperate. And she needed to leave this shop before she dropped her salmon a second time. Smiling at Hamish, she walked towards the door.

'Wait a minute, Nurse Jenna.' Hamish called after her. 'Has Dr McKinley asked you to the beach barbecue? Because if he hasn't, he's certainly been meaning to.'

Did everyone on Glenmore interfere with everyone else's lives?

Jenna looked at Ryan, who looked straight back at her, his expression unreadable.

Realising that Hamish had put them both in an impossible position, Jenna was about to formulate a response when Ryan straightened.

'It's on Saturday. In aid of the lifeboat. You should come.'

Knowing he'd only invited her because Hamish had pushed him, Jenna shook her head. 'I'm busy on Saturday.'

Hamish tutted. 'How can you be busy? Everything shuts early. Everyone on the island will be there. There's nothing else to do. Young thing like you needs a night out. You've done nothing but work since the day you stepped off that ferry.'

A night out?

When she finally felt ready for a night out it wouldn't be with a man like Ryan McKinley. When and if she did date a man again, she'd date someone safe and ordinary. Someone who didn't make her tongue knot and her insides turn to jelly. And preferably someone who didn't put her off her food.

He was watching her now, with that steady gaze that unsettled her so much. 'The islanders hold it every year, to raise funds for the lifeboat and the air ambulance. You're supposed to bring a dish that will feed four people. And wear a swimming costume.'

'Well, that's the end of that, then.' Somehow she kept it light. 'I can bring a dish to feed four people, but I don't own a swimming costume.'

'Swim naked,' Hamish said. 'Been done before.'

'And the culprits spent the night sobering up in one of Nick's four-star cells,' Ryan drawled, a sardonic gleam in his eyes. 'It's a family event. You can buy a costume from the Beach Hut, four doors down from here.'

Jenna had been into the Beach Hut twice, to buy clothes for Lexi. She hadn't bought anything for herself. 'Well—I'll think about it, thanks.'

Hamish scowled. 'You *have* to go. Isn't that right, Dr McKinley?'

Ryan was silent for a moment. 'I think Jenna will make her own decision about that.'

Jenna flushed. He wasn't going to coerce her. He wasn't going to tell her whether she should, or shouldn't go. He was leaving the choice up to her.

And that was what she did now, wasn't it? She made her own choices.

She decided whether she owned a dog and whether she was going to eat fish.

She shivered slightly, barely aware of the other customers who had entered the shop. She was only aware of Ryan, and the multitude of confusing feelings inside her. If she had to make a decision, what would it be?

She wanted to ask him whether he wanted her to go. She wanted to apologise for the fact that the islanders were match-making. She wanted him to know it had nothing to do with her.

Hideously embarrassed, she muttered that she'd think about it and walked out of the shop, her cheeks flushed.

It was crazy to feel this way about him, Jenna thought faintly. A man like him wasn't going to be interested in a divorced woman with a teenage daughter. And anyway, for all she knew he could be involved with someone. She couldn't imagine that a man like him could possibly be single.

Frustrated with herself, she hurried to her bike. She had to stop thinking about him. Even if he were interested in her, she wouldn't follow it through. For a start being with him would make her so nervous she wouldn't be able to eat a morsel, and to top it off Lexi was only just starting to settle into her new life. She could just imagine her daughter's reaction if her mother started seeing a man.

Thinking about Ryan occupied her mind for the cycle home, and she was still thinking about him as she propped her bike against the wall of the cottage and picked some flowers from the garden.

She walked into the kitchen to find Lexi sprawled on the kitchen floor, playing with Rebel.

Jenna put the flowers in a vase. 'How was the archaeology dig today?' Despite her complaints, it had taken Lexi only a matter of days to settle in and start enjoying herself. 'Did you have fun?'

'Yeah. Fraser found a piece of pot—everyone was really excited. I'm going to meet him for a walk on the beach later. I'll take Rebel. What time are we eating? I'm starving.'

Fraser? Lexi wanted to go for a walk on the beach with a boy?

'We're eating in about twenty minutes. So...' Retrieving the salmon fillets from her bag, Jenna tried to keep her voice casual. 'You haven't mentioned Fraser before. Is he nice?'

'He has a nose ring, five tattoos, long hair and swears all the time.' Lexi rubbed Rebel's glossy fur with her hands. 'You're going to love him—isn't she, Reb?'

With a wry smile, Jenna put the salmon under the grill. 'Lexi, you wait until you're a worried mother—'

'I'm not going to be like you. I'm going to trust my kids.'

Jenna sensed this was one of those moments when it was imperative to say the right thing. 'I trust you, Lexi,' she said quietly. 'You're a bright, caring, funny girl. But you're still a child—'

'I'm nearly sixteen—you're so over-protective.'

'I care about you. And you *are* still a child. Child going on woman, but still... I know all this has been hard on you. And being a teenager isn't easy.'

'What? You remember that far back?' But Lexi was smiling as she picked up Rebel's bowl. 'We're having fish again? I'm going to start swapping meals with the dog.'

'I thought you liked fish.'

'I do. But you never used to cook it in London. Now we have it almost every meal!'

'I didn't cook it in London because Dad hated it.' But Clive wasn't here now, and she was cooking what she wanted. And loving it, Jenna mused, mixing a teriyaki sauce to add to the salmon.

'Given that you're into all this healthy lifestyle stuff, I assume I *can* go for a walk on the beach with Fraser later?'

Jenna felt as though she was treading over broken glass. If she said no, she'd be accused of not trusting, and that could trigger a rebellious response. If she said yes, she'd worry all evening. 'Yes,' she croaked, washing a handful of tomatoes and adding them to the salad. 'All I ask is that you're home before dark.'

'Why? I can have sex in daylight just as easily as in the dark.'

Jenna closed her eyes. 'Lexi—'

'But I'm not going to. Credit me with some sense, Mum. You know I'm not going to do that. You've given me the sex, love, marriage talk often enough.'

'You've got it in the wrong order,' Jenna said weakly. 'And you've missed out contraception.' It was impossible not to be aware that Lexi was only a couple of years younger than she had been when she'd become pregnant.

Lexi rolled her eyes and then walked over and hugged her. 'Just chill, Mum.'

Astonished by the unexpected show of affection, Jenna felt a lump in her throat. 'That's nice. A hug.'

'Yeah—well, I'm sorry I was difficult about moving here. It's a pretty cool place. I didn't mean to be a nightmare.'

Jenna felt a rush of relief. 'You're not a nightmare, baby. I'm glad you're settling in.'

'It would be great if you could worry less.'

'It would be great if you could give me less to worry about.'

'OK. If I'm going to do something really bad, I'll warn you.'

'Lexi—about Fraser…'

'If you're going to talk to me about boys, Mum, don't waste your time. I probably know more than you anyway.'

Jenna blinked. That was probably true. She'd only ever had one boyfriend, and she'd married him at eighteen.

And he'd left her at thirty-two.

Lexi stole a tomato from the salad. 'We're just friends, OK? Mates. He's really easy to talk to. He really *gets* stuff. His dad—' She broke off and then shrugged. 'His dad walked out, too. When he was nine. That's why his mum came here.'

'Oh...'

What had happened to her had happened to millions of women around the world. She wasn't the only one in this situation. Lives shattered and were mended again, and she was mending, wasn't she? Slowly. She stared at the dog lying on her kitchen floor, and the bunch of flowers on her kitchen table. Life was different, but that didn't mean it wasn't good.

'You can go for a walk on the beach, Lexi.'

Lexi visibly relaxed. 'Thanks. We're just going to hang out, that's all. Fraser says there's really cool stuff on the beach once the tide goes out. He knows the names of everything. I feel like a real townie.'

'You'll have to teach me. Have they dug up anything else interesting at the castle yet?'

'Bits of stuff. They found these Viking combs—weird to think of Vikings combing their hair.'

'Perhaps their mothers nagged them,' Jenna said dryly, hugely relieved that Lexi appeared to be more like her old self. 'What's the castle like? I must go up there.'

'It's awesome. Fraser showed me this steep shaft into the dungeons. He fell down it a few years ago and had to have his head stitched up.'

'It sounds dangerous.'

'Only to you. You see danger everywhere.'

'I'm a mother. Worrying goes with the territory.'

'Fraser's mother doesn't fuss over him all the time. She just lets him live his life.'

Jenna bit her lip, trying not to be hurt, well used to being told what other mothers did. 'I'm letting you live your life. I'd just rather you didn't do it in a hospital or an antenatal clinic. Wash your hands, Lex—dinner is nearly ready.'

'Do you want me to lay the table or do drinks or something?'

Hiding her surprise, Jenna smiled at her. 'That would be a great help. There's lemonade in the fridge—Evanna gave it to us as a gift.'

'It's delicious. I had some at her house.' Lexi opened the fridge door again and pulled out the bottle. 'She makes it by the bucketload, all fresh lemons and stuff. She's a good cook. I told her you were, too. Are we going to the barbecue on Saturday, Mum?'

Still reeling from the compliment, Jenna turned the salmon. 'How do you know about the barbecue?'

'Fraser mentioned it.'

Fraser, Fraser, Fraser—

Still, at least Lexi seemed happy. Relieved, Jenna put the salmon on the plates. 'Do you want to go?'

'Why not? Might be a laugh.' Her eyes narrowed. 'How did *you* hear about the barbecue?'

'In the fishmonger's.' Jenna omitted to say who she'd bumped into there. 'It's amazing to be able to buy such fresh fish.'

'It's amazing what old people find exciting.' Lexi suppressed a yawn as she picked up her plate. 'Let's eat in the garden. So how many lives did you save today? Did you see Dr Hot?'

'Dr who?'

'Dr Hot. Ryan McKinley. I bet women who are perfectly well make appointments just to spend five minutes with him. Fraser says he's brilliant.'

Even at home there was no escape, Jenna thought weakly, taking her plate and following her daughter out into the sunshine.

She wasn't going to think of him as Dr Hot.

She really wasn't.

'She was playing on the deck with a water pistol and she slipped and crashed into the fence—the bruise is horrendous. I'm worried she's fractured her eye socket or something.' The woman's face was white. 'I tried to get an appointment with one of the doctors, but Dr McNeil is out on a call and Dr McKinley has a full list.'

Jenna gave her shoulder a squeeze. 'Let me take a look at it. If I think she needs to be seen by one of the doctors, then I'll arrange it. Hello, Lily.' She crouched down so that she was at the same level as the child. 'What have you been doing to yourself?'

She studied the livid bruise across the child's cheekbone and the swelling distorting the face. 'Was she knocked out?'

'No.' The woman hovered. 'I put an ice pack on it straight away, but it doesn't seem to have made a difference.'

'I'm sure it helped.' Jenna examined the child's cheek, tested her vision and felt the orbit. 'Can you open your mouth for me, Lily? Good girl—now, close—brilliant. Does that hurt?' Confident that there was no fracture, she turned to Lily's mother. 'I think it's just badly bruised, Mrs Parsons.'

'But she could have fractured it. Sorry—it isn't that I don't trust you.' The woman closed her eyes briefly. 'And I know I'm being anxious, but—'

'I know all about anxious. You don't have to apologise.' Seeing how distressed the mother was, and sympathising, Jenna made a decision. 'I'll ask Dr McKinley to check her for you. Then you won't be going home, worrying.'

'Would you?'

'I'll go and see if he's free—just wait one moment.' Giving Lily a toy to play with, Jenna left her room and walked across to Ryan just as the door to his consulting room opened and a patient walked out.

She paused for a moment, conscious that she hadn't seen him since Hamish had embarrassed them both the day before.

'Ryan?' Putting that out of her mind, Jenna put her head round the door. 'I'm sorry, I know you're busy...' And tired, she thought, looking at the shadows under his eyes. He worked harder than any doctor she'd ever met.

Or were the shadows caused by something else?

'I'm not busy—what can I do for you?' The moment he looked at her, Jenna felt her insides flip over.

'I have a patient in my room—I wondered if you could give me your opinion. The little girl is six—she's slipped and banged her face. The bruising is bad, but I don't think there's a fracture—there's no flattening of the cheek.'

Work always helped, she thought. After Clive had left, work had been her healing potion. It had stopped her thinking, analysing, asking 'what if?' And she'd discovered that if you worked hard enough, you fell into bed dog-tired and slept, instead of lying awake, thinking all the same things you'd been thinking during the day.

'Flattening of the cheek can be obscured by swelling—'

'It isn't that swollen yet. It only happened half an hour ago, and her mum put an ice pack on it immediately. I can't feel any defect to the orbit, and she can open and close her mouth without difficulty.'

'It sounds as though you're confident with your assessment.' His long fingers toyed with the pen on his desk. 'Why do you need me?'

'Because the mother is so, so worried. I thought some reassurance from you might help. I know what it's like to be a panicking mother.'

'Who is the patient?'

'Parsons?'

Ryan stood up. 'Lily Parsons? That explains why you have a worried mother in your room. Little Lily had a nasty accident a couple of years ago—almost died. She fell in deep water in the quay and a boat propeller caught her artery.'

'Oh, no—' Jenna lifted her hand to her throat, horrified by the image his words created. 'How did she survive that?'

'My predecessor, Connor McNeil—Logan's cousin—was ex-army. Trauma was his speciality, otherwise I doubt Lily would be with us today. She went into respiratory arrest, lost so much blood—'

'Were you here?'

'No. It was just before I arrived, but Connor's rescue has gone down in island folklore. Apparently Jayne totally flipped. She witnessed the whole thing—blamed herself for the fact that Lily had fallen in. The child was watching the fish, and a crowd of tourists queuing for the ferry bumped into her and she lost her balance.'

'Poor Jayne!' To stop herself looking at his mouth, Jenna walked back towards the door. 'All the more reason why you should reassure her.'

Without arguing, Ryan followed her into the room, charmed Jayne, made Lily laugh, and then checked the child's eye with a thoroughness that would have satisfied the most hyper-anxious mother.

Jenna watched, wondering why someone with his own trauma skills would give up a glittering career to bury himself on Glenmore.

Something must have happened.

Life, she thought, had a way of doling out grim surprises.

'You're right that there is no flattening of the cheek.' He addressed the remark to Jenna, gave the little girl a wink and strolled across the room to wash his hands. 'Jayne, I'm happy with her, but that bruising is going to get worse before it gets better, and so is the swelling. I'm guessing your worrying is

going to get worse before it gets better, too. I'll have a word
with Janet on Reception so that she knows to slot you in if
you feel worried and want me to take another look.'

'You don't want to X-ray her?'

'No. I don't think it's necessary.' Ryan dried his hands and
dropped the paper towel in the bin. 'Look, why don't you
bring her back to my surgery tomorrow morning anyway?
That will stop you having to look at her every five minutes
and decide whether you need to bring her back.'

Jayne Parsons gave a weak smile. 'You must think I'm a
total idiot.'

'On the contrary, I think you're a worried mum and that's
understandable.' Ryan scribbled a number on a scrap of paper.
'This is my mobile number. I drive past your house on the
way to and from the surgery—just give me a call if you're
worried and I can drop in. Take care, Lily.'

Mother and child left the room, more relaxed, and Jenna
stared at the door. 'Do you give your mobile number to every
anxious patient?'

'If I think they need the reassurance, yes. Glenmore is an
isolated island. It makes people more reliant on each other.
They're in and out of each other's lives.' He gave a faint smile.
'As I'm sure you've noticed.'

She swallowed. 'I'm sorry about Evanna and Hamish—'

'Why are you sorry? None of it is your fault.' Ryan sat
down at her desk and brought Lily's notes up on the computer
screen. 'They just can't help themselves. Matchmaking is like
eating and breathing to the people of Glenmore.'

'It happens a lot?'

'All the time—although I've pretty much escaped it up
until now. That's one of the advantages of being a doctor.
There are a limited number of people on this island who
technically aren't my patients.'

'I expect they'll back off soon.'

'I wouldn't count on it.' Ryan typed the notes with one finger. 'Do you want a lift to the beach barbecue? I could pick you up on my way past.'

'I haven't even decided if we're going.'

'If you don't go, they'll come and get you. Come. Lexi would enjoy it. All the teenagers go. She seems to have made friends. Whenever I see her, she's smiling.'

'Yes.' Jenna was starting to wonder whether there was something more to her daughter's sudden change of attitude. 'What do you know about a boy called Fraser?'

'Fraser Price?' Ryan stood up. 'He lives near you. Just along the beach. His mum is called Ailsa—she's a single parent. Diabetic. Why are you asking?'

Jenna chewed her lip. 'Lexi seems to like him—'

'And you're worrying that he has unsavoury habits?'

'I'm just worrying generally. In London, Lexi started mixing with the wrong crowd. She made a point of doing all the things she thought would upset me...'

'Why would she want to upset you?'

Jenna hesitated. 'She blames me for not trying to fix my marriage.'

'Did you want to fix it?'

Jenna thought about Clive and the scene in his office that day. *Thought about what she'd learned about her marriage.* 'No. Some things can't be fixed.' She had an urge to qualify that with an explanation, but realised that there was no way she could elaborate without revealing that her husband hadn't found her sexy. Somehow that was too humiliating. She turned away and put a box of dressings back into the cupboard. 'There's nothing to talk about. My marriage ended. It happens to thousands of people every day.'

And thousands of people got on with their lives, as she had done. Picking up the pieces, patching them together again into something different.

'Did you think about buying him out so that you could stay in the house?'

It was a practical question, typically male. 'I'm a nurse, Ryan, not a millionaire. London is expensive. And anyway, I didn't want to stay in that house. It was full of memories I didn't want. I knew if I'd stayed there I'd always be looking back. I wanted to move forward. He offered me a sum of money and I took it.'

'I'm guessing it wasn't a generous sum.' His eyes darkened, and she wondered why he'd be angry about something that wasn't his problem.

'He completely ripped me off.' Only now, after almost a year, could she say it without starting to shake with emotion. 'I was really stupid and naïve, but in my own defence I was in a bit of a state at the time. I was more wrapped up in the emotional than the practical. I shouldn't really have been negotiating a divorce settlement so soon after he'd walked out. There were some mornings when I couldn't bear to drag myself from under the duvet. If it hadn't been for Lexi I wouldn't have bothered. I left it to him to get the valuations. And he took advantage.' She lifted her chin. 'He used his friends—fiddled with the numbers and offered me a sum that was just about plausible. And I took it. So I'm to blame for being a push-over.'

'You weren't a push-over. You were in shock, and I'm guessing you just wanted it to end.'

'I didn't want it dragging on and hurting Lexi. The whole thing was very hard on her.' Jenna rubbed her hands up and down her arms. 'And she was so angry with me.'

He took a slow breath. 'You did a brave thing, coming here. Was it the right thing to do?'

She considered the question. 'Yes. Yes, it was. We're healing.' The discovery warmed her. 'The best thing I did was to get Rebel. Lexi adores him. So do I. And we love living in

the cottage. Having the beach on our doorstep is like heaven.
And I'm relieved Lexi is happy, although I'm worrying that
has something to do with her new friend.'

'I don't think you have to worry about Fraser. He's pretty
responsible.'

'Well, if he's the reason Lexi is happy, then I suppose he
has my approval.'

Ryan strolled towards the door. His arm brushed against
hers and Jenna felt the response shoot right through her body.
Seeing the frown touch his forehead, she wondered if he
did, too.

'Our receptionist Janet was saying how smoothly everything is running since you arrived. The islanders love you.'

'Everyone has been very kind.' She wondered why she felt
compelled to look at him all the time. If he was in the room,
she wanted to stare. Every bit of him fascinated her, from
his darkened jaw to his thick, lustrous hair. But what really
interested her was him. The man.

She wanted to ask why he'd chosen to come to Glenmore,
but there was something about him that didn't invite personal questions.

Respecting his privacy, she smiled. 'We'll see you at the
barbecue on Saturday.'

'Good.' He watched her for a long moment and she felt
that look all the way down to her bones.

'Thanks for seeing Lily.'

He stirred. 'You're welcome.'

The sun was just breaking through the early-morning mist
when she walked Rebel early the following day. The garden
gate no longer creaked, thanks to a regular dose of oil, and
Jenna paused for a moment to admire the pinks and purples
in her garden before walking along the sandy path that led
through the dunes to the beach. The stretch of sand was de-

serted and she slipped off her shoes and walked barefoot, loving the feel of the sand between her toes. Rebel bounded ahead, investigating pieces of seaweed and driftwood, tail wagging. Every now and then he raced back to her, sending water and sand flying.

Huge foaming breakers rolled in from the Atlantic, rising high and then exploding onto the beach with a crash and a hiss. Jenna watched as a lone surfer achieved apparently impossible feats in the deadly waves. Admiring his strength and the fluidity of his body, she gave herself a little shake and turned her attention to the beach. After twenty years of not noticing men, suddenly she seemed to do nothing else.

Seeing a pretty shell poking out of the sand, she stooped to pick it up. The pearly white surface peeped from beneath a layer of sand and she carefully brushed it and slipped it into her pocket, thinking of the chunky glass vase in her little bathroom, which was already almost full of her growing collection of shells.

She was pocketing her second shell when Rebel started to bark furiously. He sped across the sand towards the water just as the surfer emerged from the waves, his board under his arm.

Recognising Ryan, Jenna felt her heart bump hard against her chest and she forgot about shells. She should have known it was him from the visceral reaction deep in her stomach. It wasn't men in general she was noticing. It was just one man.

Without thinking, she dragged her fingers through her curls and then recognised the futility of the gesture. She was wearing an old pair of shorts and a cotton tee shirt. Running her fingers through her hair wasn't going to make her presentable. For a moment she regretted not spending a few moments in front of the mirror before leaving her cottage. Thinking of herself doing her morning walk in lipgloss and a pretty top made her smile, and she was still smiling when he ran up to her.

'What's funny?'

'Meeting someone else at this time of the morning.'

He put his surfboard down on the sand. 'It's the best time. I surf most mornings, but I've never seen you out before.' The wetsuit emphasised the width and power of his shoulders and she looked towards the waves, trying to centre herself.

'Normally I'm a little later than this but I couldn't sleep.' Because she'd been thinking about him. And then pushing away those thoughts with rational argument. But now those thoughts were back, swirling round her head, confusing her.

'You couldn't sleep?' His tone was amused. 'Maybe you were excited about the barbecue tomorrow.'

'That must have been it.' As Rebel bounded up to her, she sidestepped, dodging the soaking wet tail-wagging animal. 'Sit. *Sit!*' Ignoring her, Rebel shook himself hard and sprayed them both. 'Oh, you—! Rebel! I'm so sorry.'

'More of a problem for you than me. I'm wearing a wet-suit.' His eyes drifted to her damp tee shirt and lingered. 'Obviously the dog-training is progressing successfully.'

'It's a disaster. He obeyed me that day at Elaine's just to charm me into giving him a home. Since then he's been a nightmare.' Giggling and embarrassed, Jenna grabbed Rebel's collar and glared at him severely. 'Sit! Sit, Rebel. I said sit!'

The dog whimpered, his entire body wagging, and Ryan sighed.

'Sit!'

Rebel sat.

'OK—that's annoying.' Jenna put her hands on her hips. 'I've been working non-stop with him and you just say it once. What do you have that I don't?'

'An air of menace. You're kind and gentle. A dog can sense

you're soft-hearted. Especially a dog like Rebel, who has had his own way for far too long.'

'You think I'm a push-over?'

'I don't see you as tough and ruthless, that's true.'

Her heart was pounding as if she'd run the length of the beach. 'I'll have you know I'm stronger than I look!'

'I didn't say you weren't strong.' The pitch of his voice had changed. 'I know you're strong, Jenna. You've proved your strength over and over again in the last month. You've dragged up your roots and put them down somewhere new. That's never easy.'

His eyes were oceans of blue, waiting to draw her in and drown her.

The want inside her became a desperate craving, and when his arm curled around her waist and he drew her towards him she didn't resist. Her thinking went from clear to clouded, and she waited, deliciously trapped by the inevitability of what was to come. She watched, hypnotised, as he lowered his head to hers. His mouth was warm and skilled, his kiss sending an explosion of light through her brain and fire through her belly.

It should have felt wrong, kissing a man. But it felt right— standing here with his lips against hers and nothing around them but the sound and smell of the sea.

Jenna dug her fingers into the front of his wetsuit, felt the hardness of his body brush against her knuckles. The fire spread, licking its way through her limbs until she was unsteady on her feet, and his grip on her tightened, his mouth more demanding as they kissed hungrily, feasting, exploring, discovering.

Rebel barked.

Ryan lifted his mouth from hers, his reluctance evident in the time he took. Dazed and disorientated, Jenna stared up at him for a moment and then at his mouth.

Now she knew how it felt...

Rebel barked again and she turned her head, trying to focus on the dog.

'What's the matter with you?' Her voice was croaky and Ryan released her.

'People on the beach.' His voice was calm and steady. 'Clearly we're not the only early risers.'

'Obviously not.' She knew she sounded stilted but she had no idea what to say. Were they supposed to talk about it? Or pretend it had never happened? 'I should be getting home. Lexi will be waking up...' Feeling really strange, she lifted a shaking hand to her forehead. The kiss had changed everything. Her world had tilted.

'Jenna—'

'I'll see you tomorrow.'

His gaze was disturbingly acute. 'You'll see me at the surgery today.'

'Yes—yes, of course I will. That's what I meant.' Flustered, she called to Rebel, who was nosing something on the sand, apparently oblivious to the fact that his owner's life had just changed.

Ryan seemed about to say something, but the people on the beach were moving closer and he shook his head in exasperation. 'I've never seen anyone else on this beach at this hour.'

'It's a very pretty place.' Babbling, Jenna backed away. 'You'd better go and have a shower—warm up—you can't do a surgery in your wetsuit—I really ought to be going—' She would have tripped over Rebel if Ryan hadn't shot out a hand and steadied her. 'Thanks. I'll see you later.' Without looking at him, she turned and almost flew over the sand after Rebel, not pausing until she was inside the cottage with the door shut firmly behind her.

'Mum? What's the matter with you?' Yawning, Lexi stood there in tee shirt and knickers.

'I've been—' Kissed, Jenna thought hysterically. Thoroughly, properly, deliciously kissed. '—for a walk. On the beach. With Rebel.'

Lexi threw her an odd look. 'Well, of course with Rebel—who else?'

'No one else. Absolutely no one else.' She needed to shut up before she said something she regretted. 'You're up early.'

'I'm going over to Evanna's to give the children breakfast before I go to the dig. She has that appointment thing today on the mainland so she took the first ferry.'

'Yes, of course. I know. I remember.' Her lips felt warm and tingly, and if she really concentrated she could still conjure up the feel of his mouth against hers. 'I have to take a shower and get ready for work.'

'Are you all right? You look—different.'

She felt different.

Up until today she'd felt as though she was surviving. Now she felt as though she was living.

Everything was different.

CHAPTER SIX

Too dressy.

Too casual.

Too cold—

Jenna threw the contents of her wardrobe onto her bed and stared at it in despair. Was it really that hard to decide what to wear to a beach barbecue? It was so long since she'd been out socially she'd lost her confidence. But she knew that the real reason she couldn't decide what to wear was because Ryan would be there and she wanted to look her best. Without looking as though she'd tried too hard.

Infuriated with herself, she reached for the first skirt she'd tried on, slipped it over her head and picked a simple tee shirt to go with it. The skirt was pretty, but the tee shirt was plain—which meant that the top half of her was underdressed and the bottom half was overdressed.

Looking in the mirror, Jenna scooped up her hair and piled it on top of her head. Then she pulled a face and let it fall loose around her shoulders. She gave a hysterical giggle. Maybe she should wear half of it up and half of it down.

'Mum?'

Hearing Lexi's voice, Jenna jumped guiltily and scooped the discarded clothes from the bed. She was just closing the wardrobe door on the evidence of her indecision when Lexi sauntered into the room.

'Are you ready?'

'Nearly.' Jenna eyed the lipgloss that she'd bought. It was still in its packaging because she hadn't decided whether or not to wear it. 'I just need to do my hair.' Up or down?

'Can I go ahead? I'm meeting Fraser.'

'We'll go together,' Jenna said firmly. With no choice but to leave her hair down, she grabbed a cardigan and made for the stairs. 'I'd like to meet him.'

'We're just mates,' Lexi muttered, sliding her feet into a pair of pretty flip-flops. 'We're not quite at the "meet the parents" stage.'

Jenna picked up her keys and the bowl containing the strawberries. 'This is Glenmore. On an island this size you have no option but to meet the parents. Everyone meets everyone about five times a day.' She wished she hadn't left her hair down. It made her feel wild and unrestrained, and she wanted to feel restrained and together.

'Are you all right, Mum?'

'I'm fine. Why wouldn't I be?'

'I don't know…' Her phone in her hand, Lexi frowned. 'You just seem jumpy. Nervous. You've been acting really weird since yesterday.'

'Nervous? I have no reason to be nervous!'

'All right, calm down. I realise it's a big excitement for you, getting out for an evening. Don't be too embarrassing, will you?'

Jenna locked the door because she hadn't got out of the London habit. 'I'm meant to be the one saying that to you.'

'Going out with your mother would never happen in London. Just promise me that whatever happens you won't dance.'

* * *

Ryan watched her walk across the sand towards him.

She'd left her hair loose, the way she'd worn it on the day she'd arrived on the island.

Feeling the tension spread across his shoulders, he lifted the bottle of beer to his lips, thinking about the kiss. He hadn't intended to kiss her but the temptation had been too great, and now he couldn't get it out of his mind.

He wondered why this woman in particular should have such a powerful effect on him. Not for one moment did he think it was anything to do with her gorgeous curves—he'd met plenty of women with good bodies and none of them had tempted him past the superficial. But Jenna...

Maybe it was her generous smile. Or her air of vulnerability—the way she was so painfully honest about the things that had gone wrong in her life when most people just put up a front. Or the way she put herself last. Either way, she was sneaking under his skin in a way that should have set off warning bells.

If his aim was to protect himself, then lusting after a recently divorced single mother with a teenage daughter was probably the stupidest thing he'd ever done.

She was clearly desperately hurt after her divorce, and any relationship she entered into now would be on the rebound.

But his body wasn't listening to reason and he felt himself harden as he watched her approach. She'd dressed modestly, her summery skirt falling to her ankles, her tee shirt high at the neck. But the Glenmore breeze was designed to mock modesty and it flattened the skirt to her legs, found the slit and blew it gaily until the soft fabric flew into the air, revealing long slim legs and a hint of turquoise that looked like a swimming costume.

Ryan saw her clutch at the skirt and drag it back into position, her face pink as she pinned it down with her hand, defying the wind.

For a girl who was fresh out of the city, there was nothing city-slick about her. She was carrying a large flowery bag over one shoulder and she looked slightly uncertain—as if she wasn't used to large gatherings.

He was fully aware that she'd avoided him the day before at the surgery, going to great lengths to make sure they didn't bump into one another. Seeing her now, the emotion he felt was like a punch in the gut. He was attracted to her in a way he hadn't been attracted to a woman in years.

'She'd be perfect for you.' Evanna's voice came from behind him and he turned, keeping his expression neutral.

'You never give up, do you?'

'Not when I think something is worth the effort.' Evanna replied. 'Don't be angry with me.'

'Then don't interfere.'

'I'm helping.'

'Do you think I need help?'

'When you first came here, yes. You were so angry,' she said softly. 'I used to hear you sawing wood and banging nails. You swung that hammer as if you hoped someone's head was underneath it.'

Ryan breathed out slowly. 'I hadn't realised anyone witnessed that—'

'I came down to the lighthouse from time to time, trying to pluck up courage to ask you to join us for supper, but whenever I saw you your expression was so black and you were so dark and scary I lost my nerve.'

'I didn't know.' He'd been aware of nothing, he realised, but his own pain. 'So, have you become braver or am I less scary?'

Her smile was wise and gentle. 'You banged in a lot of nails.'

'I guess I did.' He respected the fact that she hadn't pushed him for the reason. She'd never pushed him. Just offered unconditional friendship. Humbled once again by the generosity of the islanders, he frowned. 'Evanna—'

'Just promise me that if I back off you won't let her slip through your fingers.'

'Life doesn't always come as neatly wrapped as you seem to think.'

'It takes work to wrap something neatly.' She stood on tiptoe and kissed his cheek. 'You've been here for two years. It's enough. Don't let the past mess up the future, Ryan.'

'Is that what I'm doing?'

'I don't know. Are you?'

Ryan thought about the kiss on the beach and the way he felt about Jenna. 'No,' he said. 'I'm not.'

He knew Jenna was nothing like Connie. And maybe that was one of the reasons he was so attracted to her.

'Is my wife sorting out your love-life?' Logan strolled over to them, Charlie on his shoulders.

'Who? Me?' Her expression innocent, Evanna picked up a bowl of green salad. 'Can you put this on the table, please? Next to the tomato salsa. I'm going to meet Jenna and make her feel welcome. She looks nervous. I'm sure she feels a bit daunted by the crowd.'

Ryan was willing to bet that her nerves had nothing to do with the crowd and everything to do with the kiss they'd shared. He'd flustered her.

He gave a faint smile. And he was looking forward to flustering her again.

'What does tomato salsa look like?' Logan's expression was comical as he steadied Charlie with one hand and took the salad from Evanna with the other. 'Is that the mushy red stuff?' Leaning forward, he kissed her swiftly on the mouth and Evanna sighed and kissed him back.

Watching them together, seeing the soft looks and the way

they touched, Ryan felt a stab of something sharp stab his gut and recognised it as envy.

Even in the early days, his relationship with Connie had never been like that. They'd never achieved that level of closeness. They'd been a disaster waiting to happen. If he hadn't been so absorbed by his career maybe he would have picked up on the signs. Or maybe not. Connie had played her part well.

Lifting the bottle to his lips again, he watched as Evanna sprinted across the sand to meet Jenna—watched as she gave her a spontaneous hug and gestured with her hands, clearly telling her some anecdote. He had no idea what she was saying, but it had Jenna laughing, and her laugh was so honest and genuine that Ryan felt every muscle in his body tighten. He doubted Jenna had ever manipulated a man in her life. She wouldn't know how—and anyway, such behaviour would go against her moral code.

As they approached he could hear Evanna admiring Jenna's skirt, the conversation light and distinctly female in tone and content. Jenna responded in kind, handing over a bowl of rosy-red strawberries and chatting with the group gathered around the food table as if she'd been born and raised on the island.

It took less than a few seconds for him to realise that she was looking at everyone but him. Talking to everyone but him.

Aware of Evanna's puzzled expression, Ryan sighed. If he didn't do something, the situation would be taken out of his hands.

He strolled over to Jenna, who was busily sorting food on the long trestle table, carefully ignoring him.

'Where's Rebel?' Ryan felt the ripple of tension pass through her body and she carefully put down the bowl she was holding.

'Lexi has him on a lead. I thought all those sausages and

steaks on the barbecue might prove too much of a temptation for a dog with a behavioural problem.'

'You could be right.' He noticed that her cheeks had turned
a soft shade of pink and that she was making a point of not
looking at his mouth.

No, he thought to himself. Jenna would never play games
or manipulate. She was honest and genuine—surprisingly
unsophisticated for a woman in her thirties.

Lexi strolled up to the table, earphones hanging from her
ears, her iPod tucked into the back pocket of her jeans, her
head bobbing to the rhythm. She was hanging on to Rebel,
who was straining to run in the opposite direction. 'Hi, Ryan.'

Jenna looked embarrassed. 'Dr McKinley—'

'Ryan is fine.' He bent down to make a fuss of Rebel, who
looked him in the eye and immediately sat.

'Mum, did you see that? He sat without even being told!'
Lexi gaped at the dog. 'Given that he's behaving, you can
hold him. I'm going to see my friends.' Without waiting for
a reply, she pushed the lead into her mother's hand, took the
cola Evanna was offering her with a smile of thanks and
strolled across the sand to join a group of teenagers who
were chatting together.

'I have a feeling it was a mistake to bring a dog—this
particular dog, anyway—to a barbecue.' Gripping the lead
until her knuckles were white, Jenna was still concentrating
on Rebel. 'Hopefully your influence will prevail and he'll
behave.'

'I think you may have an exaggerated idea of my power.'

'I hope not or I'm about to be seriously embarrassed.'

'I think you're already embarrassed.' Ryan spoke quietly,
so that he couldn't be overheard by the people milling close
to them. Keeping his eyes on her face, he watched her reaction. 'And there's no need to be. Just as there was no need to
run off yesterday morning and avoid me all day in surgery.'

She took a deep breath, her gaze fixed on Rebel. Then she glanced sideways and checked no one was listening. Finally, she looked at him. 'I haven't kissed, or been kissed, for a long time.'

'I know.' He watched as the tension rippled down her spine.

'I wasn't sure how I felt about it— I mean—' Her colour deepened. 'Obviously I know how I felt, but I wasn't sure what it all meant. I hadn't expected—'

'Neither had I.' Suddenly he regretted starting this conversation in such a public place. He should have dragged her somewhere private where he could have matched actions with words.

'Everyone is trying to pair us up.'

'I know that, too.'

'Doesn't that put you off?'

'I didn't kiss you because it was what other people wanted, Jenna. I kissed you because it was what I wanted.' And he still wanted it, he realised. Badly. Maybe two years of self-imposed isolation had intensified his feelings, but he had a feeling that it was something more than that.

'Is everyone watching us now?'

'Ignore them. What can I get you to drink?'

'What are you drinking?'

'Ginger beer,' he said dryly, 'but I'm on call. How about a glass of wine?'

She hesitated for a moment, and then something sparked in her eyes. 'Actually, I'd like a beer,' she said firmly. 'From the bottle. Don't bother with a glass.'

Hiding his surprise, Ryan took a bottle of ice-cold beer from the cooler and handed it to her. Maybe he didn't know her as well as he thought. She certainly didn't strike him as a woman who drank beer from a bottle.

'Thanks. Cheers.' Her grin was that of a defiant child, and

she took a large mouthful and proceeded to spill half of it down her front. 'Oh, for goodness' sake!'

Struggling to keep a straight face, Ryan rescued her beer before she spilt the rest of it. 'You haven't done that before, have you?'

Pulling a face, she tugged her wet tee shirt away from her chest. 'What a mess! Everyone is going to think I'm an alcoholic.'

'Alcoholics generally manage to get the alcohol into their mouths, Jenna. I gather your husband was more of a wine in a glass sort of guy?' Ryan put their drinks down on the table and grabbed a handful of paper napkins.

'How do you know what my husband drank?'

'It's a wild guess, based on the fact you seem to be doing the opposite of everything you ever did with him.' He pressed the napkins against the damp patch, feeling the swell of her breasts under his fingers.

'Am I?'

'You got yourself a dog, you're drinking beer from the bottle for the first time in your life, you eat fish three times a week and you never used to eat fish—' He could have added that she'd kissed a man who wasn't her husband, but he decided it was better to leave that alone for now.

'How do you know how often I eat fish?'

'Hamish mentioned it.'

Her gasp was an astonished squeak. 'The islanders discuss my diet?'

'The islanders discuss everything. You should know that by now.'

'In that case you should probably let me mop up my own wet tee shirt.' She snatched the napkins from his hands, their fingers brushing. 'If we're trying to kill the gossip, I don't think you should be doing that.'

'Do you care about the gossip?'

'I care about Lexi hearing the gossip.'

'Ah—' He noticed the pulse beating in her throat and knew she felt the attraction as strongly as he did. He retrieved his bottle from the table. 'Can I get you something different to drink?'

'Absolutely not.' There was humour in her eyes. And determination. 'I'm not a quitter. If you can drink from the bottle without dribbling, then so can I.' She lifted the bottle carefully to her lips and this time didn't spill a drop.

His body throbbing, Ryan stood close to her. 'You were late. I thought you weren't coming.'

'I was working in the garden, and then Lexi had to change her outfit four times. And I wasn't sure if it was a good idea...' She paused, staring at the label on the bottle. 'This stuff is disgusting.'

'It's an acquired taste. And now?'

'I still don't know if it's a good idea. I've never been so confused in my life.'

Evanna was back at the table, rearranging salads and plates. Ryan saw the happy smile on her lips and ground his teeth. Suddenly he felt protective—Jenna ought to be able to get out and spread her wings socially without being made to feel that everything she did was being analysed and gossiped about.

He was about to intervene when Kirsty, Evanna's six-year-old daughter, sprinted across the sand and launched herself at Lexi. 'Lex—Lex, I want to show you my swimming.'

Ryan watched as the teenager stooped to pick the little girl up. 'Wow. Lucky me. I can't wait to see.' She was a million miles from the moody, sullen teenager who had dragged her feet off the ferry a month before.

The little girl's smile spread right across her face as she bounced in Lexi's arms. 'I can swim without armbands.'

'Really? That's cool.'

'Watch me.'

'Please would you watch me.' Evanna tipped dressing from a jug onto a bowl of salad leaves. 'Manners, Kirsty.'

'Pleeeease—'

Lexi grinned. 'Sure. But don't splash me. It took me ages to get my hair straight.' Her face suddenly turned scarlet, and Ryan glanced round and saw Fraser strolling across the sand towards them, a lopsided grin on his face.

'Hey, if it isn't the city girl.' He wore his board shorts low on his hips and carried a football under his arm. 'We were wondering when you were going to get here. You going to swim for us, Kirst?'

Ryan felt Jenna tense beside him and saw Lexi's shoulders stiffen.

'This is my mum—' She waved a hand awkwardly towards Jenna. 'This is Fraser.'

'Hi, Fraser.' Jenna's voice was friendly. 'Nice to meet you.'

'Hi, Mrs Richards.' With an easy smile Fraser pushed his sun-bleached hair out of his eyes and kicked the football towards his friends. 'Evanna, is it OK if we take Kirsty swimming?'

'You'd be doing me a favour.' Evanna didn't hesitate. 'Don't let her get her own way too often.'

With Kirsty still in her arms, Lexi slid off her shoes and walked barefoot across the sand with Fraser. Close, but not touching.

Watching Jenna sink her teeth into her lower lip, Ryan sighed. 'Relax.'

'Lexi isn't old enough to have responsibility for Kirsty. I'd better follow them.'

He wondered who she was worried about—Kirsty or her own daughter.

'She'll be fine,' Evanna said calmly. 'Fraser is very responsible. The beach here is pretty safe, and Ryan can keep an eye on them—he's the strongest swimmer round here.' Smiling, she gave Ryan a little push. 'Go on. You're on lifeguard duty.'

Ryan glanced at Logan, who was expertly flipping steaks on the barbecue.

'Your wife is a bully.'

'I know. I love a strong, forceful woman, don't you?'

It was a flippant remark, with no hidden meaning, but Ryan felt his jaw tighten as he considered the question. He liked a woman to be independent, yes. Strong? He had no problem with strong—he knew from experience that life dealt more blows than a boxer, so strong was probably good. But forceful? Was forceful a euphemism for selfish and single-minded? For doing absolutely what you wanted to do with no thought for anyone else? If so, then the answer was no—he didn't like forceful women.

The question killed his mood, and he was aware that Jenna was looking at him with concern in her eyes.

'I'll keep you company. You made me buy a swimming costume so I might as well use it.' She put her drink down. 'If you're really on lifeguard duty then you can come in the water with me. It's so long since I swam I'm probably going to need my own personal lifeguard.'

Wanting to escape his thoughts, Ryan put his drink down next to hers. 'All right.'

They walked across the sand and she quickened her pace to keep up with him.

'You seem upset.' She kept walking. 'Is something wrong?'

Startled by her insight, Ryan frowned, his eyes on the sea, where Lexi was dangling a shrieking Kirsty in the water. 'What could be wrong?'

'I don't know. I just thought—you seem very tense all of a sudden. I thought maybe you needed some space.' She took a deep breath. 'If you want to talk to someone, you can talk to me.'

Ryan turned his head in astonishment and she bit her lip, her smile faltering.

'I know, I know—men don't like to talk about their problems. But you've listened to me often enough over the past month—I just want you to know that the friendship works both ways.'

'Friendship?' He realised that he was looking at her mouth again, and the strange thing was he didn't need to look. He'd memorised everything about it, from the way her lips curved to the soft pink colour. 'Is that what we have?'

'Of course. I mean, I hope so. You've certainly been a friend to me since I arrived here.'

He stared down into her eyes and something shimmered between them. Something powerful. So powerful that if they hadn't been standing in the middle of a crowded beach with the entire population of Glenmore watching he would have kissed her again.

Unsettled by his own feelings, Ryan shifted his gaze back to the sea. 'I don't have any problems.' His tone was rougher than he'd intended and he heard her sigh.

'You've known me long enough to kiss me, Ryan,' she said quietly. 'Hopefully you've also known me long enough to trust me.'

He was about to say that it was nothing to do with trust, but he was too late. She was already walking ahead, her hair tumbling down her back, sand dusting her toes.

Wondering whether he'd hurt her feelings, Ryan followed her to the water's edge, relieved when she smiled at him.

Clearly Jenna Richards didn't sulk. Nor did she bear grudges.

Fraser and Lexi were either side of Kirsty, holding her hands and swinging her over the waves while she squealed with delight. All of them were laughing.

Ryan was about to speak when he caught the wistful expression on Jenna's face. Her eyes were on Kirsty, and she had that look on her face that women sometimes had when they stared into prams.

He wondered again why she'd only had one child when she was clearly a born mother. Patient, caring, and unfailingly loving.

Pain shafted through him like a lightning bolt and he watched as she lifted her skirt slightly and tentatively allowed the waves to lick her feet. With a soft gasp of shock she jumped back, her eyes shining with laughter as she looked at him.

'It's freezing! Forget swimming. I'll definitely turn to ice and drown if I go in there!'

Forcing aside his dark thoughts, Ryan strode into the waves. 'No way are you using that pathetic excuse.' He took her hand and pulled her deeper. 'You get used to it after a while.'

'After losing how many limbs to frostbite?' Still holding his hand, she lifted her skirt above her knees with her free hand. 'I'm not going to get used to this. I'm losing all sensation in my feet.'

'What are you complaining about?' He tightened his grip on her hand. 'This is a warm evening on Glenmore.'

'The evening may be warm, but someone has forgotten to tell the sea it's summer. My feet are aching they're so cold.' Her laughter was infectious, and Ryan found that he was laughing, too.

Laughing with a woman. That was something he hadn't done for a long time.

He intercepted Lexi's shocked stare and his laughter faded. She glanced between him and her mother, suspicion in her eyes.

Jenna was still laughing as she picked her way through the waves, apparently unaware of her daughter's frozen features.

'We wouldn't be doing this in London, would we, Lex?'

'Pull your skirt down, Mum,' Lexi hissed, and Ryan watched as Jenna suddenly went from being natural to self-conscious. The colour flooded into her cheeks and she released the skirt. Instantly the hem trailed in the water. Flustered, she lifted it again.

'Lexi, watch me, watch me—' Kirsty bounced in the water, but Lexi stepped closer to her mother and dumped the child in Jenna's arms.

'Here you are, Mum. You take her. You're good with kids. Probably because you're old and motherly.'

Ryan was about to laugh at the joke when he realised that no one was laughing.

Old and motherly?

Was that how Lexi saw her mother? Was that how Jenna saw herself?

How old was she? Thirty-two? Thirty-three? She could have passed for ten years younger than that. She had a fresh, natural appeal that he found incredibly sexy. And, yes, she was different from Connie.

His jaw hardened. Connie wouldn't have paddled in the sea—nor would she have appeared in public with a face free of make-up. And he couldn't remember a time when she'd giggled. But that might have been because Connie wasn't spontaneous. She was a woman with a plan and nothing was going to stand in her way. Certainly not their marriage.

'I can't believe you're brave enough to swim!' Jenna was beaming at Kirsty, as if the child had done something incredibly clever. 'I'm so cold I can barely stand in the water, let alone swim.' She sneaked a glance after her daughter, who was walking away from them, Fraser by her side.

'I swim with my daddy.' Keen to demonstrate her skills, Kirsty wriggled in Jenna's arms and plunged back into the water, thrashing her arms and kicking her legs.

Drenched and shivering, Jenna laughed. 'Kirsty, that's fantastic. I couldn't swim like that at your age. And never in sea this cold.' The water had glued the skirt to her legs and Logan looked away, forcing himself to concentrate on something other than the shape of her body.

A crowd of locals were playing volleyball, and he could see Evanna handing out plates of food. 'I smell barbecue,' he said mildly. 'We should probably go and eat something. Sausages, Kirsty?'

The child immediately held out her arms to Jenna, who scooped her out of the water and cuddled her, ignoring the damp limbs and soaking costume.

Ryan felt his body tighten as he watched her with the child.

It was such a painful moment that when the phone in his pocket buzzed he was grateful for the excuse to walk away.

'I'm on call. I'd better take this.' He strode out of the water and drew the phone from his pocket. Was he ever going to be able to look at a mother and child without feeling that degree of agony? He answered his phone with a violent stab of his finger. 'McKinley.' It took him less than five seconds to get the gist of the conversation. 'I'll be right there.' Even as he dropped the phone into this pocket, he was running.

Cuddling a soaking wet Kirsty, Jenna watched as Ryan took off across the beach. It was obvious that there was some sort of emergency. Knowing he'd probably need help, she waded out of the water as fast as her soaked skirt and the bouncing child would allow. Once on the sand, she put the little girl down and ran, holding the child's hand.

'Let's see how fast we can reach Mummy.' At least an emergency might stop her thinking about that kiss. Nothing else had worked so far.

They reached Evanna as she was handing Ryan a black bag.

'What's wrong?' Jenna handed Kirsty over to her mother. 'Is it an emergency?'

Ryan glanced at her briefly. 'Ben who runs the Stag's Head has a tourist who has collapsed. Logan—' He raised his voice. 'I'm going to the pub. Keep your phone switched on.'

'I'll come with you.' Jenna glanced across at Evanna. 'Lexi's walked off with Fraser—will you keep an eye on her for me?'

'Of course.' Looking worried, Evanna held toddler Charlie on her hip and a serving spoon in her other hand. 'I hope it turns out to be nothing. We'll hold the fort here, but if you need reinforcements call.'

Hampered by her wet skirt, Jenna sprinted after Logan and it was only when her feet touched tarmac that she realised she'd left her shoes back at the barbecue. 'Ouch!' Stupid, stupid. 'I left my shoes—'

The next minute she was scooped off the ground and Logan was carrying her across the road.

She gave a gasp of shock. 'Put me down! I weigh a ton!'

'You don't weigh anything, and it's good for my ego to carry a helpless woman occasionally.' He was still jogging, and she realised how fit he must be.

'I'm not helpless, just shoeless.'

'Cinderella.' With a brief smile, he lowered her to the pavement and strode into the pub.

Jenna followed, feeling ridiculous in a wet skirt and without shoes. But all self-consciousness faded as she saw the man lying on the floor. His lips and eyes were puffy, his breathing was laboured and noisy, and the woman next to him was shaking his shoulder and crying.

'Pete? Pete?'

'What happened?' Ryan was down on the floor beside the patient, checking his airway. His fingers moved swiftly and skilfully, checking, eliminating, searching for clues.

'One moment he was eating his supper,' the landlord said, 'and then he crashed down on the floor, holding his throat.'

'He said he felt funny,' his wife sobbed. 'He had a strange feeling in his throat. All of a sudden. I've no idea why. We've been on the beach all afternoon and he was fine. Never said a thing about feeling ill or anything.'

'Anaphylactic shock.' Ryan's mouth was grim and Jenna dropped to her knees beside him.

'Is he allergic to anything?' She glanced at the man's wife. 'Nuts? Could he have been stung? Wasp?'

The woman's eyes were wild with panic. 'I don't think he was stung and he's not allergic to anything. He's fine with nuts, all that sort of stuff—is he going to die?'

Ryan had his hand in his bag. 'He's not going to die. Ben, call the air ambulance and fetch me that oxygen you keep round the back.' Icy calm, he jabbed an injection of adrenaline into the man's thigh, working with astonishing speed. 'Pete? Can you hear me? I'm Dr McKinley.'

Catching a glimpse of the role he'd played in a previous life, Jenna switched her focus back to the man's wife. 'What were you eating?' She looked at the table. 'Fish pie?'

'Yes. But he'd only had a few mouthfuls.'

'Are there prawns in that fish pie?'

'Yes.' Ben was back with the oxygen. 'But they were fresh this morning.'

'I'm not suggesting food poisoning,' Jenna said quickly, 'but maybe shellfish allergy?'

Covering the man's mouth and nose with the oxygen mask, Ryan looked at her for a moment, his eyes narrowed. Then he nodded. 'Shellfish. That's possible. That would explain it.' He adjusted the flow of oxygen. 'I'll give him five minutes and then give him another shot of epinephrine. Can you find it?'

Jenna delved in his bag and found the other drugs they were likely to need.

SARAH MORGAN

'Shellfish allergy?' The wife looked at them in horror. 'But—this isn't the first time he's eaten shellfish—can you just develop an allergy like that? Out of nowhere?'

'Jenna, can you squeeze his arm for me? I want to get a line in.'

'Actually, yes.' Jenna spoke to the woman as she handed Ryan a sterile cannula and then watched as he searched for a vein. 'Some adults do develop an allergy to something that hasn't harmed them before.'

'The body just decides it doesn't like it?'

'The body sees it as an invader,' Jenna explained, blinking at the speed with which Ryan obtained IV access. Her fingers over his, she taped down the cannula so that it wouldn't be dislodged, the movements routine and familiar. 'It basically overreacts and produces chemicals and antibodies. Dr McKinley has just given an injection to counter that reaction.'

The woman's face was paper-white. 'Is it going to work?'

'I hope so. This is quite a severe reaction, so I'm giving him another dose.' Ryan took the syringe from Jenna. 'And I'm going to give him some antihistamine and hydrocortisone.'

'Air ambulance is on its way,' Ben said, and at that moment Jenna noticed something. Leaning forward, she lifted the man's tee shirt so that she could get a better look.

'He has a rash, Ryan.'

'I think it's safe to assume we're dealing with a shellfish allergy—when you get to the mainland they'll observe him overnight and then make an appointment for you to see an allergy consultant. Where do you live?'

'We're from London. We're just here for a holiday. We have another week to go.' The woman was staring at her husband's chest in disbelief. 'I've never seen a rash come on like that.'

'It's all part of the reaction,' Jenna said quietly. 'The drugs will help.'

'How long do you think they'll keep him in hospital?'

'With any luck they'll let you go tomorrow and you can get on with your holiday—avoiding shellfish.' Ryan examined the rash carefully. 'The hospital should refer you for allergy testing so you can be sure what you're dealing with. You may need to carry an Epipen.' He checked the man's pulse again. 'His breathing is improving. That last injection seems to have done the trick.'

'Thank goodness—' The woman slumped slightly and Jenna slipped her arm round her.

'You poor thing. Are you on your own here? Do you have any friends or family with you?' She tried to imagine what it must be like going through this on holiday, far from home, with no support.

'My sister and her husband, but they've gone to the beach barbecue.'

'I'll contact them for you,' Ben said immediately, taking the details and sending one of the locals down to the beach to locate the woman's family.

Once again the islanders impressed Jenna, working together to solve the problem in a way that would never really happen in a big city.

By the time the air ambulance arrived the man had regained consciousness and the woman had been reunited with her family. Jenna listened as Ryan exchanged information with the paramedics and masterminded the man's transfer. As the helicopter lifted off for the short trip to the mainland, she turned to him.

His face was tanned from the sun and the wind, his dark hair a surprising contrast to his ice-blue eyes.

Trapped by his gaze, Jenna stood still, inexplicably drawn to him. She forgot about the small stones pressing into her bare feet; she forgot that she was confused about her feelings.

She forgot everything except the astonishing bolt of chemistry that pulled her towards Ryan.

She wanted to kiss him again.

She wanted to kiss him now.

Feeling like a teenager on her first date, she leaned towards him, melting like chocolate on a hot day. His hands came down on her shoulders and she heard the harshness of his breathing.

Yes, now, she thought dreamily, feeling the strength of his fingers—

'Mum!'

The voice of a real teenager carried across the beach, and Jenna jumped as if she'd been shot as she recognised Lexi's appalled tones. For a moment she stared into Ryan's eyes, and then she turned her head and saw her daughter staring at her in undisguised horror.

'What are you doing?'

Her heart pounding and her mouth dry, Jenna was grateful for the distance, which ensured that at least her daughter couldn't see her scarlet cheeks.

What *was* she doing?

She was a divorced mother of thirty-three and she'd been on the verge of kissing a man with virtually all the islanders watching.

'We probably ought to get back to the barbecue...' Ryan's tone was level and she nodded, feeling numb.

'Yes. Absolutely.' If Lexi hadn't shouted she would have put her arms around his neck and kissed him.

And what would that have done for her relationship with her daughter, let alone her relationship with Ryan?

This was her new life and she'd almost blown it. If Lexi hadn't called out to her she would have risked everything. And all for what? A kiss?

'If they've eaten all the food, I'll kill someone.' Apparently suffering none of her torment, Ryan turned towards the steps that led down to the sand, as relaxed as if they'd been having a conversation about the weather. 'How are things, Jim?'

Jim?

It took Jenna a moment to realise that the ferryman was standing by the steps, chatting to another islander. Had he been that close all the time? There could have been a fire, a flood and a hurricane, and all she would have noticed was Ryan.

'Another life saved, Doc.' Grinning, Jim scratched the back of his neck and looked up at the sky, where the helicopter was now no more than a tiny dot. 'Another good holiday experience on Glenmore. They'll be coming back. I overheard someone saying on the ferry this morning that they'd booked a short break here just so that they could ask a doctor about a skin rash, because you lot always know what you're doing.'

Ryan rolled his eyes. 'I'll mention it to Logan. We obviously need to make more of an effort to be useless.'

Jenna produced a smile, pretending to listen, wondering whether she could just slink onto the ferry and take the first sailing back to the mainland in the morning. Maybe distance would make her forget the kiss, because nothing else was working—not even an emergency.

Lexi was waiting for them at the bottom of the steps. 'Mum? What were you doing?'

'She was debriefing with Dr McKinley,' Evanna said smoothly, and Jenna jumped with shock because she hadn't seen Evanna standing next to her daughter. Last time she'd looked Evanna had been serving sausages and salad. But somehow the other woman had materialised at the foot of the steps, Charlie in her arms. 'I gather everything went smoothly, Jenna? Rapid response from the air ambulance? Did things go according to plan?'

Grateful as she was for Evanna's focus on the professional, Jenna didn't manage to respond.

Fortunately Ryan took over. 'Things don't always go according to plan,' he said softly, 'but that's life, isn't it? Ideally I would have liked to lose the audience, but you can't choose where these things happen.'

Jenna couldn't work out whether he was talking about the medical emergency or the fact she'd almost kissed him. They'd had an audience for both. and she was painfully aware that she'd embarrassed him as much as herself. These were his friends. His colleagues. No doubt he'd be on the receiving end of suggestive remarks for the rest of the summer. Yes, he'd kissed her on the beach, but that had been early in the morning with no one watching.

Because Lexi was still looking at her suspiciously, Jenna forced herself to join in the discussion. 'I—it was a bit unexpected. I'm not used to dealing with emergencies.' And she wasn't used to being attracted to a man. She'd behaved like a crazed, desperate woman.

'From what I've heard you were fantastic—a real Glenmore nurse.' Evanna was generous with her praise. 'We're expected to be able to turn our hands to pretty much anything. People are already singing your praises all over the island.' She tucked her hand through Jenna's arm, leading her back across the beach as if they'd been friends for ever. 'Word travels fast in this place. How are your feet?'

Jenna glanced down and realised that she'd forgotten she wasn't wearing shoes. 'Sore. I need to find my sandals.' Her face was burning and she didn't dare look round to see where Ryan was. Hiding, probably—afraid of the desperate divorcee who had tried to attack him. As for Lexi, she still wasn't smiling, but the scowl had left her features. Which presumably meant that Evanna's explanation had satisfied her.

'Your Lexi is so brilliant with the children.' Evanna led her back to the food and heaped potato salad on a plate. 'Logan—find something delicious for Jenna. She's earned it.'

Jenna accepted the food, even though the last thing she felt like was eating. She just wanted to go home and work out what she was going to say to Ryan next time she saw him on his own.

She had to apologise. She had to explain that she had absolutely no idea what had happened to her. Yes, she'd got a dog, she ate fish three times a week and she'd drunk beer from a bottle, but kissing a man in public…

Lexi flicked her hair away from her face. 'I'm off to play volleyball.' With a final glance in her direction, her daughter sauntered off across the sand towards Fraser, who was laughing with a friend, a can of cola in his hand. 'See you later.'

Jenna wanted to leave, but she knew that would draw attention to herself, and she'd already attracted far too much attention for one evening. Even without turning her head she was painfully aware of Ryan talking to Logan, discussing the air ambulance.

She wondered whether she should request that the air ambulance come back for her when they'd finished. She felt as though she needed it.

'Have a drink.' Clearly reading her mind, Evanna pushed a large glass of wine into her hand. 'And don't look so worried. Everything is fine. You and Ryan were a great team.'

Jenna managed a smile, but all she could think was, *Why am I feeling like this?*

She had to forget him. She had to forget that kiss.

Thank goodness tomorrow was Sunday and she didn't have to work. She had a whole day to talk some sense into herself.

CHAPTER SEVEN

10 reasons why I shouldn't fall in love with Ryan:
I've been divorced less than a year
I am too old
I'm ordinary and he is a sex god
Being with him puts me off my food
I have Lexi to think of
I need to act my age
I have to work with the man
He'll hurt me
I'm not his type

'MUM?'

Jenna dropped the pen before number ten and flipped the envelope over. 'I'm in the kitchen. You're up early.' Too early. Deciding that she couldn't hide the envelope without looking suspicious, Jenna slammed her mug of tea on it and smiled brightly. 'I was expecting you to sleep in.'

'I was hungry, and anyway I'm meeting the gang.' Yawning, Lexi tipped cereal into a bowl and added milk. 'You're up early, too.'

'I had things to do.' Like making a list of reasons why she shouldn't be thinking of Ryan.

Her head throbbing and her eyelids burning from lack of sleep, Jenna stood up and filled the kettle, bracing herself for the awkward questions she'd been dreading all night. 'You normally want to lie in bed.'

'That's only during term time, when there's nothing to get up for except boring old school.' Lexi frowned at her and then eyed the mug on the envelope. 'Why are you making tea when you haven't drunk the last one?'

Jenna stared in horror at the mug on the table.

Because she wasn't concentrating.

She'd been thinking about the kiss again.

Exasperated with herself, she picked up the half-full mug and scrunched the envelope in her hand. 'This one is nearly cold. And anyway, I thought you might like one.'

Lexi gaped at her. 'I don't drink tea. And why are you hiding that envelope? Is it a letter from Dad or something?'

'It's nothing—I mean—' Jenna stammered. 'I wrote a phone number on it—for a plumber—that tap is still leaking—'

Lexi's eyes drifted to the tap, which stubbornly refused to emit even a drop of water. 'So if there's a number on it, why did you just scrunch it up?'

'I only remembered about the number after I scrunched it up.'

Lexi shrugged, as if her mother's strange behaviour was so unfathomable it didn't bear thinking about. 'I won't be back for lunch. I'm meeting Fraser and a bunch of his friends up at the castle ruins at nine. We're making a day of it.'

'It's Sunday. Archaeology club isn't until tomorrow.'

'Not officially, but the chief archaeologist guy is going to show us the dungeons and stuff. Really cool.'

'Oh.' Still clutching the envelope, Jenna sat back down at the table, relieved that there wasn't going to be an inquisition about the night before. 'I was going to suggest we made a picnic and went for a walk on the cliffs, but if you're meeting your friends—well, that's great.'

Lexi pushed her bowl away and stood up. 'Do I look OK?'

Jenna scanned the pretty strap top vacantly, thinking that the blue reminded her of Ryan's eyes in the seconds before he'd kissed her on the beach. Had she ever felt this way about Clive? Was it just that she'd forgotten? And how did Ryan feel about her?

'Mum? What do you think?'

'I think he's a grown man and he knows what he's doing.'

'What?' Lexi stared at her. 'He's fifteen. Same age as me.'

Jenna turned scarlet. 'That's what I mean. He's almost a man. And I'm sure he's responsible.'

'But I didn't ask you—' Lexi shook her head in frustration. 'What *is* wrong with you this morning? Mum, are you OK?'

No, Jenna thought weakly. She definitely wasn't. 'Of course I'm OK. Why wouldn't I be? I'm great. Fine. I'm good. Really happy. Looking forward to a day off.'

Lexi backed away, hands raised. 'All right, all right. No need to go overboard—I was just asking. You look like you're having a breakdown or something.'

'No. No breakdown.' Her voice high pitched, Jenna pinned a smile on her face. She was good at this bit. Feel one emotion, show another. She'd done it repeatedly after her marriage had fallen apart. Misery on the inside, smile on the outside. Only in this case it was crazy lust-filled woman on the inside, respectable mother on the outside. 'Have a really, really nice day, Lexi. I'm glad you've made friends so quickly.'

Lexi narrowed her eyes suspiciously. 'What? No lecture? No "Don't go too near the edge or speak to strangers"? No "Sex is for two people who love each other and are old enough to understand the commitment"? Are you sure you're OK?'

Back to thinking about Ryan, Jenna barely heard her. 'I thought you wanted me to worry less.'

'Yes, but I didn't exactly expect you to manage it!'

'Well, you can relax. I haven't actually stopped worrying—I've just stopped talking about it.' Still clutching the envelope, Jenna stood up and made herself another cup of tea. 'I've brought you up with the right values—it's time I trusted you. Time I gave you more independence and freedom to make your own mistakes.'

'Mum, are you feeling all right?'

No. No, she wasn't feeling all right.

She was feeling very confused. She was thinking about nothing but sex and that just wasn't her, was it? Had Clive's brutal betrayal left her so wounded and insecure that she needed affirmation that she was still an attractive woman? Or was it something to do with wanting what you couldn't have?

Lexi folded her arms. 'So you're perfectly OK if I just spend the day up at the castle, taking drugs and making out with Fraser?'

'That's fine.' Thinking of the way Ryan's body had felt against hers, Jenna stared blindly out of the kitchen window. 'Have a nice time.'

'OK, this is spooky. I just told you I'm going to use drugs and make out and you want me to have a *nice time*?'

Had she really said that? 'I know you wouldn't do that.' Jenna mindlessly tidied the kitchen. 'You're too sensible. You're always telling me you're going to have a career before children.'

'Sex doesn't have to end in children, Mum.' Lexi's voice was dry as she picked up her phone and her iPod and walked towards the door. 'One day, when you're old enough, I'll explain it all to you. In the meantime I'll leave you to your incoherent ramblings. Oh, and you might want to remove the teabags from the washing machine—you'll be looking for them later.'

She'd put the teabags in the washing machine?

Jenna extracted them, her cheeks pink, her brain too fuddled to form an appropriate response. 'Have fun. Don't forget your key.'

'You're acting so weird.' Lexi slipped it into her pocket, staring at her mother as if she were an alien. 'You know—last night, for a moment, I really thought—'

Jenna's breathing stopped. 'What did you think?'

'I thought that you—' Lexi broke off and shrugged. 'Never mind. Crazy idea, and anyway I was wrong. Thank goodness. What are you planning to do today?'

Chew over everything that had happened the night before; try not to spend the day thinking of Ryan; remind herself that she was too old to have crushes on men— 'Housework,' Jenna muttered, staring blindly at the pile of unwashed plates that were waiting to be stacked in the dishwasher. 'Catch up on a few things. The laundry basket is overflowing, and I need to weed the herbaceous border.' It all sounded like a boring day to her, but her answer seemed to satisfy Lexi.

Clearly Lexi had been reassured by Evanna's assertion that the two of them had been discussing the emergency they'd dealt with. Either that or she'd just decided that no man was ever going to be seriously interested in her mother.

'I'll see you later, then. Do you mind if I take Rebel?' Grabbing his lead, Lexi whistled to the dog and sauntered off to meet Fraser and his friends at the castle, leaving Jenna to face a day on her own with her thoughts.

And her thoughts didn't make good company.

Tormented by the memory of what had happened the night before, she pulled out one of the kitchen chairs and sat down with a thump. Then she smoothed the crumpled envelope she'd been clutching and stared at her list. She'd started with ten but there were probably a million reasons why it was a bad idea to kiss Ryan McKinley.

With a groan, she buried her face in her hands. She had to stop this nonsense. She had to pull herself together and act like an adult. She was a mother, for goodness' sake.

'You're obviously feeling as frustrated as I am.' His voice came from the doorway and Jenna flew to her feet, the chair crashing backwards onto the tiled floor, her heart pounding.

'Ryan!' The fact that she'd been thinking about him made the whole thing even more embarrassing—but not as humiliating as the fact that she was wearing nothing but her knickers and the old tee shirt of Lexi's that she'd worn to bed. Jenna tugged at the hem, until she realised that just exposed more of her breasts. 'What are you doing here?'

'Trying to have five minutes with you without the whole of Glenmore watching.' He strode across the kitchen, righting the chair that she'd tipped over. Then he gave her a wicked smile. 'Nice outfit.'

Too shocked to move, Jenna watched him walk towards her, dealing with the fact that a man was looking at her with undisguised sexual interest and he wasn't Clive. There was no mixing this man up with Clive. Her ex-husband was slight of build, with pale skin from spending most of his day in an office. Ryan was tall and broad-shouldered, his skin bronzed from the combination of wind and sun. When she'd looked at Clive she hadn't thought of sex and sin, but when she looked at Ryan—

He stopped in front of her. 'You have fantastic legs.'

A thrill of dangerous pleasure mingled with embarrassment. 'How did you get in?'

'The usual way—through the door.' Before she could say a word, he caught the front of her tee shirt in his hand, jerked her against him and brought his mouth down on hers. A thousand volts of pure sexual chemistry shot through her body and thoughts of sex and sin exploded into reality.

Jenna gripped his arms, feeling hard male muscle flex under her fingers. 'I've been thinking about you—'

'Good. I'd hate to be the only one suffering. You taste so good...' Groaning the words against her lips, Ryan sank his hands into her hair and devoured her mouth as if she were a feast and he was starving. His kiss was hot and hungry, and she felt her knees weaken and her heart pound. Flames licked through her veins and Jenna tightened her grip on his arms, grateful that she was leaning against the work surface.

Engulfed by an explosion of raw need Jenna wrapped her arms around his neck and pressed closer. His hands came round her back and he hauled her against him, leaving her in no doubt as to the effect she had on him. Feeling the hard ridge of his erection, Jenna felt excitement shoot through her body.

Dizzy and disorientated, she moaned against his mouth and he slid his hands under the tee shirt, his fingers warm against her flesh. She gasped as those same fingers dragged over her breasts, moaned as he toyed and teased. And still he kissed her. Mouth to mouth they stood, the skilled sweep of his tongue driving her wild, until she squirmed against him, the ache deep inside her almost intolerable.

Dimly, she heard him groan her name, and then he was lifting her tee shirt over her head and his mouth was on her bare breast. Jenna opened her mouth to tell him that it felt good, but the only sound that emerged was a faint moan, and her breathing became shallow as he drew the sensitive tip into his mouth. Her fingers sank into his thick dark hair as the excitement built, and suddenly she was aware of nothing but the heavy throb in her body and the desperate need for more. Every thought was driven from her mind, but one—

She wanted him. She wanted sex with him, and she didn't care about the consequences.

His mouth was back on hers, the slide of his tongue intimate and erotic.

Shaking now, Jenna reached for the waistband of his jeans and felt his abdomen clench against her fingers. She fumbled ineptly for a few moments, and then his hand closed around her wrist.

'Wait—God, I can't believe the way you make me feel.'

She moaned and pressed her mouth back to his, their breath mingling. 'I want to—'

With obvious difficulty he dragged his mouth from hers. 'I know you do, and so do I, but this time I really don't want to be disturbed—how long is Lexi out for? Is she going to be back in the next few hours?'

'Lexi?' Disorientated, Jenna stared at him for a moment, and then shook her head and rubbed her fingers over her forehead, trying to switch off the response of her body so that she could think clearly. 'Lexi.' She felt as though her personality had been split down the middle—mother and woman. 'She's out, but— What on earth am I doing?' Realising that she was virtually naked, Jenna quickly retrieved her tee shirt from the floor, but she was shaking so much that she couldn't turn it the right way round.

'I wish I hadn't said anything.' His tone rough, Ryan removed it gently from her hands, turned it the right way round and pulled it carefully over her head. 'I just didn't want her walking in on us.'

'No. And it's ridiculous. This whole thing is ridiculous— I'm— And you're—'

He raised an eyebrow. 'Is there any chance of you actually finishing a sentence, because I have no idea what you're thinking.'

'I'm thinking that this is crazy.' Jenna straightened the

tee shirt and flipped her hair free. 'I'm thinking that I don't do things like this.'

'That doesn't mean you can't. You hadn't owned a dog or eaten fish until a month ago.'

She gave a hysterical laugh. 'Having sex is slightly different to getting a dog or eating fish.'

'I should hope so. If a few hours in my bed is on a par with eating fish or getting a dog, I'll give up sex.'

'That would be a terrible waste, because you're obviously very good at it.' Jenna slammed her hand over her mouth and stared at him, appalled. 'I can't believe I just said that.'

But he was laughing, his blue eyes bright with humour. 'I love the way you say what you think.'

'What I think is that I don't know what you're doing here with me.' With an embarrassed laugh, she yanked the tee shirt down, covering herself. 'I'm not some nubile twenty-year-old. I'm a mother and I'm thirty-three...' The words died in her throat as he covered her mouth with his fingers.

'You're incredibly sexy.'

Staring up into his cool blue eyes, Jenna gulped, still coming to terms with the feelings he'd uncovered. He'd had his hands on her, and as for his mouth... An earthquake could have hit and she wouldn't have noticed. In fact, she felt as though an earthquake *had* hit.

Everything about her world had changed and it was hard to keep her balance.

But she had to. She couldn't afford the luxury of acting on impulse. She wasn't a teenager.

Thinking of teenagers made her groan and close her eyes.

'Ryan, what are you doing here?' She jabbed her fingers into her hair, horrified by what could have happened. 'We could have— Lexi might have—'

'I saw her leave. And before you panic, no, she didn't see me. I stayed out of the way until she'd disappeared over the horizon. Given the way she guards you, I thought it was wise. She obviously doesn't see her mother as a living, breathing sexual woman.'

'That's because I'm not. I'm not like this. This isn't me.'

'Maybe it *is* you.' His eyes lingered on her mouth. 'Do you want to find out?'

Her heart bumped hard. 'I can't. I have responsibilities.'

'Talking of which, did she give you a hard time about last night?'

'She started to say something and then decided that she'd imagined it all. Thanks to Evanna. But—I'm sorry about last night. I was going to apologise to you.'

'Don't.' His mouth was so close to hers that it was impossible to concentrate.

'You must be furious with me for embarrassing you in public—'

His hand was buried in her hair, his lips moving along her jaw. 'Do I seem furious?' His mouth was warm and clever, and Jenna felt her will-power strained to the limit.

She put a hand on his chest, trying to be sensible. Trying to ignore the way he made her feel.

Then he paused and stooped to retrieve something from the floor. It was her envelope. He would have discarded it had she not given an anguished squeak and reached for it.

'That's mine.'

'What is it?'

'It's nothing.' Jenna snatched at it but he held it out of reach, unfurling it with one hand.

'If it's nothing, why are you trying to stop me reading it?' He squinted at the crumpled paper. '"10 reasons why I shouldn't fall in love with Ryan—" Ah.'

With a groan, Jenna covered her face with her hands. 'Please, just ignore it—'

'No.' His voice was calm and steady. 'If you can make a

list of ten reasons not to fall in love with me, I have a right to know what they are.' He scanned the list and frowned. 'I put you off your food? That's why you don't eat?'

Mortified, Jenna just shook her head, and he sighed and tucked the mangled envelope into the back pocket of his jeans.

'If you want my opinion, I don't think it matters that you've been divorced for less than a year, nor do I think your age has any relevance. The fact that I put you off your food might be a problem in the long term, but we won't worry for now. As for Lexi—' He stroked his fingers through her hair. 'I can see that might be a problem. That's why I stopped when I did. I didn't want her to walk in.'

'So you're not just a sex god.' She made a joke of it. 'You're thoughtful, too.'

'For selfish reasons. I want you, and you come with a daughter.'

Did he mean he *wanted her* body or he wanted her? She was afraid to ask and she found it hard to believe that he wanted her at all. 'Why do I always meet you looking my worst?' Jenna couldn't believe the unfairness of it all. He looked like a living, breathing fantasy and she was wearing Lexi's cast off tee shirt.

'I think you look fantastic.' Ryan slid his hand into her hair, studying each tangled curl in detail. 'Does your hair curl naturally?'

'Yes, of course. Do you think I'd pay to make it look like this?' She snapped the words, embarrassed that she was looking her worst when he was looking his best, and really, really confused by the way he made her feel.

'I really like it.' His smile was slow and sexy. 'You look as though you've had a really crazy night in some very lucky man's bed.'

Jenna couldn't concentrate. His fingers were massaging

her scalp and she felt his touch right through her body. How did he know how to do that? Her eyes drifted shut and suddenly the impact on her other senses was magnified.

'As a matter of interest, what did you wear to bed when you were married?'

Jenna gulped. 'A long silky nightdress that Clive's mother bought me for Christmas. Why do you want to know?'

'Because I suspect this is another of your little rebellions. And now we've established that Lexi isn't coming back in the immediate future...' His voice husky, Ryan slid his hands under the offending tee shirt and she gasped because his hands were warm and strong and her nerve-endings were on fire.

'Ryan—'

His fingers slid down her back with a slow, deliberate movement that was unmistakably seductive. 'I hate to be the one to point this out, but I have a strong suspicion that neither Clive nor his mother would approve of your current choice of nightwear.'

'They'd be horrified—'

'Which is why you're wearing it.'

Jenna gave a choked laugh. 'Maybe. In which case I'm seriously disturbed and you should avoid me.'

Ryan lifted her chin so that she had no choice but to look at him. 'Is that what you want?'

All the pent-up emotion inside her exploded, as if the gates holding everything back had suddenly been opened. 'No, that isn't what I want! Of course it isn't. But I feel guilty, because I know I shouldn't be doing this, and confused because I've never lost control like that before. I'm angry with myself for being weak-willed, terrified that you'll hurt me—'

'Ah, yes—number eight on your list. Why do you assume I'll hurt you?'

Jenna thought about Clive. If Clive had found her boring,

how much more boring would this man find her? 'I'm not very exciting. I'm sure I'm all wrong for you.'

'In what way are you wrong for me?'

'For a start I've never had sex on a desk,' she blurted out, and then paled in disbelief. 'Oh, no—I can't believe I said that—'

'Neither can I. You're saying some really interesting things at the moment.' To give him his due, he didn't laugh. But he did close his hands around her wrists and drew her closer. 'I'm guessing that statement has some significance—am I right?'

Jenna stared at a point on his chest. 'I walked in on them,' she breathed. 'She was lying on his desk.'

'And you think that's what was wrong with your marriage?'

'No. The problems in our marriage went far deeper than that. I wouldn't have wanted to have sex on a desk with Clive, whereas—' She broke off, and he was silent for a moment.

Then he lifted his hand and slowly dragged his finger over her scarlet cheek. 'Whereas you do want to have sex on a desk with me?'

'Yes,' she whispered. 'Well, I don't mean a desk specifically—anywhere… But that's crazy, because I'm just not that sort of person and I know I'm really, really not your type.'

'Number nine on the list. So what *is* my type, Jenna?'

'I don't know. Someone stunning. Young. You're disgustingly handsome and you're sickeningly clever.' She mumbled the words, making a mental note never to commit her thoughts to paper again. 'I may be naive, but I'm not stupid. You could have any woman you want. You don't need to settle for a mess like me. And now you ought to leave, because all I ever do when you're around is embarrass myself. I need to get my head together and think about Lexi.'

'Why do you want to think about Lexi? She's out enjoying herself.'

Jenna felt her heart bump against her chest. 'I don't want to hurt her.'

'Is it going to hurt her if you spend the day with me?' His head was near hers, their mouths still close.

'No. But it might hurt me. I find this whole situation scary,' she confessed softly. 'What if I'm doing this for all the wrong reasons?' She looked up at him. 'What if I'm trying to prove something? What if I'm just using you to prove to myself that someone finds me attractive?'

'That objection wasn't on your list.' His mouth was against her neck, his tongue trailing across the base of her throat. 'You're not allowed to think up new ones.'

'I can't think properly when you do that—'

'Sorry.' But he didn't sound sorry, and he didn't stop what he was doing.

Jenna felt her insides melt but her brain refused to shut up. 'What if I'm just doing this because I'm angry with Clive?'

With a sigh, Ryan lifted his head. 'You're suggesting that kissing me is an act of revenge?'

'I don't know. I have no idea what's going on in my head. What I'm thinking is changing by the minute.'

There was a trace of humour in his eyes as he scanned her face. 'When you kissed me were you thinking of Clive?'

'No! But that doesn't mean it isn't a reasonable theory.'

'Answer me one question.' His mouth was against her neck again and Jenna closed her eyes.

'What?'

'If Lexi wasn't part of the equation—if it were just you and me—what would you like to do now?'

'Spend the day together, as you suggested. But somewhere private. Somewhere no one will see us.' She sighed. 'An impossible request on Glenmore, I know.'

'Maybe not.' Stroking her hair away from her face, Ryan gave a slow smile. 'In fact, I think I know just the place.'

The lighthouse was perched on a circle of grass, and the only approach was down a narrow path that curved out of sight of the road.

'It's the most secluded property on the island.' Ryan held out his hand as she negotiated the stony path. 'Even Mrs Parker has never been down here.'

Jenna shaded her eyes and stared up towards the top of the lighthouse. 'It's incredible. I can't believe it's a house.'

'It used to be fairly basic, but I made a few changes.' Ryan opened the door and she walked through, into a beautiful circular kitchen.

'Oh, my!' Stunned, she glanced around her. It was stylish and yet comfortable, with a huge range cooker, an American fridge and a central island for preparing food. By the window overlooking the sea the owner had placed a table, ensuring that anyone eating there could enjoy the fantastic view. 'A few changes?'

'Quite a few changes.' Ryan leaned against the doorframe, watching her reaction. 'Do you like it?'

'I love it. I had no idea—from the outside it looks...' Lost for words, she shook her head. 'It's idyllic.'

'Do you want breakfast now, or after you've looked round?'
'After...'

'Oh, yes—objection number four.' He gave a faint smile and urged her towards an arched doorway and a spiral staircase. 'I put you off your food. I don't suppose you'd like to tell me why? I don't think I've ever made a woman feel sick before.'

She giggled. 'You don't make me feel sick. You make me sort of churny in my stomach.'

'Sort of churny?' He lifted an eyebrow at her description. 'Is that good or bad?'

'Good, if you're trying to lose weight.'

'Don't. I like you the way you are.' He was right behind her on the stairs and it was impossible not to be aware that it was just the two of them in the house.

'So no one overlooks this?'

'It's a very inhospitable part of the coast of Glenmore—hence the reason they built a lighthouse here originally. This is the living room.'

Jenna emerged into another large, circular room, with high ceilings and glass walls. It had been decorated to reflect its coastal surroundings, with white wooden floors, seagrass matting and deep white sofas. Touches of blue added colour and elegant pieces of driftwood added style. A wood-burning stove stood in the centre of the room. 'This is the most beautiful room I've ever seen. I can't imagine what it must be like to actually live somewhere as special as this.'

'It was virtually a shell when I bought it from the original owner.' Ryan strolled over to the window, his back to her. 'It took me a year to make it properly habitable.'

'Where did you live while you were renovating it?'

'I lived here. Amidst the rubble.'

'You did most of it yourself?'

'All of it except the glazing. I used a lot of glass and it was too heavy for one person to manipulate.'

Stunned, she looked around her. 'You did the building—the plumbing, electricity?'

'I'm a doctor,' he drawled. 'I'm used to connecting pipes and electrical circuits. Building a wall isn't so different to realigning a broken bone—basically you need the thing straight.'

Jenna shook her head in silent admiration and carried on up the spiral staircase. She pushed open a door and discovered a luxurious bathroom, complete with drench shower. Another door revealed a small guest bedroom. Deciding that she'd never seen a more perfect property in her life, Jenna took the final turn in the staircase and found herself in paradise.

The master bedroom had been designed to take maximum advantage of the incredible view, with acres of glass giving a three-hundred-and-sixty-degree outlook on Glenmore.

Speechless, Jenna walked slowly around the perimeter of the breathtaking room. Out of the corner of her eye she was conscious of the enormous bed, but she was also acutely conscious of Ryan, watching her from the head of the spiral staircase. The intimacy was unfamiliar and exciting.

Hardly able to breathe, she stared out across the sparkling sea, watching as the view changed with every step. Far beneath her were vicious rocks that must have sent so many boats tumbling to the bottom of the ocean, but a few paces on and she had a perfect view of the coast path, winding like a ribbon along the grassy flanks of the island. A few more steps and she was looking inland, across wild moorland shaded purple with heather.

'It's like living outside.'

'That was the idea.'

'I can see everything,' she whispered, 'except people. No people.'

'Just beyond the headland is the Scott farm.' Ryan was directly behind her now, and he closed his hands over her shoulders, pointing her in the right direction. 'But everything here is protected land. No building. No people. Occasionally you see someone on the coast path in the distance, but they can't get down here because the rocks are too dangerous. The path we took is the only way down.'

'I've never been anywhere so perfect.' Acutely aware of his touch, Jenna could hardly breathe. He was standing close to her and she could feel the brush of his hard body against hers. Her heart racing, she stared up at the roof—and discovered more curving glass. 'It must be wild here when there's a storm. Is it scary?'

'It's tough glass. You'd be surprised how much sound it blocks out. Do you find storms scary?' He turned her gently, and suddenly she thought that what she was starting to feel for him was far scarier than any storm.

'I don't know.' Looking into his eyes, she felt as though everything in her life was changing. And not only did she not trust her feelings, she knew she couldn't have them. She had to think about Lexi. But Lexi wasn't here now, was she? Maybe there was no future, but there could be a present. She was a woman as well as a mother.

His mouth was close to hers but he didn't kiss her, and she wondered whether he was waiting for her to make the decision.

Jenna lifted her hand to his face, the breath trapped in her throat. His jaw was rough against her fingers and she felt him tense, but still he didn't kiss her. Still he waited.

Consumed by the thrill of anticipation, she wrapped her arms around his neck and lifted her mouth to his, feeling her stomach swoop. It was like jumping off a cliff. As decisions went, this was a big one, and deep down in her gut she knew there would be a price to pay, but right now she didn't care. If she had to pay, she'd pay.

As her lips touched his she felt the ripple of tension spread across his shoulders—felt the coiled power in his athletic frame.

'Be sure, Jenna…' He breathed the words against her mouth, his hand light on her back, still giving her the option of retreat.

But the last thing she had in mind was retreat. She kept her mouth on his and he slid his hands into her hair and held her face still, taking all that she offered and more, his kiss demanding and hungry.

Someone groaned—her or him?—and then his arms came around her and he held her hard against him. The feel of his body made her heart race, and Jenna felt her linen skirt slide to the floor, even though she hadn't actually felt him undo it. And suddenly she was acutely aware of him—of the strength of his hands, the roughness of his jeans against the softness of her skin, the hard ridge of his arousal—

'Jenna—I have to—' His hands were full of her, stripping off her skirt, peeling off underwear until she was naked and writhing against him. And her hands were on him, too, on his zip, which refused to co-operate until he covered her hands with his. This time instead of stopping her, he helped her.

Hearts pounding, mouths fused, they fell to the floor, feasting.

'The bed is a metre away—' Ryan had his mouth on her breast and pleasure stabbed hard, stealing her breath. 'We should probably—'

'No—too far.' Terrified he'd stop what he was doing, Jenna clutched at his hair, gasping as she felt his tongue graze her nipple. Sensation shot through her and he teased, nipped and sucked one rigid peak while using his fingers on the other. The burn inside her was almost intolerable. Her hips writhed against the soft rug and she arched in an instinctive attempt to get closer to him. But she wasn't in charge. He was. Maybe there was some pattern to what he was doing, some sequence, but for her it was all a blur of ecstasy.

The words in her head died as his hand slid between her legs.

It had been two years since a man had touched her intimately, and even before that it had never felt like this. Never before had she felt this restless, burning ache.

'Ryan—' The slow, leisurely stroke of his skilled fingers drove her wild. 'Now.'

'I haven't even started…' His voice was husky against her ear, and his fingers slid deeper. Heat flushed across her skin and her breathing grew shallow. Her hand slid down and circled him and she heard him catch his breath.

'On second thoughts—now seems like a good idea…' He slid his hand under her bottom and lifted her, the blunt head of his erection brushing against her thigh.

Trembling with expectation, Jenna curved one thigh over his back and then groaned when he hesitated. 'Please…'

'Forgot something—' His voice hoarse, he eased himself away from her, reached forward and grabbed something from the cupboard by his bed. 'Damn!' He struggled with the packet while he kissed her again.

Jenna was panting against his mouth. 'Just—can you please—?'

'Yeah, I definitely can.' He hauled her under him, dropping his forehead to hers. 'Are you sure?'

'Is that a serious question?' She was breathless—desperate—conscious of the press of his body against hers. 'If you stop now, Ryan McKinley, I swear, I'll punch you.'

His laugh was low and sexy, and her stomach flipped as she stared into those blue, blue eyes. And then she ceased to notice anything because the roughness of his thigh brushed against hers and then he was against her and inside her and Jenna decided that if sex had ever felt like this before then she must have lost her memory.

Heat spread through her body and she tried to tell him how good it felt, but the sleek thrust of his body drove thought from her brain. He kissed her mouth, then her neck, ran his hand down her side and under her bottom—lifted her—

She moaned his name and he brought his lips back to hers, taking her mouth even as he took her body, and the pleasure was so intense that she could hardly breathe. Her nails sank into his back and the excitement inside her roared forward like a train with no brakes—

'Oh— I—' Her orgasm consumed her in a flash of brilliant light and exquisite sensation and she heard him growl deep in his throat, surging deeper inside her as she pulsed around him. She sobbed his name, tightened her grip and felt him thrust hard for the last time. They clung, breathless, riding the wave, going where the pleasure took them.

With a harsh groan Ryan dropped his head onto her shoulder, his breathing dragging in his throat. 'Are you OK?'

'No, I don't think so.' Weak and shaky, Jenna stared up at the ceiling, shell shocked, stunned by the intensity of what they'd shared. 'It's never been like that before.'

'That's probably because you've never made love on a wooden floor.' Wincing slightly, Ryan eased his weight off her and rolled onto his back, his arms still round her. 'I need to buy a different floor covering. This was designed for walking on and aesthetic appearance, not for sex. Do you want to move to the bed?'

'I don't want to move at all.' She just wanted to lie here, with him, staring up at the blue sky and the clouds above them. It seemed a fitting view. 'It's perfect here.'

'Perfect, apart from the bruises.'

'I don't have bruises, and even if I do I don't care.' She turned and rested her cheek on his chest, revelling in the opportunity to touch him. 'This morning I was wondering whether I ought to kiss you again—'

'And what did you decide?'

'You interrupted me before I'd made my decision.'

'If you want my opinion, I think you should definitely kiss me again.' His eyes gleamed with humour and he lifted her chin with his fingers and kissed her lightly. 'And again.'

Jenna shifted until she lay on top of him. 'I've never done this before.'

He raised an eyebrow. 'You have a child.'

'I mean I've never been so desperate to have sex I couldn't make it as far as the bed—never lost control like that.' She kissed the corner of his mouth, unable to resist touching him. 'I've never wanted anyone the way I want you. Ever since I arrived on the island I've wanted you. I thought I was going crazy—'

'I was going crazy, too.' He sank his hands into her hair and kissed her. 'Believe me, you're not the only one who has been exercising will-power.'

'I wasn't sure this was what you wanted.' She was conscious that she still knew next to nothing about him, and suddenly a stab of anxiety pierced her happiness. 'Can I ask you something?' Through the open window she could hear the crash of the waves and the shriek of the seagulls, reminding her how isolated they were.

'Yes.'

'Are you married?'

He stilled. 'You think I'd be lying here with you like this if I were married?'

'I don't know. I hope not.'

'And I hope you know me better than that.'

'Now I've made you angry.' Suddenly she wished she hadn't ruined the mood by asking the question. 'I'm sorry—I shouldn't have—' She broke off and then frowned, knowing that her question was a valid one. 'You have to understand that I thought I knew Clive, and it turned out I didn't.'

'Jenna, I'm not angry. You don't have to talk about this.'

'Yes, I do. You thought it was an unjust question, but to me it wasn't unjust and I need you to understand that.' Her voice was firm. 'I lived with a man for sixteen years and I thought I knew him. I married him and had his child, I slept in his bed—we made a life together. And it turned out he had a whole other life going on that didn't involve me. He had three affairs over the course of our marriage, one of them with a friend of mine. I didn't find out until the third.'

Ryan pulled her back down into the circle of his arms. 'You have a right to ask me anything you want to ask me. And I'm not married. Not any more.'

'Oh.' Digesting that, she relaxed against him, trailing her fingers over his chest, lingering on dark hair and hard muscle. 'So it went wrong for you, too?'

'Yes.'

She waited for him to say something more but he didn't, and she lay for a moment, listening to his heartbeat, her fingers on his chest.

Obviously that was why he'd come here, she thought to herself. Like her, he'd found comfort in doing something, found a channel for his anger. He'd built something new.

Ryan sighed. 'I'm sure there are questions you want to ask me.'

But he didn't want to answer them; she knew that.

'Yes, I have a question.' She shifted on top of him, feeling his instant response. 'How comfortable is that bed of yours?'

'Fruit, rolls, coffee—' Ryan started loading a tray. 'How hungry are you?'

'Not very. You put me off my food, remember?' Having pulled on her linen skirt and tee shirt, Jenna sat on a stool watching him.

'You just used up about ten thousand calories. You need to eat.' Ryan warmed rolls in the oven, sliced melon and made a pot of coffee. 'This should be lunch rather than breakfast, but never mind.'

'Lunch? But we—' Her gaze slid to the clock on the wall and her eyes widened. 'Two o'clock?'

'Like I said—ten thousand calories.' And ten thousand volts to his system. He couldn't believe he wanted her again so quickly, but he could happily have taken her straight back to bed.

Ryan grabbed butter and a jar of thick golden honey and then handed her some plates and mugs. 'You can carry these. I'll bring the rest.'

She stood still, holding the plates and mugs, staring at him.

Removing the rolls from the oven, he glanced at her. 'What's wrong?'

'Nothing.' Her voice was husky, and he frowned as he tipped the warm bread into a basket.

'Honesty, Jenna, remember?'

'It feels strange,' she admitted, 'being here with you like this.'

'Strange in a good way or strange in a bad way?'

'In a scary way. I was with Clive for sixteen years and he was my only boyfriend.'

Thinking about it, he realised he'd probably known that all along, but hearing it was still a shock. 'Your only boyfriend?'

'I met him when I was sixteen. I had Lexi when I was eighteen.'

Ryan wondered whether her selfish ex-husband had taken advantage of her. 'Does that have anything to do with why you have a difficult relationship with your mother?'

'I've always disappointed her.'

He frowned. 'I can't imagine you disappointing anyone.' But he could imagine her trying to please everyone, and her next words confirmed it.

'My parents had plans for me—which didn't involve me getting pregnant as a teenager.' Her head dipped and she pulled a pair of sunglasses out of the bag on her lap. 'Are we eating outside? I'll probably need these. It's sunny.'

He remembered the conversation she'd had with her

mother. How distressed she'd been. 'So what did they want you to do?'

'Something respectable. I had a place lined up at Cambridge University to read English—my parents liked to boast about that. They were bitterly upset when I gave it up.'

'Did you have to give it up?'

'I chose to. Everyone thought I'd be a terrible mother because I was a teenager, and it made me even more determined to be the best mother I could be. I don't see why teenagers can't be good mothers—I'm not saying it's easy, but parenthood is never easy, whatever age you do it.' Tiny frown lines appeared on her forehead. 'I hate the assumption that just because you're young, you're going to be a dreadful parent. I know plenty of bad parents who waited until their thirties to have children.'

Ryan wondered if she was referring to her own. 'For what it's worth, I think you're an amazing mother.'

'Thank you.' Her voice was husky as she cleaned her sunglasses with the edge of her tee shirt. 'I don't think I'm amazing, but I love Lexi for who she is, not what she does. And I've always let her know that.'

'Who she is, not what she does...' Ryan repeated her words quietly, thinking that his own parents could have taken a few lessons from Jenna. In his home, praise had always revolved around achievement.

Jenna fiddled with her glasses. 'My parents were always more interested in what I did than who I was, and I was determined not to be like that. Clive worked—I stayed at home. Traditional, I know, but it was the way I wanted it.'

'Can I ask you something personal? Did you marry him because you loved him or because you were pregnant?'

She hesitated. 'I thought I loved him.'

'And now you're not sure?'

'How can you love someone you don't even know?' Her

voice cracked slightly and Ryan crossed the kitchen and dragged her into his arms.

'The guy is clearly deranged.' Dropping a kiss on her hair, he eased her away from him. 'So now I understand why you asked me that question. You must find it impossible to trust another man.'

'No.' She said the word fiercely. 'Clive lied to me, but I know all men aren't like that—just as not all teenage mothers are inept and not all boys wearing hoodies are carrying knives. I won't generalise. I don't trust him, that's true, but I don't want Lexi growing up thinking the whole male race is bad. I won't do that to her.'

Her answer surprised him. He'd met plenty of people with trust issues.

He had a few of his own.

'You're a surprising person, Jenna Richards.' Young in many ways, and yet in others more mature than many people older than her.

'I'm an ordinary person.'

He thought about the way she loved her child, the way she was determined to be as good a mother as she could be. He thought about the fact that she'd been with the same man since she was sixteen. 'There's nothing ordinary about you. I'm intrigued about something, though.' He stroked her hair away from her face, loving the feel of it. 'If you were at home with Lexi, when did you train as a nurse?'

'Once Lexi started school. I had a network of friends— many of them working mothers. We helped each other out. Sisterhood. They'd take Lexi for me when I was working, I'd take their children on my days off. Sometimes I had a house full of kids.'

He could imagine her with children everywhere. 'Can I ask you something else? Why didn't you ever have more children? You obviously love them.'

'Clive didn't want more. He decided Lexi was enough.'

'Like he decided that you weren't going to have a dog or eat fish?'

She gave a shaky smile. 'Are you suggesting my final act of rebellion should be to have a baby? I think that might be taking it a bit far. And anyway, I couldn't do that now.'

'Why not?'

'Well, for a start, I'm too old.'

'You're thirty-three. Plenty of women don't have their first child until that age.'

She looked at him, and he knew she was wondering why he was dwelling on the subject. 'And then there's Lexi. If I had a baby now, it would be difficult for her.'

'Why?'

'Because there have been enough changes in her life. I suspect that at some point, probably soon, her father is going to have another child. I don't want to add to the confusion. I want her relationship with me to be as stable as possible. Why are you asking?'

Why *was* he asking? Unsettled by his own thoughts, Ryan turned his attention back to his breakfast. 'I'm just saying you're not too old to have a child.' He kept his voice even. 'Put your sunglasses on. You're right about it being sunny outside.'

CHAPTER EIGHT

IT WAS an affair full of snatched moments and secret assignations, all tinged with the bittersweet knowledge that it couldn't possibly last.

At times Jenna felt guilty that she was keeping her relationship with Ryan from Lexi, but her daughter was finally settled and happy and she was afraid to do or say anything that might change that.

She just couldn't give Ryan up.

They'd meet at the lighthouse at lunchtime, make love until they were both exhausted, and then part company and arrive back at the surgery at different times.

And, despite the subterfuge, she'd never been happier in her life.

'I actually feel grateful to Clive,' she murmured one afternoon as they lay on his cliffs, staring at the sea. Her hand was wrapped in his and she felt his warm fingers tighten. 'If he hadn't done what he did, I wouldn't be here now. I wouldn't have known it was possible to feel like this. It's scary, isn't it? You're in a relationship, and you have nothing to compare it to, so you say to yourself this is it. This is how it's supposed to feel. But you always have a sense that something is missing.'

'Did you?'

'Yes, but I assumed it was something in me that was lacking, not in my relationship.'

'Life has a funny way of working itself out.' He turned his head to look at her. 'Have you told Lexi about us yet?'

A grey cloud rolled over her happiness. 'No,' she said. 'Not yet.'

'Are you going to tell her?'

'I don't know.'

'You're afraid of her reaction?'

'Yes. She was devastated when Clive left. Horrified that he was involved with another woman. Apart from the obvious issues, teenagers don't like to see their parents as living, breathing sexual beings.'

And she didn't know what to say. *I've taken a lover...*

What exactly was their relationship? What could there be?

Ryan rolled onto his side and propped himself up on his elbow so that he could see her. 'I want to be with you, Jenna. I want more than lunchtimes and the occasional Sunday afternoon when Lexi is with her friends. I want more.'

Looking into his blue eyes, she felt her heart spin and dance. 'How much more?'

'I love you.' Ryan touched her face gently, as if making a discovery. 'I've loved you since you stepped off that boat looking like someone who had walked away from an accident.'

'You love me?' Jenna was jolted by a burst of happiness and he smiled.

He looked more relaxed than she'd ever seen him. 'Is that a surprise?'

'I didn't dare hope. I thought it might be just—' She was whispering, afraid that she might disturb the dream. 'I love you, too. I've never felt this way about anyone before. I didn't know it was possible.'

'Neither did I.' He kissed her gently, stroked her hair protectively with a hand that wasn't quite steady. Then he gave a shake of his head. 'You've never asked me about my marriage or why I ended up here. I'm sure there are things you want to know about me.'

'I assumed that if there was anything you wanted me to know, you'd tell me when you were ready.'

'You're a very unusual woman, do you know that? You're able to love me, not knowing what went before?'

'It's not relevant to how I feel about you.'

He breathed in deeply, his eyes never shifting from hers. 'I was married—to Connie. She was a very ambitious woman. Connie was born knowing what she wanted in life and nothing was going to stand in her way. We met when we were medical students. We were together briefly, and then met up again when we were both consultants in the same hospital. Looking back on it, we were a disaster waiting to happen, but at the time I suppose it must have seemed right.'

Thinking of her own situation, Jenna nodded. 'That happens.'

His laugh was tight and humourless. 'I think the truth is I was too busy for a relationship and Connie understood that. I was fighting my way to the top and I didn't need a woman asking me what time I'd be home at night. Connie didn't care what time I came home because she was never there to see. She was fighting *her* way to the top, too.'

Jenna sat quietly, letting him speak. She had an image in her head. An image of a beautiful, successful woman. The sort of woman she'd always imagined a man like him would choose. The cream of the crop. Bright and brilliant, like him. They would have been a golden couple. 'Was she beautiful?'

'No.' His hand dropped from her face and he sat up. Stared out across the sea. 'Physically I suppose she would be considered beautiful,' he conceded finally. 'But to me beauty is so much more than sleek hair and well-arranged features. Connie was cold. Selfish. Beauty is who you are and the way you behave. We were both very wrapped up in our careers. We worked all day, wrote research papers in what little spare time we had—our house had two offices.' He frowned and shook his head. 'How could I ever have thought that what we had was a marriage?'

'Go on...'

'I wanted us to start a family.'

'Oh.' It hadn't occurred to her that he might have a child. That was one question she hadn't asked. 'You have—?'

'I brought the subject up one night, about a week after I'd made Consultant. I thought it would be the perfect time.'

'She didn't agree?'

He stared blindly across the ocean and into the far distance. 'She told me she'd been sterilised.'

Jenna sat up. 'She— Oh, my gosh—and you didn't know?' She licked her lips, digesting the enormity of it.

'At medical school she decided she didn't ever want to have a baby. She wanted a career and didn't want children. In her usual ruthlessly efficient way she decided to deal with the problem once and for all. Unfortunately she didn't share that fact with me.' The confession was rough and hoarse, and she knew for sure he hadn't spoken the words to anyone else. Just her. The knowledge that he'd trusted her with something so personal was like a gift, fragile and precious, and Jenna tried to understand how he must be feeling, unwilling to break the connection between them by saying something that might make him regret his show of trust.

In the end she just said what was in her heart. 'That was wrong. Very wrong.'

'Some of the blame was mine. I made assumptions—didn't ask—I suppose I could be accused of being chauvinistic. I presumed we'd do the traditional thing at some point. It came as a shock to discover she had no intention of ever having a family.'

Jenna reached out a hand and touched his shoulder. 'She should have told you.'

'That was my feeling. I suddenly realised I'd been living with a stranger. That I didn't know her at all.' He gave a wry smile. 'But you know how that feels, don't you?'

'Only too well. I was living in this imaginary world—thinking things were fine. But Clive was living a completely different life. A life I didn't even see.' She looped her arms around her legs and rested her chin on her knees. 'I suppose part of the problem was that we just didn't communicate. We fell into marriage because I was pregnant and because it was what my parents expected. I made assumptions about him. He made assumptions about me.' Jenna turned her head and looked at him. 'So you told Connie you wanted a divorce?'

'Yes. I discovered that although I'd achieved what could be considered huge success in my professional life, my personal life was a disaster. I hadn't even thought about what I wanted, and suddenly I realised that what I wanted was the thing I didn't have—someone alongside me who loved me, who wanted to share their life with me. I wanted to come home at night to someone who cared about what sort of day I'd had. I didn't want our only communication to be via voice-mail. And I wanted children. Connie thought I was being ridiculous—her exact words were, "It's not as if you're ever going to change a nappy, Ryan, and I'm certainly not doing it, so why would we want children?"'

'She didn't want a divorce?'

'I was flying high in my career and she liked that. I looked good on her CV.' There was a bitter note to his voice and his eyes were flint-hard. 'Being with me opened doors for her.'

'Did she love you?'

'I have no idea. If she did then it was a very selfish kind

of a love. She wanted me for what I added to her, if that makes sense.'

'Yes, it makes sense. I don't know much about relationships…' Jenna thought about her own relationship with Clive '…but I do know that real love is about giving. It's about wanting someone else's happiness more than your own. If you care about someone, you want what's right for them.'

And that was the way she felt about Ryan, she realised. She wanted him to be happy.

Ryan put his arm around her shoulders and drew her against him. 'That's what you do with Lexi, all the time. You're lucky to have her. Lucky to have that bond.'

'Yes.' She melted as he kissed her, knowing that everything was changing. Once again life had taken her in a direction she hadn't anticipated, but this time the future wasn't terrifying. It was exciting. 'I'm going to talk to her. I've decided. I think maybe she's old enough to understand.' Strengthened by her feelings and his, she suddenly felt it was the right thing to do.

'You're going to talk to her about us?'

'Yes. This is what life is, isn't it? It's the happy and the sad and the unpredictable. It would be wrong to pretend anything different. Lexi needs to know that life is sometimes hard and that things can't always stay the same. She needs to know that change isn't always bad and that the unfamiliar can become familiar. And she needs to know that my love for her will never change, no matter what happens to the way we live.'

Ryan stroked his fingers over her cheek. 'You're the most selfless person I've ever met. When your husband walked out, who supported you? Not your mother, I assume. Your friends?'

'For a while. Then I discovered that they'd all known he was having the affair and that they'd known about his other affairs and hadn't told me.' Jenna pulled away from him. 'I found that hard. That and all the advice. "Turn a blind eye." "Dress like a pole dancer and seduce him back—'"

There was amusement in his eyes. 'Did you adopt that suggestion?'

'Of course—I went around wearing nothing but fishnets and a basque.' Pleased that she was able to make a joke about something she'd never thought would seem funny, she wound a strand of hair around her finger. 'To be honest, I didn't want him back. Not after I found out that he'd had a string of affairs throughout our marriage. But the worst thing of all was the way he behaved towards Lexi—it was as if he suddenly just washed his hands of her. His own daughter!' Humour faded and anger flooded through her, fresh as it had been on that first day. 'Whatever he felt about me, that was no excuse for cutting Lexi out of his life.'

'Forget him now.' His voice was rough as he pulled her back to him. 'He was your past. I'm your future.'

Jenna stared at him, silenced by the possibilities that extended in front of her. She wanted to ask what he meant. She wanted to ask whether the future meant a few weeks, or more than that, but she was terrified of voicing the question in case the answer was something she didn't want to hear.

He was watching her, absorbing her reaction. 'Jenna, I know this is soon, but—' There was a buzzing sound from his pocket, and Ryan swore fluently and dragged out his phone. 'Maybe there are some advantages to living in a city—at least someone else can carry the load when you want some time off.' He checked the number and frowned. 'It's Logan. I'd better take this—sorry.'

As he talked to the other doctor, Jenna gently extracted herself from his grip, wondering what he'd been about to say. It was obvious that she wasn't going to find out quickly, because Ryan was digging in his pocket for his car keys as he talked, the expression on his face enough for her to know that the phone call was serious.

He sprang to his feet. 'I'll get up there now.' His eyes flickered to hers. 'And I'll take Jenna with me—no, don't worry, we'll handle it together.'

Realising that she was supposed to help him with something, Jenna stood up and brushed the grass off her skirt.

Ryan was already striding towards the path that led up to his car. 'Have you done any emergency work?'

'Sorry?' Jenna jammed her feet into her shoes and sprinted after him, wondering how the tone of the afternoon could have shifted so quickly.

Glenmore, she thought, and its ever-changing moods.

Even the weather had changed. While they'd been talking the blue sky had turned an ominous grey and the sea a gunmetal-blue.

There was a storm coming.

'Did you ever work in an emergency department?' His mouth grim, Ryan was in the car and firing up the engine before she had time to answer the question.

'Yes. But it was quite a few years ago. What do you need me to do?' Her head smacked lightly against the headrest as he accelerated along the empty road, and Jenna felt the power of the car come to life around her. She felt a shimmer of nerves mingled with anticipation. What if she wasn't up to the job?

To give herself confidence she cast a glance at Ryan, looking at his broad shoulders and strong, capable hands. He shifted gears like a racing driver, pushing the car to its limits as he negotiated the tight turns and narrow roads that led from the lighthouse. Even after a comparatively short time she knew he would be able to handle anything he encountered, and that knowledge gave her courage. 'Tell me what's happened.'

'Group of teenagers tombstoning on the Devil's Jaws. It's close to here.'

'Tombstoning?' Jenna rummaged in her pocket and found something to tie back her hair. 'What's that?'

'It's when they stand on the top of a cliff and jump into the sea.' Ryan slowed to take a sharp bend. 'The problem is the depth of the water changes according to the tide. Even when the tide is on your side it's a dangerous activity. And the Devil's Jaws is the most dangerous place you could wish for. It's narrow there—the cliffs have formed a tight channel, so not only can you kill yourself when you hit the bottom, if you get really lucky you can kill yourself on the way down.'

'Kids are doing that? Can't they fence the cliffs off or something?'

'It *is* fenced off. The place is lethal. No one is meant to go within a hundred metres of it, but you know teenagers.' He swung the car into a space at the side of the road and killed the engine. 'We have to walk from here. Are you afraid of heights?'

'I don't know. I don't think so.'

'Watch your footing. To add to the fun, the rocks are crumbling.' Ryan opened his boot and Jenna blinked as she saw the contents.

'You carry ropes in your boot?'

'I climb sometimes.' Without elaborating, he selected several ropes and started piling equipment into a large rucksack. Then he opened his medical bag and added another series of items, including drugs he thought he was going to need. His movements were swift and economical, brutally efficient.

Jenna focused on the drugs. 'Ketamine?'

'I prefer it to morphine. It doesn't produce respiratory depression or hypotension, and in analgesic doses it produces a mild bronchodilator effect.'

'Translate that into English?' A voice came from behind

them and Jenna turned to see Nick Hillier, the island police-man. Only today he wasn't smiling.

'It means it controls the pain without affecting the breath-ing.' Ryan hoisted the bag out of the boot. 'Is it as bad as they say?'

'Worse. Two in the water—one trapped halfway down the cliff. They're right in the Jaws.'

'Of course they are—that's where they get the maximum adrenaline rush.'

'The one stuck on the cliff might be all right, as long as he doesn't let go, but he's getting tired. Coastguard helicop-ter has chosen today to have a technical problem—they're fixing it, but the cavalry isn't going to be arriving any time soon.' Nick sucked in a breath. 'I don't want anyone going near the edge. I don't want more casualties. We're going to wait and hope to hell they get that helicopter airborne in the next ten minutes. I think this is a rescue best carried out from the air or the sea.'

'I'll take a look at it. Then I'll decide.' Ryan lifted the rucksack onto his back and walked over the grass towards a gate. A sign warned the public that the area was dangerous. Dropping his rucksack onto the other side, Ryan vaulted the gate. Nick climbed over slightly more awkwardly, holding out a hand to Jenna.

She wondered who was going to have the last say on this one. The law or the doctor.

His mind clearly working in the same direction, Nick be-came visibly stressed. 'Ryan, you know how risky it is. A climber was killed abseiling from here earlier in the sum-mer—the rocks sawed through his rope.'

'Then he didn't have his rope in the right place.' Ryan dropped his rucksack again, onto the grass a safe distance from the edge. 'There are injured kids, Nick. What do you expect me to do? Leave them?'

'My job is to make sure we rescue them with minimum further casualties—that doesn't involve you abseiling down a sheer, crumbling rock face.'

Listening to them, Jenna felt her heart race, and she wondered if she was going to be any use at all.

Yes, she'd worked in an emergency department for a short time, but working in a well-equipped department was quite different from giving pre-hospital care on a sheer cliff face.

She was so busy worrying about her own abilities that it was a few seconds before she noticed the teenager sitting on the grass. He was shivering and his face was white.

Focusing on his face, Jenna recognised Fraser and her stomach dropped. Suddenly everything seemed to happen in slow motion. She was aware of the guilt in Fraser's anguished glance, and of Ryan turning his head to look at her.

And those looks meant only one thing—

That it was Lexi who was lying in the grip of the Devil's Jaws.

Maternal instinct overwhelming everything else, Jenna gave a low moan of denial and stepped towards the edge, unthinking.

Ryan caught her arm in an iron grip.

'Don't take another step.' His hand was a steadying force and his voice was hard, forcing itself through the blind panic that clouded her thinking. 'Breathe. Up here, you don't run. You take small steps. You look where you're going and you make sure it's safe underfoot. I'll get her. I swear to you I'll get her. But I can't do it if I'm worrying about you going over the edge.'

Jenna stood still, held firm by the strength of his hand and the conviction in his voice.

Fraser struggled to his feet, his lips dry and cracked from the wind and the sun. 'You don't understand—she didn't jump. Lexi was trying to stop Matt doing it—we both were.

But he did it anyway—he jumped at the wrong moment. You have to get it exactly right or you hit the rocks.' His voice shook. He was a teenager on the cusp of manhood, but today he was definitely more boy than man. 'Lexi went down there to save Matt. We could see him slipping under the water. He was going to drown. Jamie tried first, but he lost his nerve halfway down and now he can't move. I dunno—he just freaked out or something. So Lexi did it. She insisted. She was dead scared about getting down there, but she said she'd done first aid so she should be the one.'

'She climbed down?' There was a strange note in Ryan's voice and already he had his hands in his rucksack. 'Fraser, take this rope for me.'

'You should have seen her—she was amazing. Just went down slowly, hand and foot, hand and foot, muttering "Three points of contact on the rock face…" or something.'

'She did a climbing course last summer,' Jenna said faintly. Last summer—just before everything had fallen apart. 'It was indoors on a climbing wall in London.'

Nowhere near greasy, slippery rocks or furious boiling sea.

Ryan's gaze met hers for a moment. 'I'd say that was money well spent.'

Fraser was sweating. 'I almost had a heart attack watching her. I'm not good with heights since I fell into that dungeon.' He looked at Jenna, shrinking. 'I'm really sorry. I tried to stop her…'

'It isn't your fault, Fraser.' Jenna's lips were stiff and her heart was pounding. 'Lexi is not your responsibility. She's old enough to make her own decisions.'

'She's as sure-footed as a goat.' There was awe in Fraser's voice. 'Matt was face-down in the water and she dragged him towards the rocks. She's been holding him, but he's too heavy for her to get him out by herself and the tide is coming in. The water level is rising. The ledge they're on will be underwater soon.'

That news made Jenna's knees weaken with panic, but Ryan was icy calm. When he spoke there was no doubt in anyone's mind who was in charge of the rescue.

'Fraser, I want you to stay here and act as runner. Is your mobile working?'

'Yes, the signal is good.'

'Keep it switched on. Dr McNeil is bringing equipment from the surgery. If the helicopter is delayed, then that will change the way we manage Matt's injuries.' Ryan stepped into a harness and adjusted it with hands that were steady and confident. 'Keep the phone line clear—if I need to talk to you, I'll call.'

Nick stepped forward and caught his arm. 'Ryan, for goodness' sake, man, I'm telling you we should wait for the helicopter.'

Jenna couldn't breathe. If Ryan agreed to wait for the helicopter then Lexi might drown. But if Ryan went down there—if he put himself at risk for her daughter and the two boys...

'You're wasting time, Nick.' His eyes flickered to hers and for a brief moment the connection was there. 'It will be all right. Trust me.'

And she did. Although why she should be so ready to trust a man she'd known for weeks when a man she'd known for years had let her down, she didn't understand. But life wasn't always easy to understand, was it? Some things happened without an explanation.

'What can I do?' Her mouth was so dry she could hardly form the words. 'How can I help?'

'You can stay there, away from the edge.'

Nick caught his arm. 'Ryan—'

'I'm going to abseil down, and I want you to lower the rest

of my pack.' He adjusted his harness for a final time and held out his hand. 'Do you have a radio for me?'

Nick gave up arguing, but his face was white and his eyes flickered between the rising tide and the sky, obviously looking for a helicopter. Hoping.

Jenna felt helpless. 'I want to do something. If the boy is badly injured you'll need help. I can abseil down, too—'

Ryan didn't spare her a glance. 'You'll stay here.'

'It's my daughter down there.'

'That's why you're staying up here. You'll be too busy worrying about her to be any use to me.'

'Don't patronise me.' Anger spurting through her veins, Jenna picked up a harness. 'You need me down there, Ryan. Two of them are in the water, one of them injured, and one of them is stuck on the rock face. He could fall at any moment. You can't do this by yourself, and Lexi is just a child.'

Ryan paused. Then he looked over his shoulder, down at the jagged rocks. 'All right. This is what we'll do. I'll go down there first and do an assessment. If I need you, Nick can get you down to me. But watch my route. Have you abseiled before?'

Jenna swallowed, wishing she could tell him she'd scaled Everest four times without oxygen. 'Once. On an adventure camp when I was fifteen.'

'I love the fact that you're so honest. Don't worry—Nick can get you down there if I need you. Hopefully I won't.'

He went over the edge like someone from an action movie and Jenna blinked. Clearly there was plenty she still had to learn about Ryan, and the more she knew, the more she liked and admired him.

'I should have stopped him,' Nick muttered, and Jenna lifted an eyebrow because the idea of stopping Ryan doing something he was determined to do seemed laughable to her.

'How?'

The policeman gave a short laugh. 'Good question. Still, what Ryan doesn't know about ropes and climbing isn't worth knowing. I'm going to get this on you Jenna.' He had a harness in his hands. 'Just in case. I have a feeling he's going to need you. I can't believe I'm doing this.'

'If he's going to need me, why didn't he just say so?'

'Honestly? I'm guessing he's being protective. Either that or he doesn't want any of us to know how easy it is.' With a weak grin, Nick adjusted the harness and glanced at her face. Jenna wondered if he knew that there was something going on between them or whether he was matchmaking like the others.

Ryan's voice crackled over the radio. 'Nick, do you read me? I need you to lower that rope to me, over.'

'What he really needs is a miracle,' Nick muttered, lowering one end of a rope down to Ryan and securing the other end to a rock. 'That should keep the boy steady while Ryan finds out what's going on. I hope he does it quickly. There's a storm coming. Great timing. Can today get any worse?'

Only an hour earlier she'd been lying on the grass on Ryan's cliffs, bathed in sunshine and happiness.

Eyeing the rolling black clouds, Jenna approached the edge cautiously. Peering over the side, she caught her breath. Here, the cliff face was vertical. The rocks plunged downwards, the edges ragged and sharp as sharks' teeth, ready to razor through the flesh of the unwary. Her stomach lurched, and the sheer terror of facing that drop almost swallowed her whole.

'I can't believe they thought they could jump down there,' she said faintly, biting her lip as she saw Ryan attaching the rope to a boy clinging halfway down. Then her gaze drifted lower and she saw Lexi's small figure, crouched on an exposed rock at the bottom. The girl had her arms around a boy's shoulders, holding him out of the water, straining with the effort as the sea boiled and foamed angrily around them, the level of the water rising with each incoming wave.

Watching the waves lick hungrily at her daughter, Jenna felt physically sick. 'That boy is going to be under the water in another few minutes. Lexi isn't strong enough to pull him out. And she isn't going to be strong enough to keep herself out.' Feeling completely helpless, she turned to Nick. 'Get me down there now. Don't wait for Ryan to talk to you. He has his hands full. I can help—I know I can.'

'I'm not risking another person unless I have to. It's bad enough Ryan going down there, but at least he knows what he's doing. You have no cliff rescue skills—'

'I'm her mother,' Jenna said icily. 'That counts for a great deal, believe me. Get me down there, Nick.'

He slid his fingers into the collar of his jacket, easing the pressure. 'If someone has to go it should probably be me.'

'You need to stay up here to co-ordinate with the coast-guard. I don't know anything about that—I wouldn't have a clue.' Jenna glanced down again and saw that Ryan had secured the boy and was now abseiling to the bottom of the cliff. He landed on shiny deadly rock just as another enormous wave rushed in and swamped both teenagers.

Instantly Ryan's voice crackled over the radio. 'Get Jenna down here, Nick. It's an easy abseil—'

Easy? Torn between relief and raw terror, Jenna switched off her brain. To think was to panic, and she couldn't afford to panic. Her daughter had climbed down there, she reminded herself as she leaned backwards and did as Nick instructed. All the same, there was a moment when her courage failed her and she thought she was going to freeze on the black forbidding rock.

'Just take it steady, Jen.' Ryan's voice came from below her, solid and secure. 'You're nearly there.'

To stop would be to disappoint him as well as risk lives,

so Jenna kept going, thinking to herself that if he genuinely thought this was easy she wouldn't want to do a difficult abseil. The cliff fell away sharply and she went down slowly, listening to Ryan's voice from below her, thinking of Lexi and not of the drop, or of the man who had died when his rope was severed. As her feet finally touched the rocks strong hands caught her. Ryan's hands.

He unclipped the rope and the sea immediately swamped her feet. If he hadn't clamped an arm around her waist she would have stumbled under the sudden pressure of the water. As it was, the cold made her gasp. Above her the cliff face towered, blocking out the last of the sunshine, revealing only ominous clouds in the chink of sky above. Here, in the slit of the rock, it was freezing.

She guessed that if the helicopter didn't manage to get to them soon, then it would be too late. The weather would close in and make flying impossible.

And then what?

'The tide is coming in—Ryan, I can't hold his head any longer—' Lexi's voice came from behind them and Jenna turned, her stomach lurching as she saw the blood on her daughter's tee shirt.

'It's not mine.' Lexi read her mind and gave a quick shake of her head. 'It's Matt's. His legs—both of them, I think. He jumped in and hit rock under the surface. I didn't know what to do—he's too heavy. Mummy, do something!'

Mummy. She hadn't heard 'Mummy' since Lexi was about six, and it sent strength pouring back through her rubbery legs.

'Just hold on, Lexi.' Her voice was firm and confident, and Ryan gave her a brief smile and released her, checking that she was steady on her feet before crossing the rocks to the two teenagers.

'You're a total star, Lexi. I just need you to hold on for

another minute. Can you do that?' He ripped equipment out of the rucksack as he spoke, and Jenna saw Lexi swallow as she stared up at him.

'Yes.'

'Good. We're going to get him out of the water now, and you're going to help.' Ryan had a rope in his hand. 'Just do everything I say.'

Jenna saw the fierce light of determination in her daughter's eyes—saw the faith and trust in her expression as she looked at Ryan.

Gone was the child who moaned when she couldn't get a mobile phone signal.

Jenna's flash of pride lasted only seconds as she saw another huge wave bearing down on them.

She saw Ryan glance at Lexi and then back towards her, trying to make a decision.

Jenna made the decision for him. 'Hold onto the children!' She slithered towards the rock face and managed to get a grip just as the wave rose in height and started to break. With a ferocious roar it crashed onto the rocks with an explosion of white froth, as if determined to claim its prize. Jenna clung, feeling the water pull at her and then retreat.

Wiping salt water from her face, she looked over her shoulder and saw that Ryan had his hands on Lexi's shoulders, holding her. As soon as the wave receded he turned his attention to Matt. The boy was moaning softly, his body half in and half out of the water.

'My legs—I can't put any weight—'

'Yeah—we're going to help you with that.' Ryan glanced around him, judging, coming up with a plan. 'If we can get him clear of the water and onto that rock higher up, that should give us at least another ten minutes before the tide hits us again. Enough time to check the damage and give him some pain relief.' He spoke into the radio, telling Nick what he was doing and listing the equipment he needed. 'While they're sorting that out, I'm going to get a rope on you, Matt.'

'Just leave me.' His face white with pain, the boy choked the words out. 'I don't want anyone to drown because of me.'

'No one is drowning today.' Ryan looped the rope under the boy's shoulders and secured it to a shaft of rock that jutted out of the cliff. Then he did the same to Lexi. 'The rope is going to hold both of you if another wave comes before we're done. We're going to get you out of the water, Matt. Then I'm going to give you something for the pain.' He questioned the boy about the way he'd landed, about his neck, about the movement in his limbs.

Jenna wondered why he didn't give the boy painkillers first, but then she saw another wave rushing down on them and realised that the boy was only minutes from drowning. Rope or no rope, if Ryan couldn't lift him clear of the water the boy was dead.

As the wave swamped all four of them Jenna held her breath and gripped the rock tightly. The tide was coming in. They didn't have much time.

'What can I do?'

'Do you see that narrow ledge just under the waterline? Stand on it. I need you to hold his body steady so that we move him as little as possible.' As a precaution, Ryan put a supportive collar around Matt's neck.

Jenna stepped into the water, gritting her teeth as the ice-cold sea turned her legs numb. If she felt this cold, how must the children be feeling? She steadied Matt's body, her hands firm. 'I'm ready.'

'I'm going to lift—try not to let his legs drag against the rocks.'

Using nothing but brute strength and hard muscle, Ryan hauled the boy out of the water. Matt's screams echoed

around the narrow chasm, bouncing off the rocks and adding to the deadly feel of the place.

Her heart breaking for him, Jenna gritted her teeth, wanting to stop but knowing they couldn't. They had to get him
clear of the water. He'd already been in there too long. Even
as Ryan lifted him she saw the terrible gashes on the boy's
legs and knew they were dealing with serious injuries. Blood
mixed with the water, and as they laid him flat on the rock
Matt was white-faced, his lips bloodless.

'Shaft of femur—both legs.' Now that he could see the
damage, Ryan worked swiftly, checking for other injuries
and then examining the wound. 'Jenna, we need to control
the bleeding on his left leg and cover that wound. Get me
pads and a broad bandage out of the rucksack. I'm going to
give him some Ketamine. Matt, this will help with the pain.'

Matt groaned. 'I'm going to die. I know I am—'

'You're not going to die.' Seeing Lexi's horrified look,
Jenna spoke firmly, and Ryan gave the boy's shoulder a quick
squeeze.

'No one is dying on my shift,' he said easily, and Matt
made a sound that was halfway between a sob and a moan.

'If the pain doesn't kill me, my mum will.'

Jenna closed her hand over his, checking that Lexi was
safely out of the water. 'Your mum won't kill you,' she said
huskily. 'She's just going to be relieved you're OK.'

Ryan's gaze flickered to hers and she read his mind.

Matt was far from OK. He had two fractured femurs and
he was still losing blood. Knowing that she had to help, Jenna
let go of the boy's hand and dug into the rucksack, finding
what she needed. Thinking clearly now, she ripped open the
sterile dressings and talked to her daughter. 'Lexi? Do you
have your digital camera with you?'

'What?' Soaked through and shivering, Lexi stared at her

mother as though she were mad. 'Matt's bleeding half to death here and you want me to take a photo of the view?'

'He's not bleeding to death.' Taking her cue from Ryan, Jenna kept her voice calm. 'I don't want you to take the view. I want you to take a picture of Matt's legs. It will help the ER staff.'

'Good thinking.' Ryan injected the Ketamine. '*Do* you have your camera, Lex?'

'Yes—yes. But...' Baffled, Lexi cast a glance at Matt and rose to her feet, holding the rocks so that she didn't slip. She was wearing jeans, and the denim was dark with seawater. 'In my jacket pocket. What do you want me to do?'

'Take several pictures of the wounds. I'll do it, if you like.' Jenna was worried about her daughter seeing the extent of the injuries, but Lexi just gritted her teeth and pointed her digital camera. She took several photos and checked them quickly.

'OK. It's done.'

'Good.' Now that the pictures were taken, Jenna covered the wounds. 'It saves the receiving team in the hospital from removing the dressings from his legs to see what's going on.'

'Oh. I get it.' Several shades paler than she'd been a moment earlier, Lexi nodded. 'What else can I do?'

'Stay out of reach of the waves,' Ryan said immediately, his hands on Jenna's as they packed the wound, using a bandage to hold it in place. 'Any change—tell me. Jen, I'm going to splint both legs together.'

They worked as a team, Jenna following his instructions to the letter. It didn't matter that she'd never done anything like this before because his commands were clear and precise. Do this. Do that. Put your hands here—

Later, she'd look back on it and wonder how he could have been so sure about everything, but for now she just did as she was told.

Checking the pulse in both Matt's feet, she nodded to Ryan. 'His circulation is good in both legs.'

'Right. Lex, take this for me.' Ryan passed his radio to Lexi, freeing up his hands. Then he turned back to the boy. 'Matt, you've broken both your legs. I'm going to put a splint on them because that will reduce the bleeding and it will help the pain.' He looked towards Lexi. 'Logan should be up there by now. Make contact and tell Nick I need a towel.'

A towel? Glancing at the water around them, Jenna wondered if he'd gone mad, and then reminded himself that everything he'd done so far had been spot-on.

Worried that all this was too much for Lexi, Jenna was about to repeat the instructions but Lexi was already working the radio. Doing everything she'd been asked to do, she talked to Nick and relayed messages back and forth, copying the radio style she'd heard Ryan use.

'Dr McNeil is there. He wants to know what you need.'

'I'll have a Sager splint, if he has one, otherwise any traction splint. And oxygen. And ask Nick if we have an ETA on the helicopter.'

'Sager?' Jenna handed him a Venflon and Ryan slid the cannula into the vein in Matt's arm as smoothly as if he was working in a state-of-the-art emergency unit, not a chasm in the rocks.

'It's an American splint. I prefer it.'

'They're lowering it down now. I'll get it.' One eye on the waves, Lexi picked her way across the slippery rocks like a tightrope walker and reached for the rucksack that had been lowered on the end of a rope.

Watching the boiling cauldron of water lapping angrily at her daughter's ankles, Jenna prayed that she wouldn't slip. Pride swelled inside her and she blinked rapidly, forcing herself to concentrate on her part of the rescue. 'Is it possible to apply a splint in these conditions with just the two of us?'

'I can do it in two and a half minutes, and it will make it easier to evacuate him by helicopter.' Ryan took the rucksack Lexi handed him and opened it. Using the towel, he dried Matt's legs and then opened the bag containing the splint. In a few swift movements he'd removed, unfolded and assembled the splint. 'OK, that's ready.' He positioned it between Matt's legs, explaining what he was doing.

Hearing the sound of a helicopter overhead, Jenna looked up, relief providing a much-needed flood of warmth through her body. 'Oh, thank goodness—they're here.'

Ryan didn't look up. 'They can take Jamie off first. By the time they have him in the helicopter Matt will be ready.' He wrapped the harness around the boy's ankles. 'Lexi, tell Nick.' He was treating the girl like an adult, showing no doubt in her ability to perform the tasks he set.

Without faltering Lexi spoke into the radio again, obviously proud to have something useful to do.

Jenna helped Ryan with the splint. 'How much traction do you apply?'

'Generally ten per cent of the patient's body weight per fractured femur.' Eyeing Matt's frame, Ryan checked the amount of traction on the scale. 'I'm making an educated guess.'

The noise of the helicopter increased, and Jenna watched in awe as the winchman was lowered into the narrow gap between the cliffs. In no time he had a harness on Jamie and was lifting him towards the helicopter.

'At least there's no wind.' Ryan secured straps around Matt's thighs until both legs were well supported.

Staggered by the speed with which he'd applied the splint, Jenna took Matt's hand. 'How are you doing?'

'It feels a bit better,' Matt muttered, 'but I'm not looking forward to going up in that helicopter.'

'You're going to be fine. They're experts.' Ryan watched as

the winchman was lowered again, this time with a stretcher. 'We're going to get you on board, Matt, and then I'll give you oxygen and fluid on our way to hospital. Once we're on dry land, we can make you comfortable.'

Jenna looked at him, his words sinking home.

Ryan was leaving them.

She gave herself a mental shake. Of course he had to go with the casualty. What else? But she couldn't stop the shiver, and her palms dug a little harder into the grey slippery rock as she kept hold.

Ryan helped the winchman transfer Matt onto the stretcher. They had a conversation about the injury, the loss of blood—Jenna knew they were deciding whether it was best to have a doctor on board. The winchman was a paramedic, but still—

She watched as Matt was lifted slowly out of the narrow gap between the rocks, the winchman steadying the stretcher.

Once he was safely inside the helicopter, Ryan turned to Jenna.

Seeing the indecision on his face, she didn't hesitate.

'You should go! He might need you. You have to leave us here while you get him to hospital.'

Ryan's face was damp with seawater, his hair soaked, his jaw tense. 'I can't see any other way.' Already the winchman was being lowered for the final time.

Jenna lifted her chin. 'You're wasting time. We'll be fine, Ryan. We'll climb a little higher and the helicopter will be back for us soon. They're ready for you.' She watched, dry-mouthed, as the winchman landed on the rocks. 'Go.' To make it easier for both of them, she turned away and picked her way over the rocks to Lexi.

The girl was shivering, although whether it was from the cold or shock, Jenna didn't know.

She was shivering, too.

'They'll be back for us ever so quickly. You did so well,

Lexi. I was so proud of you.' She wrapped her arms around her daughter and rubbed the girl's back, trying to stop the shivering. 'Oh, you're soaked through, you poor thing. How long have you been in that water? You must be freezing.'

'Is Matt going to die, Mum?' Lexi's teeth were chattering and her long hair fell in wet ropes around her shoulders. 'There was so much blood—'

'That's because the seawater made it seem like more.' Jenna's protective instincts flooded to the surface as she heard the fear in Lexi's voice and decided this was one of those times when it was best to be economical with the truth. 'He isn't going to die. He is seriously injured, and he's going to be spending quite a bit of time in hospital, but he'll be all right, I'm sure. Largely thanks to you. How did you do it, Lexi? How did you climb down here?' Her stomach tightened at the thought.

'He was just lying there, Mum. I had to do something.'

Jenna hugged her tightly. 'You saved his life.'

'Not me. Ryan.' Lexi hugged her back. 'Did you see him come down that cliff face, Mum? It was like watching one of those special forces movies. Commandos or something.'

'Yes, I saw.' Jenna closed her eyes, trying to wipe out the image of her daughter negotiating those deadly, slippery rocks without a rope.

'And he knew exactly what to do—'

'Yes.'

Lexi gave a sniff and adjusted her position on the rock. 'He's so cool. And you were good, too, Mum. I've never seen you work before. I didn't know you were so—I dunno—so great.'

Jenna smiled weakly. 'It's amazing what you can do when the tide is coming in.'

'You and Ryan get on well together. You look like—a team.'

Jenna stilled. Had Lexi guessed that her relationship with Ryan had deepened into something more? 'We are a team. A professional team,' she said firmly, and Lexi lifted her head.

'Do you like him, Mum?'

Oh, no, not now. 'Of course I like him. I think he's an excellent doctor and—'

'That wasn't what I was asking!' Lexi's teeth were chattering. 'He was really worried about you. You should have seen the look on his face when he had to decide whether to hang onto me or you. He never took his eyes off you. If you'd been swept into the water he'd have been in there after you. What's going on?'

This was the perfect time to say something.

Jenna licked her lips. 'Do you like Ryan, sweetheart?'

'Oh, yes. And I like Evanna and the kids, and Fraser. Loads of people, actually. I never thought this place would be so cool.' Lexi clung tighter. 'I've got used to it here, Mum. I like Glenmore. And do you know the best thing?'

Ryan, Jenna thought. He was the best thing. 'Tell me the best thing for you.'

'The fact that it's just the two of us. I love that.'

Just the two of us.

Jenna swallowed down the words she'd been about to speak.

How could she say them now?

Lexi buried her face in Jenna's shoulder. 'Dad was awful to you. I see that now. He didn't even tell you stuff face to face. He just let you find out.'

'I expect he did what he thought was best.' Burying her own needs, Jenna watched as the sea level rose. 'Don't think about it now.' They needed to climb higher, she thought numbly, glancing upwards with a sinking feeling in her stomach. Now that the immediate crisis was over, the impossibility of it overwhelmed her.

'I want to talk about it, Mum!' Lexi seemed to have forgotten her surroundings. 'You're always protecting me, but I want the truth.'

Shivering, wet, chilled to the bone, Jenna tried to stop her teeth from chattering as she searched for the right thing to say. 'Dad— He— Actually, Lex, I don't know what happened with your dad. The truth is that sometimes the people we love disappoint us. But I'm not going to do that. I will always be here for you. Always. You'll have a home with me always.' She smoothed the girl's soaking hair. 'Even when you're off at university, or travelling the world, you'll still have a home with me.'

If they survived.

If they didn't both drown in this isolated, godforsaken gash in the cliff face.

'Dad just acted like he didn't have a family—' Lexi's voice jerked. 'I mean, he made you sell the house so that he could have the money, and he didn't even want me to go and stay with him this summer. That's why we came up here, isn't it? You made it impossible for me to get back there, so I wouldn't find out the truth. But when I rang him he told me it wasn't convenient for me to come—he didn't want me around, and that's why we came up here.'

Jenna stroked her daughter's soaking hair, smoothing it away from her face. 'I don't know what's going on in your dad's head right now, sweetheart, but I do know he loves you. You need to give him time to sort himself out.'

'He loves me as long as I don't mess up his new life.' Lexi scrubbed tears away with her hand. 'I'm sorry I was so difficult. I'm sorry I made it hard for you.'

'You didn't. It always would have been hard. Having you is what's kept me going. Having you is the best thing that ever happened in my life.' With a flash of relief, Jenna saw the helicopter and drew Lexi back against the rock face. 'Right. They're going to get us out of here. You go first.'

Lexi clung to her mother. 'I don't want to leave you here—'

'I'll be right behind you, I promise.'

As Lexi was clipped onto the rope and lifted into the helicopter Jenna had a few moments alone on the rock.

Looking at the swirling, greedy sea, she knew that she was facing the most difficult decision of her life. She thought back to the moment when Ryan had been forced to choose between holding her and holding her daughter and the injured boy. That was life, wasn't it? It was full of tough decisions. Things were rarely straightforward and every decision had a price.

If she told Lexi about her relationship with Ryan, she'd threaten her daughter's security and happiness. And what could she offer Ryan? He wanted a family. Babies. Even if she was able to have more children, how could she do that to Lexi?

There was no choice to make because it had already been made for her.

Clinging to the rock, Jenna watched Lexi pulled to safety inside the helicopter, the seawater mingling with her tears.

CHAPTER NINE

OVERNIGHT, Lexi became a heroine.

As word spread of her daring climb down the cliffs to save Matt, Jenna couldn't walk two steps along the bustling quay without being stopped and told how proud she must be feeling. Every time she opened her front door there was another gift lying there waiting for them. Fresh fruit. Cake. Chocolate. Hand-knitted socks for Lexi—

'What am I expected to do with these? They're basically disgusting!' Back to her insouciant teenage self, Lexi looked at them in abject horror. 'I wouldn't be seen dead in them. Who on earth thinks I'll look good in purple and green? Just shoot me now.'

'You'll wear them,' Jenna said calmly, and Lexi shuddered.

'How to kill off your love-life. If I'd known there was going to be this much fuss I would have let Matt drown.' She grabbed a baseball cap and pulled it onto her head, tipping the brim down. 'If this is how it feels to be a celebrity, I don't want any of it. Two people took photos of me yesterday, and I've got a spot on my chin!'

Jenna smiled at the normality of it. It helped. There was an ache and an emptiness inside her, far greater than she'd felt after Clive had left. One pain had been replaced by another. 'Ryan rang.' She kept her voice casual. 'He thought you'd want to know that Matt's surgery went well and he's definitely not in any danger. The surgeons said that if he'd lost any more blood he might have died, so you really are the hero of the hour.'

'It wasn't me, it was Ryan.' Obviously deciding that being a heroine had its drawbacks, Lexi stuffed her iPod into her pocket and strolled towards the door. 'I'm meeting Fraser on the beach. At least that way I might be able to walk five centimetres. And, no, I'm not wearing those socks.'

'You can wear them in the winter.'

'Any chance of us moving back to London before the weather is cold enough for socks?' But, despite the sarcasm, there was humour in her eyes and Lexi gave Jenna a swift hug and a kiss. 'What are you doing today?'

'Nothing much. Just pottering. I might go for a walk.' To the lighthouse, to tell Ryan that their relationship had to end.

Jenna watched as Lexi picked up her phone and strolled out of the house, hips swaying to the music which was so loud that Jenna could hear it even without the benefit of the earphones.

Her daughter was safe, she thought. That was all that mattered. Safe and settled. And as for the rest—well, she'd cope with it.

Ryan was standing on the cliffs, staring out over the sea, when he heard the light crunch of footsteps on the path. Even without turning he knew it was her. And he knew what she'd come to say.

Bracing himself, he turned. 'I didn't think you'd be coming over today. I assumed you'd be resting—that's why I rang instead of coming round.'

'We appreciated the call. We've both been thinking about Matt all night.' She was wearing jeans and her hair blew in the wind. She looked like a girl, not a mother. 'Lexi has gone for a walk and I wanted to talk to you.'

He wanted to stop her, as if not giving her the chance to say the words might change things. But what was the point of that? Where had denial ever got him? 'Are you all right after yesterday? No ill effects?'

'No. We were just cold. Nothing that a hot bath didn't cure. Ryan—'

'I know what you're going to say, Jenna.'

'You do?'

'Of course. You want to end it.'

She took so long to answer that he wondered if he'd got it wrong, and then she made a sound that was somewhere between a sigh and a sob. 'I have to. This just isn't a good time for me to have a new relationship. I have to think of Lexi. She's found out just how selfish her dad has been—she feels rejected and unimportant—if I put my happiness before hers, I'll be making her feel as though she matters to no one. I can't do that. She says she likes the fact that it's just the two of us. Our relationship is her anchor. It's the one thing that hasn't changed. I don't want to threaten that.'

'Of course you don't.' Ryan felt numb and strangely detached. 'I love you—you know that, don't you?'

'Yes.' Her feet made no sound in the soft grass as she walked towards him. 'And I love you. And that's the other reason I can't do this. You want children. You deserve children, Ryan. I'm thirty-three. I have no idea whether I can even have another child. And even if I could—and even if Lexi accepted our relationship in time—I couldn't do that to her. She'd feel really pushed out.' The hand she placed on his arm shook. 'What am I saying? I'm talking about children and a future and you haven't even said what you want—'

'I want you.' It was the one question he had no problem answering. In a mind clouded with thoughts and memories, it was the one thing that was shiny and clear. 'Have you talked to Lexi about it at all?'

'No. No, I haven't.'

'Maybe you should.' Refusing to give up without a fight, he slid his hands into her hair and brought his mouth down on hers. The kiss was hungry and desperate, and he wondered if by kissing her he was simply making it worse for them both. He tasted her tears and lifted her head. 'Sorry. That wasn't fair of me.'

'It isn't you. It isn't your fault.' She scrubbed her palm over her cheek. 'But we're grown-ups. She's a child. This whole situation is terrible for her, and I'd do anything to change it, but I can't. The one thing I can do is not make things worse.' Her voice broke. 'She is not ready for me to have another relationship.'

'Are you telling me that you're never going to have another relationship in case it upsets Lexi?'

'One day, maybe. But not yet. It's just too soon. I won't do anything that makes this whole thing worse for her. I suppose I could hide our relationship, but I don't want to. I don't want to sneak around and live a lie. We deserve better.' Jenna lifted her fingers to her temples and shook her head. 'This is ridiculous. I may be thirty-three but I feel seventeen. And I never should have started this. I never should have hurt you—'

'You've always been honest with me, and that's all I ask.' The hopelessness of it made the moment all the more intense, and their mouths fused, their hands impatient and demanding as they took from each other. Urgent, hungry, they made love on the grass, with the call of the seagulls and the crash of the sea for company.

Aferwards they lay on the grass in silence, because there was nothing more to say.

When Jenna stood up and walked away he didn't stop her.

* * *

The following day Jenna was half an hour late to surgery because everyone had kept stopping her to ask her for the details or give her another bit of gossip. Feeling numb inside, she'd responded on automatic, her thoughts on Ryan. 'Thank you—so kind—yes, we're both fine—no permanent damage—Matt's doing well—'

The effort of keeping up a front was so exhausting that she was relieved when she finally pushed open the glass doors to the Medical Centre. Hurrying through Reception, she was caught in an enormous hug by a woman she'd never met before.

'Nurse Jenna—how can I thank you?'

'I—' Taken aback, Jenna cast a questioning glance at Janet, the receptionist, who grinned.

'That's Pam. Matt's aunt. He has four aunts living on the island, so there's going to be more where that came from.' Janet handed a signed prescription to one lady and answered the phone with her other hand. 'There's a crowd waiting for you here, Jenna.'

Matt's aunt was still hugging her tightly. 'It's thanks to your lass that our boy's alive. I heard she climbed down—and then you went down that rope after her.'

'Lexi was brave, that's true—I'm very proud of her. And Ryan. But I didn't do anything.' Embarrassed by the fuss, desperate to be on her own, Jenna eased herself away from the woman, but people still crowded around her.

'Can't believe you went down that rope—'

'Lexi climbed down without any help—'

'Anyone who says today's teenagers are a waste of space has never met a Glenmore teenager—'

'Devil's Jaws—'

'Been more deaths there than any other part of Glenmore—'

Jenna lifted a hand to her throbbing head. 'Maybe I'd rather not hear that part,' she said weakly, remembering with horrifying clarity the moment when she'd stepped over the edge of the cliff. 'I'm just so pleased Matt's going to be all right. Dr McKinley rang yesterday and the hospital said surgery went well.' After a summer on Glenmore she knew better than to bother worrying about patient confidentiality. If she didn't tell them what was going on they'd find out another way, and the information would be less reliable. 'I'm just sorry I'm late this morning. If everyone could be patient...'

'Don't give it a thought.' Kate Green, who ran the gift shop on the quay, waved a hand. 'Won't kill any of us to wait. Anything we can do to help? We're sorting out a rota to make food for Matt's family when they're back from the mainland. They won't want to be fussing with things like that.'

Jenna looked at them all—looked at their kind faces, which shone with their eagerness to support each other in times of crisis. It was impossible not to compare it to the surgery she'd worked at in London, where patients had complained bitterly if they were kept waiting more than ten minutes. In London everyone led parallel lives, she thought numbly. Here, lives were tangled together. People looked left and right instead of straight ahead. They noticed if things weren't right with the person next to them. They helped.

Someone pushed something into her hand.

Jenna opened the bag and saw two freshly baked muffins.

'My mum thought you might not have had time for breakfast. We made you these.' The child was no more than seven years old, and for Jenna it was the final straw. Too emotionally fragile to cope with the volume of kindness, she burst into tears.

'Oh, now...' Clucking like a mother hen, Kate Green urged her towards the nearest chair.

'Shock—that's what it is. It was her lass who stayed with Matt. Saved him, she did. That's a worry for any mother.'

'Tired, I expect...'

'I'm so sorry.' Struggling desperately to control herself, Jenna rummaged in her pocket for a tissue. Someone pushed one into her hand. 'Just leave me for a minute—I'll be fine.' Oh, God, she was going to crack. Right here in public, with these kind people around her.

Evanna hurried out of her clinic, alerted by Janet. 'Jenna? Are you all right?'

Jenna blew her nose. 'Just being really stupid. And making my clinic even more behind than it is at the moment.'

'Then perhaps we can get on with it? I'm first.' Mrs Parker's crisp voice cut through the mumbling and the sympathy. 'And I've been standing on this leg for twenty minutes now. I'm too old to be kept waiting around. It isn't the first drama we've had on Glenmore and it won't be the last.'

Even the gentle Evanna gritted her teeth, but Jenna stood up, grateful to be forced into action.

'Of course, Mrs Parker. I'm so sorry. Come with me. The rest of you—' she glanced around the crowded waiting room '—I'll be as quick as I can.'

Following Mrs Parker down the corridor to her room, Jenna braced herself for a sharp rebuke and a lecture.

Instead she was given a hug. 'There, now...' Mrs Parker's voice shook slightly, and her thin fingers rubbed Jenna's back awkwardly. 'Those folks think they're helping, but they're overwhelming, aren't they? I've lived on this island all my life and there are times when I could kill the lot of them. You must feel like a crust of bread being fought over by a flock of seagulls.' With a sniff she pulled away, leaving Jenna with a lump in her throat.

'Oh, Mrs Parker—'

'Now, don't you get all sentimental on me, young lady.' Mrs Parker settled herself in the chair. 'Sentimental is all very well once in a while, but it doesn't solve problems. I'm guessing those tears have nothing to do with that foolhardy rescue or lack of sleep. Do you want to talk about it?'

Jenna blew her nose again. 'I'm supposed to be dressing your leg—'

'You're a woman. Are you telling me you can't talk and bandage a leg at the same time?'

Jenna gave a weak smile and turned her attention to work. Washing her hands, she prepared the equipment she needed. 'It's just reaction to yesterday, I'm sure. And I am a little tired. Really.'

'I'm old, not stupid. But not so old I don't remember how it feels to be confused about a man. You came here as a single mother. I'm guessing you're rethinking that now.'

Jenna's hands shook as she removed the bandage from the old lady's leg. 'No. No, I'm not rethinking that. Lexi and I are a team.'

'So you're going to let a strong, impressive man like Dr McKinley walk away from you?'

Jenna stilled. She thought about denying it and then realised it was useless. 'Does everyone know?'

Mrs Parker sighed. 'Of course. This is Glenmore. What we don't know is why you're not just booking the church. The Reverend King is quite happy to marry you, even though you've been divorced. I asked him.'

'You—?' Jenna gulped. 'Mrs Parker, you can't possibly— you shouldn't have—'

'You have a daughter. You need to keep it respectable. One bad marriage shouldn't put you off doing it again.' Mrs Parker glared at her. 'What? You think it's right, teaching that girl of yours it's all right to take up with whoever takes your fancy? You need to set an example. If you like him enough to roll around in his sheets with him, you like him enough to marry him. And he certainly likes you. There's a bet going on down at the pub that he's going to ask you to marry him. You'd better have your answer ready.'

'It would have to be no.'

Mrs Parker looked at her steadily, her customary frown absent. 'As we've been drinking tea together for almost two months now, perhaps you'd do me the courtesy of explaining why you'd say no to a man most women would kill to be with.'

Jenna didn't pause to wonder why she was talking to this woman. She needed to talk to someone, and Mrs Parker had proved to be a surprisingly good listener. 'Because of Lexi.'

She blurted it all out. Everything she was feeling. The only thing she didn't mention was Ryan's past. That wasn't hers to reveal.

Mrs Parker listened without interrupting. Only when Jenna had finished and was placing a fresh dressing on the wound did she finally speak. Her hands were folded carefully in her lap.

Age and wisdom, Jenna thought, wondering what secrets Mrs Parker had in her past. She was a girl once. A young woman. *We see them as patients, but they're people.*

'Tell me something.' The old lady looked at her in the eye. 'Do you plan to try and shield your daughter from everything that happens in life?'

Jenna swallowed. 'If I can.' Then she gave a sigh. 'No, of course not. Not everything, but—I love her. I want her to be happy.'

'Has it occurred to you that she might like a new man around the house?'

'I think it would unsettle her.' Jenna finished the bandage, concentrating on the job. 'Is that comfortable?'

Mrs Parker put her weight on her leg. 'It's perfect, as usual.' Her voice calm, she picked up her handbag. 'You're not the only one who can love, you know. And if love is want-

ing someone else's happiness, maybe Lexi should be thinking of yours. Maybe you should give her the chance to worry
about you for a change. I want you to think about that.'

'Mrs Parker—'

'Just think about it. I'd hate to see you turning your back
on something special. I'll send the next person in, shall I?
Don't forget to drop in for tea when you're passing.' With a
quiet smile, the dragon of Glenmore opened the door. 'I happen to know that Rev King has a date free in December. I
always think a winter wedding is romantic. And I expect an
invitation. I have a particularly nice coat that I haven't had
reason to wear for at least two decades.'

'He rolled in a pile of something gross and now he stinks—
Mum, are you listening to me? Basically, the dog is rank.'
A frown on her face, Lexi helped herself to crisps from the
cupboard and waved them under her mother's nose. 'Junk
food alert! Time to nag!'

Her mind miles away, Jenna stared out of the window,
trying to find the right way to say what needed to be said.

'On my fourth packet—' Lexi rustled the bag of crisps
dramatically. 'Might add some more salt to them just to make
them extra yummy—'

'Lexi…' Her strained voice caught her daughter's attention.

'What? What's wrong?'

'I—there's something I need to talk to you about.
Something very adult.'

'Is it about the fact you're having sex with Ryan? Because
honestly, Mum—' Lexi stuck her hand in the crisp packet
'—I don't want to know the details. I mean, I love you, and
I love that we talk about stuff, but I don't want to talk about
that. It would feel too weird.'

Stunned, Jenna felt her face turn scarlet. 'You— I—'

'Don't get me wrong. I'm basically cool with it, Mum. I'm

pleased for you.' Grinning, Lexi nibbled a crisp. 'It's nice for someone of your age to have some excitement.'

Jenna moved her lips but no sound came out.

Lexi squinted out of the window. 'Better pull it together fast, Mum, lover-boy is strolling up the path. I'll go and let him in, shall I?' She sauntered towards the door, crisps in her hand. 'Hi, Ryan. I'm glad you're here, because Mum so needs a doctor. She's acting weird. I've waved, like, five packets of crisps under her nose and she hasn't even reacted. Normally she'd be freaking out and going on about too much salt, too much fat. Today—nothing. What's the matter with her?'

'Perhaps you'd better leave us for a moment.' Ryan dropped his car keys on the table, but Lexi shook her head and plopped onto a chair by the kitchen table.

'No way. I'm fed up with being the last person to know stuff around here. If you want to get rid of me you'll have to kick me out, and that will be child abuse.'

A smile flickered at the corners of Ryan's mouth. 'Presumably that wouldn't be a good start to our relationship.'

Lexi looked at him thoughtfully. 'You've got a thing for my mum, haven't you?'

Ryan winced, and Jenna came to her senses. 'Lexi!'

'It's too late for discipline. I'm already full of crisps.' Lexi folded her arms. 'It would be great if someone around here would give me a straight answer for once. I know you like my mum, so there's no point in denying it.'

'That isn't quite how I'd describe it,' Ryan said carefully, and Jenna felt the pulse beat in her throat.

Lexi didn't pause. 'What words would you use?'

'I love your mum.' Ryan spoke the words calmly, with no hint of apology or question. 'I love her very much. But I realise that the situation is complicated.'

'What's complicated about it? She's divorced, and you—' Lexi frowned. 'Are you married or something?'

'No. I was in the past.'

'So, basically, you're free and single?' Lexi grinned cheekily. 'I missed out the "young" bit, did you notice?'

'I noticed. Remind me to punish you later.' A sardonic smile on his face, Ryan sat down at the table. 'I'm not sure what order to do this in. If you want to be part of a family that already exists, do you propose to the woman or the daughter?'

'Don't waste your time proposing to me,' Lexi said casually. 'You may be hot, but you're way too old for me. How old *are* you?'

'Thirty-six.'

Lexi shuddered. 'You'd go and die, or something, while I was still in my prime. Mind you, that has its advantages. Are you rich?'

'Lexi!' Jenna finally found her voice. 'You can't—'

'Actually, I am pretty rich. Why does that matter?' Ryan's long fingers toyed with his keys. 'Are you open to bribery and corruption?'

'Of course. I'm a teenager. The art of negotiation is an important life skill.' Lexi grabbed a grape from the fruit bowl and popped it in her mouth. 'So how big a bribe are we talking about? If I let you marry my mum you'll buy me a pink Porsche?'

Ryan grimaced. 'Not pink. Please not pink.'

Glancing between the two of them in disbelief, Jenna shook her head. 'Can we have a proper conversation?'

'We are having a proper conversation.' Lexi looked at Ryan speculatively. 'What music do you like?'

'I have eclectic tastes.'

'In other words you'll pretend to like anything I like.'

'No. But I'm sure there would be some common ground.'

'If I let you marry my mum, will you teach me to abseil?'

Jenna felt faint. 'Lexi—Ryan—for goodness' sake—'

'I don't see why not.'

'And surf?'

'Your balance was pretty impressive on those rocks, and you don't seem to mind being swamped by seawater.' Ryan gave a casual shrug and a smile touched his mouth. 'Looks like I'm going to be busy.'

'And you promise not to tell me what time to go to bed or nag me about my diet?'

'You can eat what you like and go to bed when you like.'

Lexi fiddled with his car keys. 'Do I have to call you Dad?'

'You can call me whatever you like.'

'I never thought about having another father.'

There was a long silence, and then Ryan stirred. 'How about another friend? Have you thought about having another one of those?'

Lexi gave a slow smile and stood up. 'Yeah,' she drawled huskily, 'I could go with that. I'll leave you two alone now. The thought of watching a man kiss my mum is just a bit gross. I'm taking Rebel down on the beach to wash off whatever it is he's rolled in. I reckon it's going to take me at least two hours to get him clean, and I'm going to bang the front door really loudly when I come back.' Grinning wickedly, she scooped up the lead and then walked over to Jenna. 'Say yes, Mum. You know you want to.' She glanced over her shoulder to Ryan. 'And he's pretty cool—for an older person. We're going to do OK.'

Jenna couldn't find her voice. 'Lex—'

'You're almost too old to have another baby, so you'd better not waste any time,' Lexi advised, kissing Jenna on the cheek.

Sensing Ryan's eyes on her, Jenna swallowed. 'Lexi, we won't—'

'I hope you do. Think of all the money I'd earn babysitting.' Lexi grinned. 'How much would you pay me to change nappies? I'll think about a decent rate while I'm scrubbing

Rebel. See you later.' She sauntered out of the house, leaving the two of them alone.

Aware of Ryan still watching her, Jenna opened her mouth and closed it again.

He stood up and walked across to her. 'I had an unexpected visitor this morning.'

'You did?'

'The Reverend King.' There was a gleam of humour in his eyes. 'He wanted to know exactly what time we wanted the church on Christmas Eve. Apparently it's been reserved provisionally in our name. His suggestion was just before lunch, so that the entire island could then gather for food at our expense. I wondered what you thought.'

Jenna swallowed. Then she turned her head and stared into the garden, watching as Lexi put Rebel on his lead and led him through the little gate towards the beach. 'I think that life sometimes surprises you,' she said huskily. 'I think that just when you think everything is wrong, it suddenly turns out right. I think I'm lucky. What do you think?'

Ryan closed his hands over her shoulders and turned her to face him. 'I think we only have two hours before Lexi comes home.' His fingers were strong, and he held her as though he never intended to let her go. 'We should probably make the most of it. Especially if we want to make a baby before we're both too old.'

She made a sound that was somewhere between a laugh and a sob and flung her arms around his neck. 'What if I can't? What if I *am* too old? What if I can't give you a family?'

His hands gentle, he cupped her face and lowered his mouth to hers. 'Marry me and you will have given me all the family I need. You. Lexi.'

'But—'

'Sometimes we don't begin a journey knowing where it's

going to end,' he said softly, resting his forehead against hers as he looked down at her. 'Sometimes we don't have all the answers. We don't know what the future holds, but we do know that whatever it is we'll deal with it. Together. The three of us. And Rebel, of course.'

The three of us.

Holding those words against her like a warm blanket, Jenna lifted her head. 'The three of us,' she whispered softly. 'That sounds good to me.'

* * * * *

If you enjoyed **Summer Kisses**,
why not share your thoughts with
hundreds of other Sarah Morgan
fans and post a review at:

Don't miss Sarah Morgan's first, irresistible O'Neil brothers story

Enjoy more sizzling summer stories from Sarah Morgan